KNIGHTS CORRUPTION MC SERIES

JAGGER

S. NELSON

Jagger
Copyright © 2016 S. Nelson

Editor
Hot Tree Editing

Cover Design
CT Cover Creations

Interior Design & Formatting
Christine Borgford, Perfectly Publishable

Jagger/ S.Nelson.—1st edition
ISBN-13: 978-1537360249
ISBN-10: 1537360248

Jen, without our little brainstorming session I probably never would have stumbled across the idea which ended up being one of the most unique parts of this story. Thanks schmoopie! ☺

PROLOGUE

"WORTHLESS PIECE OF SHIT!"

I swore those were my father's favorite words. His preferred insult. Normally, he spewed the offense alone, but then there were times, like now, when he followed them with his fists. The contact with the side of my face jolted me back, the sting of pain forcing me to feel something. Anything. Otherwise, I remained in a constant state of numbness, my own kind of self-preservation.

Hitting the wall behind me, my head thumped off the plaster and created a small dent, but I didn't dare move; if he saw what I'd done, he'd become even more irate. If that were at all possible.

I'd come to expect his outbursts, especially when he drank. Which happened to be most of the time. Growing up with an alcoholic parent was tough, and that was putting it lightly. He'd hated me my entire life, his abuse escalating the older I became. He blamed me for everything that went wrong in his life, from the death of his wife, my mother, to gambling debts he'd incurred, to losing his job. I couldn't win, no matter what I said or tried to do to help.

I'd gotten a paper route at the tender age of eleven, handing over all my wages, but all that earned me was a swift backhand. He thought I was being disrespectful, essentially telling him he couldn't take care of us. Which was the absolute truth, but I never uttered those words. We'd lost our house soon after and had been moving from place to place ever since. My father couldn't hold down a job because of his excessive drinking, and no matter how much I tried to stay out of the way, he'd always find fault with something I did, punishing me so badly sometimes I didn't dare go out in public for fear people would see the damage he'd caused.

For as horrible as my father treated me, he was the devil I knew. The thought of being yanked from the only life I'd known and placed with strangers was enough to cause me to silently endure all of his beatings.

Both verbal and physical.

He'd told me my entire life that I would never amount to anything. That I'd probably drop out of school and end up being a bum for the rest of my life.

But I'd proved him wrong.

Holding my cap and gown, I'd thought my graduation day would have finally made him proud of me, but instead my accomplishment only made him rant his insults harder and faster.

"You think just because you skated by and passed by the skin of your teeth that means you're somethin' special?" he roared, his spittle hitting my cheek he was standing so close. His version of "skating by" was me graduating with second honors, and while most kids would be proud of that achievement, I had to hide it from him. Otherwise, he'd think I was boasting, rubbing it in his face that I was smart.

I stood in front of him with my head hung low, knowing better than to answer. He'd already struck me once, and although his fists didn't hurt as much as when I was younger, I still didn't want to have to deal with any more. I'd never retaliated against my father. Never raised my own fists in return. No, I took his rage because a part of me thought I deserved it.

Guilt ate at me from the inside that I was the reason my mother had died. I'd killed her simply by being born, and my father never let me forget it. Unfortunately, his lack of love for me fueled my anger toward others. It was why I'd been expelled from more than a few schools, constantly getting into fights with kids who'd picked on me because of the shoddy clothes my father forced me to wear. He simply refused to spend money on his growing son.

But something good came from my rage. I'd perfected my fighting skills, often sparring against other kids for money. Some were my age and some were years older, but no matter what, I'd win every time.

Every opponent was my father.

Every knockout was my father hitting the floor.

Every win was my way of telling my father to go fuck himself.

My father staggered backward in his drunken state, bumping into the kitchen table before stabilizing himself. Running his pale hand over his balding head, he looked like he was going to explode. Gritting his teeth, he stepped closer. "I hope you don't think you're gonna live under my roof now that you're grown," he seethed, his bloodshot eyes looking like they belonged to some sort of demon. "Well? Answer me, boy," he demanded, stepping even closer. He reeked like alcohol, the smell making me instantly nauseous.

"No," I answered, keeping my head down so I didn't have to look at the loathing in his eyes, his hatred making me feel the way he truly saw me.

Worthless.

Dreadful silence danced around the both of us, the drumming of my heart the only sensation I allowed myself. I'd shut down, but in the next few minutes I'd be free forever from the evil bastard standing in front of me.

Spitting at my feet, he shoved past me, but not before driving the emotional knife in deeper, slicing me apart from the inside. "Get your fuckin' shit and get out." A ragged breath passed. *Here it comes.* "It should have been you who died that day," he said, venom cutting each word perfectly. I wished I could have said he'd never spoken those words before, but then I would have been lying.

He said them often.

Only that time would be the last I'd have to hear them.

CHAPTER ONE

Jagger

"KILL HIM!" THE WORDS ECHOED in my ears, the air swirling around me suddenly thicker than it was seconds before. I dismissed the lump forming in my throat and focused all of my attention on pummeling my opponent, my fists flying so fast his blood coated the ground beneath us in no time. Taking a quick reprieve, I allowed him a few precious seconds to regain his footing; otherwise, our bout would be over too fast. And where would be the fun in that?

So many people united in the thrill of the fight. They'd paid good money to witness bloodshed, to be part of something they were too terrified to do themselves.

Fight.

For sport.

But not me. I lived for the surge of adrenaline that slithered through my veins. To know my skills outmatched anyone who had stepped in the ring with me. Plus the prize money wasn't anything to sneeze at.

I'd been involved in the underground world of MMA fighting for a few years, and I was undefeated. Confidence and cockiness were often separated by a thin line, but I wasn't in it for the recognition, or the women, or the power trip it gave most fighters. To me, the ring was the one place I could release all my pent-up rage. A place I could lose myself to the chants of the crowds and the smell of blood and sweat.

A place where I wasn't . . . worthless.

A sharp pain in my side shoved me back into the heat of the fight. The kid in front of me was two years younger and certainly not as skilled, even though he'd just managed to catch me off guard. But it wouldn't happen again. I knew his weaknesses—his left knee, for one. He'd hurt it badly a year back and unfortunately for him, I was gonna make him relive that excruciating pain. The other obstacle working against him was that he was a known drug addict, fighting strictly for money to fuel his demons. While he possessed some talent, he wasn't focused or disciplined. Two things working in my favor right then.

Locking eyes with the guy who would give me my next win, I faked an uppercut, drawing his attention to my hand while my foot shot out and connected with his previously injured knee. As soon as his leg bent in the wrong direction, I knew the fight was over, but just to lock in the victory I finished him off with my infamous right hook.

He never saw it coming.

And I never expected for my hit to be the final blow.

The final action which stripped his soul from this life.

An unnerving sound reverberated in the air around me. No one else heard it, but the crackling noise boomed inside my ears, pounding so fiercely inside my head I thought for sure everyone knew what I'd just done.

I hadn't meant to.

All I'd wanted to do was make sure I remained at the top of my game. There was no saving him, though. I jumped back and watched his body free fall in slow motion. His head hung from his shoulders while his body twisted in an awkward position, his legs bending while the pull of gravity embraced him.

So many people cheered, the applause and shouts making me feel as if my ears were bleeding. My heart pounded inside my chest so fiercely I feared I was gonna join him in the afterlife if I didn't get a fucking grip on my new reality.

Blood poured from his nose and mouth, but there was no other sign of life emanating from him.

He'd broken his neck. Or rather, *I'd* broken his neck.

His body lay limp on the ground.

Not a twitch.

Not a breath.

No hope whatsoever that it was all a bad dream.

Death.

He was dead.

I'd killed him.

I'd only intended to put him out of commission from fighting, not from life itself. My wrapped hands pulled at the sweaty strands of my hair, blowing out a disbelieving gush of air as I tried to wrap my head around what just happened. I'd never killed anyone before. Well, let me clarify—I'd never killed anyone *in the ring* before.

Outside the solace of the ropes, I'd snatched a few lives alongside my brothers of the Knights Corruption.

A strong grip ripped me backward toward the ropes, making me stumble and fall onto the stool in my corner of the ring. I heard someone speaking but the sound was muffled, as if their hands were covering their mouth while they yelled incoherently.

My body shook under the solid hold of someone, and it wasn't until I finally raised my head that I saw who it was. Stone, the VP of our club, stood over me with an intense worried look in his eyes. His lips were moving but I couldn't make out what he was saying. Then, without warning, all the muffled noise came into focus and it suddenly became too much to bear. My hands hastily covered my ears, drowning out the sound of the chaos of what I'd done.

The shock of killing my opponent twisted me in ways it shouldn't have. As I said, I'd killed before, but it was always justified; battle of the clubs warranted fatalities now and again. But when I was in the ring, my ultimate goal was to win. To be the victor and to show everyone I excelled at something. To prove to those around me that I had amounted to something because my entire life my father had drilled the exact opposite into me, telling me I was a mistake and would either end up in jail or dead. He told me once he hoped it was the latter. I was only ten when I first heard those words, and while I'd tried not to let him see me upset, tears spilled forth at the very notion that my own father hated me.

It was his face I saw most often when I beat the hell out of someone, wishing my fists pulverized the man who'd given me life.

"Jagger!" Stone shouted. "We have to go. Now!" He held the ropes open for me and once my feet hit the ground, two men flanked me, one on each side. Ryder and Tripp. I hadn't even known they were there that evening, my focus solely on my fight and nothing else.

"Let's grab your winnings," Tripp yelled in my ear, "then we can get the hell outta here." As soon as I came out of the office with my prize money, we hastily headed toward the back of the warehouse, the red blinking exit sign my sole focus. But our escape was interrupted by someone blocking our path.

Hyped from my fight, with disgust and a twinge of guilt shooting through me, I hardened my restraint when I realized the man standing in front of us was none other than Snake, the brother of the guy I'd just killed. And as luck would have it, Snake just so happened to be part of our most hated enemy.

The Savage Reapers.

Normally, members of the two clubs would never be in the same vicinity, not unless we were warring. But the unspoken rules were bent under these types of circumstances. The underground fighting world brought out all sorts of characters, and unfortunately for us, it meant the scum of the Reapers often visited the fights. I tried to keep that part of my life separate from the club, although the two worlds were blending more and more recently. Plus I knew if our president, Marek, found out he might've put a stop to me participating in the bouts. He already didn't like me, suspecting I held certain feelings toward his wife. Feelings he'd misread. Regardless, I didn't want to give him any reason to take away one of the few things in life I thoroughly enjoyed.

But now that secret was out in the open. Stone, Ryder and Tripp circled me, a protective gesture which wasn't needed, but was definitely appreciated.

"What the fuck are you doing here?" Stone seethed, clenching his fists at his sides as he glared at Snake. "Do you have a death wish?" Tripp and Ryder stayed close, prepared to jump in if anything popped off. Even though the Reaper was surrounded by the enemy, it didn't seem to faze him. In fact, he looked like he was enjoying himself, knowing his presence was pissing us off even more.

Completely ignoring Stone's question, Snake turned his stare to me, puffing up his chest and stepping toward me. "You killed my little brother," he gritted, strands of his long dark hair falling loose from the tie that held it away from his face.

I wanted to tell him it wasn't on purpose, that it was an accident, but I didn't dare open my mouth to explain. It would be portrayed as weakness, so I kept my lips sealed.

I meant to keep my eyes on Snake, but I was curious to see what my brothers' reactions were to his statement. Now that they knew the man I'd killed was a sibling to a Reaper, they had to have guessed I knew our enemy had visited the fights. Would they rat me out to our leader? And if so, would I be kicked out of the club? Surely my omission would be the proverbial nail in the coffin. The final straw that would allow Marek to get rid of me.

I'd heard stories of other clubs never allowing their members to leave in anything other than a body bag. But I knew Marek didn't rule like that. Brothers who no longer wanted to be part of the life simply left, no bad feelings or ill wishes. The club wasn't for everyone and Marek knew it. Although I could've counted the number of men who'd left on one hand, and none since I'd been accepted as a prospect two years ago.

A quick hit to the chest pushed me back a step, and I was thrust out of the ramblings inside my own head and back into the situation. He'd dared to put his hands on me, and because I was distracted he'd been able to do so. Before anyone else could react, I shoved past the bastard and walked toward the exit. Some might have construed my actions— or lack thereof—as a pussy move, but I needed air. I needed to clear my head, and the last thing I needed was to take out all my frustrations and shock on the brother of the man I'd just killed.

Thankfully, Stone, Ryder and Tripp followed me without so much as a word, lining up alongside me as we escaped the confinements of the old, abandoned warehouse.

"The next time I lay eyes on you, you're fucking dead," Snake shouted after me. He continued to spout off at the mouth, but the harsh click of the metal door closing behind us cut him off.

Hunching forward in the backseat of Stone's truck, I rested my head in my hands and prayed that some potent alcohol would help me lose myself. Even if just for an evening.

I'd deal with life, and the consequences, when the sun came up.

CHAPTER TWO

Jagger

THE MORNING LIGHT INFILTRATED THE common room, my hungover ass burrowing further into the couch and shielding my eyes just so I didn't have to witness the dawn of another day. Because I wasn't a full-fledged member, I didn't have my own room at the club, so taking the couch was my only option.

After my fight the prior evening, the guys had brought me back to the clubhouse instead of dropping me off at my dismal apartment all by myself. They knew I'd have a problem with what I'd done, even though it hadn't been intentional. Still, to kill by accident was much worse than when it was done on purpose.

Tripp and Ryder had joined me while I'd drowned myself in alcohol. Stone on the other hand had to get back home to Adelaide and their new baby, Riley. I viewed the VP of my new family like a brother, even more so than the other men. We had a special bond. Maybe it was because we were both skilled fighters, or maybe it was because Stone had taken me under his wing when I'd first become part of the club, looking out for me when things went a little off the rails.

The cushion near my feet dipped, the weight of someone who I'd yet to identify taking up some of my personal space. Shoving at my legs, a rough voice vibrated through the air, and even though my eyes were still shielded, I knew exactly who it was.

My fellow drinking buddy. Ryder.

Thankfully, he'd stuck to beer; otherwise last night would have had a much more dire outcome. Ryder didn't do well with hard alcohol and we all knew it.

"You gettin' up anytime soon, prospect? It's just after two. You've slept the majority of your day away," he chided. Kicking at him only made him laugh, punching my leg before slouching back on the couch.

So much for losing myself to slumber for the rest of the day.

Before long, other voices filled the room, rousing me from my half sleep once and for all. Sitting upright, my hands instantly cradled my head, the intense pounding threatening to stay with me for hours.

"Wow, buddy, you look like shit."

When I spread my fingers to look and see who'd given the compliment, I saw it was Hawke. The wide grin he sported soon disappeared when his crazy woman, Edana, walked up behind him. She mumbled under her breath before shoving past him, heading toward his room at the back of the club, her wild auburn hair flowing behind her while she strode off with purpose. The pissed-off look on her face was telling. Those two had such an explosive relationship; I had no idea why he kept her around. "Great pussy" was something I'd heard him say before, but ain't no pussy worth putting up with that much shit on a daily basis. The fact that Hawke never kept his dick in his pants just added fuel to that out-of-control fire. But to each their own.

Hawke's eyes darkened before he dropped his head and followed Edana, probably gearing up for another all-out brawl from the look on his face.

Slowly rising from the couch, I walked toward the kitchen in search of food. I needed something to settle my stomach, and I'd found that greasy food always did the trick. Although I doubted I'd come across something already made and waiting for me to snatch up.

My head was buried in the refrigerator when I heard someone enter. Paying no attention to who it was, I continued to scour the shelves, hoping there was something edible for me to digest. Rooting through the choices, I decided to grab one of the small cardboard containers from the bottom shelf—leftover Chinese food of some sort. I opened the lid and gave it a whiff before deciding it was still good enough to eat. Someone was gonna be pissed I ate the rest of their chicken and broccoli, but I was too hungover to care.

Closing the fridge door, I turned around to find a fork when I came face-to-face with Sully. Her sweet smile calmed me some, my headache becoming a dull annoyance more than anything. For some inexplicable reason, any anxiety I'd carried around on a daily basis was lessened whenever she was near. I didn't understand it, and I stopped trying to months ago. It started when Marek summoned me to watch over her while he was away on club business with Stone after she had first come to stay with us. I'd thoroughly enjoyed our time together, loving that I'd been able to bring her out of her shell a bit by making her laugh. Normally, I was pretty reserved, but every now and again I could shoot the breeze with the best of them, coming up with witty banter just like everyone else.

Our budding friendship had been cut short, however, when Marek got it into his head that I had feelings for his new wife.

Was he right?

Sort of.

To myself, I would admit I found Sully very attractive, and while she was thinner than what I normally went for, she had a great body. Come on, I'm a young, red-blooded male after all. I noticed. What can I say? I won't apologize for it, although I would never make my appreciation known out loud for fear of retaliation from my president. I valued the club—and my life—way too much to do something so stupid.

But it was more than Sully's physicality that drew me in. It was something inside her which spoke to me, an inexplicable pull. Maybe it was the way I truly let my guard down in the presence of a female for once, not second-guessing whether she wanted to get into my pants or simply use me as a stepping stone to gain some kind of status within the club.

Maybe it was the short role of protector I was forced into while I watched over her for those few days. I'd seen how broken she was when she'd come to be with us, and even though she seemed much stronger and happier with each passing day, I'd discovered some of the things she'd had to endure at the hands of her club. Mainly her father and Vex. Thankfully, Vex was dead; if Marek hadn't already disposed of him, I probably would have.

I'd also been at the club the day the leader of the Los Zappas cartel visited, along with his right-hand man, Rico Yanez. Apparently, Yanez had raped Sully before Marek had stolen her, a situation which played heavily on our leader's mind day in and day out—anyone with eyes could see it. He'd changed over the time she'd come into his life. There were times he seemed lighter, but as soon as he'd found out what had happened to her, finding himself face-to-face with one of the men who'd violated her, something inside him had turned off—or on, depending on how you looked at it.

The need for vengeance and blood was strong with him, and I couldn't say I blamed him. I just hoped when the time came he would allow me to assist in the demise of that worthless piece of shit.

"Hi, Jagger," Sully's soft voice greeted me, looking toward the door to see if anyone else was going to enter. For the time being, we were alone, which probably wasn't the safest thing. If Marek walked in and saw us together, he'd flip out. And although his demeanor around me wasn't as aggressive as it had been initially when all the shit went down about my new friendship with his wife, the tension between us still bristled whenever we were near each other. I just didn't want to do or say anything which would shove me back into "I'm gonna fuck you up" status.

"Hey." I gave her a tight smile before moving past her, continuing to look for a fork. "How are you?" I asked, keeping my eyes diverted just in case someone did interrupt us. At least they couldn't say we were engaged in anything inappropriate.

"I'm good." She hesitated before speaking again, and I had a good idea why. It was obvious she knew what had happened at the fight, and was deciding whether or not she should ask me about it. Leaning against the counter, I shoved food into my mouth while I waited for her to say something, daring to finally look at her.

Worry laced the faint lines of her expression and I wanted nothing more than to comfort her. To tell her I was okay . . . or at least I would be. I was a survivor. If my bastard of a father had taught me anything, it was how to throw up walls to protect myself from the harshness of the world. Most of the time it worked, but there were instances—like with my interactions with Sully—where the walls started to crack.

"I heard about last night," she confessed, taking a few steps closer until she reached out and placed her hand on my shoulder—an action which was definitely appreciated, but not necessary. I didn't want anyone's pity, most of all hers.

Shrugging away from her touch, I gave her another tight smile before nodding. Continuing to eat was the distraction I needed, and thankfully Sully picked up on the vibe I'd thrown out. She probably thought I was scared to talk to her, but that was only partly true. While I could hold my own with Marek—and when I say hold my own, I mean letting him treat me any way he saw fit without retaliation—the last thing I wanted to do was cause Sully more heartache by creating an argument between them. She had enough to deal with, and I didn't want to add to it.

"No big deal," I lied. "Part of the risk we all take when we step into the ring."

Her lips parted to respond when someone barreled through the kitchen door, locking eyes on me as soon as I came into view.

"Yo," Breck interrupted. "Prez wants to see ya." He glanced quickly to Sully, then back to me before exiting the room.

"Fuck," I cursed, slamming the container of food on the nearby counter. Marek either wanted to see me because I was alone with his wife, or for the previous night. And seeing as how no one knew we were alone in the kitchen, my bets were on the latter.

"I'll go talk to Cole before he sees you," Sully offered, turning toward the door before she allowed me to respond.

Quickly walking past her, I reached for her arm to stop her. "No," I gritted. "I'll deal with it. Besides, I doubt it has anything to do with you."

Choosing not to utter another word, I pushed the door open and walked into the common room. I was halfway toward Chambers when

I heard Marek shout, "Where the fuck is he?"

Great! Nothing like walking into the lion's den, and apparently he was hungry.

Blowing out a frustrated exhale, I breached the threshold of the room where we held all our meetings.

This should be fuckin' good.

CHAPTER THREE

Jagger

AS SOON AS I STEPPED inside Chambers, I noticed that almost everyone was present, with the exception of Cutter and Trigger. I hadn't even seen the majority of the members milling around the club, but then again, I was too busy trying to function with a raging hangover.

To say Marek was beside himself was quite the understatement. He looked ready to rip someone apart. Sections of his dark hair stuck up, his hands gripping his head in frustration as he paced in front of everyone present.

His blue eyes darkened as soon as he saw me, halting his anxious stride before making a beeline in my direction. I didn't flinch, even though the furious look on his face unnerved me. An unkempt beard covered his face, his eyes red and haggard-looking. He wasn't getting any fucking sleep and his body paid the price. I knew he was biding his time until he could make Yanez pay for what he did to his wife once and for all. And if I'd overheard Stone correctly, his wish was gonna come true any day now.

Grabbing my cut, he drew me close. Ominous silence stretched between us while he prepared the words he wished to spew at me. His brow furrowed and the muscle in his jaw ticked, but still I showed no fear. To show weakness was detrimental, not only in the club but in life in general. That much I knew.

I could have shrugged Marek off me but I didn't dare, and the reason boiled down to one thing and one thing only.

Respect.

"Why the hell didn't you tell us the Reapers were hangin' around your fights?" He shoved me before giving me a chance to explain, and I was oddly thankful for the space he'd offered. Straightening my vest, I steeled my resolve and stood up straight, looking him in the eyes the entire time.

Words zipped through my brain at warp speed, and while I tried to nail down enough of them to form a coherent sentence, Marek shouted, "Answer me, goddamnit!"

His spike in temper forced me to speak right away.

"I didn't know any of those bastards were there until last night. I swear. I never pay attention to anyone other than who I'm fighting. Never get distracted by the noise," I said, turning to the VP of the Knights for affirmation. "Right, Stone?" I asked, hopeful he would back me up right then.

Stone gave me a simple nod, followed by a quick smirk.

Slamming his hand down on the table, Marek shot daggers toward all of us before speaking. "You need to be on guard every fucking second of the day. You need to make sure you know who is around you at all times. Do I need to remind any of you what's at stake?" Silence followed his outburst. "Do I?!" he roared, the vein in his temple threatening to burst if he didn't calm the hell down.

"No," everyone collectively answered, including me.

"Those bastards still haven't made a move for my wife, and every day that passes puts me even more on edge, just waiting for what they're gonna try to force me into. Force *all* of us into," he corrected. Plopping down in his chair, he expelled a breath and leaned forward, his fisted hands resting on top of the oblong table. "Get your heads right, fucking pay attention and be ready for anything."

No one broke the intensified silence, instead nodding and waiting for direction. And Marek gave it with a slam of the gavel, the boom ringing out and dismissing all in attendance.

As we headed toward the door, Marek's harsh tone stopped a few of us. "Stone, Jagger and Tripp, stay behind."

Once everyone else had left, the three of us turned all our focus toward the man who commanded our attention.

"I want you guys at every one of his fights," he said, pointing at me. "If there are Reapers showing up, we need to make our presence known. Stay in the background, though. Watch. Listen. We need as much information as we can get to make sure we're prepared for whatever they're planning. And trust me, they're planning something. Psych Brooks won't leave his daughter alone much longer." Gripping his chest, he affirmed, "I can feel it."

We each nodded our understanding before he dismissed us.

"You got off lucky," Tripp mused, slapping my back hard before shoving past me toward the common room. The nomad was quickly becoming a friend, even though he gave me shit all the time. Whenever he saw me sparring in the ring we'd constructed in the corner of the lot of the clubhouse, he teased that he could take me down, telling me I hit like a little girl. Yet he hadn't made good on his threat, still hadn't stepped up to show me what he was made of. Don't get me wrong; the guy was huge, standing at six-four and easily weighing in at two-twenty. But although he was a great match for me, he didn't intimidate me. I may have been a bit smaller, but I was quicker, a trait I used to my advantage every time an opportunity arose.

Taking a right, I walked toward the exit, needing some air to help soothe everything tumbling around inside my head. I was still unnerved about what had happened the night before. I'd tried to forget by losing myself to the bottle, but all that did was give me a wicked headache. No, I needed to do something else, but I wasn't sure what that was right then.

This fuckin' sucks.

"Yo, Jagger," Stone shouted from behind me. "Wait up."

Turning on my heel, I watched him slowly jog toward me, a pensive look on his face the closer he came.

"Sup?" I mumbled, just wanting to leave. I needed to take a ride, but where I was gonna go I had no idea.

"You okay? You don't look so great," he acknowledged.

"I'll be fine. It's just. . . ." I cut myself off because I didn't want to verbalize what was bothering me. I was sure Stone knew what the problem was, so there was no need for me to elaborate.

"I get it, man," he consoled, grabbing my shoulder for a quick show of support. Stone's friendship rattled me sometimes, but in a good way. I wasn't completely used to having someone show a genuine interest in my well-being.

"Did you want to talk to me about something?" I asked, gripping the back of my neck to help assuage the knotted muscles.

"When's your next fight?" Without even saying it, I knew having to accompany me to each of my upcoming bouts was the last thing Stone wanted to do, even though he enjoyed a good show. He had a new family waiting for him at home, a situation I very much wanted for myself. Well, maybe not the baby part, but definitely a woman. I was lonely, plain and simple. Sure, I had chicks throwing themselves at me all the time, but I was tired of pump-and-dumping every woman who spread her legs for me. I was looking for something more—which I was sure sounded odd coming from a twenty-two-year-old guy, but there it was. I knew enough not to verbalize that to anyone, however. If I did, I'd never hear the end of what a pussy I was, or whatever other clever names they'd come up with.

No, I'll keep my thoughts to myself.

"Two days."

"That's kind of soon, isn't it?" he asked, a confused look distorting his expression.

"It is, but ever since . . . well, what went down, I'm apparently a hot ticket. The purse has nearly tripled, and while I don't want to fight again so soon, I just can't pass up the opportunity at that kind of money." Looking sheepish for a second, I added, "I don't have the financial security you guys do. Just trying to make my way and all."

Stone nodded. "I get it." He swung his arm around my shoulder and pulled me close. "I do, but don't do it for the money. Not if you're not right in here," he said, tapping the side of my head with his finger.

"Easy for you to say," I grumbled. "You don't have to worry about money." I shoved him away, the annoyance with my situation propelling my anger further. "I don't want to keep living like this, Stone."

"Like what?"

"I live in a shithole. My president can't stand me. Hell, I'm surprised he hasn't kicked me out of the club by now. I ain't got no woman," I exclaimed, throwing my hands out to the sides. "I fight 'cause it's my escape, but if I kill again, in the ring, I won't even have that anymore." Clutching my chest, a sharp pain shot through me. I knew it was just nerves, though. Anxiety. "And if I can't fight, I don't know what I'll do."

Baring my soul to someone was new to me, and had it been in front of anyone else, I would've kept my mouth shut. But I knew Stone wouldn't give me shit like the others would.

Sympathy washed over him while he stared at me, trying to think of a retort to my mini outburst. "First, if you don't like your place, fucking move. Second, Marek doesn't *hate* you." I cocked my head to the side in disbelief. "Well, you're not his favorite person, but he acts better toward you than he did. He knows you're loyal to the club, that you would do anything for your brothers. Plus, you bring in a nice chunk of change." Stone grinned, but his smirk was fast replaced with a solemn look.

"Then why haven't I been fully patched in yet?"

"Time, brother. Give it time. You know Marek doesn't just patch someone in because they think they're due. But I promise it'll happen." I knew Stone couldn't guarantee such things, but I appreciated his faith in me, and in our leader. "Now," he said, "as far as a woman goes, you have your pick. What's wrong? I see the way all these chicks throw themselves at you, panting for your dick." He laughed, but I didn't find it funny.

I know, I know—poor young, good-looking guy. Pussy all around, wantin' to fuck me. I get it.

I just . . . I just want something more.

"It's not what I'm interested in anymore. I want what you guys have." Right then, Sully and Marek came strolling outside, his arm wrapped protectively around her waist as they approached. I couldn't help it; my eyes instantly latched on to hers, and while she gave me a quick smile, she looked away just as fast. And thankfully, so did I. Focusing back on Stone was my safest bet.

I thought Marek was gonna say something to us, but all he did was nod at Stone and give me a quick scowl before leading his wife toward his bike. They were gone before I registered that Stone had started talking again.

" . . . so you just have to wait until the time is right." I completely missed what he'd said, the lost look on my face telling him everything. "You didn't hear a word of that, did you?"

"Sorry, man. My mind is firing off in all different directions."

"I said"—he took a deep breath—"you'll find someone to settle down with when the time's right." He slapped me on the back. "Besides, aren't you a bit young to be thinking about getting married and having kids?"

The look on my face was comical, I was sure. "What the fuck? I'm not looking to get married and start breeding," I practically shouted, then lowered my voice. "I just want to have some kind of connection with someone, in addition to sexual." A cocky grin spread wide on my face. "I wanna be interested in fucking her *and* hearing what she has to say about stuff, you know?"

"Yeah, I know."

Taking a few more steps, Stone gave me a quick look before straddling his bike. I walked toward my own ride, grabbing my helmet when my friend's voice broke the silence. "About the fights," he started. "Don't worry about what *could* happen, Jagger. Just give it your all and everything else will fall into place."

CHAPTER FOUR

Jagger

NORMALLY, THE ENTIRE WORLD DWINDLED away when I prepared for a fight. An unusual peace rained down over me, as if all my troubles had faded into obscurity, my only focus defeating my opponent.

It fueled me.

I craved it.

The adrenaline was my drug of choice, my shield against the world.

Sitting in one of the empty back rooms of the warehouse, however, all I could concentrate on was whether or not this fight would end up with another fatality. My internal warring weighed heavily on me, and right then I desperately prayed for a distraction. But the close confines of the tiny room offered nothing.

Thankfully, before I went out of my mind waiting to be summoned, Stone and Tripp strolled into the room, closing the door behind them so we could have some privacy before the bout.

"How ya feelin'?" Tripp asked, leaning against the wall while Stone sidled up next to me.

"Good."

"You sure?" Stone asked, grabbing the wraps from the table and raising my fists. Normally I took care of wrapping my own hands, had been doing it since I started fighting, but that night I let Stone do it. I had a lot on my mind and could use his help with the simple, yet important task.

"Yeah," I muttered. Not really having much else to say, I remained quiet, my pulse quickening with each tick of the clock. Each pass of the second hand was like a boom inside my head. Breathing deeply, I closed my eyes and tried to will my pounding heart to calm the fuck down.

Tightly grasping my shoulder, Stone leaned in close and calmly said, "You'll be fine, brother. Stop freakin' out." While my demeanor was calm, my face expressionless, he knew exactly what was going on inside me without me saying so. He could read me better than I'd expected, but for some reason that didn't shock me. Stone was very perceptive, although he tried to hide it most times—not wanting to get mixed up in other people's drama, I was sure.

The click of the door startled me, my gaze flying toward whoever had entered the room. It was Marty, one of the organizers for the fight. He was in his late forties, a sorry excuse for a comb over covering the top of his head. He reminded me of someone who lived alone, eating a ton of microwavable dinners while watching *Jeopardy!* Ask me why I pictured him in that scenario and I'd tell you I had no idea. It just fit.

"Five minutes," he announced, leaving the door open after he exited.

Before long I heard the announcer say my name. The floor beneath my feet vibrated, the excitement from the crowd undeniable. Their hype only served to unnerve me more than I already was, but I had to push past my apprehension if I was going to keep my undefeated status.

I was fighting Marcus Hill, an underground up-and-comer who had only lost one out of his last fifteen fights. Having done my own research, I'd been able to easily identify his weakness—his right shoulder, which was injured six months back. Since then, it popped out of its socket if twisted the wrong way. Or right way, depending on who was inflicting the damage.

Jumping up, I cracked my neck from side to side before throwing out a few shadow punches. Pushing out the breath I'd held hostage in my lungs, I locked eyes with Stone and Tripp before walking toward the door.

Here goes nuthin'.

Barreling my way through the crowd, my brothers tight on my heels, I focused on the guy already dancing around inside the ring. *Never get distracted by the noise.* It was a mantra I'd adopted from Stone. He'd yelled it at me a few times when we started sparring together, and it just stuck. It made total sense, and it always kept my attention on what was right in front of me, whether it was in the ring or handling club business.

Marcus hyped up the crowd, trying his hand at some fancy foot-work and entertaining the audience until I approached. Once I was close enough, he stopped jumping around and turned fully toward me. Raising his arm, he pointed at me and shouted, "You're dead." I was surprised I heard him over the sound of everyone screaming. And the fact that he would use those exact words had me instantly furious. The fuck-er was going down hard—in and out, quick defeat. Then I'd escape and drown myself in a bottle of whatever would do the trick that evening.

Tripp grabbed the ropes and parted them enough for me to pass through, planting my feet directly in the corner while waiting for the fight to begin. Since I was involved in the underground fighting aspect of MMA, there weren't many rules. Actually, there weren't any rules to speak of, but I was sure it was frowned upon to kill someone during a fight.

Even in the absence of guidelines, the people who set up the bouts tried to pair the fighters as best they could, putting them in similar class-es. Ours was the middleweight category, putting us both around a hun-dred and eighty-five pounds. Marcus and I were similar in stature, him only standing an inch shorter than my six-foot frame. While we were both lean, I was cut everywhere it counted. Marcus was in decent shape, although he carried a few extra pounds around his belly. It was in that added weight I would find more weakness.

I barely heard the ring announcer finish his speech, spouting off our names and fight histories, before it was time to put this guy on his ass and claim my prize money. Slowly approaching, we sidestepped each other, our gazes locked and ready for any unexpected moves. He was quick . . . but I was quicker. I kicked out and slammed the top of my foot into his ribs, making him stumble backward, a grimace instantly lighting up his face. Not taking a few seconds to compose himself before coming at me was his mistake. He should have thought about his next strategic move, but he was eager to show everyone what he could do.

Too eager.

And it was his downfall in the end.

Rushing toward me, he managed to land a blow to my side, but when he attempted to strike again, he missed as I danced away. While he staggered forward, I surprised him with a few rapid blows to the kidneys, knocking the breath from his body before he even realized he'd been hit.

While I normally reveled in the thrill of the fight, stretching out my time in the ring as long as possible because it was the only place I'd actually felt at home, that time was different. The fear of accidentally killing someone else drove me to distraction.

All I wanted to do was end the bout, lose myself to a few stiff drinks and possibly give in to one of the wannabes who'd been shamelessly throwing themselves at me. I could use a warm body for an hour or two.

Deciding enough was enough, I struck like a coiled snake. With a sudden right hook, I knocked Marcus flat on his back, dazed and confused. While he tried to right himself, I dropped to the mat, wrapped my legs around his body and captured his right arm, rotating it harshly in the wrong direction. As soon as I heard his shoulder pop out of place, I knew the fight was over.

With his free hand, he tapped the mat, signaling his submission.

I jumped to my feet and strode to my corner of the ring, waiting for my name to be announced as the winner. Stone and Tripp were there, huge smiles of pride on both their faces as they slapped my shoulder and shouted out congratulations, making me grin for a brief moment.

I turned toward the center of the ring to see what was going on. As soon as my eyes connected with Marcus's, I sort of felt bad, but only for a brief moment. Anyone looking at him could tell he was in agony, one of his buddies trying to pop his shoulder back into place. Contrary to

popular belief, I didn't get off on going around hurting people. Yes, inju-
ries—and apparently death—were all on the table as soon as we stepped
into this ring, but that didn't mean the smell of blood made me high.
No, I honed my skill to the point that I was undefeated in this world,
and all I wanted was to go against a worthy opponent. So far, I hadn't
had many.

Jerking my head toward Stone and Tripp after I'd been declared the
winner, I silently communicated for them to follow me. All winnings
were picked up in the back office, and while the door was guarded by
two large buffoons, I wasn't scared in the least. Knowing I could take
them both out in five seconds flat hitched a swagger to my gait.

"Tripp, can you do me a favor and grab my bag from the room?" I
asked before disappearing inside to grab my prize money.

"You got it," he replied. "Be right back." He disappeared while
Stone stood outside, waiting for me to re-emerge. No one was allowed
to accompany the fighters inside the office. They'd been robbed in the
past, hence the two roided-out guys standing watch.

The purse that night amounted to fifteen thousand dollars, the
most I'd won to date. I wasn't stupid; I knew the result from my last
fight upped the ante. At least something good had come out of it.
Morbid way to look at the situation, but it was all I had.

Tripp walked toward us, my duffel bag slung over his shoulder.
He threw it to me and I stuffed the envelope full of cash inside, zipped
it back up and headed toward the exit. There were a few more fights
scheduled for that evening, but I wasn't stickin' around. All I wanted to
do was go back to the clubhouse to hopefully get drunk and get laid, in
no particular order.

"At least we didn't see any of those fuckin' Reapers here tonight."

"Yeah, one less thing we have to worry about right now, at least."
I had no idea who was saying what, Stone's and Tripp's voices melding
together at some point. All I could focus on was getting out of there,
the smell of piss, smoke and body odor more potent the longer I remained inside the confines of the old, dilapidated building.

Just as we were about to walk through the door and escape, a flurry
of movement to my left caught my attention. Then I heard a panicked

female voice saying something I couldn't quite make out, but I knew enough to recognize that she was in some sort of trouble. There were throngs of people milling around all over the place, so I wasn't quite sure why the hairs on the back of my neck bristled. Something warned me to stop and take notice, though. And the closer I stepped, pushing past some of the people blocking my view, the more amped up I became.

"Why won't she look at me?" a gruff voice shouted. Shuffling closer, my brothers close on my heels, I could finally see what was happening. Initially, they'd been confused as to why I'd turned around, but as soon as they'd heard what I had, they'd followed me, ready to jump into action if necessary.

"Because she doesn't want to have anything to do with you," one of the women yelled back. "She hasn't responded to any of your texts, so take the hint." A spitfire with shoulder-length blonde hair stood toe to toe with none other than Marcus Hill, challenging him as best she could. Physically she was no match, but that didn't stop her.

I caught bits and pieces of their argument, realizing she wasn't fighting for herself, but for another person. But who? And where were they? Stepping so close I was standing directly behind the shouting female, my eyes wandered all over the place, trying to see everyone who was in close proximity.

"Well, I'm not goin' anywhere until she at least lets me explain what happened," Marcus threatened, his left hand gripping his right shoulder, pressing his fingertips into the swollen flesh. He still hadn't seen me, too focused on arguing with the blonde.

Peering over the feisty woman's shoulder, I finally saw another woman crouching in the corner, her head down and tilted to the side. All I could see of her was her long dark hair, strands that shielded her face from everyone there. Protecting her. Assessing her body language, I could tell she was frightened. The slight tremble of her shoulders infuriated me, bringing out a fierceness I'd only possessed while enthralled in one of my fights.

"If you don't leave her alone right now, I'm calling the cops," the blonde woman threatened, fisting her hands at her sides in an attempt to gain some semblance of control. Without knowing her, I instantly liked her. Anyone willing to stick up for someone else was okay in my book.

Marcus looked around at the numerous sets of eyes watching the situation unfold, angry he wasn't getting what he wanted. When his gaze landed on me, the tick in his jaw told me my presence was about to make things worse. Not only had he been denied from talking to the dark-haired woman, but the victor of his fight was watching intently, ready to pounce if given the opportunity. I knew his shoulder was still throbbing and there was no way he wanted to tussle with me again, so he smartly decided to let it go.

"Fine," he bit out. "She's a *freak* anyway," he emphasized, taking a step back. The dark-haired woman snapped her head up at his comment, and it was then I was able to finally see her. A shiver shot straight through me, an audible gasp forced from my mouth. An angelic face with the most entrancing caramel-colored eyes glared at Marcus before quickly connecting with the woman to her left, her features and expression in direct contrast to one another. Glancing back and forth between the both of them, I could tell there was some sort of relation. Sisters, maybe?

Stone and Tripp walked up beside me, watching with as much interest as I was. Marcus backed up another step after he'd seen all three of us standing side by side. He could act as tough as he wanted in front of two helpless females, but he knew I'd pound him into the middle of next week if he made a wrong move.

Before I could open my mouth to tell him to fuck off, the dark-haired female tugged on the other woman's arm, raised her hands in the air and signed something to her. The blonde woman responded, signing back at a rapid pace. I had no clue what they were saying to each other, but I was fascinated by the scene unfolding in front of me.

Idiotically, I thought that I'd be able to identify a deaf person simply by looking at them, but I now knew how stupid that assumption was. Caught up in watching the two of them communicate with one another, it took my brain a few extra seconds to register what Marcus had just said about the deaf woman.

I stepped forward and grabbed him by his throat, pushing him against the nearest wall. "Don't you ever say that about her again," I seethed. "You got it, Hill?" I said his name with disgust, shoving at his injured shoulder when he refused to answer me. Instead of words, a howl flew from his mouth, his body crumpling against the wall behind him.

When I deemed him no longer a threat, I released him and turned around, striding toward the two women. My gaze was fierce enough to deter anyone else from getting involved. The crowd who had initially been surrounding us dispersed, leaving only myself, Stone, Tripp and the two females remaining.

"Are you all right?" I asked both of them, not quite sure who to direct my question to. I knew she couldn't hear me, but that didn't stop me from flitting my attention to her as well.

"Yes, thank you," the blonde woman replied, throwing her arm over the other woman's shoulder and pulling her close.

"Do you want us to escort you and your friend outside? Just to make sure Marcus doesn't try anything else?" I waited patiently for her to let me know what my next move was gonna be.

"My sister."

"What?" I asked.

"She's my sister. Kena. And my name is Braylen."

Pointing to myself and then my buddies, I said, "Jagger, Stone and Tripp." I was talking to both of them but I'd kept my eyes on Kena, watching her every reaction. Locking eyes with me, a small smile graced her full lips, and it was right then that I knew I was done for.

Changed forever.

CHAPTER FIVE

Kena

THE THREE MEN WHO HAD thankfully come to our aid wore their appearance of intimidation well. But I guessed at a gentleness underneath, a trait I was sure not many people bore witness to. I saw it in the way they'd tried to protect my sister and me, in the softness in their eyes when they reassured us that Marcus wouldn't be a problem any longer.

I'd mistakenly gone on a date with Marcus Hill a few weeks back. He'd come into my family's restaurant a few times and had always seemed nice, never giving me any reason not to trust him. I know it sounded weird since I didn't know him, but I naively thought I could spot an asshole right out of the gate. As it turns out, some jerks conceal their assholishness during the initial encounters, sucking their victim in and revealing their true selves only when they deem it necessary. Such as when they'd had too much to drink. As was in my case.

He knew about my handicap, although if I referred to myself as impaired around my family they lovingly scolded me. Despite realizing I was different, he'd asked me out anyway, and after some persistence on his part, I'd agreed. But on one condition—that Braylen tagged along. I wanted her with me for two reasons. One, because I hadn't been on a date since my senior year of high school, and two, so she could help communicate for me.

My sister and I met him at a bar he'd chosen, which was the first mistake, because all he did that evening was throw back shot after shot. When he'd become quite intoxicated, we told him we were leaving, which was when he became a little too handsy with me, completely ignoring the horrified look on my face. He ended up shoving my sister to the side when she grabbed his arm to let me go. When I turned hysterical with fear, I must have hit a nerve because he backed away and allowed us to walk out without further incident. I had no idea if it had dawned on him just how aggressive he'd become, or if he simply thought I wasn't worth the effort after I refused his advances.

When Braylen had begged me to come out to the fight that evening, I had no idea Marcus was going to be there. He'd briefly mentioned being involved with fighting, but it was such a fleeting statement I never paid much attention to it. So imagine my surprise when I saw him saunter down the narrow walkway toward the ring. Because of where our seats had been, he hadn't seen me. Until later. As soon as I saw him, I'd wanted to leave, but the other guy who had entered the ring after him kept me glued to my rickety chair.

An undeniable fierceness shrouded him, a potency which drew me in right away. A sensation I couldn't comprehend, but I knew I had to stay until the end. Luckily, Marcus had lost, making the mystery fighter the victor. Or at least he was a mystery to me. To the fans shouting his name, he was obviously well-known.

Standing outside and finally breathing in some fresh air, I'd managed to calm down some, thankful these three men had come to our rescue. I had no idea how far Marcus would have taken it if we were left to deal with him all by ourselves. Not that I didn't have faith that Braylen would have jumped on his back like an angry spider monkey if he refused to leave me alone, of course. She was fiercely protective of me. And I loved her all the more for it.

Jagger tentatively approached me, a curious look on his face while he attempted to converse with me. He'd seen my sister and I signing to each other so he knew there was something different about me, but I bet he had no idea what it really was.

"Is she all right?" he asked Braylen, turning his head toward her at the last minute. "She's not hurt, is she?" He looked worried about me and I found it rather sweet. I didn't know him, yet there was a strange pull between us. I felt it, and I noticed he did as well. His expression was one of a child looking at something wondrous for the first time, the innocent curiosity which came from being exposed to something unknown and . . . different.

Braylen smiled at Jagger then turned her attention toward me. Raising her hands, she signed, *He's quite the hottie, isn't he? Look at those arms of his, and that butt. Wow! Did you see his butt, Kena? And what about his two buddies. Holy shit, woman. We couldn't have been saved by hotter men.*

I smiled, responding with, *Jagger is hot, for sure. I hope none of them know what we're saying.* I glanced at Jagger and saw him intently watching the exchange between Braylen and me, waiting for my sister to confirm that I was indeed all right. *Tell him I'm fine.*

Do you want me to give him your number? she asked. I looked at her like she'd lost her mind. *What? You can text, can't you?*

What I strangely felt toward Jagger was nothing I'd ever experienced before. Maybe it was simply hormones. Or maybe it was the knight in shining armor syndrome. Whatever the cause, I couldn't deny I felt something toward the mysterious fighter. So I allowed myself a moment to consider Braylen's question. But in the end I declined, not being in the right frame of mind to put myself out there.

Tapping my index and middle finger against my thumb, I signed, *No.* I saw the disappointment on her face right away, and I knew she wasn't going to let me dismiss him that easily. I would have thought she'd be onboard with my refusal because of what had transpired with Marcus, but she still pushed me.

Why not? she asked. *I really don't think he's anything like that asshat. Plus, you need to get out more. Stop hiding behind this bullshit,* she signed, pointing to my throat. *Live a little, and what better way to do that than with this fuckable man?*

My eyes widened and she laughed. I dared to glance at the guy in question, and thank goodness he still had no idea what we were saying to each other.

After Braylen gave me a subtle glare, she turned toward Jagger and said, "Kena is fine. She was a little rattled, but she's okay now. She also wants me to thank you and your friends"—she looked over at his buddies quick before locking eyes with Jagger again—"for helping us out. Kena is forever in your debt. And because of that, she wants me to give you her phone number." I grabbed her arm to try and turn her toward me, but she wouldn't budge. Instead she was smiling, extending her hand for his phone.

"How are we gonna talk on the phone?" Jagger asked slowly, as if my sister hadn't realized this.

"You can text, can't you?" Braylen retorted, smiling even wider.

The whole time they were conversing, I couldn't stop the embarrassment from creeping up and stealing over my skin, my face no doubt bright red. Continuing to try and get my sister's attention was futile; she was dead set on fixing me up with Jagger. After she'd finally put my number in his phone, he raised his head and pinned me with his entrancing amber-colored eyes. Biting down on his lower lip, he seemed to be struggling with something. Maybe he only took my number to be polite. Or maybe he wanted to speak to me. I had no idea, but I wasn't complaining about having to look at him for a few more minutes.

"I don't know if I can do this," he suddenly blurted. My heart fell, rejected before he even got to know me. I should have felt nothing, since I was the one who had initially refused my sister's persistence, but his dismissal hurt all the same. "I think she's absolutely beautiful, and I would love to get to know her, but how the hell am I gonna talk to her?"

I wasn't quite sure who exactly Jagger was talking to, because his eyes roamed from Braylen to his friends, only resting on me for a few seconds before looking at the ground. He seemed put out all of a sudden, as if it were a burden to be mixed up with someone like me.

It made me feel less than.

Inadequate.

Without thinking, I grabbed Braylen's arm, and that time she gave me her attention. I signed furiously. *You tell him not to bother with me then. Don't call me. I'm not someone to be tolerated. To hell with him if he doesn't want to get to know me.*

Braylen looked at me strangely. "I'm sure that's not what he meant,

Kena." She didn't sign to me that time.

"What did she say?" Jagger asked, suddenly looking interested again.

"Nothing. Don't pay attention to her. She's just flustered. It's been a long day." I tried to turn Braylen toward me once more so I could tell her something else, but she refused. "I'm not looking at you, little sis, so stop trying." Stomping my foot like an errant child did nothing but make her laugh. "Not gonna work, so stop it," she chided. Folding my arms over my chest, I blew a strand of hair out of my face before turning and walking away. If she wasn't going to listen to me, I was done. My feelings had been hurt, and all I wanted to do was go home. Maybe soak in a hot bath before turning in for the night. The thing was . . . I knew Jagger would run on a constant loop in my head until I finally succumbed to sleep. Even while still being upset with him, as well as with my sister.

Maybe I'd taken what he'd said the wrong way. Or maybe I hadn't. Either way, I was used to people ignoring me, never giving me the time of day because I was different.

I briskly walked away from the small group, but didn't get very far before a firm yet gentle hand wrapped around my upper arm, stopping me.

When I turned my head, I saw Jagger staring at me like I was a piece of lost treasure. His eyes roamed my face, focusing a little too long on my lips before connecting with my eyes.

Everyone else stood back while we had our own private moment. "I'm sorry if I offended you, Kena. That wasn't my intention at all. It's just . . . I'm not sure how to talk to you. Look at me now. You can't hear anything I'm saying and I have no idea how to tell you . . . well . . . anything. You're so fucking beautiful that I'm losing all my sensibilities just being near you." He stepped closer, his scent wafting around me and making me dizzy. In a good way. "I guess there's no harm in telling you that I'd love nothing more than to kiss you, to feel the warmth of your mouth against mine. I have no idea why I'm saying this, except for that I guess I'm safe to do so because you can't hear me. Which sucks, by the way." The more he spoke, the more uncomfortable he appeared.

"Listen to me ramble on. Sorry, I have no idea why I keep talking except that I have this overwhelming need to tell you that you do something to me. You make me feel . . . relevant. If that makes any sense at all, which it probably doesn't." His tongue snuck out and ran over his bottom lip, immediately drawing my attention to his delectable mouth.

As if a lightbulb had switched on inside his head, he suddenly asked, "Can you read lips?" Turning around to look for my sister, he yelled, "Can she read lips?"

"No, she never bothered to learn." Jagger instantly relaxed, but it was short-lived. "But she can hear everything you're saying." Braylen strolled up behind Jagger, put her hand on his shoulder and leaned in close. "You see, Kena's not deaf. She just can't speak. Whatever you just told her is now ingrained in that brain of hers, so it better have been good." My sister chuckled as she grabbed my hand and pulled me away. "Time to go now, boys. Thanks again for your assistance." She looked back at Jagger. "You better text her. You'd be a fool not to."

Daring to take a look back at the guy who just threw my world into chaos, I saw the wheels turning, watching him come to the realization that I'd heard him tell me he wanted to kiss me. That I made him feel relevant.

I had no doubt he would have never told me those things if he thought I could hear, but I loved that he'd bared a piece of himself. Even though he thought his words fell on deaf ears.

Every pun intended.

Before we slipped inside Braylen's car I heard one of his friends say, "Looks like you'll be learnin' some sign language, my man."

CHAPTER SIX

Kena

WHY DID YOU GIVE HIM *my number?* I asked Braylen while she flitted around her room trying to get ready for work. It'd been two days since I'd met Jagger and still he hadn't reached out. I tried to convince myself that I didn't care, that it was for the best, but I was disappointed. He'd been attracted to me; he'd said so. He told me he wanted to kiss me, so why the silence?

My sister ignored me, mumbling words every now and again. She drove me nuts refusing to answer. Before she became even more distracted, I grabbed her arm and spun her toward me, letting her know I wasn't going to let up until she answered my question.

Sighing overdramatically, she tucked her hair behind her ear and stared at me for countless seconds before opening her mouth. "Because you need to get out, Kena. You need to stop shying away from people and put yourself out there more. Hiding at work and then back at home is not doing you any good." Braylen only signed to me when we were in the company of others, and when she wanted to talk about them. Otherwise, she spoke to me like any other normal person, something I thoroughly appreciated.

I'm not hiding.

"You are. I love you, but you're in denial, sis." Throwing a pair of jeans on her bed, she brushed past me toward her closet to search for a shirt.

When she emerged, I signed more emphatically. *I would have thought you wanted me to stay clear of all fighters, especially after what happened with Marcus.* Shifting from one foot to the other, I patiently waited for the line of crap she was going to lay on me.

"You can't group all of them together. Plus, I don't know . . . ," she stalled. "There's something about Jagger I found calming. Weird choice of word for his type, but there it is. Plus, the way he was watching you when you weren't paying attention was endearing."

Endearing or stalker-ish? I smirked before she tossed a pillow at my head. *Either way, I'm not getting mixed up with him. You say there's something calming about him, but I detect there's a very dangerous element surrounding him.* What I'd really been referring to was him being hazardous to my heart.

"It's up to you either way. I think you should give him a shot if he texts you, though. Take it slow. Give it time and get to know him. If you're not interested, let it go. But if I'm right about him, and I really think I am, he could be good for you." After Braylen finally decided on an outfit, skinny jeans and a red tank top, she threw on her sneakers and grabbed her smock. She was running late and would have to leave right away if she was going to make it to work on time. Thankfully, her best friend owned the hair salon, Transform, where she worked.

Sensing there was nothing left to say, I followed her toward the front door, walking past her while she locked up. Happy to head into work, I started my trusty Nissan and decided I would welcome the distraction of my job; otherwise, I'd overthink the entire situation involving Jagger.

Braylen and I hadn't ventured far from the nest, renting a house ten minutes from my parents, eight minutes from the restaurant and five minutes from the salon.

I never had any big dreams of traveling around the world, or going away to school far from home. I was a homebody, attending a nearby college and earning my accounting degree, which enabled me to take care of the finances for my parents' lucrative restaurant. They were doing so well there were plans to branch out a few towns over. They paid me a nice salary, so I couldn't complain. Sure, I could have gotten a job at a large accounting firm, but because of my "challenge" I was simply more comfortable around my family.

In most cases, I coped rather well in life, but there were moments, like with the altercation with Marcus, where I found myself shutting down. I hated that I couldn't scream at him to leave me alone, leaving my older sister to fight my battles for me yet again. She'd been the first one to stick up for me, defending me against the bullies at school. Little did she know, sometimes she did more harm than good. When she called out those little bastards, they teased me relentlessly whenever she wasn't around. I never told her because I didn't want to make her feel bad.

My parents wanted me to have as normal a childhood as possible, which was why they had enrolled me in public school. Sure I couldn't talk, but I could hear just fine. I'd write down any questions I had for the teachers, and everything worked out fine until fifth grade, when the bullying just got worse. The kids called me a mute, which I was, but the way they said it made me feel like a freak, as if I had a choice in what had happened to me.

When I was an infant, I'd contracted a viral infection which had damaged the nerves in my larynx. A freak thing. There was optimism that the damage wouldn't be permanent, but as the years passed and I still wasn't able to form a sound, the doctors said there was no more hope. Because of that, I'd never spoken a day in my life. In the past, I often wondered what my voice would have sounded like, fantasizing about all the things I would've loved to say to my family, and to the few friends I'd made growing up. To tell someone I loved them, for them to hear me say the words, was what I had dreamed about the most. But it would never happen, so I let those fantasies die long ago. No use dwelling on the impossible.

The bullying had gotten so bad that one day during sixth grade my parents found me bawling my eyes out, tucked into the far corner of my closet. After some prodding, I finally spilled the beans, signing so fast I was surprised they understood me at all. Finally deciding enough was enough, they'd moved me to a school for the deaf. At least there I'd be around kids who had to communicate the same way I did.

Signing was my main way of communicating, but for my family, since I could hear what they were saying, they'd simply spoken. Occasionally, there were times when they would talk, stop to sign, and then go back to talking.

Almost like speaking Spanglish, but for sign language.

CHAPTER SEVEN

Kena

PULLING INTO THE PARKING LOT of the restaurant, I noticed we were rather busy. Crowds sometimes gave me anxiety, so I was thankful there was a back entrance, something I used quite a bit. Walking down the short hallway toward my office, I heard my phone ding, alerting me to a text message. Rooting through my purse, I found the device buried at the bottom. I hurriedly swiped the screen, thinking it was Braylen switching plans for later, but to my astonishment the message was from an unknown number. All it said was *Hello.*

My heart thumped against my chest, my breathing suddenly coming in short spurts. *Is this him?*

Closing the door behind me, I walked across the room and sat behind the desk. My office was small but it did the trick, locking me away from everyone else. The walls were painted a neutral tan color, which I found oddly soothing. My desk was big enough to house a computer, phone and lamp. I often listened to music while I worked, so I had a docking station as well, which charged my phone while Pandora played.

Five minutes had passed and I still hadn't responded to the text. There was a chance it could be a wrong number, but deep inside I knew it wasn't. Still . . . I hesitated.

Did I want to start talking to Jagger?

Open myself up only to be disappointed in the end?

Being guarded was a natural defense, but after warring back and forth with myself for another ten minutes, I finally gave in and typed a response.

Kena: Who is this?

Three little dots appeared on the screen.

Unknown: Jagger.

Unknown: How are you?

My breath caught in my throat, small beads of perspiration forming by my hairline. I had a sneaking suspicion it was him, so why was I so nervous? What about him had me suddenly flustered? Closing my eyes, I brought forth the memories of when I'd met him two nights prior. Fast-forwarding past the unfortunate encounter with Marcus, I focused on when my eyes first met his. I'd been so infuriated after hearing that ass call me a freak that I hadn't seen anything but red. Still in the throes of anger, I soon calmed when I'd realized that someone had come to our rescue.

A stranger.

A gorgeous, tattooed, tough and intimidating-looking fighter.

The first thing I noticed about Jagger was his eyes. I knew it sounded all dreamy and lovely and cliché, but it was the truth. His eyes captivated me as soon as our gazes met, the amber color almost mesmerizing. The shade was beautiful, but it was the intensity behind them which drew me in and held me prisoner.

To what, I had no idea.

Not yet, at least.

I'd only had seconds to rake in his entire being before I came across as some sort of visual stalker, so I'd made it count. My eyes darted from his dark golden hair, to his strong jaw, to his full and inviting lips. Then my gaze went lower, noticing his muscular arms which were covered in ink before dropping to the cut physique hidden underneath his clothing. I'd seen him earlier in all his glory while he was in the ring, only wearing a pair of black shorts, his chest bare and on display for all to see.

Based on the shouts of the women, they were enthralled with him as well—not that he paid any attention. And not that I'd noticed.

Kena: I'm fine.

Shaking my head, I'd instantly wanted to delete my response, but it was too late. I was sure he'd already seen it, seen what a doofus I was. Not having used that word since I was a kid, it seemed to fit perfectly. My lack of flirting, even over text, proved how out of practice I'd been. Not that I'd ever had much experience, of course.

Throwing my phone in my desk drawer, I busied myself with numbers. Work needed to be done, plus I needed a very real distraction. My impatience to hear Jagger's response annoyed me, though, and it was simply one more thing to add to the growing list of reasons why I'd chosen to keep myself hidden from the world as much as possible. My family didn't understand it—Braylen, mainly—but they didn't have a handicap they had to endure. Sorry, not handicap . . . challenge. No, to hell with that. It was a handicap, no matter how they tried to spin it. Don't get me wrong, I wasn't a "poor me" type of girl, but I hid behind it when it suited me. Which was quite often.

My cell vibrated inside the drawer, drawing me back from my internal deliberations. Closing my eyes, I willed my inner strength to barrel forth, to deter me from glancing at his response, but it was futile. Curiosity won out and I pulled the drawer open to retrieve my phone, swiping the screen so I could see his reply.

Jagger: I'll text you later. Have to take care of something.

The door to my office came crashing open, my surprise at the intrusion swallowing the disappointment I felt reading Jagger's last text.

Mom, you scared me, I signed before relaxing in my chair.

"Sorry, sweetie, the door flung open too easily," she said, smiling widely as she approached. My mom, Caroline, was a beautiful woman. While she was short in stature, matching my five-foot-three frame, she made up for it with her feistiness, a trait my father often told us he loved. Although there were a few times I was sure he wasn't a big fan, mainly when they argued. Thankfully, those occasions were few and far between.

Did you need me? I asked, waiting to find out why she'd burst in.

Rounding the desk, she came to sit on the corner, tucking an unruly strand of hair behind my ear. She hesitated before speaking, which told me she was going to say something I didn't want to hear.

"Kevin is going to be an hour late for his shift," she said, turning her eyes away from mine for a brief moment. "He said he has personal business to attend to that he can't get out of." Fidgeting, she finally looked at me again before asking, "Do you think you can help out in the kitchen until he gets here?"

I knew my mom wouldn't ask me to help out unless she absolutely had to, so as it turned out I really didn't have a choice at all. Well, I did, but I'd do anything to eliminate the look of worry in her eyes right then. My dad wasn't feeling well so he hadn't come in, and my sister was already at her other job. So it was either I help out or my mother would have to run back and forth between the kitchen and helping wait tables, since we were down a waitress at the moment. Given the option, I would much rather help cook than take people's orders, seeing as how I couldn't answer any of their questions and all.

Our regulars knew I couldn't speak, but whenever newbies came in . . . Let's just say I was thankful for my office hidden in the back of the restaurant.

Who's going to be helping me out until Kevin gets here?

"Eddie. It's a little busy right now, but it's starting to calm down. The two of you will be fine. Then when Kevin gets in, you can come back here and finish up."

I liked Eddie a lot. He'd always managed to make me laugh, entertaining me with one of his crazy, adrenaline-infused stories. Plus, he wasn't too bad to look at. With shoulder-length black hair—which he always had tied back when working—and brown eyes, he was certainly a cutie. Not my type, but good-looking nonetheless.

Okay, just give me two minutes and I'll be right there.

She leaned over and kissed my cheek. "Thanks, sweetheart. I really appreciate it." Giving my mom a faint smile, I waited until she left my office before taking a few deep breaths to steel my nerves.

I wasn't a recluse or someone who shied away from all social interactions, but I did become slightly unnerved when thrown into a situation I wasn't completely comfortable with. I'd get over it, though. I always did.

Tying my hair back, I ventured out toward the front of the restaurant. Ten minutes later and I was in full swing, helping cook some of the lunch specials for the day. The time flew by. Between orders, Eddie regaled me with stories of his latest thrill-seeking adventure. A month back he went base jumping with a few buddies of his, said the feeling was unlike anything he'd ever experienced. I listened attentively, nodding and smiling so he knew I was paying attention.

Although Eddie was only twenty-four, three years older than me, he seemed much older—not necessarily looks-wise, but in experience. I guessed it had to do with him living his life to the fullest. I was sure he had fears, everyone did, but he never exposed them or let them hold him back.

Glancing at the clock, I noticed two hours had passed. As I was about to search for my mother, Kevin barreled into the kitchen, furiously tying his apron around his back so he could take over. Leaning in, he kissed my temple and gave me a thousand-watt smile.

"I'm so sorry I'm late, Kena. Please forgive me," he pleaded, holding his hand over his heart while he gave me the puppy dog eyes. And boy, what eyes they were. Pools of dark blue which promised wicked nights of fun, with full, lickable lips to match. Kevin was quite the sight, standing before me awaiting my faux absolution. Little did he know I could pardon him almost anything, his dimpled cheeks persuading me rather quickly.

He remained motionless until I smirked and signed, *You're lucky I like you.*

Kevin had learned sign language when he was a kid. His aunt Louise had been born deaf, so communicating with her that way had simply become second nature for him and his entire immediate family.

Love you, pumpkin, he hastily signed before taking the spatula from my hand. I laughed at his ridiculous nickname for me, shaking my head and walking back toward my office.

Braylen had often asked me why I never gave him a chance, seeing as how he'd asked me out a few times in the past. Repeatedly I'd explained that while he was rather attractive, much more so than Eddie—not that I was comparing them to each other—I simply wasn't interested. To clarify, I *had* been interested in accepting one of his invitations for dinner and a movie, but after I saw the way women threw themselves at him after one of his shows, I decided not to put myself into a situation which would only serve to hurt me in some way.

Kevin was the lead guitarist for a local rock band called Breakers, and they had quite the following. Braylen and I had gone to a few of their gigs, and had really enjoyed ourselves. The last time he asked me out, which was two months ago, I'd finally told him the reason why I wouldn't accept. Instead of trying to convince me otherwise, he simply nodded and kissed my cheek, telling me if I ever changed my mind, he would be the happiest man alive.

After another couple hours, I'd finally finished my work, so I texted Braylen and told her to meet me at home when her shift ended. Checking my phone one more time, I saw Jagger hadn't texted again, and it was with vast disappointment that I drove home. I vowed right then not to allow myself to get all worked up over some guy I didn't even know.

CHAPTER EIGHT

Jagger

ANNOYED I HAD BEEN PULLED away from texting with Kena, I tossed my cell on the table outside Chambers before entering. No one was allowed to bring their phones inside when we were discussing club business except on rare occasions, which always had to be approved by our president.

Walking around the large oblong meeting table, I settled into my assigned seat and impatiently waited to find out why we'd all been gathered last-minute.

The men filed in one after another, taking their seats and conversing amongst themselves. Marek and Stone were the last to arrive, their expressions hiding the direness of what was about to unfold.

Once our leader pulled his chair closer to the table, he rested his folded hands on top of the etched wood. A frown decorated his face, his dark hair disheveled and sticking up in several places. There were a few more lines around his eyes than from months prior, telling the amount of stress he'd been under. Steering the club away from the Los Zappas cartel was taxing, and even more so on Marek and Stone, since they worked so closely together. I knew our prez was still waiting for the green light to snatch Rico Yanez's life, and then he would focus his attention on ridding the world of Psych Brooks, Sully's father. If anyone could even call him that. The man made the Devil look like a pussycat.

"I have news," Marek announced, silencing those who were holding their own sidebar conversations. Everyone turned toward the head of the table, eagerly awaiting the next words to fall from his mouth. Brief silence danced around the room, each member taking comfort in the unknown, for as brief as it was. "I got the call I've been waiting for." After briefly locking eyes with his second in command, he leaned forward and pinned the rest of us with his intensity. "Rafael Carrillo called me to tell me we could have Yanez." Everyone remained silent, fearing they'd miss something if they uttered a word or moved a muscle. "He instructed a few of his men to follow Yanez, gathering his own intel to support our claim that his right-hand man was continuing to deal with the Reapers after he'd cut off all dealings with them. Apparently he found what he was looking for."

Marek turned his head toward Zip. "Good work." Two words and the youngest member beamed with pride.

Zip had been tasked with following Yanez a while back, trying to obtain any kind of evidence he could to give to Marek, who in turn would bring it to Carrillo to show him just how disloyal the shady bastard had been to the cartel. He'd snapped pictures of Yanez with Sam Koritz, a corrupt DEA agent who'd raided our club, as well as photos with Psych Brooks. It was those pics with the president of the Savage Reapers which had apparently spurred the cartel to take action.

Looking from one man to another, I wasn't quite sure where to rest my attention. The room had remained silent, Marek's words festering for all of us. He was finally going to get justice for his wife, and while the thought pleased me, I wasn't afraid to admit to myself that I was a bit unnerved at what it could mean for our club. With an integral part of the cartel now being extinguished, would they look to make up for the loss?

I knew Marek and Carrillo had some sort of agreement, the head of the cartel releasing us from their grip because of it, but I still didn't trust the guy. Who was to say he wouldn't go back on his word in the future, forcing us back under their wing whenever he deemed necessary? I hadn't been privy to any of the meetings that had taken place, so

I only had my suspicions to go on, but I prayed with everything inside me that my concerns would remain unjustified.

"Don't make any plans," Stone said, directing his instruction to the entire room. "We're gonna need you all ready to go when the time comes. Some will come with us to the safe house, others will stand guard at various locations. If anything pops off, we need to be ready." Stone nodded at Marek before leaning back in his chair.

The club kept a safe house an hour away, a place that was used in cases of emergency. It was situated in the middle of a residential area, hidden in plain sight. With a soundproof basement, it was perfect for dealing with unsavory people. The last time I knew of anyone making use of it was when Marek and Cutter had tortured and killed Vex, the guy who'd tormented Sully while she lived with her club.

The boom of the gavel sounded, signaling the meeting was officially over. Rising from my seat, I walked toward the exit, my mind on what was going to happen in the next few days. I was eager to assist Marek in resolving the issue of Yanez, even though I was positive he would never ask for my help, content with leaving me in the background when it came to club business.

As soon as I walked from the room, I grabbed my cell from the table where I'd left it and glided my fingers over the keyboard to text Kena. Just as I was about to hit Send, the phone was suddenly ripped out of my hands. Snapping my head up, I saw Tripp grinning, rifling through my privacy.

"Is this the chick we met at your fight? The deaf one?" he asked, continuing to smile at my unease. Why I was nervous I couldn't say. I just was.

"She's not deaf," I snapped. "She just can't speak."

"So, you gonna fuck her or what?"

"Gimme back my phone," I demanded, my anger rising the longer he held my cell captive. The bastard towered over me, but if he didn't watch it I'd knock him on his ass. Or at least imagine such a thing. While I was quite lethal in the ring, Tripp could certainly give me a run for my money if we ever got into a serious altercation.

"Answer my question first."

"None of your business," I quipped. A need to defend Kena abruptly took over, even if Tripp had just been messing with me.

Looking at my phone, he chuckled before tossing it back to me. "If you need help with sexting, just let me know." He walked away before I could respond, his cocky gait making me want to throw something at the back of his head.

Sending Kena a quick text, I hoped she was near her phone so she could respond. Walking toward the bar, I nodded toward Trigger to pour me a drink. I liked the resident member of the club, his no-nonsense attitude quite amusing most of the time. Thankfully, I'd never been in his line of sight before. Stone took the prize for that one. Ever since he got with Adelaide, Trigger's niece, there's been an all-out battle between the two of them, Trigger going as far as shooting the VP when he found out. Although, since the birth of Stone and Addy's daughter, the tension has seemed to lessen between the two men, only erupting when Stone wanted to get a rise out of Trigger, and vice versa. Using Adelaide as leverage, of course.

> Jagger: Did you officially add my number to your phone so you don't think some random creep is texting you? LOL

LOL? I'm not an LOL kind of guy.

Throwing back a shot, I nodded for Trigger to hit me again.

"You know it's still early, right?" he asked, flinging a white dishtowel over his shoulder. He could ask me all the questions he wanted, as long as he poured me a drink.

"So?"

"Don't you have to train or something for your upcoming fight?"

"That's not for another two weeks," I retorted, growing agitated that I had to explain why I wanted another shot. I knew I was just the prospect of the club, but although the guys treated me well, it was times like this that I felt as if they undermined me. Or was that just concern? I had no idea and didn't have enough energy to deem it one way or the other right then.

Sliding the drink toward me, I tossed it back then slammed the glass on the bar before leaving my seat and walking toward the couch.

Plopping down, I gripped my phone, willing Kena to respond so I had something to occupy my time. I didn't have anything planned for that evening. No fights, and it appeared as if my services weren't needed with the club yet. Having no desire to sit in my small apartment by myself, I lounged on the sofa and waited.

Thankfully, I didn't have to wait too long.

Kena: Who is this?

Did she have that many guys texting her that she honestly didn't know who it was? That we hadn't just been communicating before? And why did that thought irritate me?

Jagger: It's Jagger. Did you really forget about me that fast? Or do you have a slew of men begging for your attention?

No way was I gonna come across as insecure. Chicks hated that shit, right?

Kena: I know who it is. I'm just playing with you. Plead the fifth on the last question.

Before I could read too much into her last text, another one came through.

Kena: And yes, I added you to my phone. Hopefully, you won't make me delete you.

She certainly had some spunk, a trait I hadn't expected. I liked it.

Jagger: I'll try not to.

"Ask her to send you a pic of the twins," Tripp shouted as he walked past me on the way to the bar.

"What are you, fifteen?" I yelled back.

"No, I just haven't seen a nice pair of tits in a while, and from what I remember, she looked like she had some nice ones." I knew Tripp was just bustin' my balls, but his comments made me want to punch him in the face.

"Don't pay the nomad any attention," Stone instructed, sitting down next to me. "He likes to get under my skin with Addy, and he's just doin' the same shit with you. You texting that girl from the other night?"

"Yeah."

"You like her?"

"Yeah," I repeated, counting the seconds until she responded.

Oh God, I can feel myself growing a vagina.

"Then why don't you ask her to do something?" he asked, slinging his arm over the back of the couch and settling in.

"Because I can't talk to her in person. I know she can hear, but what about when she tries to say something to me? I-I mean . . . communicate with me, I know she can't speak," I explained, frustration tripping up my words. "I won't be able to understand her and I'll look like an idiot." Leaning my head back against the cushion, I let out a breath and tried to figure out what to do. I really wanted to get to know Kena, but would it ever go further than just texting?

"Do you like her?" Stone asked a second time, arching his brow in waiting.

"I already told you I did," I snapped.

"Then get off your ass and figure it out," he chided, rising to his feet and towering over me. Confident he'd given me the best advice known to man, he walked toward the exit of the clubhouse.

As I parted my lips to shout after him, my phone chimed.

Kena: Do you have any plans tonight?

Jagger: Why do you ask? Way to play it cool.

Kena: Friend's band is playing. Wanna go?

Jagger: I'm not into chick music, but I'll go if you want me to.

I frowned after re-reading my response, realizing I'd probably come off like a douche.

Kena: Ouch! I think you just shit all over my gender's music. BTW, my friend isn't a girl.

Jagger: Sorry, that didn't come out right. What's the name of the band?

Kena: I don't know if I should tell you now.

Is she seriously pissed off?

Radio silence for what seemed like forever. Just when I thought I'd blown my chances of seeing her that evening, an occurrence I hadn't even thought possible until her suggestion, she responded.

Kena: Breakers.

Jagger: I know them. Who's your friend?

How did she know any of the members? Did she go to school with them? Did she date one of them? More than one? Were they friends with her sister instead? So many questions rattled me.

Kena: Kevin. He works at my family's restaurant.

Jagger: Which restaurant?

Kena: Nope. Not gonna tell. You could be a crazy person. Don't need any sexy fighters showing up and stalking me.

There was no way to identify a tone through text, but I knew she was only messing with me. I wouldn't push for the information, however, in case she was being slightly serious. Plus, I didn't blame her. At least she was being safe, even though it was directed toward me.

Jagger: Smart move. You think I'm sexy?

Kena: :)

Allowing her compliment to boost my ego, I wanted to go out on a high note, ending our messaging tryst with one final request.

Jagger: Text me the name of the bar and the time to meet you. If I can get away, I'll see you later.

Appearing aloof had always worked in the past in garnering female attention, and I prayed my indifference worked with Kena. With each stroke of the keys I knew I was putting myself out there more than I'd initially intended, but I couldn't help myself. My heart pounded at the very thought of seeing her again, her communication with me crystalizing the possibility as a very real one.

Tucking my phone into my back pocket, I leaned forward and rested my forearms on my thighs. Bowing my head, I threaded my fingers through the strands of my hair in distraction. It wasn't a smart move to appear too eager, and although I looked forward to seeing her again, I tried to convince myself that she was just another girl.

A vibration thrummed against my lower back, but I ignored it.

Let's see how well restraint works in my favor.

CHAPTER NINE

Kena

OH MY GOD! GIVE ME back my phone. My hands were going a million miles a minute, my aggravation prevalent in the way my fingers danced through the air and created words. Sentences. Threats to my sister for stealing my phone and texting Jagger.

Only Braylen would be so carefree, flirting with him via messaging. She knew damn well I would've kept my responses short and sweet. And although I probably would've sounded like a dork, it was me and I wasn't going to change for anyone. A stubborn trait which irritated my older sister to no end.

But she didn't understand.

She didn't have anything holding her back from being "normal." While I longed to join the rest of society, I was forced into the shadows, watching everyone else live the life I wish I could. Warped or not, it was my view of the world.

Braylen danced around me, dizzying me into submission, if only until I regained my senses. "Oh, come on, lil' sis. You know damn well you would've let him slip through your fingers with your nonchalant responses and ill-conceived notions of what you think flirting is." She laughed harder with my pathetic attempts to tackle her and retrieve my cell.

Huffing, my face turning a light shade of red, I finally stood still and glared at my infuriating sibling. You would think being three years my elder would've made her more mature, but nope. I'd give her credit, though; with every birthday that passed, she refused to shed her child-like enthusiasm for unexpected situations. I guessed she viewed my predicament as such.

With my hands on my hips, I refused to plead again, instead choosing the effective stance of patience. Although it wasn't my strong suit. Eventually, she'd tire and pass me my phone. Moments prior, I'd caught a few of her responses to Jagger, but she'd been too quick, hopping off the bed before I could snatch the phone away from her.

Finally, after she deemed enough was enough, she crossed the small space between us and gave me a hug. Kissing my cheek, she said, "I did it for your own good. You'll thank me one day," she promised, returning my property.

Sauntering toward my closet, she disappeared inside and rooted around, the slight clang of the hangers drawing my attention. Re-entering the room, she shoved a dark purple tank top at me, flirty ruffles embellishing the front. "Wear those skinny jeans that make your booty pop. And those black heels you never wear."

Which ones? I loved how she could switch my mood from irritation to curiosity.

"The ones that make your legs look like they go on for miles, with the studded spikes on the back."

I'll break my neck. There's a reason I only wore them once. I cringed, remembering the time we'd gone out for drinks and I'd tripped walking back from the ladies' room, almost falling on my face.

"Stop being a baby and just get them. We have a few hours before we have to leave, so make sure you sex it up."

Taking my time, I indulged in a long shower. Thoughts of the upcoming evening took hold as the foam from my vanilla-scented shower gel coated my skin, lost in hopes that something good would finally happen. Not that I'd had a bad life, because I certainly had not. But most days, it seemed like I was simply existing, trudging from one day to the next with snippets of joy laced between.

I wanted to experience all life had to offer.

Passion.

Drama.

Love.

Okay, maybe not the drama piece so much, but the other two would be wonderful.

An hour later, I curled the last strand of my dark hair, flinging it behind my shoulder and integrating it with the rest, using my fingers to soften the look. I slipped on my heels, smoothed down my shirt and checked out my butt. Hey, I had to make sure the jeans still did their job. Deeming myself presentable, I snatched my wristlet from my dresser, flicked off my bedroom light and strode down the short hallway to my sister's room.

Pushing open her door, Braylen gave me an enormous smile when her eyes landed on me.

An impervious whistle cut through the air. "Now that's what I'm talking about," she exclaimed. "Wait until he gets a load of you. He's gonna bust a nut for sure." She teasingly smacked my ass on her way toward the front door. "Let's go, chica. There is some fun to be had."

———◆———

NERVES SHOOK ME THE FURTHER we walked toward the entrance to Rustic, the trendy bar where Kevin's band was set to play that evening. I'd wanted nothing more than to lay eyes on Jagger again, but with every swift tick of the clock, reservation suffocated my hope. In its place, anxiety and fear riddled me, threatening to shut down my evening before it even started.

"Calm down," she soothed. "I see you're getting nervous. Don't get lost inside that head of yours tonight," she said, tapping my temple to help shock me out of my own inner paranoia. "If he shows, great. If he doesn't, we're gonna drink and be merry. Even flirt a little with whoever catches our fancy." She laughed, seizing my hand and dragging me through the entry, steering me directly toward the bar ahead. "Let's get started, shall we?"

There were a few different levels to Rustic, making it a popular hangout for the locals. The first floor housed the main bar and the stage where the bands played, numerous high-back booths as well as tables and chairs scattered throughout providing plenty of seating for the patrons. If people wanted to experience more of a club feel, they ventured down to the basement where another bar stole the entire back wall, a large dance floor stretching across the majority of the open space. The seating on the lower level was selective, only a few couches spread out around the room.

Two cosmopolitans in and I felt nice. Relaxed. Ready to allow the night to unfold and thrust me into unforeseen possibilities—of the good kind, of course. Listening to Braylen chatter on about some of her salon clients, my nerves lessened, having something other than my anxiousness to focus on. Plus, the alcohol licked my veins, pulling me into a nice fog. In the middle of my sister telling me about some hot guy who'd walked into her work, a strong hand clutched my waist, pulling me back into a strong chest. Stumbling backward a step, the mystery guy helped to steady me before making his identity known. My sister was all smiles.

Turning my head to the side, I saw Kevin grinning at my shocked reaction. Leaning in, he kissed my temple before releasing me.

"I'm so happy you two made it," he said, leaning his hip against the bar so he was facing both of us. "You haven't been to a show in a few months." Quirking his brow, he looked lost in thought for a moment. "Yeah, it's been at least six months," he affirmed, a beaming smile lighting up his face once more.

As I brought my hands up in front of me, preparing to sign, an eager-looking redhead sauntered past, eyeing Kevin like she wanted to eat him up. "Hi, Kevin," she cooed, pushing her tits out to make herself more tempting. She was attractive enough, if you found desperation appealing.

"Hi, sweetheart," he answered, winking at her before turning his focus back on us. "Fans," he chuckled. "Comes with the territory."

You certainly don't mind, I signed, smirking at the way he tried to look affronted.

"I'd give it all up in a heartbeat if you'd agree to be mine, pump-kin," he teased, encircling my waist with his arm and pulling me close, kissing the top of my head. "Just say the word." I knew Kevin was at-tracted to me, but I also realized he was only playing, enjoying getting a rise out of me whenever he could.

You'd never be able to live without all the fans fawning at your feet night after night, I jested, resting my hand on his upper arm in a comfortable touch of friendliness.

Contemplating a retort, he wiggled his brows and bit his bottom lip. "Yeah, you're right." I enjoyed the easiness between us, thankful Braylen had convinced me to come out. Plus, Kevin took my mind off Jagger, which was a good thing.

After five minutes of easy banter between the three of us, Kevin spotted his buddies, announcing he had to do some last-minute sound checks before the show. Once we readily agreed to stay until their set was over, he embraced the both of us before sauntering across the room and hopping on stage with his bandmates.

"You having fun?" Braylen asked, bumping my shoulder with hers, a hopeful look in her eye that her baby sister was letting loose and en-joying herself.

I really am. I smiled, harboring a deep appreciation toward her for constantly looking out for me. *I can't believe I'm saying this, but thanks for forcing me out tonight.*

"You're welcome, sweetie. I just wanna see you live a little, ya know?"

Nodding, I turned my attention toward the drink she pushed my way, sliding it across the dark polish of the bar. The alcohol promised an eventful night, dark liquid fingers dragging me into a soft oblivion if I wasn't careful.

Last one. I don't want to get drunk, I signed.

"Why not? It's not like you have to go into work tomorrow if you don't want to." Chewing on her straw, she took quick sips before plac-ing the drink back on the bar. "What's the harm in totally losing your-self tonight?"

Well, for one, I don't want to be throwing up all night. And two . . . , I stalled, *there's no two. I just don't want to be sick and then feel like crap all day tomorrow. Plus, you know what a lightweight I am when it comes to drinking.* Bringing my hands down to rest on the edge of the bar, I reached for my third and final drink of the evening, circling my fingers around the cool glass and gingerly bringing it to my lips.

"Well, you might change your mind," she prompted, her eyes suddenly fixated on someone across the room. Grinning from ear to ear, she looked back at me before broadcasting, "Someone decided to show up after all. And he looks fine as hell."

Slowly turning my head, my eyes locked on Jagger propped against the wall behind him, hands in his pockets and looking quite magnificent. Even from across the room, I knew his gaze rested on me, his beautiful eyes so intense it made me shudder. An undeniable pull existed between us, and all I wanted to do was go to him.

Or run and hide.

I couldn't decide yet.

CHAPTER TEN

Jagger

I WASN'T GONNA LIE. FOR as tough as I appeared, I was a nervous wreck on the inside. Self-doubt propelled itself forward, casting me in the unrelenting shadows of unworthiness. What if she became frustrated because I couldn't communicate with her? Would she deem me undeserving and move on? Even over the distance separating us, I witnessed the comfortability that existed between her and Kevin. His attraction to Kena was obvious, but was she to him? It sure looked like it.

The aloofness I played while texting her came back to kick me in my stubborn ass. Maybe I shouldn't have ignored her last message. Maybe I should have let her be the one to end the back and forth between us. Either way, it was too late now; what was done was done. If she had certain feelings about it, or me, I was sure she'd let me know as soon as I approached.

I hid in the dimness of the bar until Kevin left. Only then did I reveal myself, still while hanging back and watching her. Parts of me felt like a creeper, but when it came to Kena, all bets were off.

Hopefully she's still interested; otherwise, I fear stalking charges in the near future.

Dispelling all unsure thoughts, I shoved off the wall once I knew Kena and her sister had seen me. While I took my time reaching them,

I calmly repeated, *Don't fuck this up. Don't fuck this up. This one is special.* My little mantra had the opposite effect, though. My sudden nerves ricocheted inside me, my heart thumping hard against my chest and threatening to stop altogether the closer I advanced.

Expelling a quick breath, I dodged the ever-growing crowd and finally came to rest a few paces from Kena. Braylen's stare was intense, but the lilt of her smile helped to ease some of my trepidation. I realized Kena would consider her sister's advice when it came to interacting with me, so I knew I had to impress both of them.

"Hi," I greeted, standing so close to Kena our shoulders brushed. Her body trembled from the touch and I prayed it was from excitement, not regret of having invited me that evening. Not wanting to come across as lustful as I felt being near her, I kept my eyes on her face, drinking in her image as best I could before moving on to her sister. Giving them both a genuine, yet apprehensive smile, I eased a little when I saw they both appeared happy to see me.

"Thank God you came," Braylen gushed. "I was beginning to lose all faith in your intentions toward my sister." She laughed, throwing her arm over Kena's shoulder and pulling her close—a protective stance of sorts. Right away, I liked Braylen. A fire lit behind her eyes in warning, although hope danced alongside. The warring emotions both confused and elated me. She loved Kena more than anything, and while she wanted her to be happy, she would slay anyone who hurt her.

"I wouldn't miss seeing you again," I admitted, meeting Kena's eyes briefly before looking away again. Not wanting to reveal too much, I changed the subject. "What are you both drinking?" I asked, signaling for the bartender who was chatting it up with some chick.

Kena raised her hands and signed something to her sister, a look of hesitancy holding her captive.

Braylen responded before turning her attention to me. "She's fussing because she doesn't think she should drink anymore, but I told her to relax and live a little. You never know what can happen," she goaded.

Kena gave Braylen a death stare of sorts before shyly looking over at me, the uncertainty in her beautiful caramel-colored eyes undoing me. The need to assure her that everything would be fine overwhelmed me, a strong urge of protectiveness wrapping its warmth around me. I couldn't explain it, and I didn't think I wanted to; if I unraveled those feelings too much, they might float away and leave me in a place where I no longer wished to exist.

Before my brain could filter my words, I opened my mouth and said, "I won't let anything bad happen to you." I hadn't meant to be so forward, but every syllable was the absolute truth. She smiled at me before looking back to Braylen.

It was clear Kena was nervous, but did she realize I was as well?

Hiding my emotions had been ingrained in me since I was a kid, my father's constant hurtful words toughening me up faster than was deemed healthy. The only time I'd let my guard slip was when I'd met Sully. Like Kena, she'd elicited my protective side, and just like this situation, I couldn't explain it.

"Kinda heavy for a first date," Braylen chuckled. "But I like it." Kena hurriedly signed something again, embarrassment stealing over her skin like a cloak. If I had to guess why, I would have said it was because her sister referred to this as a date, something I wasn't completely opposed to. Ignoring Kena, Braylen looked at me when she said, "I'm going to go check out when the band's gonna start. Be back soon." On her last word, she smiled at her sister before walking toward Kevin and his bandmates.

I'd known Kevin for a few years, as we went to the same high school. He was slightly older than me, and while we weren't technically friends, we'd been to a lot of the same functions—football games and parties, to be specific. I had no issues with him, and I wasn't aware of any negativity he harbored toward me.

I'd chosen not to wear my Knights Corruption cut to the bar that evening, not wanting to draw any unnecessary attention to myself. Don't get me wrong, the pride I felt toward my club would never waver, even though I still only held the title of prospect. Something I hoped changed in the near future. But we didn't have the best reputation around the area, and I didn't want to scare Kena off before she had the chance to get to know me.

The silence between us was palpable, and a tad uncomfortable. I could speak to her, but she couldn't reply—not in a way I understood, at least.

Not yet.

I vowed to rectify that soon, though.

Hoping to rely on body language and common sense, I took a chance and started speaking. "You look beautiful, Kena," I said, figuring it best to start off with an honest compliment.

She blushed before bringing the pads of her fingers of her right hand to her chin, touching briefly before pulling them away. After the gesture, she looked surprised she'd done it, probably because she knew I didn't know what it meant. But I could have guessed, given what I'd just said to her.

"Does that mean 'thank you?'" I asked, smiling when she emphatically nodded. "There's hope for me yet, isn't there?" I saw the quake of her chest, and her lips kicking up in a smile, realizing she was laughing, although not a single vibration of noise escaped. For the first time since I'd met her, her eyes lit up with a subtle hint of joy. Granted, this was only the second time I'd been in her presence, but she wore her emotions on her sleeve—which I found perfect since it made reading her moods much easier. And the more I got to know her, the easier it would become. I was sure of it.

Because I wanted to find out more information about her relationship with Kevin, I decided to cut to the chase and simply ask her, a yes or no the only response necessary.

"So, you and Kevin . . . Are you strictly friends?"

She swiftly nodded.

The bartender finally broke away from the chick he was fawning over and approached. I placed my order for a beer and for him to refill whatever it was Kena was drinking, before returning my full attention back to her.

"Did you ever date him?"

She shook her head.

"Did he ever ask you out?"

She briefly averted her gaze before looking me in the eyes again.

She nodded.

The air thickened around us as I prepared to ask my next intruding question, but I couldn't help myself; I needed to know. Curiosity as well as ego propelled me forth.

"Did you *want* to date him?" I intended to be casual but the more I engaged her, the more I wanted to know about the nature of their relationship.

Looking hesitant, she finally nodded, just as my fingers brushed over hers on top of the bar. An electric jolt passed between us—literally. I shocked her and she pulled her hand back before giving me an innocent smile.

Damnit! She had wanted to be with Kevin at some point. Did she still? I had to find out before I pursued this thing between us.

"Why didn't you, then? Be with him, I mean?" It wasn't until she frowned that I realized she couldn't answer me; I'd strayed off the path of simple yes and no questions. Reverting back, I changed my inquiry. "Do you still want to date him?"

No time passed before she shook her head, placing her hand on my wrist before pulling back once she realized she'd touched me. She looked confused, like she didn't understand her own reaction.

Her response soothed me, and from the intensity in her eyes, I knew she was being truthful. For some reason, she'd wanted to take things beyond friendship with Kevin, but had chosen not to.

Assuming, I pressed, "Was the reason why you chose not to be with him have anything to do with him being in Breakers?" *Depending on her response, I might be in the same boat, once she finds out about my club.*

Another nod.

Choosing not to rush things, and needing to save the information of my being involved with the Knights Corruption for another time, I offered a nod of my own before taking another pull of my beer. I dissuaded myself from interrogating her more about Kevin, not wanting to come off like an untrusting asshole.

Moments passed before Braylen returned. While I wanted to spend more time alone with Kena, there were only so many questions I could ask before our encounter would turn even more awkward.

"What are you two talkin' about?" she asked, taking a healthy sip from her drink, eyeing me first before looking at her sister. Kena signed something, and Braylen glanced at me skeptically before speaking. "Jagger, let me ask you something." *This should be good.* "My sister tells me you were asking her about her relationship with Kevin. Do you believe her when she tells you they're just friends?" Placing her hand on her hip, she leaned in to her sister while waiting for my lips to part and answer.

"Yeah." I wanted to add "For now," but thought wisely against it.

"Good. Because the last thing Kena needs is some possessive ass trying to stake some kind of claim on her. Understand?"

Kena shifted her feet, not sure who to look at.

"Completely."

"Are you possessive and territorial?" she threw at me, taking me by complete surprise.

"Not typically, no."

"What does that mean?" Kena's hands worked feverishly, but Braylen wasn't paying attention, her focus on me and me alone.

"I haven't met someone I've wanted to protect before. That's what I meant." I knew I'd stretched the truth a little when I'd answered. Sully popped into my mind, but I wasn't about to bring her up, because I didn't want the both of them getting the wrong idea. Besides, the way I felt toward Sully was completely different from the way I felt about Kena.

Worlds apart.

"I vouched for you, so don't mess this up," the feisty blonde said, taking a step back and finally turning toward Kena. Braylen shook her head and signed back to her sister. Whatever they were saying, they wanted to keep secret.

Note to self: learn sign language as soon as possible.

CHAPTER ELEVEN

Kena

FINDING A BOOTH CLOSE TO the stage with a perfect view of Kevin and his band, I sat next to Jagger, Braylen sitting across from us. I'd become flustered when Jagger started asking about Kevin, but I didn't want to lie. Yes, I'd been attracted enough to want to date the guitarist, but I decided against it because I didn't want to have to deal with all the drama that came with his fans. Namely the brazen women fawning all over him. So instead, we'd remained friends, and it was the furthest our relationship would ever develop.

I found nothing wrong with his questions on the subject, but apparently Braylen did. She liked Jagger, had encouraged me to give him a chance, but as soon as she found out he was asking about my feelings toward Kevin, the protective side of her busted through. And while she hadn't been aggressive with Jagger, her tone indicated her seriousness. It both comforted and irritated me.

I'd pleaded with her to let it go, and we had a mini argument of sorts. Thankfully it was quickly resolved, with me promising not to take things further with the fighter if I felt he was turning into a jealous freak.

An hour later, the band was in full swing. While I tried to lose myself to their music, all my attention was geared toward the devilishly handsome guy to my left. Jagger wore a dark green, button-down shirt with the sleeves rolled up, exposing the ink on his skin. And every time he moved his hand, I saw the muscles in his forearm twitch.

Playing with the stem of my glass, I tried not to pay too much attention to him, but it was impossible. Every so often, he'd nudge my arm or brush my shoulder, asking if I was enjoying myself. My only response was a curt nod. I knew he gazed at me, and each time I turned my head to check, he would simply smile and occasionally lick his lips, which then made me think naughty thoughts.

My imagination ran wild, picturing his naked body. Images of how he'd look hovering over me while he spread my legs, impaling me onto him until he filled me completely. I fantasized what his kiss would taste like. Was he aggressive or gentle, or a little bit of both? The thoughts shocked me, mainly because I'd never felt the touch of a man before. Yes, I'd kissed a few boys when I was younger, but because I shielded myself from normal dating situations, I'd never found myself in the position where I was thoroughly tempted to go all the way. Not that I didn't think about it. Often. Because I did. Being a twenty-one-year-old virgin was a status I wanted to rid myself of, but not with just anyone. While I wanted to shed my innocence, I wanted it to mean as much to the person I'd chosen to give it to as it did me.

Brushing my hand with his, Jagger called my focus when he leaned in close and asked, "Do you want another drink?" His warm breath danced over the side of my face and made me shiver. Finding the perfect opportunity to gaze at him openly, I turned toward him and we locked eyes. Gently shaking my head, I waited for him to speak again, to say anything that would keep me engaged so I didn't have to look away.

His hand lingered near mine and I didn't pull away. I loved the contact more than I let on because I didn't wish for him to view me as clingy. I had no idea what he thought of me, other than I believed he found me attractive.

"Do you want some water instead?" Realizing I definitely should have some, I nodded. Since I blocked his exit, I shuffled to the edge of the booth and stood when I cleared the table. "Braylen, do you need another drink?" he politely asked, scooting the rest of the way out of the booth until he stood directly beside me, his hand resting on my lower back. The warmth from his touch instantly ignited my desire, and it was difficult to keep such a thing in check.

But I managed.

Barely.

"Thanks, but this should be my last," she responded, holding up her drink for him to see. "But I'll take a water as well, if you don't mind."

"Not at all." He smiled at me before walking toward the bar.

A second after I sat back down, my eyes following every move Jagger made, my sister burst in on my visual stalking.

"Wow!" she exclaimed, hitting the top of the table with her hand. "You really like this one, don't you?"

Shrugging, I tried my best to play nonchalant, but she saw straight through me.

"Don't play coy with me, missy. I see the way you keep trying to sneak a peek at him. Even now, you can't keep your eyes off him, probably staring at his ass. But hey, I don't blame ya. He's gorgeous. Plain and simple."

He's certainly attractive, but I'm not gaga over him if that's what you're implying. So what if I'd told her a little white lie. I thought I was trying to convince myself more than her.

"Uh-huh," she mumbled, following my line of sight to Jagger, which only confirmed she knew I'd just fibbed. "Either way, it's nice to see you having a good time for once." Bringing the glass to her lips, she tipped it back and swallowed the rest of her drink.

I have fun, I argued, my hands taking on the frustration my voice wouldn't allow.

"When?"

When we go shopping or watch a movie. When we're just hanging out.

"That's not the same thing, Kena, and you know it. All I'm saying is that it's nice to see you interested in getting out there, putting your heart on the line, no matter the risk."

Whoa, slow down. Let's not get crazy. I smiled at her assumption that I was diving headfirst into the thought of me with Jagger. It was only the second time I'd seen him, and although I wanted there to be more occasions of the same, I wasn't naïve enough to think he'd break down all my walls with a few encounters.

Before Braylen and I could continue our conversation, Jagger sauntered back over with our waters in hand. He'd also gotten himself another beer. He didn't appear inebriated in the least, even though I'd witnessed him put away at least four of them. It should have alarmed me, but his actions and words hadn't been anything shy of respectful, so I pushed the thoughts from my mind as soon as they appeared.

I slid into the booth, allowing him to take the seat near the edge. Bringing the cool liquid to my lips, I swallowed a few sips before placing it on the table. *Thank you*, I signed, hoping he remembered what it meant.

He smiled. "How do you sign "you're welcome?"" he asked, never taking his eyes off me.

I brought the pads of my fingers to my chin, like before, and then pulled them away.

"I thought that was "thank you"," he said, rather confused, glancing back and forth between me and Braylen.

"It is. You can use the same simple gesture to reply after someone signs "thank you,"" Braylen explained. "It's similar to when people say "aloha" for hello and goodbye."

Jagger thought Braylen's clarification was amusing, the corners of his full lips kicking up into a breathtaking smile.

"I guess that's easy enough," he chuckled, bringing his fingers to his chin and forming the gesture. "Did I do it right?" he asked, uncertainty scouring his face as he looked at me afterward. A simple nod from me and he relaxed, reaching for my hand and giving it a small squeeze.

His touch warmed me. I liked him, but I didn't really know him. I wanted more than anything to see him again, but I also didn't want to appear desperate. My battling feelings drove me crazy.

When he withdrew his hand, I had to resist appearing distraught. To distract myself I ran my fingers up and down my glass of water, the condensation making the pads of my fingers slippery.

"So," Jagger blurted suddenly, "are you two going anywhere afterward?"

I shook my head, all the while silently pleading with my sister to back me up. While I thoroughly enjoyed my time with Jagger, it was emotionally draining. I needed the rest of the night to decompress, maybe talk it out with my sister back at home.

"It's been a long day, so we're just gonna head on home in a few minutes," Braylen affirmed, tapping her fingers against the wood of the table. Every once in a while she'd turn her attention to the band, trying to give Jagger and me some privacy, even though we were all sitting together.

Ten minutes later, we rose from the booth and started walking toward the exit. I glanced back over my shoulder to make eye contact with Kevin, trying to let him know that we were leaving. Initially we'd told him we'd stay until the end, but Braylen was right; it'd been a long day and while I wanted to spend more time with Jagger, I was tired. Kevin acknowledged our good-bye with a jerk of his head, but when his eyes fell on the guy walking behind us—my "date," of sorts—a frown painted his expression. I wasn't sure why, though. Maybe he thought we'd picked up some random guy, or maybe he thought we were leaving because he'd been bothering us. I wasn't sure, and right then I didn't have enough energy to care.

Even though the warmth of the night air was soothing, a shiver shot through me at the close proximity of Jagger's body to mine. There was certainly a connection between us, but would it move past that evening? I figured only time would tell.

"Well, I had a great time," he stated, reaching for my hand once more. Holding it tight, he gave me a sultry smile. "Thanks for inviting me." I hadn't revealed that it was in fact Braylen who had invited him, but I guessed none of that mattered now.

A fleeting moment passed when I thought he was going to lean in and kiss me. My heart leapt in anticipation, but that was quickly squelched when Jagger's eyes darted past my sister and me and locked on someone behind us.

"Fuck," I heard him grumble. I tugged on my hand, still clasped tightly in his, but he ignored me. Instead, he shoved me behind him in one quick move, my sister standing close by me. Jagger shielded the both of us, and I had no idea why.

Until a man stood two feet from him and shouted, "This is payback for killing my brother." As his words nestled deep in my brain, the man pulled a gun from his waistband and pointed it at Jagger's head.

CHAPTER TWELVE

Jagger

EVERYTHING HAPPENED IN A SPLIT second. I went from thanking Kena for inviting me out to shielding her and Braylen from Snake, his gun pointed right in my goddamn face.

There was no getting out of this without someone hitting the ground. And that someone wasn't gonna be me.

Threat aside, I understood the man's hatred toward me, but that didn't give him the right to pull up on me right out in the open. If he wanted to exact his revenge against me, he needed to step inside the ring in an attempt to right the so-called wrong I'd done him.

"Are you out of your fucking mind?" I yelled, releasing Kena's hand and throwing my body toward him, catching him off guard, and in the process knocking the gun from his hand. There was no reasoning with the guy and I knew it, making a snap decision in order to spare not only my life but everyone else present. Mainly the two women behind me.

Snake was part of the Savage Reapers. Even if he didn't have a beef with me for accidentally killing his brother, his hatred toward our club would be enough of a reason to pull the trigger, possibly killing anyone else who got in the way.

I heard a few screams behind me, and I was sure one of them came from Braylen. Not having enough time to turn around and explain, I followed Snake to the ground, landing on top of him to break my fall. My fist connected with his face before he had time to react, blood spurting from his nose and mouth and covering my shirt. But I didn't care. Not only had I probably blown any shot I had of seeing Kena again, I was enraged this bastard had the balls to pull a gun on me. He knew the dangers of the ring as well as I did; he couldn't possibly have thought I killed his brother on purpose. Either way, I showed him I wasn't gonna tolerate being threatened. Add in the fact he was part of our most hated enemy and my aggression poured from me with ease, beating the man unconscious. He never had a chance, which was why he'd brought his weapon with him in the first place.

Two bouncers rushed outside in the midst of the commotion, and luckily for Snake they pulled me away before I killed him. It would have been another accident, so to speak, although I wouldn't have let his death eat at me like his brother's did.

Staggering to my feet, I ran my bloodied hand through my disheveled hair, trying my best to catch my breath. Once security realized I'd calmed down, they approached the limp body lying on the sidewalk, grabbing the fallen weapon before tucking their hands under his arms and dragging him around the corner, away from any spectators.

Turning around, I assumed I'd be met with the absence of Kena and her sister, but they were still there, staring at me with matching looks of horror. Braylen more so than Kena.

Taking a tentative step forward, I threw my hands up in surrender, showing them no more threat was present. "Are you okay?" I asked to no one in particular, although my question should have been poised directly to Kena. She looked down at the ground as soon as I took another step closer, her shoulders trembling in fear.

Regret shrouded me that she had to witness what just happened, but I didn't have another choice, unless she wanted to see my brains strewn all over the sidewalk. Call me crazy, but I thought that would have been more disturbing.

Braylen stepped in front of her sister, shielding her entirely from me as I approached. "Don't take another step," she warned. When I stopped, she came at me, albeit verbally. "What the hell was that,

Jagger? What are you into? Did you really kill someone? Are you part of a gang?" She peppered me with question after question, her ranting making me mentally dizzy. Never allowing me a chance to respond or explain, she seized Kena's arm and dragged her away. "Don't contact her again or else," she threatened, both of them disappearing around the corner before I could even think to stop them.

I reached for my phone to text her when all of a sudden it rang, the shrill sound slicing through the air and distracting me enough to answer it.

"Yeah," I shouted, clutching the cell to my ear so tight my lobe started throbbing. I'd welcomed the pain.

"Hey, man," Stone chastised. "What the hell's up your ass?" I opened my mouth to answer when he cut me off. "Doesn't matter. Get to the clubhouse. Now. We're making a plan tonight." Silence greeted me on the other end as he hung up.

———— ◆ ————

ARRIVING AT THE COMPOUND, I parked my bike and rushed inside to find out what the hell was goin' on. I had a feeling, but I wanted to hear it from our leader's mouth. Throwing my cell on the table outside Chambers, I rounded the table and took my seat. Hawke, Ryder and Zip strode in behind me, Trigger and Cutter following after them. Marek, Stone, Breck and Tripp were already seated. Once everyone was prepared to start, Marek uttered four words which would change the course of our night completely.

"We're pickin' him up." Resting against the worn leather of his seat, he thrummed his fingers on the tabletop, the rhythm he created hypnotic. A calm descended over our prez, and I knew why. Finally, after what seemed to be forever, he was gonna seek the justice he needed to avenge what had happened to his wife. Hopefully after the deed was done, they could both start to heal and move on.

The need to desecrate the man who'd violated Sully ran deep in my veins. Adrenaline coursed through me in waves and I prayed Marek would allow me to be part of Yanez's death in some way, although I'd never request such a detail. He tolerated me, his harsh demeanor toward me lessening each time we interacted, but I didn't want to do anything to jeopardize our "progress."

"Where?" Stone asked, worry etching deep into the lines of his face. He had more to lose than most of us, Addy and his daughter waiting for him at home. I couldn't even imagine how he felt, realizing he was walking into an unpredictable situation. But I was sure Marek wouldn't send us into enemy territory. Not intentionally, at least.

"Reynosa," he answered, expelling a deep breath.

"Fuckin' Mexico!" Trigger shouted, lowering his voice once he saw the glare on Marek's face.

"Yeah, fuckin' Mexico," he yelled back. "Carrillo is doin' me a favor by handing Yanez over so we can finish him off. He's been holding him for the past four days, delivering his own brand of justice for going against the cartel." He took a moment to compose himself. "He said if we want him, we have to come and collect him. Obviously, I agreed."

Leaning forward and resting his arms on the table, he laid out the carefully orchestrated plan. "Stone, Tripp, Ryder and I are takin' the cage." Pointing at Cutter, he said, "You take Trigger and Breck to the safe house and get set up." Turning his head toward Zip and Hawke, who were sitting side by side, he instructed, "You two are gonna stay behind and man the compound. No one knows about the trip, so you shouldn't have an issue with any surprise attacks. But just in case, I put a call in to our Laredo chapter. Salzar is bringing ten of his best guys with him. They'll be here tomorrow night."

A solemn air fell all around us, thoughts of the assigned duties driving home the severity of the upcoming event. And by event, I meant the torture and death of Rico Yanez.

Marek had stopped talking to the group at large, instead having his own sidebar with his VP. It appeared everyone had their orders—everyone but me, that was. Chancing an argument, or the silent treatment, I interrupted Marek and Stone.

"Prez," I called out, counting my heartbeats until he looked my way. "What do you want me to do?" I held my breath in anticipation. He could dismiss me altogether, or acknowledge me and treat me as a rightful part of this club, even though I wasn't fully patched in.

Stone nudged his friend with his arm, leaning in and whispering into his ear. Marek nodded before turning his attention back on me.

"You'll go to the safe house. We need someone to clean up, after all." A cocky grin tilted his lips, and I realized he was giving me a shit job. But I'd take it. When I disposed of Yanez, I'd gain my own sense of closure over what had happened to Sully, burying the bastard where no one would ever find his body—or what was left of it.

"When do we leave?" Trigger asked, smoothing his straying hairs back into place.

"We leave first thing tomorrow. You guys will head to the house later on. So get as much rest as you can because we have a long couple days ahead of us." Striking the gavel against the wood signified our meeting had come to an abrupt end. The sound boomed, slicing through hesitation and tension. Everyone knew what they had to do, and because we were loyal to our leader, we all did as asked without a second thought.

With everything else going on, I barely had enough mental energy to deal with the issue with Kena. Thinking I'd completely blown my shot with her, I threw all caution to the wind and decided I didn't have anything to lose. It'd been a couple hours since the incident at Rustic, and there was a good chance she'd turned in for the evening, but I decided to contact her anyway.

Jagger: Are you awake?

I ventured home after our big meeting, but instead of passing out for the evening, I stayed awake in the hopes I'd get the opportunity to explain myself to Kena. All different excuses ran through my mind, but none of them were any good. Some were the truth, some elaborations on fact, but all were clearly not sufficient enough to warrant her ever giving me another chance.

An hour passed.

Then another.

And another.

As I sprawled across my bed, phone clutched tightly in hand, my eyes drifted close. The faint light in my bedroom slowly becoming dimmer, until there was nothing left except blackness. A few more minutes and I would've been out cold, but the alert from an incoming message jolted me back awake. I swung my hand up so fast to check that the cell slipped from my fingers and plonked me right in the face. Curses flew from my lips while I clutched the bridge of my nose, massaging away the quick bite of pain. When I finally swiped the screen, I saw a response from Kena. Wasting no time, I checked her message.

Kena: I don't want you to contact me anymore.

Jagger: You don't? Or Braylen doesn't?

Kena: Both.

I had to convince her to let me fully explain myself, but I sure as hell didn't want to do it over text. I wanted to do it in person, but that wouldn't be for another few days at least, depending on how long Marek was gonna keep me at the safe house.

Jagger: I have to go away for a few days, but when I get back can we please meet up? I need to explain what happened. And if you don't want to see me ever again after that, then I won't bother you. But please just give me a chance to tell you my side.

Breathing had quickly become difficult. My palms started to sweat the longer I waited for her to respond. Having no clue why it meant so much to me to have Kena hear my excuses threw me into instant aggravation. I hated feeling defensive, like I had to justify my life to someone, but I also knew she was different. I couldn't explain it, though; I just . . . felt it. Deep inside.

A text popped up, and with it hope that she'd give me an opportunity to right what she thought was a wrong.

Kena: Kevin said you're part of an illegal biker gang. Is that true?

Fuckin' Kevin.

Jagger: Yes and no. Yes, I'm part of a biker club. Not gang. And no, it is not illegal.

May as well disclose everything.

Jagger: Not anymore.

The detail about finishing off Yanez I'd keep to myself. Residual tactics had to be dealt with, but the Knights were more legit than not.

Twenty excruciating minutes passed before my cell dinged again. I really should have put the issue on the back burner until I was able to give her my full and undivided attention, but the need to explain weighed heavy on me.

Kena: I don't know.

Jagger: You don't know what?

Kena: If I should see you again.

I hated that I couldn't talk to her, that she couldn't hear the sincerity in my voice when I explained I would never hurt her. That I didn't want to scare her. I just wanted one more chance. My fingers slid over the keys when a thought popped to life.

Jagger: Can I call you?

Kena: Did you forget I can't speak?

Jagger: No, but I have an idea.

CHAPTER THIRTEEN

Kena

UNEASE SETTLED AROUND ME WHILE I curled up in the corner of the couch. Phone clasped in hand, I stared at the screen, re-reading Jagger's texts. There wasn't a lot of information in them, but for some reason the strange need to allow him to explain possessed me. Plus curiosity pushed me to hear his side of the events.

Danger had never been a friend of mine. Nor was drama. I stayed tucked away in my own little bubble, never venturing too far outside my comfort zone. Then one day I allowed Braylen to convince me to go to an abandoned warehouse where men would pummel each other for money. And it was at that match that Jagger had come to my rescue. Fighting whatever feelings he'd evoked within me, I'd never retracted my sister's invite for him to meet us at Rustic.

Even now, I still had this pull toward him. My head told me to run far, far away from the sexy, dangerous fighter, but my heart told me to take a chance and hear him out.

Damn emotions.

He wanted to call me. I had no idea what he thought he'd achieve by doing so, but again, I was intrigued as to what would happen. The one thing I was positive about was that his voice would surely undo me, destroying any uncertainties I had toward giving him another chance.

The rasp in his tone did strange things to me, and I knew if I heard him on the other end of the line that I'd cave and give in to whatever he asked of me.

Before I typed my reply, my mind wandered to Braylen and how upset she'd seemed on the ride home. She'd ranted all the way back to our house about how I'd better never see "that lunatic" again. She confessed her initial judgment of him had been misconceived, and I lost count how many times she apologized for pushing me toward going out with him. Seeing someone pull a gun so close to where we were standing shocked and terrified her, as it did to me. But whereas she closed the door on Jagger altogether, I left it open just a crack. I wasn't ready to shut him out completely. Not just yet. Not until I'd at least heard what he wanted to tell me.

Making sure my door was shut, I walked back to my bed, crawled on top and rested against the headboard, my phone staring at me like it held the answer to some great riddle.

Blowing errant strands of hair away from my face, I chose two letters which just might change my world as I knew it.

Kena: Ok.

A few seconds passed before my phone rang. I had no idea how to lower the volume, seeing as how no one had ever called me. For obvious reasons. But no mind; I swiped the Answer button and held the device to my ear.

Then waited.

"Kena, thank you so much for taking my call," he said breathlessly. Even if my voice had worked, I wouldn't have been able to speak right then, nerves strangling my thoughts, let alone any words I would have been able to form in my throat. "I know you can't answer me in the traditional way, so I thought if I asked you a yes or no question, you could tap one of the buttons as your response. One tap for yes and two for no. Can you do that? Does that make sense?"

I waited a heartbeat before hitting a key one time. I swore I heard the smile in his voice when he spoke again.

"Good. That's good," he affirmed, his deep breaths helping to soothe my wayward nerves. He had no idea what he did to me. Even now, he had no clue that my heart raced inside my chest, that my breathing had become erratic at hearing the growl in his tone. My mind raced with images of him, picturing him sitting next to me at the bar, the way his touch jolted me when he brushed his fingers over mine, or when he clasped my hand in his. How warm I'd felt from the contact.

"I wanted to tell you how sorry I am that you had to see that. I'm sure you were scared, and I hate that I put you in that position." He sounded sincere, and I couldn't help but feel as if I should've been the one comforting him in some way. "Anyway, I wanted to know if I could see you again when I get back in town. Shouldn't be any more than a week, at most. Please let me apologize in person, Kena. Then, if you never want to see me again, I won't bother you. I promise."

Silence made the hairs on the back of my neck stand at attention. Contemplating his request, I mentally weighed the pros and cons, the cons vastly outweighing the pros. Something dangerous surrounded Jagger, and the night's events only proved my suspicions. He belonged to a biker gang—sorry, "club." Although I had no idea what the difference was. Kevin told me they were into some illegal shit, but wouldn't explain any further. Maybe he didn't know, or maybe he'd tried to spare me the gory details. Either way, he had warned me away from the likes of Jagger, promising nothing good would come from seeing him again. Kevin told me they'd gone to the same high school, and while he wasn't friends with him, per se, he told me Jagger was always getting into fights, trouble following him all the time. Then there was the little fact that a scary-looking man had tried to shoot him, out in the open, without a care in the world, screaming that Jagger had killed his brother.

Red flags littered my internal struggle, shrouding me in waves of uneasy doubt. And even though I shouldn't have ever granted his request to call me, I had. For some inexplicable reason. And because confusion over my lack of sense baffled me, I decided to give in to him once again, agreeing to see him so he could apologize in person.

Only then would I know how I wanted to proceed.

My forefinger hovered over a key, prepared to answer his question. It was a simple response but one which eluded me. His voice cut through the line again, startling me before I'd made my decision.

"Please," he begged. "Can I see you again? To explain?" The voice drifting through my ear was poignant. Gentle. Convincing.

Without hesitation, I pushed a random number key.

One time.

Yes.

A quick exhale of relief barreled down the line. "You won't regret it. I promise. I'll text you in a few days and you can decide where you want to meet. Good night, Kena," he said before disconnecting the call. He hurried off, but I couldn't say I blamed him, probably afraid I would change my mind if given more time to think about it. And while I appreciated he didn't keep me on the phone, I hated the absence of his voice.

Lying in bed, I stared off into the darkness and prayed I'd just made the right choice. Although I was sure Braylen would tell me otherwise.

CHAPTER FOURTEEN

Jagger

RAMPANT THOUGHTS KEPT ME AWAKE the rest of the evening, sleep continuing to evade me. Taunting me with promises of submersion, only to be thrown back into consciousness. Even lying in the pitch black, my shallow breaths the only sound cutting through the air around me, I couldn't let go and give in. My mind raced, first to thoughts of Kena and how she felt about everything she'd seen, then to how she truly felt about me.

Was she as intrigued with me as I was with her?

Did she feel the same pull toward the unknown like I did?

Did she rationalize against it?

When I wasn't thinking about Kena, my brain switched to thoughts of Sully. I couldn't even imagine what she was going through. I would've loved nothing more than to be her true friend, out in the open, but her husband wouldn't allow it. Maybe once he saw I was interested in someone, he'd rid himself of the silly notion that I was in love with his wife.

Knowing the men didn't divulge club business to their women or families, I wondered if Marek had hinted at the reason for his departure. Maybe she'd want to know that the man who'd attacked her would be disposed of, never to walk the earth or breathe the same air as the rest of us again. It would give her solace. Some, at least.

Before long, the soft burn of the sunrise sliced across the horizon. An orange glow lit up the sky, the white haze of light filtering through my bedroom like fog billowing across the moors. Stretching, I yawned and allowed my body to flex and constrict before finally mustering enough energy to rise from the bed. Planting my feet firmly on the ground, I massaged the back of my neck. Tight muscles had always been my dead giveaway of the stress I'd harbored inside, whether from an upcoming fight, tension whenever Marek and I were in close proximity to each other or impending club business.

Specifically revenge.

Padding across my bedroom, the worn carpet cushioning the soles of my feet, I walked into the hallway, lost in thought of the upcoming hours . . . days. Not only did I have to do my part in the death and disposal of Yanez, but I had to convince Kena of my regret at her having witnessed something which most likely terrified her. If I weren't in the lifestyle I was, I would've been unnerved, and that's putting it lightly. Though I knew the threat against the club was dwindling, after what transpired with Snake, how did I convince her she'd be safe with me? That I could protect her? Because honestly, I had my doubts at times.

My life was my own. I took care of myself the best I could, but I hadn't thought about what it would mean to bring someone else into my world. For as bad as I wanted her, for as desperate as I was to have her in my life, I could admit the thought of something happening to her frightened me.

Don't get ahead of yourself. She just agreed to hear you out. Nothing more.

How people outside my club perceived me had never mattered before. I was proud of being involved with the Knights Corruption, even at the prospect level, and being an undefeated fighter in the underground world always spoke volumes to the type of man I wanted to become. One who had the loyalty of his brothers, and someone who was feared in the ring.

Turning on the water, I busied myself with brushing my teeth until the temperature warmed. Finally stepping inside the shower, I exhaled a satisfying groan, the spray helping to ease the stiffness from my limbs. I stood still and let the water cascade over my body, my head hung low while the heat drenched my hair. If I could've stayed in there until it was time to travel to the safe house, I would have.

My hands skated over my chest, then my arms, around to my back, then finally down my legs. I washed away not only the prior evening, but the early morning residual sleep as well.

Fully awake, my thoughts returned to Kena. Her beauty stunned me. Her body turned me on, but she was more than her physical appearance. A quiet desperation lived behind her eyes, a plea to be more like everyone else—to be "normal," without a handicap. But in reality, everyone had their own challenge to overcome; some were physical, while others were mental or emotional. She didn't strike me as someone who felt sorry for herself, but I had a funny feeling she hid from the rest of the world, only showing a close few her true self.

I want to be included in her inner circle.

New goal: penetrate Kena's world.

Oddly enough, or expectedly enough, my brain instantly flooded with images of her naked, fantasizing what she would look like silently pleading with me to possess her. Before I realized, my fingers circled my arousal and I pumped it from root to tip. My grip tightened the more I pictured her underneath me, writhing in pleasure as she clawed at my back, hooking her legs around my waist and anchoring herself to me. With every jerk of my hips, I imagined thrusting inside her, the warmth of her flooding over me and ruining me for all others. I wanted to draw out my pleasure, but my orgasm threatened to rock through me at any moment. My spine tingled while my balls drew tight. My stomach muscles clenched, an ache I hadn't realized was present until it was too late. Kena's delectable mouth was the final image I saw before my release rushed forth, my moans infiltrating the enclosed space, echoing against the easy thump of the water hitting the tiles.

Damn, I needed that.

As soon as my breathing slowed, I shut off the water and stepped from the shower, doing a quick pat down before tying the white towel around my waist. Shuffling down the hall, I entered my room and rooted through my closet, grabbing the first pair of jeans I could find. Opening the drawer of the only dresser housed inside my small bedroom, I grabbed a pair of socks, boxer briefs and a plain white T-shirt, quickly dressing before shoving my feet inside a worn pair of brown boots.

I lounged around for the remainder of the day, ordering takeout to ensure I had something in my belly before I got the call. Who knew when I'd eat again? Or would want to, for that matter. Having no idea what type of actions I'd be expected to perform, I wanted to at least have the vigor to contemplate the severity of them. Nervous energy surrounded me while I watched the sun disappear, its soft glow illuminating the night, promises of calm and tranquility a lie.

Passing out on my worn fabric couch, I awoke to the piercing sound of my cell. Rubbing the sleep from my eyes, I turned the phone over and saw Cutter's name flash across my screen. The man rarely called me, but since he was assigned to the safe house, along with his son, Breck, and Trigger, it wasn't a complete shock that he'd called me.

With a flick of my finger, the call connected. Before I could say hello, however, his raspy voice paraded down the other end of the line.

"Get a move on, prospect. We're headin' to the safe house in an hour. Meet you there," he said before hanging up. I'd quickly learned Cutter was a man of few words. I'd heard he had a daughter he never saw, but other than that personal tidbit of information, the man was a mystery to me.

Rising from the sofa, I took a quick look around and counted my blessings, as meager as they may be. While my apartment was humble, at least it provided me with a roof over my head. I preferred to spend my time at the clubhouse as much as I could, though, simply because I was around other people. When I was home, I was alone. And if the solidarity wasn't enough to deter me from staying there a lot, the lack of décor amped up my loneliness. Finally having some money in the bank, courtesy of the fights, I thought it was time I seriously considered buying a few things to spruce up the space. But who would help me? I didn't know the first thing about tackling such a feat.

The couch I'd crashed on earlier was a dark green sofa. Or at least it had been, the color fading over the years since I'd bought it. Even then, it was secondhand. A barely held-together TV stand and an end table were the only other items in the living room. My bedroom consisted of a simple queen-sized mattress, sans frame and box spring, a small dresser and nightstand.

I didn't require much, but some new things would certainly put me in better spirits when I stepped foot inside my home.

Snatching my keys, I twirled them around my finger while I walked toward the front door, locking up before I headed outside.

While I straddled my bike, I prayed everything would go according to plan and that I could put the upcoming days behind me as soon as possible.

CHAPTER
FIFTEEN

Jagger

WE'D BEEN AT THE SAFE house for almost two days, impatiently awaiting Marek's return. Which wouldn't be for quite some time yet. He wanted everyone ready to go, and while Trigger, Cutter and Breck occupied themselves with games of poker, I vegged out in front of the television, watching hours of mindless shows. But at least we'd kept up with the cable; otherwise, I would've been sitting around twiddling my goddamn thumbs.

The safe house had timers for everything, from the sprinkler system, to the lights, to the television. It always appeared as if someone lived here, or the neighbors would be a bit more suspicious than I was sure they already were.

As the many hours ticked by, the building eagerness rattled me. While I wasn't a newbie when it came to killing, torture was a whole new ball game. And if I knew anything about Marek and what he'd been through, Yanez would beg for death more often than not. I knew where our leader's head was at; he wanted justice for Sully. While I was completely onboard, the unknown distressed me, something I kept secret for fear the other guys would think me to be soft.

And how would it look like if the fighter of the group showed an ounce of indecision? Bad. It would look bad. No, I'd buck up and help orchestrate Yanez's demise when the time came, if Marek wanted my help at all. He might just need me to clean up like he'd mentioned during our last meeting.

"Yo, prospect," Breck shouted from the kitchen. "Grab me a beer." The only reason I didn't tell him to get fucked was because I knew my place in the pecking order. Still trying to prove myself, I had to take orders, no matter how small, like this one. What Marek would require of me later would be considered a big one.

Night and day, but I was obligated to do both.

Normally, I liked Breck, but during times like this I wanted to show him how much damage I could do to him with a quick shot to the jaw. Slowly rising off the couch, I walked the short distance to the kitchen where he was playing cards with his father and Trigger. Even though the fridge sat directly behind them, I still proceeded without a single complaint uttered. Internally, I told him right where to go. Roughly pulling open the door, I reached inside and grabbed a beer, flicking off the top before slamming it down on the table in front of him.

No "Thanks."

No "Bout time."

Just a cocky smirk before he tipped the bottle to his lips and swallowed half of the alcohol in a few short gulps. Wiping his mouth with the back of his hand, he focused back on the game, his face scrunching up in concentration as he tried to win the pot of money in the center of the table.

Twisting an empty chair around, I straddled the seat and rested my arms over the back. "Who's winning?" I asked, looking first over Trigger's shoulder and then Breck's.

"I am," Cutter divulged. "These two bastards been losin' their money to me all evening." After fifteen minutes of watching them bluff and curse each other, I'd had enough.

"Do you guys need me for anything? If not, I'm gonna catch some shut-eye until they get here." As I hopped up from the chair, Trigger's phone rang. He glanced at the screen, then quickly at all three of us, a warning look in his eyes he couldn't hide even if he wanted to.

"Yeah?" he answered, nodding while intently listening to whoever had called. A few more intense seconds of waiting and Trigger finally ended the conversation.

"They're a few hours away." He jerked his chin in my direction. "Brew some coffee, prospect. It's gonna be a long fuckin' night."

———————◆———————

HEADLIGHTS LIT UP THE DARKNESS, and everything became real when the heavy garage door started to open. Then the screech of the van's engine sounded as it lurched inside. We all scrambled to our feet, wired and ready to jump into action. Flinging open the door which separated the house from the garage, we rushed forward, coming to a dead stop when we saw Marek and Stone heave a limp body from the side of the vehicle.

Yanez.

His head was down, and at first it appeared as if he were unconscious. But when they jostled him, soft, pained moans escaped his mouth. Dropping him, Yanez hit the ground with a heavy thud, more groans cutting the otherwise silent air. Seizing his arms, Tripp and Ryder pulled him behind them as they walked up the three steps into the house. Yanez's body awkwardly slid over every bump and rigid surface as he was dragged through the kitchen and eventually down into the soundproof basement below. As I walked behind them, careful to keep my distance and not get in their way, I heard Yanez's head hit off every single step, the sharp thud jolting me each and every time. Don't get me wrong, the despicable piece of shit deserved whatever Marek had planned, but that didn't stop my body from reacting. My heart hammered double time, my palms starting to sweat in expectancy.

"Put him on the table," our leader shouted, switching the light on and walking across the small room. Shrugging off his cut, he laid it across the chair in the corner, cracking his neck briefly before fiddling with what sounded to be knives of some sort. His back faced me, and while Tripp and Ryder heaved the barely alive man onto the table, Stone walked up behind Marek, talking so low I couldn't make out a single word.

Cutter walked past me, his shoulder brushing against mine when he entered the dank room. The light above slightly illuminated the space, shadows dancing next to us and creating the perfect atmosphere.

For death.

"What you gonna do to him, Prez?" Cutter asked, rounding the table and glaring down at Yanez, although the barely breathing man hadn't taken notice. Instead, he turned his head to the side, the loud clanking sounds Marek made drawing his attention. I moved closer while still being mindful to stay in the background until instructed otherwise. Not sure whether or not I wanted to witness Yanez's ultimate demise, I pushed all doubt to the side and just watched the scene unfolding in front of me.

Turning around, Marek stepped toward the table, a pair of pliers in his hand. He spun them around and around before lightly tapping them against his temple. In the soft light, the leader of the Knights Corruption resembled a deranged lunatic, the lost look in his blue eyes hazed over with a sort of delirium. Fear ripped through me right then, and I had no doubt his victim felt it as well. In that moment I couldn't help but envision hearing Rob Zombie, the unease of his music a perfect fitting to the horror-type scene unfolding.

Shaking my head to rid myself of the odd thoughts, I glanced toward the men milling about the room. All of them were there because of their loyalty to Marek, as was I. Even though I knew he didn't like me, I would do what was asked of me without second-guessing him.

Locking eyes with Cutter, Marek's voice finally rang out, hatred and desperation mixing together to form an odd sound. "Remember what we did to Vex?" Cutter nodded right away. "Worse than that," Marek declared.

"Fuck," I heard Tripp and Ryder mutter. Everyone, including myself, heard about what Marek and Cutter had done to Vex. After carving the letters 'KC' into his chest, they finished him off by using a bat. And not by beating him with it.

Marek stood next to the table, Yanez's beady eyes intently trying to watch him as best he could given the damage to his face. Carrillo's ex right-hand man was beaten to a pulp, both of his eyes so swollen I was surprised he could see anything at all. He was littered with cuts and burn marks, on his face as well as his neck and what I could see of his chest, his tattered shirt torn to reveal parts of his damaged skin. Normally, I would have hated to see someone treated like this, but he certainly deserved it for what he'd done to Sully. And if I had to wager a bet, she wasn't the first woman he'd brutalized.

Rico Yanez lived in darkness, his soul blackened with what I was sure he'd done during his wretched life.

Raising Yanez's hand, Marek inspected it briefly before letting it drop back to the table. "Looks like Carrillo beat me to it," he mumbled, walking around the table to look at the man's other limb. I moved closer, wanting to see what he meant, but before I opened my mouth to ask Stone, who stood in front of me, I saw it.

Yanez's fingers were missing.

All ten of them.

Whoever had cut them off had also cauterized the wounds. My guess was so he didn't bleed out, ending his torturing sessions too early.

"Oh well," Marek said dismissively, waving his hand through the air like it was no big deal. "Looks like we'll just have to get right to it, then." A glaze washed over our leader's face, and right before my very eyes I saw him shut down, going into whatever headspace would allow him to deliver justice for his wife. Briefly turning around, he fiddled with a few things before donning a pair of latex gloves. Then he reached for a dull scalpel-type knife as well as a vice grip before walking back toward Yanez's limp body. "Prospect," he addressed, turning his gaze to me. "Grab some gloves, then yank down his pants."

My mind was a flurry of thoughts, but I had no time to indulge any of them. Hurrying across the room, I threw on a pair of the same gloves, a bead of perspiration trickling down the side of my face. Hesitation held me prisoner until I heard Stone clear his throat behind me.

"You good?" he asked, concern slithering around those two words. I quickly turned around and saw him quirking his brow in wait.

"Yeah," I muttered before taking the few steps necessary to put me right next to the table. I had an idea what Marek had planned, and while the thought sickened me, I knew it was the only way for him to purge.

My fingers fumbled with Yanez's belt buckle, and once it was undone, I popped open the button of his jeans and tore the zipper down. After dragging the material down his legs, I stepped back, my eyes locked on my president.

"The underwear too," he instructed, a sick sort of smile tilting up the corners of his lips. Marek looked haggard, deep stress lines marring his face. His eyes were bloodshot and his hair stuck up around the edges of his head. Again, he looked a bit deranged, but plotting revenge and then finally seeing it through had to take some sort of toll on the mind and body. Hell, probably even the soul.

Yanking down the man's briefs made him come to life—well, whatever was left of him, at least. He tried to struggle, but his strength eluded him. Instead his eyes bulged as best they could and he tried to speak, his garbled voice incoherent to the rest of us. I thought he said, "Please, don't," but I couldn't be sure. Either way, it didn't matter; his fate had been decided, and no amount of begging would change it. If anything, his whimpers would do more harm than good, although I couldn't fathom what "more harm" would entail at that point.

Marek stretched his arm across the table and passed me the vice grip. "Put his dick in this, then grab his balls tight."

Those were the ten most menacing words I'd ever heard.

Yanez knew what was coming, and although he tried to fight again, it was useless. His death was imminent, but how long would it be before the reaper came to steal him from this life?

With every slice Marek made, separating two of the three body parts which made Yanez a man, he whimpered uncontrollably, thrashing as much as he could while in our grasp. There was an unwritten rule among men: Never go for the nuts. That being said, what Marek was doing to Yanez was justified. In our eyes, at least.

My arm jerked back when Marek had finished, my eyes instantly going to the area between Yanez's legs. Blood poured forth in spurts. It would only be a matter of minutes before he bled out completely, I was sure of it.

With his free hand, our president wrenched a piece of duct tape he'd pre-cut from the edge of a utility cart. "Tripp," he called, "open his mouth." The nomad jumped into action, prying Yanez's jaw wide and holding steady while Marek shoved the man's balls past his stretched lips. As soon as Tripp released his grip, our leader slapped the piece of duct tape over his mouth, pressing down to make sure it was securely in place.

Stepping back, Marek gazed at his handiwork, a look of satisfaction covering his face as his eyes roamed the full length of his victim. Nodding hastily, as if he'd agreed with a silent conversation he'd been having with himself, he jerked his chin toward Stone and Ryder.

"Bring him to the corner so we can string him up," Marek instructed. The two men shot into action, dragging the ex-cartel member from the table and across the room. Standing him upright, they placed his wrists in the shackles built into the wall, letting him dangle once they'd released him. The position would allow him to bleed out quicker than lying on the table. And if blood loss wouldn't cause his demise, then suffocation would.

We all stood there watching Yanez struggle during the last minutes of his life. Silence comforted us while we witnessed the warranted punishment.

Five minutes turned into ten, which turned to twenty.

He still breathed.

Another five minutes passed.

Finally deciding enough was enough, Marek walked toward the strung-up man and raised his hand to Yanez's nose, pinching his nostrils to hurry his death along.

A slight twitch was the only form of life still left inside him.

Two minutes later, he was dead.

Finally.

CHAPTER SIXTEEN

Kena

"WHAT?" BRAYLEN SHOUTED. "ABSOLUTELY NOT. Don't you even think about it, Kena," she continued, pacing in front of me while she tried to control her sudden outburst. "There is no way in hell I'm going to allow you to meet him. No," she said, suddenly stopping to look me in the eye. "He's not the guy I thought he was. You have to see it too." She resumed pacing. "You just have to." Pushing loose blonde strands away from her eyes, she pinned me with a concerned look. "I made a mistake when I encouraged you to give him a chance, a mistake I regret with every fiber of my being. Putting you in harm's way is the last thing I ever wanted. And now you're telling me you want to hear him out? No," she repeated, shaking her head in earnest.

Because my sister's back was to me, I couldn't respond. Breaching the few steps between us, I reached for her shoulder. Turning her around, I narrowed my brows and cocked my head slightly to the side.

I know you're concerned for me, but I'm a big girl. I can make my own decisions, so stop treating me like a child. My hands fell to my sides in exasperation. I parted my lips, expelling the air from my throat, but no matter how much I willed the words to take flight, it was utterly useless. Most days I accepted and even reveled in being mute, but then there were instances where the silence kept me chained to a frustrating existence.

Stilling her movements, Braylen unexpectedly pulled me into a hug, wrapping her arms tightly around me as if she thought I would disappear. After countless seconds she pulled back, her warm breath fanning the side of my face. "It's my job as your big sister to look out for and take care of you." I tried to distance myself to respond, but her hold on me intensified. "I know you're not a kid anymore. I do," she said dejectedly, as if she wished the opposite were true, "but that doesn't mean I won't stop trying to protect you. I don't care if you're fifty. I'll always look out for you." A small smile tipped her lips upward, the love she held for me shining brightly in her brown eyes. "And as such, I'm warning you to stay away from Jagger. For your own good." She finally took a step back, allowing me the distance I craved in order to respond to her ludicrous threat.

Every muscle in my body locked up, anger dancing on the edge of every gesture I made. *And if I don't? What will you do?*

At first I thought my sister had been bluffing, mere worry for me pushing her toward an argument. But it wasn't until her next statement that I completely understood how far she'd go to make me comply.

"I'll tell Mom and Dad."

My mouth dropped open, and it was a good thing for her right then that I couldn't speak because I'd be cursing her every which way to Sunday. So instead, as usual, my hands were a flurry of activity, gesturing so fast I was sure she missed most of what I told her.

I can't believe you would stoop so low as to tattle on me like some five-year-old brat. You know damn well Mom and Dad would worry themselves sick if you filled their heads with lies. She started to speak but I cut her off with a fierce scowl. *While I realize what happened was bad, the last thing they need to do is worry about me. You telling them would only make things worse. Please.*

I started off angry, but by the end I pleaded with her not to interfere. I couldn't explain my incessant need to see Jagger again, not even to myself, but the one thing I did know was that I'd never felt this way toward anyone. Even with my lack of experience with the opposite sex, I felt the pull, the undeniable connection between us, and I wanted to see him again to make sure I hadn't made it up in my mind, that I wasn't crazy.

Braylen just stood there, hands planted firmly on her hips, waiting. For what I wasn't sure, but at least in silence I could hope she relented. I should've known better, though.

"I swear I'll bring our parents into this if you agree to see him, Kena," she warned. A standoff ensued between us, her unwavering and me staring at her in utter disbelief. When I realized she wasn't going to give in, I offered what I thought was a fair compromise. At least I hoped she would see it as such.

How about if you come with me when I meet him? That way, you'll know I'm safe. Plus you'll hear what he wants to tell me and find out for yourself that he's not someone I should be afraid of.

"I don't think *Jagger* is the person you should fear, but the types of people he surrounds himself with. But then again, what the hell do I know? I thought he was a safe bet. His coming to our rescue that night fooled me. I let my guard down because I saw the way he looked at you, and I wanted so badly for you to open up to someone. To really start living, experiencing life, instead of hiding away in the back of the restaurant all the time."

If I looked up "stubborn" in the dictionary, there would be a picture of Braylen, smiling and flipping off the reader. I knew whatever reply I gave wouldn't deter my sister, but I tried anyway. *Don't judge him on one incident.*

"That was a pretty big fucking incident," she yelled, anger wrapping around her like a blanket. Waving my hand in her direction in frustration, dismissing our entire conversation, I walked past her, my shoulder bumping into hers as I headed out of her bedroom. She saw the look on my face, I was sure, anger mixed with sadness. "Kena!" she shouted. "Wait."

I ignored her, snatched my keys from the table near the door and rushed out of the house. Clicking the key fob to my car, I got in and turned over the engine, sitting in silence for a few minutes. Maybe I'd hoped Braylen would chase me outside and plead with me to forgive her. What did I get instead? A lousy text message telling me she wouldn't budge, no matter how angry I was with her. She was only looking out for me, blah, blah, blah. I didn't need her love and protection, though. Even though I didn't have much experience when it came to guys, I really thought I could handle myself. Being mute didn't thwart my knee from connecting with Jagger's balls if I felt I needed to fight back for some reason. Although, the last thing I wanted to do was hurt his family jewels. No, I could think of many other things I wished to do with that region of his body.

Simply thinking of him caused a warmness to float through me, shivers of delight shooting to my own nether region. Lost in dirty thoughts of writhing around with the fighter, the sudden knock on my window made me jolt. My hand flew to my chest in surprise and I inhaled a quick breath of air. Glancing to my left, I saw Braylen watching me, probably wondering what the hell I was doing just sitting in the car. Thank God she wasn't a mind reader; otherwise she'd be giving me the riot act about my daydreams.

Her fist pounded again, that time with a bit more urgency. Finally lowering the window, I expected to hear an apology, but no such words came out of her mouth. She did say something that made me happy, however.

"Okay. Fine," she relented. "I'll go with you to meet him. But it has to be out in the open with lots of people around, and it has to be in broad daylight. Preferably Neelan Park."

I could certainly accommodate her request, especially if it meant I could see Jagger again without worry she'd find out and make good on her threat to bring my parents into the situation.

Braylen never waited for my response, instead turning on her heel and walking back inside the house. But that was okay; I'd gotten the answer I'd wanted.

Now all I had to do was wait for Jagger to contact me again. He'd told me he'd be away for a few days, but if he didn't text me soon, my sister would surely tell me "I told you so," and the last thing I wanted was for her to be right about him.

I wanted to prove her wrong in the worst way.

CHAPTER SEVENTEEN

Jagger

EVERYONE HAD LEFT THE SAFE house except for Cutter and me. It was up to us to dispose of Yanez's body. Well, to be more factual, it was my job to get rid of him, but Cutter volunteered to help. I had no idea why, but I welcomed his assistance nonetheless.

Silence teased us while we busied ourselves in unchaining Yanez from the wall, laying him on top of the thick green tarp we'd readied, rolling him up and carrying him out to the garage. The guys who'd gone to pick up the ex-cartel member caught rides back with Breck, who'd thought ahead and brought his truck, leaving the van for us to use. Stuffing the dead man in the back of the vehicle was the easy part. When Cutter sat his ass down in front of the television, I knew I was on my own with cleaning up the mess in the bowels of the house.

Oddly enough, while I hosed the blood off the concrete ground, the red-tinged water sliding across the surface and disappearing down the drain set in the floor, Kena popped into my head. At first, it disturbed me that I thought of her while cleaning up after a kill, but it was exactly why the images of her bombarded me.

The world I'd immersed myself in was dangerous, no doubt about it. I realized selfishness drove me to pursue her, even though I knew she didn't belong anywhere near me. Yes, the Knights were going legit, but we still had shit to clean up, and until everything was put to bed, the threat against all of us was grave.

Yanez had finally been dealt with, which meant there was only one remaining loose end to tie up.

Psych Brooks.

Sully's bastard of a father.

When and where that man would cease to exist still baffled me, as I was sure it did Marek and the rest of the guys. Everyone itched to finish the war between us and the Savage Reapers, and we all realized more blood would be shed before it was over.

But how much, and whose, were the real questions.

Throwing the rags I'd used to clean off the table into a nearby garbage bag, I glanced around the room one last time to make sure I hadn't missed anything. Shutting off the light, I ascended the stairs and announced I'd finished. Clicking the remote, Cutter rose from the sofa and led the way back out to the garage.

The club's safe house wasn't used for disposal of bodies, and from what I'd heard, there had been quite a few. You don't shit where you eat, so to speak, so we drove for an hour before turning down a partially hidden dirt pathway. The secluded area was perfect, far away from both of the areas the club used.

Tossing me a shovel from the back, Cutter and I made quick work of finding the perfect spot to bury Yanez. Flashlights resting on the ground illuminated the darkness while we worked, flinging sodden dirt behind us while we unearthed his new home. It'd rained hours prior, which made the soil heavy, requiring a bit more muscle, but neither of us complained.

A few times I'd opened my mouth to make chitchat, but every time I ended up thinking better of it. What were we gonna talk about, the weather? No, the situation called for concentration and quiet. The quicker we finished the better.

After a grueling two hours, we'd managed to dig deep enough to conceal the body without worry, cover him back up and start the drive back to the clubhouse. I would've ridden my bike but I'd asked Stone to take it back for me, realizing I'd be in no condition to be out on the open road with a tiredness which would undoubtedly get me killed.

Resting my head against the passenger side window, I closed my eyes and wondered when my life would start to fall into place. Question after question arose.

When would Marek decide me worthy enough to patch me in as a full member, solidifying my loyalty for good?

Would Snake decide to come after me again? Would he end up getting lucky and kill me?

As slumber beckoned me, Kena's beautiful face popped into my head. In my mind she spoke, telling me how much she wanted to be with me. Fantasy, I knew, but it was the peace I needed to drift off during the last stretch of our ride. I only hoped she wouldn't go back on her promise to meet me.

———————◆———————

WITH A JOLT, THE VAN came to a stop. "Fuck," I groaned, rubbing the side of my head while Cutter grunted out some garbled noise. Clutching the door handle, I pulled the lever toward me and flung the door open, practically falling out of the vehicle I was so uncoordinated.

The last couple days had drained me, especially that evening. I was physically and mentally exhausted, and all I wanted to do was crash for the night. Didn't matter where; the couch inside the club would do just fine.

Lazily strolling across the lot, my eyes stayed on the entrance to the building with one goal in mind: forget everything that had happened in the past twelve hours.

The waiting.

The uncertainty of my role in the revenge against Yanez.

The torture.

The dismemberment.

The blood.

The burial.

The end of Yanez, once and for all.

The last part comforted me while the rest of it sickened me. I played the tough, unaffected guy, but deep down I was unsure of a lot of things in life. My sense of self had been warped since I could remember. In some small way, my father still held power over me, making me question my worth every now and again. It was why the Knights were so important to me, and why I would do whatever was asked without question.

Loyalty.

I'd never had it before I'd become a part of them. Even though I was the low man on the totem pole, tasked with the worst jobs from time to time, I knew every one of those members would have my back if and when I needed them.

It was why I held my tongue when Marek gave me a verbal lashing whenever he felt he needed to. It was why I never retaliated with my fists when he punished me for getting too close with his wife when he'd asked me to watch over her.

And it was why I respected his dislike for me, staying clear of Sully when I saw her, even though all I wanted to do was make sure she was okay. The innate need to protect her battled within, though I wasn't quite sure why. Maybe because of the way she'd looked so lost when she first came to stay with us. Or maybe it was because I saw a woman trying to make sense of her new life, silently pleading for someone to help her.

Maybe I read into things which weren't there.

Maybe I didn't.

All I did know was that as time passed, and wrongs against her were righted, she would start to heal.

"Prospect! Come here," Marek demanded, standing in the entryway to Chambers, looking beat down and tired as hell. With my shoulders squared, I huffed and silently counted to ten as I approached, dodging the throngs of men who were partying it up like we hadn't just tortured someone. Almost a dozen members from the Laredo chapter had arrived a day or so before, setting up camp to make sure nothing popped off while we were gone. And now that the ordeal was finished, it was time for them to party, to engage in a ruckus, although I wanted no part of it this time.

Standing a foot away from Marek, something in his bloodshot eyes softened when he looked at me, but it was gone before I could read further into it. Moving to the side, he allowed me to pass and enter the room where we met about all things club-related. The good and the bad.

The click of the door closing jostled me. I'd flinched, but Marek had been facing away from me so he hadn't noticed. He strode toward his seat at the head of the table, never uttering a single word while he situated himself. Still locked into place, I remained quiet until the silence tore at me, threatening to undo my sanity if he didn't speak soon. Pressing my luck where he was concerned, I opened my mouth and forced five words past my unsure lips. "Did I do something wrong?" I asked, fisting my hands and slowly unfurling them, over and over.

"Sit." He gestured toward a chair closer to him than my assigned seat at the far end of the oblong table.

Hesitation briefly gripped me, but I dismissed my reluctance before it got the better of me and sat a few seats away from him. Drumming my fingers against the wood of the table did nothing but increase my jumpiness, never mind that the noise also served to irritate Marek. A quick pull of his brow and I'd stopped the incessant tapping. Laying my palm flat, I waited for him to speak, to finally find out why he'd called me in there by myself. It'd been a long time since Marek and I had been alone together.

Not since he'd saved me from getting my ass jumped by four members of the Savage Reapers. But to be fair, I'd been the one to initially jump in and help him and Stone out when they were ambushed by a handful of our enemy's club, not realizing who they were before I stuck my nose into their business.

It seemed like forever ago, but it had only been two years since Marek had accepted me, bringing me into the club as a prospect with promises of money, loyalty and girls. And hey, what twenty-year-old guy would turn down such a proposition? I'd been undeniably grateful, humbled by his acceptance of me when all I'd received my whole life was rejection from the one person who should have been wired to love me unconditionally.

My shitbag father.

I'd learned the rules of the club quickly, thankful to have fallen upon the opportunity to finally belong somewhere. To be accepted by a group of men who emanated nothing but confidence, strength and smarts. Sure, they gave me shit from time to time, but that was all part of the ritual of belonging.

While Marek had been the one to essentially save me from myself, giving my life a purpose, it was Stone I eventually gravitated toward. Something about the VP seemed familiar to me, and while I couldn't pinpoint exactly what that had been, I welcomed his friendship with open fuckin' arms. He became more like a big brother than anything, helping me with my fighting techniques and offering his advice, even when I hadn't asked for it.

Clearing his throat, Marek brought me out of my own head and back to our impromptu meeting. Jerking his head toward me, his gaze locked on me the entire time, he asked, "You good?"

Inquiring if I was okay was his subtle way of finding out how I'd felt about everything that went down with Yanez earlier. Marek's concern was masked with aloofness, although I'd been smart enough to read between the lines. Or between those two simple words.

Was this his proverbial olive branch?

If so, I'd take it, grab on with both hands if it meant slowly creeping my way out of the dog house.

Many different words jumbled together inside my head, but for some reason none of them would leave my mouth. So instead, I simply nodded.

Leaning forward, his elbows resting against the etched wood of the table, he scrutinized me for a few seconds before continuing to speak. "What I asked you to do was a bit more than I'd ever required from you before. More . . . gruesome than what you're probably used to." Roughly running his hands through his messy dark hair, he blew out a pained breath. "Hell, maybe not. I've no idea what you've seen before you came to be part of us. Either way, it's a lot to deal with. I realize that. Just wanted to make sure you're okay with everything."

This was the most he'd spoken to me without gritting his teeth, or looking at me like he'd wanted to kill me, in a long fucking time. Stunned stupid at first, I shook off the surprise and answered with the first thing that came to mind.

"I'm fine. Nothing I can't deal with." What I didn't divulge was that I'd probably have a nightmare or two over holding Yanez's balls in my hands while Marek stole them from him.

A few more seconds passed before he rose from his chair. "Okay then." Walking toward the door, he shouted over his shoulder, "If you wanna sleep in Stone's room, go right ahead. He went home already."

Another offering I'd gladly take, seeing as how I doubted I'd make it home in one piece if I dared to ride my bike with fatigue nipping at my heels.

I'd meant to text Kena before I fell asleep, but as soon as my back hit the mattress I passed out cold, hoping the nightmares weren't waiting for me in the shadows of darkness.

CHAPTER EIGHTEEN

Kena

IT'D BEEN FOUR DAYS SINCE I'd last heard from Jagger, and I started to believe that he didn't want to meet up after all. Maybe after some consideration, he thought I wasn't worth the trouble. Why should he feel as if he had to explain anything to me? Sure, our attraction was strong—at least it was on my part—but maybe he viewed me as just another person who came across as demanding, eluding his advances until he justified himself. Perhaps he only wanted to get me into bed, and after thinking of all the work he'd have to put in, apologizing and trying to make me see things from his point of view, it was too much effort. He'd just move on to the next one; surely there wasn't a shortage of women lining up to sleep with him.

As the thought permeated my brain, I cringed. I hardly knew the guy, yet the thought of him having sex with someone tore at my heart in a big way.

Braylen stopped asking me if I'd heard from him, the disappointed look on my face enough to tell her I'd been upset at his lack of communication.

The day had passed by like the previous ones. I'd woken up, showered, gotten dressed and gone to the restaurant to work for the day, filling in for Kevin when he'd been late. Again. Thankfully, he hadn't brought up the incident with Jagger. He'd done his friendly duty in warning me against him, but he didn't bombard me with questions about the situation every time he saw me.

When I dragged myself back home, I plopped my tired ass on the sofa, leaned my head back against the soft material and closed my eyes. Thoughts of Jagger infiltrated, but I shoved them aside because I refused to keep thinking about him when I clearly wasn't on his mind. A weightlessness grabbed hold and started to pull me under. Wanting to take a quick nap, I gave in, but was quickly jostled back to reality when I heard my phone chime, indicating I'd received a text. Doing my best not to get my hopes up, thinking it was most likely Braylen messaging me, I reached over to the table near the couch where I'd thrown my purse. Rummaging through it, I pulled out my cell and stared at the screen.

The message was from Jagger.

Breath eluded me.

My mind went blank.

The heightened beat of my heart thrummed against my chest the more I stood there staring at the tiny device.

After what seemed like hours, I swiped my phone open and read his message. For a full minute, my eyes stayed focused on the first word he'd written, fearing if I read the entire text I'd be disappointed in some way. Finally, I read it all, my heart leaping in my chest as I finished.

> *Jagger: I hope you still want to meet up with me. You're all I've thought about for the past few days.*

His blatant admission surprised me, although it thrilled me just the same.

> *Kena: Yes. It's only right to hear you out, give you the opportunity to explain yourself in person. I hope you don't mind, but the only way Braylen would let me see you again is if I agreed to let her come with me.*

He texted back right away.

> *Jagger: That's absolutely fine with me. Although I'm confused as to why Braylen has any say over what you do. You're grown.*

How did I explain my sister to him in a way that wouldn't make him run for the hills? Braylen had always been there for me, sticking up for me and defending me growing up—and even as an adult, the awful encounter with Marcus the most recent. She'd attack anyone without a second thought if she thought they posed a threat toward me. I loved her for it, although it was times like with Jagger when I wished she'd take a step back and let me handle my own business.

Kena: She's only concerned for me, that's all.

I decided to downplay her protectiveness; no need to scare him off too soon.

Jagger: You're lucky to have her watching out for you, then.

An exhale of relief escaped that he understood and hadn't tried to persuade me to come to meet him alone.

Jagger: Where did you want to meet? Totally up to you. You tell me the time and place and I'll be there.

Well, he's sure accommodating.

Kena: Do you know where Neelan Park is?

Jagger: Yes.

I knew Braylen didn't have work the next day, so the timing was perfect.

Kena: Meet us tomorrow at noon by the picnic tables.

Jagger: I'll be there. Can't wait to see you.

Now all I had to do was make sure Braylen hadn't changed her mind. I fired off a quick text letting her know that Jagger had contacted me and we were going to meet him tomorrow. I gave her the time and place, although she'd insisted on the park initially. Either way, happiness danced in my heart I'd see Jagger again.

Would it be for the last time?

———◆———

A SINGLE BEAD OF SWEAT trickled down my back under the blaring sun. Thank heavens I chose to wear a tank top and shorts, or I probably would've passed out by now. The temperature had already reached the mid-eighties and it was barely noon.

Braylen and I patiently waited by the designated area for Jagger to show up. We'd decided to arrive a few minutes early; somehow my sister had convinced me we'd have the upper hand if we were there first. Because I hadn't felt like arguing, I just agreed with her.

Glancing at my watch, I saw that it was exactly noon. While we'd been waiting for the past fifteen minutes, Jagger wasn't technically late. Not yet, at least. Huffing beside me, Braylen rolled her eyes when I turned my head toward her.

Hey, you're the one who insisted on coming with me. My own frustration escaped, and if I had to sit in this heat for much longer, I feared my mood would switch from tolerable to volatile. I didn't do well with the hot weather, becoming ornery rather quickly.

"You know damn well I wasn't gonna let you come alone, so just let it go," she argued, taking a swig from her icy bottle of water. Just as I raised my hands to respond, I caught a glimpse of two men walking briskly toward us. Even though a vast amount of space separated us from them, I knew one of them was Jagger.

The closer they moved, the more anxious I became. Excited to lay eyes on him was second to the nerves gripping me from the inside. I believed Braylen's presence, along with whomever he'd brought with him, made for a very tense meeting. Flustered at what would happen in the next few moments, I closed my eyes and willed my erratic heart to stop its furious pounding. But all the will I could muster didn't matter.

My sister had finally noticed our visitors, hopping up from the picnic bench before I could beg her not to embarrass me. I followed behind, walking up to meet Jagger and his friend. Both guys looked quite menacing from afar, but up close I could see the vulnerability in Jagger's expression. His friend, on the other hand, looked like he would rather be anyplace but there with us. Both wore a leather vest with patches all over. I assumed it had something to do with their club, and because Jagger had worn it to meet me, he was essentially introducing me to that part of his life. While I appreciated the small gesture, I was sure my sister did not.

Finally standing before us, Jagger reached for my hand and pulled me close, kissing my cheek before stepping back.

"Nice to see you again, Kena," he greeted, his amber eyes glistening with appreciation. Turning toward my sister, his smile faltered slightly when he said, "Hi, Braylen. Thanks for letting Kena come and see me today."

"Uh-huh," she responded, tilting her head to the side while her hands found their way to her hips. She could be quite intimidating when she wanted to be, to men and women alike. "Who's this?" she asked, pointing toward Jagger's buddy.

"Oh, sorry. This is Ryder. He's one of my brothers."

"Didn't know you had a brother. Then again, we didn't know a lot about you, Jagger," she gritted, his name sounding like acid on her tongue. "Like you killing someone, or belonging to a gang."

Oh Lord. If I didn't shut her down she'd haul me away before he ever had the chance to explain.

"First off, *sweetheart*," Ryder chastised, stepping closer until he towered over my sister, "you don't know anything about him. Or me, for that matter. So I'd suggest you keep your mouth shut and let these two talk."

For once in my life, someone had rendered my sister speechless. Her cheeks flushed, her eyes popping wide in astonishment that someone had the balls to talk to her like that. I would've laughed if I hadn't feared the whole situation was on the verge of blowing up in my face.

Before Braylen could respond, Jagger opened his mouth and apologized for his friend's behavior. "Braylen, you'll have to forgive my friend here. You see, he's just sticking up for me, like you are for your sister." The words sounded sincere, but the smirk on Jagger's face told me they were anything but.

Reaching out, I grabbed hold of my sister's arm, jerking her to the side before she made our encounter any more awkward. Turning her fully toward me, I let my hands do the talking.

Please don't embarrass me. I'm begging you. Just ignore his friend and let Jagger and me have a few minutes alone. She stared at me with her mouth agape, probably still stunned into silence from what Ryder had just said. *Please,* I begged.

"If you think for one second I'm gonna hang back with that ass Jagger calls a friend while you two traipse off, letting him fill your head with God knows what, you're outta your mind."

"Well, nobody wants to be alone with you either," Ryder snickered, crossing his arms over his chest in a defensive stance. For some reason, his willingness to engage my sister—or better yet, *enrage* my sister—amused me. He had every right to defend his friend, even if he came off as aggressive doing it. Looking the man up and down, I decided that I kind of liked him. Short dark hair neatly adorned his head, while a shadow of a beard painted his face. He was tall; if I had to guess he was just over six feet. Well-built and handsome made him a catch for any woman. Well, anyone except my sister. She apparently didn't like his mouth, although those lips of his could certainly entice any woman out of her panties.

Oh my God! What is wrong with me, I thought, thankful no one could read my mind.

Clearing his throat, Jagger brought me back to our uncomfortable little standoff, his eyes silently apologizing for his friend's retort. He moved a step closer, and when Braylen made a move to step in front of me, I pulled her backward with more force than I thought I had in me. Seizing her arm, I dragged her away until we had some privacy.

I love you, but if you don't let me talk to Jagger alone for a few minutes, I swear I'll make you regret it. I don't know how, but I'll think of something. I mean it, Braylen. You have to back off and let me handle this.

For the second time that day, my sister was at a loss for words. I'd never been so forceful with her before, but right then I didn't have a choice. I couldn't allow her to run my life, making my decisions for me, even if she only did it out of love. Concerned or not, she had to let me live my own life without always interfering.

"Fine, but don't come crawling to me when he breaks your heart. Or worse, gets you killed because of whatever he's mixed up in."

Well, if I'm dead I won't really be complaining much, I signed quickly, more to get her goat than anything, showing her how ridiculous she sounded.

"Not funny," she replied, walking back toward the two guys waiting on us. Brushing past the both of them, she planted herself on the picnic bench, crossing her arms over her chest and mirroring Ryder. When I glanced over at him, I saw a hint of a smile lift the corners of his lips. Clearly my sister amused him, even if he gave off the impression she annoyed him. The wheels of my mind started spinning, thinking that if I could somehow hook the two of them up, maybe she would leave Jagger and me alone.

I knew I'd gotten ahead of myself, but a girl could dream, couldn't she?

CHAPTER NINETEEN

Kena

WARM BREATH FANNED ACROSS MY ear and sent a shiver of delight pulsing through me. "They'd make one helluva couple, don't ya think?" His raspy voice unraveled the last thread of restraint I held close. If I turned my face an inch to the left, Jagger's lips would brush over mine, and although I wanted that more than anything, it wasn't going to be in front of the two brooding people standing close by.

Feeling brazen after threatening my sister to cool it, I grasped Jagger's hand and led him toward a secluded area of the park not far from where we stood. Needing to be away from prying eyes, he readily followed, tightening his hold in mine the further we walked. When two enormous oak trees finally shaded us, I removed my hand from his and took a reluctant step back. My boldness slipped when I found myself alone with him, a sudden shyness wrapping around me and strangling me. I wished I could be more like other girls my age, throwing caution to the wind and just going for it, whatever the situation may be. But sadly, I didn't fall into that category.

Staring down at my shuffling feet, I startled when Jagger's fingers lifted my chin, his eyes boring into mine in the most intimate of ways. Tucking a piece of my hair behind my ear, his hand lingered near my face, almost as if he wanted to stroke my cheek. But he didn't, instead choosing to break the connection right away.

"Thanks again for agreeing to hear me out. I'd hate for you to think of me as someone I'm not," he said, biting his bottom lip in sudden nervousness. I found his uneasiness slightly endearing, rendering him the opposite of his big-bad-biker persona. There was much more than met the eye with Jagger, and I only hoped I'd have the opportunity to find out what.

For a split second I'd wanted Braylen next to me to translate, but I knew I had to do this on my own. While it had been difficult to fully communicate with him, I appreciated the attempts he'd made so far. Sure, he'd only asked me yes or no questions, but at least he'd tried.

"Well, I guess I'll get right to it so we can get it out of the way." His lips kicked up in a sexy grin, and I just about pounced on him. The way his eyes roamed over my entire body, then fixated on my face, studying every feature as if he'd never see me again, both worried and titillated me. I *wanted* to be studied by him, and I hoped this wouldn't be the last time we'd be in each other's presence.

Leaning back against one of the oak trees blocking out the blaring sun, I bent my right leg and rested my foot on its trunk, entwining my hands in front of me while I waited for him to continue.

"What you saw, what you had to witness . . . I'm so sorry that happened. Had I known he would be there, I would've made sure you were nowhere in sight. Of course, I couldn't have known he'd come after me, although I should've expected it after what happened, but still," he rambled on, then stopped himself. "I'm getting off topic. Sorry. That guy came after me because I'd accidentally killed his brother in the ring. I swear it wasn't intentional, and it's been bothering me ever since." He took a deep breath before continuing. "What else?" he asked, more to himself than to me. "I'm part of the Knights Corruption MC, and although we've been involved in some illegal shit in the past, we no longer are."

Something in the way he averted his eyes every now and again told me he omitted certain important details from his explanation, but I couldn't very well ask him about it since he would have no idea what I was trying to get at. Better left for another time, I supposed.

"I'm an underground fighter, as you well know, and currently I'm undefeated." A proud smile appeared when he spoke about being unbeatable. "My club brothers mean the world to me and I would do anything to protect them, as they would for me." He went back to biting his bottom lip, rocking back and forth on the balls of his feet while trying to figure out what to tell me next. His slight anxiety in turn made me nervous, so I stepped forward and reached for his hand. When our palms touched and our fingers intertwined, I felt an overwhelming sense of safety. As if Jagger would go to the ends of the earth to protect me from harm, much like he'd explained he'd do for the members of his club.

I smiled at him when he faltered for his next words, trying to gift him my calmness to continue. Normally, I'm a Nervous Nellie around the opposite sex, never mind someone as gorgeous as Jagger, but there was something about him which spoke to me on a level even I didn't completely understand.

His hold on my hand tightened, pulling me closer until our faces remained just inches apart. "I really like you, Kena. And I would love it if you would give me the chance to get to know you better." His subtle scent of cologne, mixed with a muskiness that was all him, invaded my nose, the smell so heady I wanted to bottle it up and inhale it whenever I thought of him. "Can you give me that chance?" he asked, his beautiful smile returning in full force.

I just couldn't say no.

I nodded, displaying my own happiness with my expression.

"Good." When he leaned in closer I swore I could taste his lips, but we were interrupted before anything happened, Braylen power-walking toward us with intent.

"Are you guys done? Because I can't take any more of that guy," she shouted, pointing over her shoulder toward Ryder. Her face scrunched in anger, and I found it funny that she'd allowed someone to rile her up so much. It had to mean something, or maybe I just hoped for something that wasn't there.

Breaking apart, our intimate moment ruined, I smiled at Jagger before turning toward the feisty blonde I called a sister.

We're finished now, thank you very much.

Glaring at the guy standing next to me, Braylen passed him some sort of silent warning before turning her attention back to me. "Are you ready to go? I have more important things to do than stand around here all day," she huffed, tapping her foot in restlessness.

"Actually, I thought I could give Kena a ride home," Jagger interrupted, stepping closer and reaching for my hand again. Braylen saw the interaction and scoffed, raising her eyes from our entwined hands to stare at me in astonishment.

"Don't tell me you let him sweet talk you?"

I tried to respond, but Jagger held on to me. It wasn't until I tugged again that he let go. "Sorry," he said, "forgot you needed that." His apologetic smile undid me, and all I wanted to do was wrap myself in his arms. But instead, I had to deal with my overprotective sister.

I didn't let anyone sweet talk me. He's nice, and I like him. That's all there is to it. So let it be.

Standing firm, I placed my hands on my hips and waited for her to give in. Thankfully, I didn't have to wait long.

"Whatever," she mumbled, as she walked away. "It's your life. You're the one who's gonna have to deal with the repercussions."

Shaking my head, I turned back toward Jagger and grinned. I hadn't felt like this . . . ever, now that I thought about it. Sure, I'd had crushes on people before, but never had I been so consumed with thoughts of someone. Especially someone I hardly knew.

Heading back to the picnic table, I saw Braylen saunter past Ryder, waving him off when he tried to touch her arm. *What the hell happened while we were gone?*

"Nice to meet you, sweetheart," Ryder yelled after her, laughing as he watched her fling open her car door.

"Can't say the same," she shouted back before starting the engine and taking off.

Lightly smacking my upper arm, Ryder continued to laugh when he said, "Wow! Your sister is a piece of work. Is she always that intense?"

I wanted to shake my head but that would have been a lie, so I settled between nodding *and* shaking my head from side to side. Indecisive, but they both understood what I meant.

"I like it," Ryder said, before clasping Jagger on the back. "Well, if you kids don't need me anymore, I'm out." Without another word, he strode across the lot and swung his leg over his motorcycle, the engine coming to life with the turn of a key. It was then I realized the bike next to Ryder was most likely Jagger's. He said he wanted to give me a ride home, but I'd never ridden on the back of something so dangerous before. They looked so unsafe, no protection from anything.

"Text me your address." I quickly pulled out my phone and messaged him the information. After he glanced at the screen, he put his phone back inside his vest. "Shall we?" he asked, placing his hand at the base of my spine and guiding me toward his ride. Reaching for his helmet, he passed it to me before swinging his leg over the impressive piece of machinery. Scooting up some, he started it up, the fierce sound of the bike startling me. Glimpsing back, he seemed confused as to why I hadn't already straddled the seat, but one glance at the reluctance on my face told him everything. "Let me guess. You've never ridden before."

I shook my head.

"Well, you're in for a treat, then. It's the best feeling in the world. Well, the second best feeling in the world," he teased, winking while a slight tinge of pink stole over my cheeks. He did his best to put me at ease, but I truly didn't think I'd be able to go through with it. *Maybe I should text my sister and ask her to come back for me,* I thought. "I won't let anything happen. I promise." He reached out, the flat of his palm facing upward, waiting for me to accept his invitation.

I trusted him to keep me safe, so I placed my hand in his and allowed him to help me onto the bike, scooting up behind him until my front pressed against his back. Having no idea what to do, I placed my hands on my thighs, waiting for further instruction.

"Wrap your arms around my waist," he said. When I'd done as he'd instructed, he pulled them snugger. "There, just like that. Hold on tight, and lean into any turns I make." My fingers grazed over his abdomen, and even though I was petrified, I quickly took the opportunity to explore the hard planes of his stomach over his shirt. I remembered exactly what his torso looked like, and a warmth spread through me the more my hands snaked around his body. He patted my hands in reassurance. "Don't worry. You'll be fine. Trust me." As the last word fell from his lips, he took off slowly, allowing me time to adjust before increasing his speed. Once he turned onto the highway, he let loose, thrusting forward with a quickness I knew had to be dangerous.

I held on for dear life, probably ensuring he would never want to have me on the back of his bike ever again. After a few minutes, however, I breathed deep and celebrated the feel of the air whipping around my body, and the freeness of the open road. The leather encasing him was warm to the touch, and I wondered what his bare skin would feel like against mine. Being so close to him toyed with my imagination, but before I could lose myself to any more of my thoughts, he turned left off the highway. We were only a few minutes from my house, and never before had I been so disappointed.

When he finally killed the engine, he unlocked my arms and helped me find my footing. After I stood without wobbling, I removed the helmet and placed it on the seat I'd just vacated. A second passed before Jagger swung his leg over and joined me on solid ground.

"So, did you enjoy your first bike ride?" He seemed hopeful, and I didn't want to disappoint him, so I nodded. "Are you lying?" he teased, reading me better than I thought possible. While I'd been terrified in the beginning, I relaxed after a few minutes and really did enjoy myself. So when I nodded again, I truly meant it. "Good, I'm glad. It's the first of many."

Shrugging, at a loss for what to do next, I pointed toward my house, signaling he had the right place.

"I'll walk you to your door," he offered.

Flashing him a genuine smile, I turned my back and started walking the few yards toward the porch. Once we stood on the bottom step, I nervously played with the flap of my cross-body purse, finally delving inside to retrieve my keys. My eyes kept flicking from his face to my hands and back again.

"Do you think I could use your bathroom quick before I head back?" Because I wanted more time with him I readily agreed, nodding before turning around to put the key in the lock. Glancing around the street, I realized Braylen wasn't home, which worked out just fine in my book.

Opening the door, I moved aside so he could enter. Our ranch home wasn't anything fancy, but it was nice. Cozy. And apparently Jagger thought so as well.

"I like your house," he said, glancing from the living room, to the kitchen and then toward the small hallway to the left. "Bathroom?"

I signed, *Second door on the left,* briefly forgetting he had no idea what I'd just told him. But instead of showing him where it was, I held up my forefinger and middle finger in a V shape, then tapped my other hand against the wood of the front door, then pointed down the hall. I wanted to see if he caught on to what I tried to tell him, although it appeared as if I'd been playing charades more than anything else.

A frown appeared, but a few seconds later he grinned. "Second door down the hall?" I nodded. I did a lot of that with him, but I had no other choice. "On the left or the right?" I pointed to the left. He walked away, and I headed straight for the kitchen. I needed a drink like nobody's business, and while I could've definitely used a glass of wine, I opted for a bottled water instead. I'd just finished half of my drink when Jagger reappeared, striding straight for me, his lips curved up in the most enticing grin. He appeared happy. Even his eyes shone brightly. Was it because of me? Or was he normally a happy-go-lucky kind of guy? I hoped for the first option. Well, and the second, but more the first.

We stared at each other for a short while, neither of us knowing what to do. Until he broke the silence, his voice wrapping around me and threatening to never let go. "Well, I guess I better get going. Have some stuff to take care of."

Again, more nodding on my part.

Looking like he battled between leaving and wanting to hang out for a little while longer, I couldn't help but share his silent indecision. Desperately wanting more time with him, my brain fired off warnings that if he didn't leave soon, I might be tempted to throw caution to the wind and do something I may regret.

Once we neared the front door, he turned around and stepped

toward me, his lips so close all I could do was stare at his mouth. Without touching me or saying a single word, he'd somehow managed to drive me insane with want. His warm breath tickled my lips, and when I'd finally dragged my eyes up to his, they bored into mine and tried to communicate a silent message of sorts.

The impending anticipation before the first kiss drove me crazy, although I'd never wanted anything more. After what seemed like forever, the both of us frozen in time for countless seconds, he placed his right hand on my waist, digging his fingers into my skin. Not hard, just the right amount of pressure to tell me he needed to touch me, to connect with me in some way before he left.

"Can I kiss you?" he asked, looking tentative, preparing himself for rejection. But it was a denial which never came. I nodded and leaned in, waiting for him to crush the remaining space. Greedily accepting my invitation, he brushed his lips against mine, the softness of them teasing me in just the right way. At first, I assumed he'd hold back, offering nothing more than a simple peck, but the longer we remained fused together, the clearer it became our first kiss would surely be electrifying.

His right hand traveled up from my waist until it rested at the nape of my neck, gripping me softly and pulling me further toward him. His lips pressed harder. When his tongue slipped from his mouth and teased my lips, I instantly opened for him. Allowing myself to lose some of my inhibitions where he was concerned was the most freeing thing that'd happened to me in a very long time. His warmth enveloped me, and we spent the next few minutes exploring one another's tastes, enjoying the other while we could. My fingers dug into his shoulders as he devoured me, his desire for me fueling my own to even greater heights. His kiss was dominant yet permissive, firm yet tender. The two wavering contradictions certainly kept me intrigued.

Jagger's free hand explored my body, yet he remained respectful. Dipping his fingers under the fabric of my shirt, he skated across my skin, eliciting goose bumps. Freeing my neck from his hold, both of his hands glided behind my back, holding tightly and pulling me impossibly close, as if he wished to meld his body with mine—and judging from the hard length poking me in the stomach, it was exactly what he wanted to do. But he never pushed me further than I was willing to go. He didn't grab my ass or grope my breasts, and while I appreciated him remaining a gentleman, there was a small part of me that wished he'd cross the line and show me just how much he wanted me.

Breaking apart, his short pants of breath hit the side of my face as his lips moved toward my ear. "I can't stop kissing you," he whispered, nipping my lobe before kissing the tender flesh just below it. Pulling back so he could see my flushed face, he asked, "Do I affect you the same way?" There was no mistaking the wanton look on my face, but just in case, I gave him a simple nod. "Good, at least it's not just me who feels like I'm going crazy," he mumbled, hitting the proverbial nail on the head. I shared in his delirium, yet I'd never been so happy.

Gifting me with one last kiss, he stepped back and adjusted him-self, sheepishly grinning when he'd been caught. "Sorry, but I couldn't help it." All I could do was rest my head against the door and smile. I wished for time to stand still, to never move from the spot where I stood. But like all good things—spectacular things, even—our connec-tion had to come to an end at some point. "Well, I guess I should go now." Disappointment snared my vision, but I quickly reeled it in. I knew he liked me, as I did him, immensely, but I also didn't want to come across as needy. Treading carefully for fear I'd offer him too much of myself, I continued to lounge against the door, doing my best to plas-ter a nonchalant look on my face. I wasn't sure if I pulled it off, though.

My body felt like jelly, so to ensure I wouldn't sink to my knees, I took a few extra seconds and gazed at Jagger. Truly looked at him. Studied him, really. I needed to commit every image I could to memory. The way his dark golden hair had flecks of sun-kissed blond spattered all around his head. The way a small dimple appeared in his left cheek when he grinned. The tiny chip in his front tooth that was unnoticeable to most, but because I'd been scrutinizing every facet of him, I'd no-ticed. Oddly, it added to his ruggedness. I glanced down and peered at his forearms, the ink and corded muscles flexing with every gesture he made. Right then his hands fisted and unclenched, over and over again, and I thought maybe it was a nervous tick.

Finally moving away from the door, I twisted the handle and opened it, waiting to hear if he'd say anything before leaving. Luckily, he didn't disappoint. "I'll text you later and we'll set up a day to do something. Sound good?" He fiddled with his own keys that time, glancing from his hands to my face, back and forth until I cupped his cheek. Smiling, I leaned forward and captured his mouth with my own, getting my fill until the next time we'd see each other. I not only found Jagger quite intriguing, but I liked the person I became when I was around him; I remained shy, but my wall of reserves faltered when in his presence. I couldn't explain it, nor did I wish to.

As my lips broke away from his, saddened at the loss, I took a tentative step backward. I wanted nothing more than to taste him again, but I realized that if I didn't allow him to leave something bigger might happen. And while I could certainly picture myself pinned beneath him, offering him my most precious gift, there was no way I wanted to rush things between us.

Not yet.

Not until we knew each other better.

Pushing a heavy sigh from his mouth, Jagger looked dazed. A fleeting look skipped across his face, one so quick it disappeared before I could dissect it. "We'll talk soon," he said, squinting his eyes shut when he realized what he'd just said. "Sorry," he apologized. "Y-you know what I mean." I simply smiled, doing my best to communicate that I didn't find offense with what he'd said. Actually, I found his screwups quite endearing.

He soon disappeared from my house, and as I watched him walk away, I couldn't help but regret my decision to let him leave.

CHAPTER TWENTY

Jagger

WITHOUT SOUNDING TOO MUCH LIKE a pussy, I felt as if I were floating on cloud nine. I spent the entire ride back to my apartment picturing her mouth against mine. The way our tongues melded together, teasing and tasting. The way her skin warmed from my touch. The look of longing on her face when she'd given in and demanded as much from me as I did from her.

The wind swathed me as I rode, the rumble of my bike's engine eradicating some of my frustrations. Of the sexual kind, of course. Wanting desperately to take Kena to bed, the image of the two of us entwined, writhing around in blissful pleasure, bombarded me while I drove. I wouldn't rush her; however, there was too much at stake, for both my head and my . . . heart?

I'd never allowed a female to consume my thoughts before, choosing only to use them for sexual gratification and nothing more. I'd also never pictured myself in a relationship before, electing to stay as detached as possible when it came to the opposite sex. Not that Kena and I were in a relationship. Well, not yet, at least. But hopefully in time, she would deem me worthy of being her man.

Although I wanted nothing more than to be with her, I knew danger lurked around every corner. Psych still hadn't made a move to come and collect Sully, something which unnerved Marek, as well as the rest of the club. Plus, Snake would surely come after me again, and where would I be the next time? At one of my fights? Out with some of the guys? Or maybe out with Kena?

While I despised the thought of putting her in that situation again, I couldn't help but be selfish.

I wanted her.

And I knew there was no way my head was going to win against my incessant need to possess her.

Before long, not remembering a single mile of the travel home, I veered up the incline of my street, whizzing past the parked cars and imagining what it would be like to live in a house filled with a family. Because my mother died giving birth to me, the only family I knew was my father. Obviously, I used the word "family" extremely loosely when referring to that man.

But then I'd stumbled upon Marek and Stone, jumping in without regard for my own safety in order to help them out. My assistance was rewarded when Marek insisted I stop by their clubhouse the following day.

As they say, the rest was history.

Or at least history in the making.

As I dismounted, clutching the black helmet in my hand, I strolled toward the front entrance, a tilted smile encroaching. For once, after a very long time, hope swirled inside me, and it happened because of one person.

The one woman who challenged me to be a better man without even realizing it.

Once inside, I pulled my T-shirt over my head, catching the faint smell of vanilla. Inhaling the only remnants of her, I took my fill before tossing the shirt to the floor in the corner of the bathroom. I imagined my sloppiness grating on her nerves, triggering many an argument, and while the subject should've served to irritate me, I could only grin. Wanting nothing more than to share my life with someone, daily struggles and all, I'd embrace each and every moment she gifted me.

To be thinking of her as if she were the one didn't scare me, although it probably should have. I was only twenty-two, too young to even think about settling down, but I knew deep inside that she differed from every other woman out there.

Felt it deep inside my broken soul.

Continued images of her lifted my spirits as I washed the day off me, my fingers circling my arousal in an attempt to tamper the need surging through me to claim her, if only in thought. Desiring someone so desperately both unnerved and exhilarated me.

Two contradictory emotions, neither of which I gave in to completely.

I had no idea what the future held for me until it smacked me in the face. Drifting off to sleep, the only thing I kept praying for was to get what I'd wanted. I figured fate would deliver soon enough.

Or not.

⸺◆⸺

"WHATCHA LOOKIN' AT?" ADELAIDE ASKED over my shoulder, snatching my phone from me before passing me her daughter. She smirked before taking a few steps back, completely out of my reach from my lounging position on her couch. I cradled Riley in my arms, the baby's presence dispelling any frustrations I'd had at Adelaide's prank. I ignored her, concentrating on trying to make the four-month-old baby smile. Normally I wasn't a kid person, but Stone and Adelaide's child was surely someone special. She had the entire protection of our club behind her, and she didn't have a clue how much shit we were gonna give any boy who came near her as she got older. Poor thing.

Riley's tiny fingers clutched my thumb, gurgling and staring at me like I was some kind of large toy. Her bright green eyes marveled at the sight of me, and I returned the favor.

"Why are you looking up books on sign language?" Glancing over my shoulder, I saw Adelaide's curiosity written all over her face, her brows knitted together while she continued to stare first at my phone's screen, then at me.

"There's this girl I met," I answered, repositioning Riley so I could turn around without fearing I was gonna squish her. I'd planned on leaving it at that, not going into too much detail, when Stone ambled into the living room, running a towel over his head to help dry his hair. Bare-chested, drops of water running down his torso, it was obvious he'd just hopped out of the shower. Thank fuck he had enough sense to put on a pair of shorts before strolling out.

"You talking about the girl from the fight?" He leaned in to give his woman a kiss before walking toward me and reaching for his daughter. If life ever granted me children, I could only hope to be half the father Stone turned out to be. He loved his daughter with a fierceness I'd never seen before, coddling and fussing over her constantly. Or at least that's the way he was whenever I was around.

"Oooo, what girl?" Adelaide teased, biting her lower lip and wriggling her brows. She passed Stone a bottle of formula, all while keeping her stare glued to me. Obviously she wasn't gonna let up until I gave her a bit of information.

"Just some girl," I replied, the words erroneously riddled with nonchalance to throw her off the trail. As soon as Stone opened his mouth again, I knew more details would be demanded, so I crossed my ankle over my knee and settled in for the interrogation.

"Just some girl, my ass," Stone mumbled, tipping the bottle higher so Riley could eat. "He's gaga over this chick. Don't let him fool ya." He sat down beside me, hitting my shoulder with his as he looked down at his daughter. If Stone wasn't such a good friend, I would've up and left the house, refusing to allow anyone to rib on me just because they felt they could. But in truth, I'd come to their house because I'd secretly hoped to talk to him about her. The other guys at the club would razz me, blowing off whatever I felt toward her as nothing more than needing to get laid.

"All right," I confessed. "So she's more than just some girl." Throwing my arm over the back of the sofa, I said, "I really like her, but. . . ."

"But what?" Adelaide asked, handing back the phone she'd grabbed from me moments earlier.

"She can't talk, so I need to learn sign language in order to understand what she's trying to tell me."

"Wait, I'm confused," Adelaide said. "Is she deaf?"

"No, she just can't speak. So while she can hear me, if I ask her anything other than a yes or no question, she has to sign. And as of right now, I only know "thank you."" Puffing out my cheeks in frustration, the stress of not being able to communicate properly with Kena already weighing on me, I threw my head back and closed my eyes.

"Sully knows sign language. Maybe she can teach you." The last word barely left Adelaide's mouth before I had already jumped to my feet. The knowledge that someone I knew could help thrilled me, but then realization hit. No way would Marek allow us time together. As quickly as I became excited, defeat rained down all over me. Slumping my shoulders, I walked toward their kitchen and pulled open the refrigerator. Grabbing a beer, I popped the top and took a big swig.

"Help yourself," Stone grunted, turning his brief attention away from me and back to his daughter.

"What's the problem, Jagger?" Adelaide asked, sitting next to her family.

"Marek will never go for it." She opened her mouth to speak but I cut her off. "Trust me, he won't, which sucks because I need to learn this shit like yesterday."

"We'll talk to him," Stone offered, passing Riley to her mother to finish the feeding. Rising, he walked past me and grabbed his own bottle of beer.

"Yeah? How long's that gonna take?"

"No time at all," he answered. "He and Sully are on their way here now."

CHAPTER
TWENTY-ONE

Jagger

I WOULD'VE BEEN LYING IF I'd said being in such close proximity to Sully and Marek together didn't play on my nerves. The only thing settling me was that he seemed to have softened toward me somewhat over the previous couple weeks. Okay, maybe softened was the wrong choice of word. His borderline hatred of me had lessened, tolerating my presence more and more as the days passed. Hey, any little bit helped.

Taking a seat in the lone recliner, facing the sofa where everyone else perched themselves, allowed me to follow along with their conversation while keeping to myself. Laughing right along with Stone and Adelaide while they regaled us with some of their stories of Riley tempered some of the tension swirling in the air. Or was that just around me?

"But when she looks at me like I'm her whole world, it just does somethin' to me, man." Stone smiled, glancing over at his best friend. Adelaide grazed the back of his head with her hand, and when he turned to look at her, she kissed him. A simple gesture of affection, but it made me long to be with Kena. I wanted so much to be wrapped up in her, just like Stone was with Adelaide. Hell, even the way Marek was with Sully.

I'd coyly snuck peeks at my prez's wife, watched her glancing at her husband every now and again, and I desperately prayed Kena would gift me with the same adoration someday. Minus the sorrow laced behind her eyes, an emotion which confused me because I had no idea where it had come from. I would like to have said Sully and I were friends, and I thought we were . . . to a point. But we'd never been able to explore and strengthen our relationship because of her husband.

Marek's stubbornness aggravated many people, but that trait had also helped the club in immeasurable ways. His quest to never give up on getting his hands on Yanez, for one. Something which had paid off, because the world was now free of such an evil, despicable human being. If I could even call him that.

Moments of fussing over Riley filled the ensuing silence, all of us fascinated with the tiny human. When the baby was placed in Sully's arms, a heart-wrenching look passed over her face, one that was gone too quickly to discern exactly what it had meant.

"So," Adelaide started, reaching over and stroking Riley's head while Sully held her close, "Stone and I wanted to know if you and Marek would be Riley's godparents." For a brief moment, I'd almost felt like I was intruding on a sacred moment between close friends, but it quickly passed when I saw the smiles light up all their expressions, especially Sully's. She was elated, and it pleased me to see her so happy.

To see all of them so happy.

"We don't go to church," Marek blurted, "but we'd do it if you could find a way around that little issue." He kissed Sully's temple before placing his hand over Riley's tiny chest. "We'd be honored, is probably the response you wanted," he chuckled.

"Well, yeah, I guess it is," Stone agreed, reaching over and smacking his friend on the back. "I don't go to church either, and while Addy is a practicing Catholic, she kind of fell off attending as well. But she has a great relationship with her church's priest, and he said he would officiate Riley's baptism, no problem."

"We were thinking of having it at the clubhouse, if that's okay with you," Adelaide said, glancing from Stone to Marek and back again.

"I'm pretty sure that question was to you, buddy," Stone said, jerking his head toward Marek.

"Of course. Yeah. Whatever you two need, we'll do it." They all continued to smile, and their joy seeped into me and calmed me further.

And then Adelaide opened her mouth and started talking to Sully.

About something which involved me. A topic which would surely get under Marek's skin and squash all the happy vibes floating around the room.

"Sully, you know how to sign, right?" Adelaide asked, continuing to stroke the top of her daughter's head, calming her as soon as Riley started to cry.

"Yeah, why?" she answered, her gaze never wavering from the child in her arms, not until Stone had cleared his throat. Even he knew what was coming, preparing himself to deal with whatever blowback would possibly occur.

"How do you know it?" I blurted out, not even realizing I'd asked the question until after the words had left my mouth. Marek picked his head up and looked at me, but thankfully his expression was void of anger. Irritation may have been at the forefront, but not anger.

"I didn't have much going on when I lived. . . ." She trailed off before taking a breath and continuing. "I had to be inventive, fill my days with something, so I watched videos and convinced my father to allow me to buy a book on the subject. I would sit in my room for hours on end and have conversations with myself just so I could practice." She smiled, but the curve of her lips waned. Handing Riley back to Adelaide, she tucked a strand of her black hair behind her ear before resting her hands in her lap.

"Why the sudden curiosity?" Marek inquired, looking at everyone, including me.

"Jagger's interested in someone, and she can't speak. So he needs to learn sign language in order to understand her," Adelaide offered. If Stone had been the one to talk, he probably would've been a bit crasser about my situation, no doubt throwing in that I wanted to get Kena into bed and needed a way to tell her so, or some shit like that.

"Is she deaf?" Sully asked, quickly glancing toward Marek to see how he was faring with her talking to me. Luckily, he didn't seem to have minded, but maybe that was because his wife and I were not alone together.

"No, she just can't speak," I responded, scratching the side of my head as a distraction.

"So she can hear, just doesn't wanna talk? Is that what it is?" Marek asked, confused by the turn of conversation.

"No," I said, a little more intensely than I'd intended. "She physically can't talk. I haven't worked up the nerve yet to ask her what happened. It might be a touchy subject." *Breathe deep.* "And yes, she can hear. But for right now, I can only ask her yes and no questions, because otherwise . . . I just can't understand her when she tries to communicate with me." Annoyance trickled through my veins because they'd forced me to talk about Kena's condition, and although the conversation was one derived from simply curiosity, I felt as if I were betraying her in some way.

"Oh, how awful for her," Sully said, a frown suddenly appearing. "I'd love to help you, but I'm not sure I can." Without realizing, she caught her husband's eye before turning back toward me. She silently asked permission with the quick look they'd shared. The last thing I wanted to do was turn the joyous nature of the day's visit into one filled with bristling tension, but I had no other choice.

With every moment that ticked by where I couldn't properly communicate with Kena, I feared she'd deem me not worthy and move on to someone who could understand her. Someone like Kevin. Someone who fully comprehended her situation and could give her something I couldn't.

So I decided to risk Marek's anger and pushed Sully on the topic.

"Anything you could teach me would be awesome. I really like her. It'd mean a lot to me." I leaned back in my seat and patiently waited to see what would happen. Thankfully, Stone's woman interjected her two cents.

"It's the perfect solution. Isn't it, Sully?" Adelaide asked, first locking eyes with her friend, then with Marek, silently challenging him to disagree. Adelaide wasn't afraid of anyone, and I truly admired that about her. She'd put Stone's volatile ass in check on quite a few occasions, and while the leader of the Knights Corruption unnerved me at times, he had no such effect on Adelaide.

Tense, uncertain seconds passed without a single word spoken from anyone. I swore they heard my heart thrumming inside my chest, felt the uneasiness wrapping around me, but still the silence continued.

Deciding to end it, I finally spoke up. "It's okay. I'll figure something else out. No biggie." Slumping back in my chair in defeat, I ran my hand through my hair in uncertainty.

"Nonsense," Adelaide pushed, handing Riley to Marek to hold. A distraction tactic at best, and I think it worked; everyone loved the little girl, Marek being no exception. "Jagger, Sully will help teach you what you need to know. It's not every day someone special falls into your lap."

"That's a whole other topic, sweetheart," Stone teased, grabbing his woman by the waist and pulling her impossibly close.

Shoving his shoulder in mock annoyance, she turned back toward me, an amused look on her face. "I'm serious. We need to help him out. And if anyone here has a problem with that, they'll have to deal with me." A smile still danced on her lips, but everyone present knew she was dead serious. Even Marek.

All heads turned toward the dark-haired leader of the club, breathlessly waiting for him to speak. Would he assert his dominance over the entire group? Or would Adelaide's not-so-subtle demands win out?

Marek's chest rose and fell, an unsettling sigh his only response until he finally opened his mouth. "At the clubhouse. Be there tomorrow at noon." Leaning forward, he pointed a dangerous finger in my direction. "If I so much as see anything inappropriate, you'll regret it, prospect."

"Oh, stop playing the big bad biker, Marek," Adelaide teased. "Save all that testosterone for when Riley starts dating." She laughed at her own joke, but her words only served to rile up her man.

"Hell no!" Stone shouted. "No dating for my baby girl. Nope. Not gonna happen."

We all laughed, even though I knew Stone stood firm behind his outburst.

Poor Riley was gonna have a hell of a time dealing with not only her father, but every other man in the club as she got older. Their protection over her already something fierce, it would only intensify as she became interested in the opposite sex.

CHAPTER
TWENTY-TWO

Kena

"I CAN'T BELIEVE THAT GUY," Braylen grated. "I mean, who the hell does he think he is?" For the past two days, my sister had been going off about both Jagger and his friend Ryder, flip-flopping between the both of them so often it was hard to keep straight who she'd been pissed at.

Who are you talking about? And why are you so upset? I'd never seen my big sister so riled up over any guy. Yeah, her concern about me getting involved with Jagger was understandable, but when it came down to it, I could make my own decisions. But for her to still be this upset over some guy she'd just met was rather telling. What had happened between them when Jagger and I left them in search of some privacy at the park? We weren't gone that long.

"I'm talking about his friend. Ryder," she blurted, running her hands through her hair in annoyance. I had no idea how we'd gotten on the topic of either one of the men, but there we were, and since she needed to get something off her chest, there was nothing I could do but sit back and hear her out. Plus, it amused me to see her so irked over Jagger's friend and club brother.

What happened between you two? I wriggled my brows in jest, but it only served to irritate her more.

"Absolutely nothing," she replied too quickly, a slight pink tinge stealing over her cheeks.

Come on, Braylen. You're not telling me everything. I rested my hands at my sides and squinted at her, doing my best to read her body language. Other than the embarrassment which covered her skin, I had no idea what else she'd been leaving out of our conversation.

"He's a pig," she'd finally disclosed. "When you guys walked away, he told me that I needed a good fuck to calm me down. He even offered to be the one to "fuck me senseless,"" she said, switching her tone to a deeper voice, no doubt imitating Ryder.

I couldn't help it.

I smiled. Big.

My sister was certainly intense, especially toward those she had an issue with, justified or not. And because Ryder had called her on her shit, he was all right in my book. Maybe my sister did need to get laid, although she'd never had any issues in that department before. If she had someone else to focus on, maybe she wouldn't be so overbearing when it came to Jagger, and my decision to keep seeing him. A decision she didn't know about yet. I hadn't even told her about the kiss. Needing to keep something to myself, I decided to tell her when I deemed necessary, or when she'd moved past her dislike for him.

I guess I shouldn't hold my breath on that one.

"It's not funny," she pouted, although the slightest hint of a smile graced her mouth.

It kind of is, I signed back. *Plus, Ryder's kind of hot.*

I half expected her to make some kind of grossed-out face, as if the mere mention of Ryder's looks would send her into a tailspin of sorts. Spouting off how much she couldn't stand the sight of him, and if she ever saw him again it would be too soon. That kind of stuff. But instead, she gave me a half smirk before turning around and walking toward the kitchen. When she returned with a bottle of unopened wine and two glasses, plopping down on the couch next to me, I couldn't help but shake my head and smile again.

Raising my hands, I signed, *You like him.* It wasn't a question, instead an observation.

"What?" she practically screeched. "You're out of your mind."

Leaning closer, she scrutinized me. "Are you already drunk, Kena? Because that's the only way you could be serious right now." When I just sat there staring, she continued with her mini outburst. "Are you for real, or are you messing with me? Because if you honestly think that I would ever like that man, no matter how good-looking and mysterious he may be, I might need to have you committed." Popping off the cork, she took a big swig straight from the bottle. Scrunching up my face, I tore the wine from her fingers and poured myself a glass before she finished off the contents.

So you do think he's good-looking?

"Duh." She rolled her eyes. "Anyone can see he's fucking gorgeous. Too bad he's crass and arrogant." Pouring herself a glass, she took a few slow sips, the look plastered across her face telling me she was contemplating an issue, an internal dialogue I was sure she wouldn't allow me to be a party to.

Settling back into the comfortable couch, I pressed the remote and flicked on the television. We'd planned on watching a movie, but something told me we'd be discussing some of the members of the Knights Corruption instead.

Placing the wine glass between my legs, I asked, *Why don't you give him another chance? If he still acts the same, then you'll know he's not right for you.*

Only my sister could chug wine and not make it look uncouth. "Give him another chance? Now I *know* you're drunk." Plunking back against the leather sofa, she folded her legs underneath her. "I don't want to be anywhere near that man. Besides, when or why would I even be in the same room with him again?" Her question lingered in the air, more of a serious inquisition than a rhetorical one.

I'm going to see Jagger again soon. I could ask him to bring Ryder along if you want. Maybe we could all grab something to eat. For a split second I believe Braylen considered it, but then her stubbornness kicked in and she tossed aside the mere notion of ever laying eyes on Jagger's friend again.

"No, thank you," she emphatically said, pouring another glass of wine. "Can we please not talk about either one of them anymore, and just watch this damn movie?"

Okay, okay. Don't get testy, I signed before pushing Play. For the next hour and a half, we lost ourselves in the comedic world of Kevin Hart.

Later that evening, as I snuggled under my thick comforter, my air conditioner on full blast, a message came through on my phone. My heart skipped a beat from the mere thought that it could be Jagger texting me. Unhooking my cell from its charger, I swiped the screen and saw it was indeed him.

> *Jagger: Would you like to grab a bite to eat next Friday? Say around seven? I'd make it sooner but I have a lot of stuff I have to deal with. Plus I have a fight coming up in a couple days I need to train for.*

When he'd left my apartment days ago, I'd expected him to contact me right away. But he hadn't, and while I'd been disappointed, I understood our situation wasn't the norm for him. Or for me either, as a matter of fact. I'd accepted my limitations, but I was smart enough to realize it might take him some more time. My condition certainly wasn't an easy thing to handle, so I silently berated myself for not being patient.

While excitement raced through me at seeing him again, my nerves also took over. There were only so many yes and no questions he could ask me in person.

> *Kena: Next Friday sounds good. See you then.*

> *Jagger: Great. I'll text you tomorrow. Good night.*

I fell asleep that evening thinking of Jagger, much like I had since the day I'd first laid eyes on him. Thoughts of him infiltrated my brain more often these days. I found it hard to concentrate at work, or while I hung out with my sister or just doing mundane everyday tasks. Consumed with when I'd see him again became my not-so-favorite pastime.

Picturing his face and remembering what his kiss tasted like lulled me to sleep, dreams sneaking out from the recesses of my subconscious and pulling me under into a blissful slumber.

CHAPTER TWENTY-THREE

Jagger

"STOP MESSIN' AROUND AND BE serious for a minute," Sully demanded, her tone belying the words she'd spoken. Trying to appear the serious teacher, her face lit up at the interaction between us. Sitting next to her on the couch in the clubhouse common room had been our daily meeting place for the past five days, and she'd taught me a lot. We'd also managed to have a bit of fun along the way as well.

"I *am* serious," I said, smirking at the disbelieving expression on her face. "I just keep forgetting some of the letters. This shit isn't easy."

"No one said it was gonna be, so stop pouting and get with it. Besides, aren't you taking her out in two days? Because that's not a lot of time to practice. I think we're gonna have to extend our sessions a bit. What do you think?" Sully glanced at the book in her lap, the one she'd been teaching me from since we started the lessons. She knew a lot without even glancing at it but because she wasn't fluent, she had to refer back to the book every now and again. But she was a much better teacher than YouTube.

"What about your husband? What's he gonna say about that?" Marek had handled our little sessions a lot better than I thought he ever would. At first he hung around, often sitting at the bar to keep an eye on us, but after the third day, he'd disappeared into Chambers, most times with Stone and Tripp, to discuss routine club business. All the important topics required all of our attendance, but thankfully that didn't happen all that often lately.

"I've discussed it with Cole already and he's fine with it. As soon as I told him how much Kena means to you, he kind of gave up the notion that you're in love with me." Sully swallowed nervously and brushed her hair from her face, glancing at me quickly. "I told him he was crazy, that you never felt that way about me, but he dismissed my ramblings. Anyway," she muttered, "he's fine with all of it."

Sully and I had talked about how Marek had treated me after the day he attacked me in his living room when he'd returned home early from his trip. Seeing his wife sleeping against my shoulder had set him off, and I caught the brunt of his anger that night. Then for the months that followed, he barely tolerated my presence. It wasn't until recently that his behavior toward me started to thaw, the turning point happening after killing Yanez.

The next two hours passed by ridiculously fast, the both of us giving it our all, communicating with nothing but our hands. We weren't allowed to speak to the other, and while I'd messed up a few times, I'd certainly made progress. An accomplishment I treasured, as did Sully, beaming brightly with her own teaching achievement.

Rising to my feet, I raised my hands above my head and allowed my muscles to stretch. Craning my neck from side to side helped to wake me, which I'd needed because I had to prepare for that evening's fight.

"Hey, Ryder!" I shouted over my shoulder as he walked by. "You seen Stone?" Figuring it was probably a good idea if I engaged in some last-minute training, I squeezed Sully's hand in thanks and went in search of my sparring buddy.

"Yeah, he's in Chambers with Marek."

Nodding my thanks, I strolled across the room, and knocked on the door before entering. Peeking my head through the small allowance, I locked eyes with Stone before turning to Marek.

"You need something, prospect?" the club leader asked, a look of irritation strangling his features. Was that for me? Or for another reason?

With no time to waste, I answered right away, hoping to get in at least an hour in the ring before I had to leave. I'd wanted to shower and contact Kena for a little bit before heading to that night's fight location.

"Yeah, sorry for interrupting. Sully and I are done for today, and I wanted to know if you," I said, switching my attention to Stone, "could go a few rounds in the ring with me."

Stone looked a bit unnerved, as if whatever he and Marek had been discussing had been heavy. But it was obvious it wasn't weighty enough to require all of us to be involved, so I dismissed it as none of my business.

"Sure. I'll be out in five," the VP acknowledged, waving toward the door, essentially dismissing me. I took the hint and closed the door, striding toward the bathroom so I could change into a pair of shorts. I planned on working up a sweat, and jeans just wouldn't be the proper attire for me to whoop on Stone.

———◆———

"WHO'S COMING TONIGHT?" I ASKED, wiping the sweat from my brow after Stone and I finished dancing around the ring, both of us energized after our little bout. My friend had a red mark forming on his side where I'd kicked him, but the bastard never even flinched, his ability to never feel pain pissing me off. Not that I wanted to harm him, but for ego sake, it would have been nice if Stone had at least made some kind of pained expression.

Normally, I wouldn't train the same night I had a fight scheduled, but I'd needed to release some of my aggression. Saving all my energy for my opponent that evening might have proved to be detrimental, and there was no way I wanted a repeat of what happened before, ending someone's life unintentionally.

"I can't make it, but Ryder and Tripp will be there with you." Stone ran a towel over his dampened hair, tossing it at me with a devious smirk on his face. "That's for good luck."

"Gross, man." Tossing his sweat rag to the floor, I threw him the middle finger before lifting the top rope of the ring so I could exit. "I'll text them the address." Jumping to the ground below, I snatched my shirt from my duffle bag and threw it on, heading toward my bike so I could make it home in time to relax before I had to leave again.

An hour later and I'd washed off the remnants of my training, my mind focused on one person and one person only. Although, given I had a fight later that evening, my mind should've been on my upcoming opponent and not on the one woman who'd captured my undivided interest.

I'd tried texting her as soon as I arrived home but she never responded. Assuming she was busy, I didn't think anything of it until my phone suddenly chimed with her reply.

Kena: Sorry, I meant to text you back earlier but I was with Kevin.

What. The. Fuck? What was she doing with Kevin? She'd told me there was nothing going on between the two of them, even though he'd asked her out and she'd been interested at some point. Had she changed her mind? About him? About me?

My fingers glided over the keys without a second thought. Normally I wasn't a jealous person, but all of that changed right then. She belonged to me, and the thought that she spent time with another guy more than irritated me.

Jagger: Why were you with Kevin? I thought you weren't interested in him.

I had a few other choice words on reserve but thought better of expressing them, especially so new into our budding relationship. Not wanting to scare her off before we'd spent more time together, I kept my temper in check. From our messages. At home alone, I brewed in my anger, cursing out loud as I paced back and forth waiting for her to respond.

Kena: I'm not. His band wrote a new song and he wanted to know if I could listen and give my honest opinion. That's all.

Jagger: Are you sure that's all it is? Because I have a right to know.

I need to calm down before I type something that'll be out there forever.

Kena: Yes. Why are you acting like this?

Why am I acting like this? Maybe because you're spending time with another guy, someone who's expressed interest in you. Wants to date and no doubt fuck you. My inner ramblings never made it into text, thank God, because if they had she might never respond. Deciding to completely ignore her question, I switched the subject and invited her to my fight. Normally I would've thought it best to keep her far away from that part of my life because of obvious danger, but I wanted to see her. To look into her eyes and see if she still felt about me the way I did about her. I had to make sure the torture that kept me awake most nights was shared. I'd meant to save my surprise for when I saw her on Friday, but because of the revelation with Kevin, someone who could readily communicate with her, I needed to show her I was on the same level.

Someone worthy of sticking with.

> *Jagger: Why don't you and Braylen come to my fight tonight? Tripp and Ryder are going. I'll make sure they watch over you two, just in case Marcus is lurking around.*

No response for ten minutes. *Maybe she's asking her sister. Hopefully that's the only reason for delay.* Finally, a message flashed across my screen, but unfortunately it wasn't from Kena.

> *Tripp: We'll meet you there a few minutes beforehand.*

I never texted him back, instead impatiently waiting for Kena to get back to me. Countless minutes passed, driving me insane with edginess. Had I fucked up calling her out like I had? I could've said so much more, but I did my best to keep it in check. My heart raced at the thought that she'd changed her mind about me, and even though there wasn't a damn thing I could do about it right then, I still berated myself for becoming so entranced with her. Nothing good was gonna come out of it, so why did I insist on pursuing her?

Because you feel something for her you can't explain.

Over the next twenty minutes, I drove myself crazy. Finally deciding I had to pull my focus back from her and onto my upcoming bout, I tossed my cell on the table near the door and walked down the hall toward my bedroom. Gripping the sides of my hair, I pulled tightly, eliciting a sting of pain which helped to soothe the rampant fire burning inside. Lost to the ramblings inside my head, I almost missed my phone ringing. Realizing it had to be someone from the club, I lazily strolled back toward the living room, grabbing my cell and turning it over so I could see who was calling.

To my surprise, Kena's name appeared on the screen, which was quite odd seeing as how she couldn't talk.

"Hello," I tentatively answered, holding my breath in confusion.

"Listen, we'll go, but you better tell that ass of a friend of yours to stay away from me because if he says the wrong thing, I'm gonna deck him. You got it?" Braylen spewed her words faster than I could understand. It took my brain a few extra seconds to comprehend what she'd said, but apparently it was too long because she started in on me again. "Jagger," she shouted. "Did you hear me?"

"Yeah, I heard ya. I'll warn Ryder that he's gonna get junk-punched if he steps over the line." He'd told me why she left the park so pissed off that day. His telling her she needed to get fucked probably hadn't sat so well with her, and while I found it funny, I cautioned him to cut the shit because he could potentially ruin things between Kena and me. Her familial loyalty to her sister no doubt surpassed anything she felt toward me.

Chuckling to myself so as not to piss her off, I complied with her amusing demands and wasn't even offended when she hung up on me. Seconds later, a text message came through.

> *Kena: Sorry about that but she refused to go unless she talked to you first.*

> *Jagger: No problem. I won't be there until nine thirty, so I'll see you then.*

A tentative smile lifted the corner of my mouth, and while I'd been thrilled Kena had decided to come that evening, I couldn't help but feel like something bad was gonna happen.

CHAPTER TWENTY-FOUR

Kena

THE ROAR OF THE CROWD should've excited me like it seemed to do for everyone else, but instead it frightened me. I hated watching grown men fight, and while I came to see and support Jagger, I couldn't wait until we could leave.

As soon as we entered the basement of the abandoned warehouse, two men in leather cuts flanked us on either side. I recognized Ryder from the park, and I believed the other guy's name was Tripp, briefly remembering him from the night I'd first met Jagger. I raised my hand to both of them in greeting and they returned the welcome with a simple nod.

I saw Ryder lean down and whisper something to my sister, the slight flush of her cheeks warning me she was set to explode. Grabbing her hand, I hurried down the narrow walkway and toward two empty seats in the middle of the growing crowd. Once seated, I raised my hands and asked, *What did he say to you?*

Biting her bottom lip, she tilted her head to the left where Ryder stood, then looked back to me before saying, "That his offer still stands in case I'm interested."

I instantly smirked, a reaction which made my sister scoff and slap my arm in irritation. Her admonishment only made me smile bigger.

While I'd thought Ryder and Tripp would sit next to us, they chose to stand on either side of the aisle instead. Our lookouts, or bodyguards I supposed. It should've been a warning of things to come, but as soon as the lights dimmed and the announcer started speaking, all I could think about was Jagger. And sure enough, as if my mind willed the sight of him, I spotted him moments later coming down the walkway, fans patting him on the back as he took his time advancing toward the ring. Women shouted obscene things, vying for even just a second of his attention. Right away, I was thrust back to the reason why I'd denied Kevin a date.

Fighters were no different than band members.

Although, what I'd felt toward Kevin didn't even compare to what I felt about Jagger. Not even in the same ballpark. So I dismissed my insecurity and tried my best to focus on him as he approached. When he turned his head to the right, we'd locked eyes and everyone else ceased to exist. I found it hard to breathe, let alone make any kind of movement while I continued to stare at him.

Jagger wore a pair of black shorts which hit just above his knees, and as my eyes traveled the length of him I noticed he was not only bare-chested but also barefoot. As naughty images of the two of us penetrated my mind, he winked before continuing toward his destination. Spreading the ropes, he stepped inside the ring and walked to the far left-hand corner, his opponent already boring holes through him like he wanted to rip him to shreds.

Both men were cut, but Jagger looked more powerful. Maybe it was the way he carried himself, confident the other guy never stood a chance. Jagger *was* undefeated, after all. I'd heard it from his mouth as well as from his buddies muttering the same before Braylen and I took our seats.

My mind raced to the explanation he'd given me about why that scary guy had pulled a gun on him, and I wondered if every time Jagger stepped foot in the ring he was worried about ending another man's life.

The sound of the bell rang out and I couldn't help but become fascinated with the dance both fighters performed. But it quickly changed as soon as Jagger's head shifted to the side after his opponent landed a punch. From that moment on, I looked away often, dreading what I'd see when I lifted my eyes to the gruesome scene in front of me. Braylen, on the other hand, cheered right along with everyone else, often standing on her seat so she could have a better view of the action. A sentiment I definitely didn't share.

While my head hung low, someone sidled up next to me. At first I had an uneasy feeling, but when I raised my head, I saw Tripp casually standing there, his hands in his pockets while he watched the fight with appreciation. When he finally turned toward me, he started to speak but because of the noise, he had to lean down quite a bit so I could hear him properly.

"Don't worry about him. He's just messin' around with the other guy. Workin' him up some for the sake of the crowd. It makes him more valuable." Leaning back, Tripp gave me a megawatt smile.

A simple nod from me and I looked to the ring in enough time to watch Jagger land a hard punch to the side of the man's face, tossing him to the ground like he weighed nothing at all.

The fans went crazy.

Jagger had just knocked out his rival.

He jumped out of the ring and walked directly toward me, not participating in any of the showboating that went along with winning. Leaning over Tripp, Jagger extended his hand to me and I readily accepted. Pulling me forward, I glanced back at Braylen to let her know we were leaving when I saw Ryder say something to her. But instead of looking pissed as usual whenever he was near, a shadow of a smile ghosted her lips. I left them to attend to whatever it was they were doing, allowing Jagger to lead me to the back of the crowded space.

"I just have to rinse off, change and grab my money. Then we're out," he said to both me and Tripp, before disappearing inside a back room. He'd emerged five minutes later fully dressed in a white T-shirt, dark jeans and worn brown boots, his hair still damp from the shower.

Damn, he was fine both in and out of clothes.

Leaving me alone again with Tripp, Jagger disappeared inside a small office. I'd fidgeted with the hem of my blue shirt, shuffling my feet anxiously waiting for him to come back.

"Want out of here that bad, do you?" Tripp asked, leaning against the wall behind him. His piercing green eyes swallowed me whole, but not in an inappropriate way. More like he'd taken over the role of protector in Jagger's absence.

Balling my fist, I placed my thumb over the rest of my bent fingers and bent my hand forward. His brows knit together in confusion. I'd realized I'd just signed *yes*, but of course he had no idea what I was trying to tell him.

Jagger reappeared quickly and translated for me, which was completely unexpected.

"She said yes," Jagger announced, grabbing my hand firmly in his before leaning in to capture my mouth. The sudden gesture surprised me, although I would have been lying if I said the kiss didn't thrill me. Even in front of hundreds of strangers. Not having enough time to even contemplate what other words he'd learned in sign language, he pulled me toward the exit, Tripp following closely. Once outside, I peered around the both of them and tried to locate my sister.

Sneaking his arm around my waist, Jagger pulled me close, planting a kiss on my temple before smiling down at me, the gesture indeed intimate. My heart sang, but my head told me to remain alert.

Ryder and Braylen suddenly appeared out of nowhere, rounding the corner of the building and heading straight for us. My sister's face was expressionless, while Ryder's was the exact opposite. In fact, he looked to be quite animated, a cocky smirk playing on his features and softening his hard-around-the-edges look.

When all three men circled around us, I couldn't help but notice the strength they emanated. Jagger was the only one not wearing his leather vest, but he looked just as intimidating as the other two. All of them were at least six-foot, Tripp being the tallest and towering over his friends by a few inches.

Jagger took a few steps forward, releasing my waist only to latch on to my hand. Intertwining his fingers with mine, he pulled me behind him, telling his buddies he'd see them the next morning. I turned my head to look back at Braylen, and it was then I saw the look she gave Ryder when she thought no one was paying any attention.

Especially him.

She liked him.

For as much as she tried to convince everyone of the opposite, the man clearly intrigued her. Catching my eye, she shrugged. It made me smile. Braylen was a tough woman, didn't take shit from anyone, so it was nice to see her express interest in someone. Someone who challenged her, albeit in a way I'd never thought she'd go for. Ryder came across as the silent type, brooding even, but when he was around my sister, something switched inside him. I didn't know him well at all, but I knew enough to see he liked her. And that was good enough for me.

If he was half the man Jagger was, he was okay in my book.

Jagger's warm breath hit my ear before I'd even realized he'd leaned in to me. "Ryder's gonna walk her to her car and follow her home. You wanna say good-bye?" he asked, taking a step back to look at my face.

I tugged my hand from his and strode back toward Braylen, Ryder stepping aside so I could talk with my sister before we parted ways.

Are you all right with this? I gestured, glancing over at Ryder and the other two who were all now huddled together and talking about something so low neither of us could hear.

"Yeah, I'm good. He's just going to walk me to my car and make sure I get home safe." When she looked down at her feet, then back up at me, she laughed and blurted, "He's not that bad, I guess."

Shaking my head in amusement, I gave her a hug before heading back toward Jagger. As our small group dispersed, a blur of commotion caught my attention, but before I could see what happened, Jagger stepped in front of me, essentially blocking my view of everyone.

"Let's go," he urged, doing his best to keep his tone casual. But a slight tremor escaped. Before I could read into it, he placed his hands on my shoulders and turned me around. Once I faced away from the crowd, he threw his arm over Braylen's shoulders and steered her away as well, the three of us walking down the sidewalk as if it had been the plan all along.

My sister tried to break free, confusion riddling her expression at the about-face, but Jagger's hold never wavered. "I'm gonna follow both of you home." He offered no other explanation. Even though I knew something happened, I didn't quite know what, and something inside my curious brain told me not to ask.

Otherwise, I feared whatever relationship I had with Jagger would go up in smoke.

CHAPTER TWENTY-FIVE

Jagger

MY SELFISHNESS TO BE NEAR her, to show her I was the man for her, put her in danger yet again. Only this time, I'd been able to shield her from what I feared could've been fatal.

Either for me or, God forbid, Kena.

Constantly questioning her safety had become the new norm for me, and while I knew deep in my soul that she'd be better off without me in her life, I just couldn't break away. No one else had managed to make me feel the way she did.

"Why did you drag us away so fast?" Braylen asked, continuing to try and glance over her shoulder every few steps. She'd clearly made some sort of plan with Ryder that evening, and because her night had switched to something else entirely, Kena's sister was not too happy.

"Ryder and Tripp forgot they had to head back to the club. Had to sort out some business." I hurried them down the remainder of the block, their car parked smartly underneath a bright street lamp. "I'm sure you'll hear from him," I tried to reassure her, but her pissed-off attitude told me she wasn't taking his abandonment lightly.

She mumbled incoherently before rounding the car to jump in the driver's seat. Reaching for the passenger handle, I waited until her sister clicked the locks before opening the door for Kena. But she didn't get in right away. Instead, she stood there looking up at me, confusion mixed with a sprinkling of fear behind her eyes. The frustrating thing was that she couldn't just come out and say what she wanted, ask me the many questions mulling around inside her head. It wasn't the time or place, anyway. I'd answer as much as I could later on, but not now. Not here.

Needing them to leave, I gestured toward the inside of the car with a jerk of my head, hoping she understood so I didn't have to push further. Averting her eyes from mine, she turned slightly to the left and took her seat inside the car.

"I'll follow you to make sure you get home safely. I'm parked down there a bit," I said, pointing back toward the warehouse. "But don't wait for me. I'll catch up." The words lingered in the air, but the swift slam of the door sliced them to pieces before another breath escaped my lungs.

The ride to their house filled me with trepidation, a feeling I was all too familiar with these days. Before Kena, I only worried about myself and my club, which was more than enough, trust me. But ever since she'd come into my life, fear riddled me. Always worrying whether or not being mixed up with me would endanger her triggered many a sleepless night.

I portrayed someone filled with confidence, a guy who took life's punches as they came—literally and figuratively—before quickly moving on.

I joked.

I laughed.

I had my brothers' backs. Always.

I got drunk occasionally.

I used to partake in the endless flow of pussy.

I tried to do right by others, shielding them the best I could, when I could.

No one ever bore witness to my insecurities. I feared I'd never be good enough for the Knights Corruption family. I feared Kena would eventually tire of me and move on, leaving me in the dust to fumble my way back toward my warped sense of reality.

There was no doubt I was a work in progress, but then again, weren't we all?

Winding down the curvy road, I finally came to stop behind Braylen's car, the small white Toyota's engine shutting off just as the driver and passenger doors sprung open.

Braylen looked back at me before turning toward the front of their house, walking briskly toward the door and disappearing inside before I'd even come to stand next to Kena. The last thing I wanted to do was explain why I'd rushed them home so fast, so I was happy Braylen left so abruptly; out of the two, she'd obviously be the one to shower me with endless questions.

One minute Kena and I were walking along, minding our own business, and the next I'd been shot a warning look from Tripp, a silent order to escort the women out of there right away. Out of the corner of my eye, I saw Snake approach our group like a man on a mission, one of his friends accompanying him this time. Before an ambush erupted, Tripp and Ryder formed a wall, essentially separating the threat from me, Kena and her sister.

Stupidly thinking the Reaper wouldn't dare show his face at one of my fights so soon after our last encounter proved to be an almost lethal mistake on my part. I had no doubt he'd come to finish what he'd started, snatching my life for killing his brother. In his head, I had to perish, and now I knew he wouldn't stop until he'd accomplished his mission.

So wrapped up in my head, Kena's warm palm on my cheek threw me back into the here and now, and I leaned in to her touch like it would give me solace. But sadly, it didn't; if anything, her concern rattled me. Looking deep into her eyes, I tried my best to smile, and for the most part I'd succeeded, even though I knew she realized something was off.

"It's getting kind of chilly out. You better head on inside," I urged, removing her hand from my face, kissing her palm before lowering it to her side. Too many contradictions flew at me, and right then I didn't have time to indulge any of them. I had to head back to the club and find out what the hell ended up happening after I'd left.

A frown knit her brow, but before she read further into my dismissive words, I leaned in and grazed my lips over hers. For a brief moment, I thought about staying right there with her, wrapping her in my arms and never letting her go. But I knew it was only a fantasy, one which had to end in mere moments.

Kena's hands snaked around my neck, her fingers threading through my hair, the strands long enough for her to tug them in excitement. Her tongue pressed against mine, the dance intoxicating and breathless. If I hadn't known better, I would've thought she was trying to convince me to stay. But was she that brazen? What would happen if I followed her inside? Would she give herself to me?

For as much as I wanted to find out, I knew I had to head back to the clubhouse so I could do my part in the situation I'd created.

Breaking free from her embrace, I silently cursed myself before looking at her beautiful face. "I'd love to stay, Kena. You have to believe me. But I have to go. I can't explain everything right now, but just know that I'd rather stay here with you." I could see she wasn't sure if I was telling the truth or not, so I pressed my entire body against hers, pinning her to the side of the car. My arousal was quite evident when pressed against her stomach. Her caramel eyes undid me, pleading for me to stay and make good on what my body promised. Or did I read her expression wrong?

No matter. I had to go. Now.

Capturing her mouth once again, I traced her luscious lips with my tongue, my hands resting on either side of her face to pin her in place. When I broke free once more, I finally took a few steps back, my hands falling to my sides in disappointment.

"I'll text you later. I promise." The only movement she made was to nod, a fallen look taking over her expression. I hated that she thought I didn't want to spend more time with her, but I couldn't get into why I had to leave. She continued to remain motionless while I watched her, and it became evident that she wasn't venturing inside anytime soon. Not without some encouragement. "Kena, I need you to go inside," I pressed. "I'll wait here until you do." Reaching behind me, I snagged my helmet and waited for her feet to carry her forward.

She remained unmoving.

And while I found her stubbornness amusing, I didn't have time to play games. Tilting my head to the side, I gave her my sternest look, but still . . . nothing.

Instead of compliance, her body straightened. Pushing back her shoulders, she held her head high and challenged me. I smirked but quickly thinned my lips to show her I'd meet her challenge head-on, eventually winning the little battle of wills she'd started.

"Kena . . . ," I warned, taking a step forward.

She signed something, her frustration pushing her to communicate even though she thought I didn't understand. But I did. I'd wanted to let her in on my surprise earlier, but then everything happened and I wanted to savor my secret until our next encounter.

However, now was as good a time as any to let her know I understood her, returning my slight annoyance with her jerky movements.

"I know you just signed my name."

Her eyes widened fractionally before switching up and squinting at me. She'd tried to hide her surprise, but I'd seen it.

Her hands were a flutter of activity after that, and while I tried to remain as serious as possible I couldn't help the laugh which erupted. No doubt she'd thought I'd learned a few simple things, like "yes" and my name. Although, she'd soon learn the opposite was true.

Taking another step toward her, I smirked before saying, "You just asked me if I wanted to kiss you again. And the answer is a definite yes." A slight blush kissed her cheeks, the tinge of color arousing me even more than I already was.

Again her hands rose and hit together, making a few sweeping motions before settling at her sides. She threw me a lopsided grin, figuring what she'd signed was too complicated for me to understand.

Without hesitation, I answered back.

"There's no way I can understand you? Is that what you just signed? Or did you ask me how it is that I can understand you? I'm still new to this, so you have to be patient." I waited for her response.

I asked you how it is that you can understand me.

I decided to test out my signing skills in response. *My friend Sully has been teaching me. How am I doing?*

Very well.

Her smile lit up the world around us, and all I wanted to do was attack her mouth again in reciprocation, but I knew if I moved toward her, I wouldn't be able to break free. Not again.

A brief moment of awareness encapsulated us, one where we realized we'd just crossed a barrier. She could communicate with me now, other than nodding in response to a yes or no question, eliminating the boundaries that had trapped us since the day I'd first met her. It was a freedom both of us felt right then, perpetuating our connection even deeper than before.

"Well," I spoke up, breaking the silence, "I do have to get going, but I promise I'll text you later. If it's not too late, message me back." Thankfully, she'd turned around after throwing me one last smile and walked toward her front door. After she'd disappeared inside, I grinned, a real weight lifted from my shoulders.

But it would soon be replaced with another as soon as I pulled into the clubhouse lot.

CHAPTER TWENTY-SIX

Jagger

I SWUNG MY LEG OVER the seat of my bike, planting both feet firmly on the ground. While walking toward the clubhouse, my phone vibrated against the inside of my pocket, startling me into the seriousness of the new situation. I had no doubt Tripp and Ryder had *detained* the two Reapers, our biggest enemy not getting the hint to go into hiding, never to resurface.

Marek had seen to it that their drug supply had been cut off from the cartel, a stipulation—or promise, depending on how we looked at it—for our prez saving Rafael Carrillo's life once upon a time. The mere inconvenience that the Reapers kept coming after us screamed how stupid they really were.

The mistake they'd made, however, was showing up to one of my fights. Yet again. Only this time, the brazen fucker had thought ahead and brought one of his pathetic brothers with him, realizing he'd get knocked the fuck out again if he came alone. But in the end it didn't matter.

Marek wouldn't allow them to go back home.

They had to die.

And I knew I was gonna have to take part in their demise, eliminating one more threat to me and my club.

Then the only danger remaining would be the guy who led the Savage Reapers.

A club that stood for nothing other than greed and bloodshed.

Psych Brooks.

"Yeah," I finally answered, gripping the handle to the clubhouse's door.

"Get to The Underground. Now. Back room." Seven words . . . then silence. At first, it sounded like Cutter, but once I'd allowed my brain to register his voice, I realized it was Ryder who'd called. Then hung up on me. The inflection in his tone left no room for argument. Besides, I knew better than to piss him off. Although he'd come across as sullen most times, joking with some of the brothers from time to time, I knew a darkness nestled deep within him. From what, I had no idea, but surely time would reveal some of his secrets.

Time, or some hard-ass liquor. A substance he definitely didn't handle well. All the brothers were aware. It was why Ryder was closely watched whenever alcohol was served, beer not only his preference to remain on the sane side, but all of ours as well.

I'd only witnessed the club's resident mechanic volatile from consumption one time, and believe me, it had been eye-opening.

Snatching my hand away from the door as if I'd been burned, I turned on my heel and walked back toward my bike, all sorts of thoughts of the long evening ahead invading my brain.

Because of the late evening hour, traffic hadn't been an issue, and I'd arrived at the establishment our club owned in no time. Striding through the door, I saw a few of the members lounging in different areas. Breck and Zip hung at the bar, talking with Barlow, The Underground's bartender, breaking the conversation between them every few seconds to laugh about something one of them had said.

Hawke slunk off his barstool and stumbled toward the hallway, no doubt headed toward the bathroom to either piss or puke. He looked like shit, no doubt drowning himself in alcohol over his woman, Edana. The two of them had made me think twice about becoming involved with someone, their crazy relationship a deterrent to most young guys. But when I looked at Marek and Sully, or Stone and Adelaide, my faith in the possibility of attaching myself to a woman had become renewed.

And then I met Kena.

Don't think about her right now. Not when you have to do something you're gonna take issue with.

No one noticed me as I slinked past toward the darkened hallway. The last room on the left called to me. Inhaling a deep breath, I grasped the handle and turned.

"Get in here and close the door," Tripp grated, circling the two guys slumped against the worn leather sofa situated in the corner of the room. As my gaze danced over them, I realized they were in pretty rough shape, although not nearly as bad off as I would've thought. The nomad, while more of a laid-back member, had a temper when prompted. And members of the Savage Reapers coming after me provoked that shielded part of his personality.

"What are we doin'?" I asked, leaning against the wall and shoving my hands in my pockets. Bending my right leg, I rested the sole of my boot behind me, locking me into place because I had no idea what else to do with myself.

"What do you think we're doin'?" Ryder spoke up that time, taking a swig from his bottle of beer before slamming it down on top of the desk. "We gotta get rid of 'em." The look on his face told me two things. One, Ryder didn't want to be there anymore than Tripp or I did. And two, he wasn't as settled with disposing of our enemies as he would've liked to portray. I honestly didn't think any member of the KC MC *liked* to kill, even if their victim was our most hated enemy. As far as I knew, no one craved bloodshed. No, if it had to be done, it had been out of necessity.

Retribution for attacking one of our own.

Revenge for Sully.

Payback for constantly threatening us, and essentially threatening our families.

Pushing off the wall, I strode toward the couch with determination. I wanted to snuff out their existence once and for all, send a message back to the Savage Reapers that every time one of them came after one of us, it would end in death. For them. But the other part of me wanted to spare their lives, give them the option to cease fire here and now. So with a tentative glare, I opened my mouth and made an offer I was sure wouldn't be accepted readily, by them or by my brothers, and essentially Marek, who I was sure knew about our little hostage situation.

"I have an offer for you, Snake. You and me. Right now. We fight, and if I win you walk away and never come after me again." Rocking on the balls of my feet, I clarified my statement. "Me or anyone in my club."

He didn't speak, but then again he didn't have the opportunity to do so because both Tripp and Ryder started shouting over each other.

"No fuckin' way, Jagger," Tripp yelled.

"Ain't gonna happen, brother," Ryder chimed in. My eyes pinged back and forth between the two of them, the muscles in my neck tensing from the added stress.

"The only way either one of them is leavin' is in a body bag." Gripping the shortened strands of his hair, Tripp blew short, rough bursts of air through his nose. Looking to the left, I saw Ryder mirroring his frustrations.

"He wants to destroy *me!*" I roared back. "Me. So give him his shot. But he'll do it with his fists and not a fucking gun like a coward." All I wanted to do was punch something, but I knew I had to save all my energy for the possibility of a fight. I feared my brothers weren't gonna give in, but eventually they accepted the offer I'd thrown out.

"Fine," Ryder gritted. "But you better fuckin' win. Or so help you." His threat left no room for argument. I knew he'd look out for me, as I would him, but right then much more was at stake than just me winning for myself.

I had to win for the good of the club.

"So, what do ya say?" I kicked Snake's boot, pulling his attention away from his friend. "Want a chance to try and take me down? Finish what your brother couldn't?"

Snake lifted his head, rage blossoming behind his eyes as he glared at me. Most times a pissed-off opponent fought sloppily. What I'd said demeaned him, in more ways than one, but I'd pulled it from my arsenal of tricks in hopes he'd make the fight an easy one. There was no doubt he'd be a poor match for me, lacking the necessary skills to fight someone of my caliber, but I knew enough not to underestimate the effect of rage. A slight possibility existed that he'd be able to best me; hatred and the need for revenge could give him the push he'd need to defeat me.

Slowly rising to his feet, Snake walked toward me, a slight limp emerging the closer he advanced. Blood crusted the corner of his lip, his left eye cut, and well on its way to becoming swollen. His shirt was torn, exposing multiple darkening bruises on his torso. But for as fucked up as he appeared, it wasn't enough to hamper him from fighting.

Standing two inches shorter than me, he almost matched my physical prowess. Almost. The Reaper was no lanky fuck, and the upcoming battle between us would most certainly make me break a sweat. Pushing strands of his long dark hair away from his face, he gave me his best scowl, and had I not been a fighter, confident in my skills, I might have been unnerved.

"Where we doin' this?"

His question had me turning toward Tripp, who happened to be standing off to my right.

"Outside," the nomad grunted.

Not five minutes later, we stood under the dark shield of night, the dim light above the back door our only illumination. Enough to see each other. Snake's buddy remained inside, Ryder keeping a close watch over him in case he tried to escape.

Foolishly I thought we'd speak before beginning, but Snake charged me, catching me completely off guard. Fuck! Stumbling backward, he'd managed to knock me off balance, but because of my training, I quickly recovered, sidestepping his next move. He tumbled forward but swung around quickly, bringing his right arm with him.

His knuckles grazed the side of my jaw, but it wasn't enough to do any damage. He hadn't even managed to stun me. Instead, all his fist did was piss me the hell off. I knew going into our fight that it wasn't gonna be pretty, and that most likely my adversary wouldn't make it out of there alive, but I kept a tiny shard of hope that I'd defeat him and he would return to his club the loser, never to come after me again.

Twisted fantasy, I knew.

"I'm gonna kill you!" Snake roared, lunging at me before he'd fully restored his balance. His technique was sloppy at best. No way in hell he would manage to take me down.

Enough shittin' around. I need to end this and do it soon. Bracing myself for his next move, I deflected his punch with a block of my arm and returned a powerful right hook, directly to the side of his face. His head snapped to the side and we wobbled but didn't fall over. The stunned look in his eyes told me I'd definitely fazed him, but unfortunately for me it wasn't enough to knock him out.

For the next ten minutes, he tried his best to hurt me, but he failed every single time. Punch for punch, I warred with him, two men battling for victory. Only I had skill on my side; he had rage, and nothing more.

Faltered steps showed me he was tired, and it was then I took full advantage. Pummeling him with my fists, his head snapped from side to side. Blood matted hair stuck to his face, hiding most of the damage from sight. But I kept at him.

A harsh gut shot.

A kick directly to his knee, bending his leg back awkwardly. The move sent him on a free fall, and on his way down I hit him with a swift, hard upper cut.

Down to the ground he went, but oddly enough he remained alert, spitting blood and attempting to rise from the dirt. "When I'm done with you, I'm goin' after that fuckin' freak you like," he growled. Spitting more red saliva on the ground, he spoke again, sealing his fate once and for all. "I'll take her back to my club and pass her around to every single member of the Reapers, but not until after I've broken her in." He smiled, one of his front teeth now missing, and thought he'd won. Stupidly thinking if he angered me in return, I'd lose all control and somehow he'd best me.

What he didn't realize was that after the last despicable word left his filthy mouth, he'd essentially chosen to give up his life. Without even realizing it, he'd played on one of my biggest fears—Kena coming to harm all because of me. Terror gripped my insides and squeezed. I saw red and before I could stop myself, I pounced on top of him, pounding him with my fists so fast I was surprised I kept my balance.

All my anger poured forth, driving directly into his jaw. His cheekbones. His nose. His temples. I would never allow anyone to touch Kena, especially this piece of Reaper shit. As the seconds passed, disorientation set in, shrouding my reality.

I heard someone yell my name, but I never stopped. The only thing I could focus on was the man lying beneath me. I had to make it so that he was no longer a threat to Kena, and if that meant beating him into unconsciousness then so be it. Doing whatever I could to protect her, I continued to desecrate his bloodied form.

"Jagger!" I heard once more, only that time strong arms wrapped around my shoulders and heaved me backward. My ass hit the dirt, my arms still swinging in front of me. Lost in a daze, it took some time before my delirium subsided. "Come on, brother. You're done."

Recognizing Tripp's voice, I blinked a few times and did my best to catch my rapid breaths. Lines of sweat dripped down the sides of my face, the ache in my hands making me wince.

"I'll kill him," I seethed, trying to rise to my feet so I could go at him again. With a stern look, warning me to stay put, Tripp leaned over Snake and placed his fingers on his neck.

"Looks like you got your wish," he stated matter-of-factly. It hadn't even dawned on me that I might actually kill him. Well . . . no, I lied. It had occurred to me that it might be the end result, but I hadn't gone into the fight planning for such a thing to happen. I truly did want him to crawl out of there afterward, return to his cesspit of a club and finally understand that he couldn't beat me. He couldn't harm me. He couldn't end me.

But he had, in a way. Threatening Kena had sliced through me, splintering me in two. And when both halves came back together, I'd become a different man.

Someone who sat on top of another and literally beat him to death with nothing but my fists.

Would I kill for Kena?

It appeared I just had.

Adrenaline coursed through me, and I hadn't even noticed that Ryder had dragged the other Reaper outside, shoving him to the ground right next to Snake. Pulling a gun from his waistband, Ryder aimed it at the guy's bald head, but before he fired, the guy sputtered something so fast I almost missed what he'd said.

"Prez is comin' for ya. He's gonna get that bitch and kill off your entire club." He spit at Ryder's feet, grinning as if his words would somehow free him from his ultimate demise.

"Well, you ain't gonna be with him when he tries," Ryder taunted, pulling the trigger before the man could reply. The blast cut through the dismal night's thickness, shards of truth falling to the earth all around me.

We'd just killed two men—albeit our enemy, but still. We'd snatched two lives, and although I'd beat myself up over the death of Snake's brother, I felt justified over these kills.

Numb even.

Without a single word spoken, I ran from the scene, hopped on my bike and raced toward Kena's house, hoping and praying she'd make me feel something again.

CHAPTER
TWENTY-SEVEN

Kena

SLEEP EVADED ME. MY EYES fluttered closed but my mind raced, thoughts of Jagger flooding in. My inner voice warned me of danger, but my soul soared whenever we were together. I found it hard to explain, even to myself, so all my inner ramblings were pushed to the wayside by my feelings for him.

Because I couldn't fall into the blissful arms of slumber, I'd decided a hot shower might calm me enough to try again. Running my hands over my soapy skin, I imagined they were Jagger's instead. My brain immediately went back to the kiss earlier that evening. The way his taste invaded my senses proved even more powerful than the last time our mouths had collided. Nipping and suckling, tasting and devouring. On top of it all, the revelation that he'd learned sign language just about undid me. My heart burst at the seams, splintering apart before becoming whole again, only this time I was more vulnerable than before. Realizing he cared for me more than I thought scared me, but only because I feared him tearing me to pieces with a simple denial. Of what magnitude I didn't dare think.

Finishing up, I finally turned the handle and shut off the water, wrapping a towel around my body before running another over my wet hair. Steam kissed my exposed skin as I stepped from the stall into the middle of the bathroom. Music drifted from my phone's speakers but when the song ended, I heard a noise coming from the living room.

Leaning my ear against the door, I heard Braylen shouting at someone. Who the hell would be here at this hour? Had Ryder found out where we lived and showed up to apologize for blowing her off? Curiosity pushed me to crack open the door, allowing the chill of the air to barrel in.

"I need to see her, Braylen. It's important. Please let me in." Jagger's gruff voice traveled down the hallway, my fear escalating as to why he'd shown up on our doorstep at nearly two in the morning. Needing to find out the reason, I threw my towel to the ground before wrapping my short black robe around me, cinching the belt at the waist before rushing toward the front of the house. In my haste, I'd almost tripped over my feet, but luckily managed to remain upright.

As soon as I entered the living room, I saw Jagger standing near the front door. Apparently his plea had convinced my sister to let him in, although her body blocked him from going any further.

What happened to you? I signed, hastening my advance toward him in desperate concern. His wet hair told me he'd recently showered, but the water didn't wash away the damage littering his body. His left eye was cut near his brow, the skin surrounding it puffy and red, well on its way to becoming a nasty black contusion. The flesh on his cheekbone and jaw was colored a dark red, the edges already turning a tinge of purple. When I glanced down at his fists, I noticed his knuckles appeared raw, as if he'd run them over a cheese grater.

When he'd left me earlier, he never mentioned having to fight that night, so I could only assume something bad had taken place. Something frightful enough to push him to come to my house afterward.

Taking a step toward me, he pulled me close and wrapped his arms around me tightly. His warm breath fanned my wet air, triggering a chill to break out all over my body. Pulling back briefly, he asked, "Can we go to your room?"

Nodding, I gave my sister a half smile before reaching for Jagger's hand, threading my fingers with his and pulling him behind me back down the shortened hallway. Once inside my bedroom, I closed the door before removing my hand from his. I walked toward the bed and sat on the edge, waiting for him to tell me why he was there. Watching him pace in front of me should've unnerved me, but the opposite was true. His anxiety calmed mine, taking my mind off my own unease and pushing the focus onto him.

When he stopped, he turned toward me and locked me in his stare. He opened his mouth to speak but no words tumbled forth, an action which happened to me more times than I could count. But I had a reason. He didn't, other than struggling with what to tell me and what to keep hidden. The more he remained still, the heavier his breathing became. I swore I saw the pulse in his neck throbbed.

What happened? I asked him again, resting my hands back in my lap after signing.

"I can't talk about it," he answered, looking regretful right away.

Why?

"Because I can't."

Then why are you here? I expected silence but instead he moved toward me, hovering so close I had no choice but to lean back on the bed, my arms behind me for support.

"Because I need you, Kena. I need you to calm me." His thumb gently stroked my bottom lip. The look in his eyes made me hyper-aware that my robe barely hid my nakedness. An ache only Jagger could elicit began, the throbbing between my legs almost unbearable. Could he sense it? Did he have any idea how he made me feel?

No more words were spoken as he kicked off his shoes, and climbed on the bed until his body hovered over mine. I'd pushed myself further back on the mattress, coming to rest when I settled in the middle. Holding himself up on his forearms, his face was mere inches from my own, his warm breath dancing over my lips.

Tempting me.

Tormenting me.

"I need you," he repeated, before crushing his lips to mine. Our kiss turned frenzy, the heat of our mouths fusing us as one. I lost myself to his taste, just like I had the other times he'd completely consumed me. My hands wrapped around his upper arms while he kissed me with such passion I'd become drunk on it.

Jagger's one arm roamed the length of my body, stopping at the hem of my robe before dipping underneath. As he explored my skin, his fingers skating higher and higher, I suddenly became nervous. I pulled my mouth from his and pressed further into the bed, gripping his bicep in slight warning.

His hand stilled on my hipbone, but his finger brushed back and forth over my heated skin. I didn't think he even realized he was doing it, so I didn't stop him.

"What's wrong?" he asked, dipping down to give me a quick kiss. A reassuring kiss, of sorts.

I didn't know how to respond so I simply shook my head. His eyes penetrated my own for a brief moment before he pushed himself off me. Standing at the side of the bed, he reached for my hand and pulled me to my feet, directly in front of him.

Clutching my robe tightly around me, I made sure my belt hadn't come undone before releasing my hands.

"What's wrong? You can tell me. Do you not want to be with me? Am I going too fast?" The look of concern on his face relaxed me. I knew I'd made a big deal of him touching me, but my inexperience made me stiffen. I wanted nothing more than to give Jagger my virginity, but I knew I should probably tell him the reason for my hesitation.

I raised my hands in front of me, his eyes lowering to watch me tell him something. *I've never done it before.* Embarrassment stole my next response, so I patiently waited for him to say something in return.

Cocking his head, his eyebrows knit together, causing him to wince from the deep cut set above it. Gently touching his wound, he gave me a lazy smile before speaking.

"Does that mean what I think it means?"

My shy expression gave him the answer.

Pulling me into his arms, he kissed the top of my head, his lips lingering for added affection. "We don't have to do anything you don't want to, baby. I would never rush you." Taking a step back while still holding my arms, he continued to comfort me. "Besides, I wouldn't want our first time together to be in the same vicinity as your sister."

He laughed. "I think she'd try and cut my dick off." He chuckled some more, making me break out in the biggest smile.

Bringing his arms around me again, he gave me a lingering hug before releasing me once more. "Do you mind if I stay over, though? I just want to be near you. I swear I won't try anything," he promised. "I just wanna hold you."

I pulled him toward my bed and threw back the covers, releasing his hand as I climbed in. Once he'd disrobed, leaving on his white boxer briefs, he snuggled in next to me. Turning on our sides, he drank in my essence, tracing his fingertips up and down my arm. My eyes started to close after a while, but quickly opened when the pad of his thumb came to rest on my throat.

"What happened, Kena? Why can't you talk?"

Swallowing against his touch, I knew I owed him an explanation. I just didn't like talking about it, fearing it made me appear weak, even though I knew the mere thought was ludicrous. I inched back a little so I could put some space between us.

When I was a baby, I contracted a viral infection. It damaged the nerves in my larynx.

"So you've never spoken? Not a day in your life?"

No. Not one word.

"Oh, man. That sucks." He closed his eyes in regret the instant he'd said it. "Sorry."

Don't worry about it. You're right. It does suck.

In order to abate the awkwardness that followed, I decided to ask him a question I'd been wondering for quite some time. Since we were sharing and all.

Is Jagger your real name?

"No."

Care to tell me what it is?

"No." His lips kicked up in the cockiest of grins. "Just kidding, although I don't like it, so please don't ever use it."

Oh this should be good. Wait, don't tell me. Let me guess. Tapping my forefinger against my lips, I appeared to be contemplating his name. *Is it Milton?*

Laughing, he quickly said, "No, but nice try."

Okay, okay, hold on. I got it. Is it Arlo?

"Arlo? What the hell kind of name is that?" He shook his head, laughing.

No more kidding around. I know your real name. I licked my lips, drawing his attention to my mouth as a distraction. *It's Beauford.*

With a faux shocked expression, he attacked me, tickling my side and throwing me into a fit of hysterics. Although he couldn't hear my laughter, he could see me smiling, writhing around uncontrollably. Finally coming to rest on top of me, he pinned my hands above my head, essentially rendering me "speechless."

"You sure do have an active imagination, woman. No, my first name is not Beauford. If you must know," he stalled, averting his eyes briefly, "it's Harold."

I wriggled my wrists in his hold, trying to let him know I wanted to respond. Releasing his grasp, I made a few quick movements with my hands. *Harold's not that bad. Why don't you want me to use it?*

A dark look stole over his face. "Because it's my father's name."

And you don't get along with your dad?

"No." His curt answer warned me not to push, but I did it anyway.

Why not?

"He hates me . . . and the feeling is mutual. Look, I don't wanna talk about him, okay?" He pushed off me, flipped over and came to rest on his back, folding his arms over his chest in unease. Upsetting him was the last thing I wanted so I nestled close, hinting that I wanted to comfort him.

Without a second thought, he unfolded his arms and pulled me to him, allowing me to rest my head on his chest. The rhythmic thumping of his heart calmed me, and a short time later, I drifted off to sleep, cushioned in the safety of Jagger's embrace.

CHAPTER TWENTY-EIGHT

Jagger

"CAN I BORROW ADELAIDE FOR a few hours?" As soon as the question left my mouth, I knew perhaps I should've rephrased it. Yeah, no doubt the way I blurted out such an odd request would surely piss off Stone.

Stalking toward me, he balled his fists at his sides while he glared at me.

"What the fuck does that mean?" he growled, advancing on me quicker than I thought possible.

I held up my hands in surrender, realizing Stone's protectiveness over his woman rivaled Marek's for Sully.

"Sorry, I didn't mean to ask like that." I smirked, although taking his anger lightly could surely prove dangerous.

"You better wipe that grin off your face, Jagger, before I wipe it off for you." Stone took another step, but halted as soon as Adelaide entered their kitchen. We both watched as she rounded the table and approached me, gently cupping the side of my face.

"You need to protect yourself more when you're fighting," she instructed, slightly shaking her head before kissing my cheek. A concerned smile graced her features when she pulled back, an expression I both appreciated and detested. I hated the thought that she might find out exactly why I'd received the cuts and abrasions, not wanting her image of me to be tainted. Irrational, I realized, but the thoughts flitted through my head nonetheless.

I'd always liked Adelaide, even more so since she'd brought such happiness into my friend's life. Although, glancing at his hardened expression, he appeared anything but right then.

"What brings you by today?" she asked, busying herself preparing a bottle to feed Riley.

"Funny you should ask," I replied, moving closer to her and further away from her man. "I need help furnishing my place and I thought that, since you did such a great job with your house," I complimented, gesturing with a wide sweep of my arm, "you could help me."

My eyes quickly surveyed the adjacent rooms, pops of color set amongst a neutral backdrop. No doubt Stone had chosen the tan wall paint, as well as the dark, brown leather furniture, but it was his woman's eye for detail which set the room apart from most. A multi-colored, intricately woven area rug sat underneath their chest-type coffee table, pulling the non-descript wall color into its design as well as the red and yellow throw pillows. Colorful artwork adorned their walls, as well as antique-looking knickknacks placed on shelves Stone had installed after Adelaide moved in. I'd seen the transformation during my visits to their house, so I knew she would be the perfect person to ask for this task.

Adelaide smiled. "Flattery will get you everywhere." I thought I heard Stone grunt, but tried not to pay him any mind. "Of course. Can you go today?"

"Yeah. Today would be perfect, in fact."

I'd wanted to invite Kena over, but no way would I expose her to the current state of my place. She deserved better. Besides, I'd meant to spruce up the place for a while now; Kena just happened to give me the push to forge ahead.

Thinking of her, I hated that I'd left her house so abruptly a few days before, but I needed time by myself to process everything that had happened. Leaving her sleeping form had been extremely difficult, but I knew if I'd stuck around, she'd somehow try to force me to explain why I'd shown up at her house in the middle of the night. And no way was

I ready to divulge that sort of information. Not now. Maybe not ever.

So I decided to leave her a note, apologizing for leaving before she woke but that I'd text her later that day. And I did, but unfortunately, all we'd been doing was texting. Realizing I hadn't been in the right state of mind, I came up with excuse after excuse as to why I couldn't see her, but I knew she'd become frustrated with my absence. Her texts proved as much, her replies short and to the point.

"Hello," Stone called out, snapping his fingers in front of my face. "What the hell are you thinkin' about?"

"What?" I startled, leaning against the counter to brace myself. "No one," I uttered.

Realizing my mistake did nothing to stop the barrage of questions Adelaide hurled my way. "No one?" she asked, smiling while she glanced back and forth between me and Stone. "This is for that girl you learned sign language for, isn't it?? Oh, this is getting serious." Clasping her hands together, she let out an endearing, albeit frustrating, yelp of glee. "It is, isn't it?"

"Stone . . . a little help here," I pleaded.

"Nope," he mumbled, opening the cabinet to hand Adelaide the top to the bottle she was making for their daughter. "You wanted her, so there you go. Take her." He grinned, earning him a slap on the arm from the mother of his child.

Tightening the lid of the bottle, she handed it over to Stone, which he readily accepted. I'd never seen a man so enthralled with the day-to-day dealings with his child as much as I'd seen with Stone. A tiny shard splintered a piece of my heart at the thought that I'd never received even an iota of compassion and love from my own father. And while I'd missed out on one of the fundamentals in life, protection and encouragement from a parent, I was thrilled Riley would receive it in spades her entire life. Not only from Adelaide and Stone but from all of us. The poor thing would be smothered in love, so much so I was sure she'd find an issue with it at some point.

"Let me get changed and we can go," Adelaide announced, gifting Stone with a quick kiss before disappearing around the corner.

As soon as she was out of sight, I leaned in close, choosing to lower my voice for what I had to say. "I'm assuming you heard about what happened a few days ago." I'd said it more as a statement than a question, garnering a raised brow from Stone.

"Of course I did," he replied, leaning against the same counter and mirroring my body language—arms crossed over the chest, muscles tensed in a touch of anxiety. Me more so than him. "You good?"

What a simple yet loaded question. How did I feel about everything that had happened in the span of less than a week? I supposed I hadn't allowed myself to fully digest what I'd done, choosing to focus on eradicating the threat to Kena more than anything else. Stone and I were locked in the same headspace when it came to destroying the risk to those we cared about, so I knew he'd understand why I'd flown into a rage and ended up killing Snake. Besides, that piece of shit belonged to our enemy. I could've walked up to him on the street and shot him dead and Stone wouldn't have looked at me twice in question. Well . . . okay, maybe not in that situation, but pretty similar.

"To be honest, I've tried to block it out. I don't have the mental energy to deal with the consequences of what I've done. All I thought about while I beat him was that I needed to eliminate any threat possible toward Kena." His confused expression spurred me to explain. "He told me he was gonna snatch her and pass her around his club, but only after he'd had his fill." I ran my hands over my face, careful not to further aggravate my cuts and bruises. "I lost it, man. My vision tunneled into near black and I let my fists take over. The only reason I stopped was because Tripp pulled me off him."

Stone slapped my shoulder, a sign of support. "You did what you had to. Don't ever doubt that. I know it, and Marek will too as soon as you explain what happened."

Shit! I'd completely forgotten about Marek and what his reaction would be to us killing two of our enemy. He held great contempt for them as well, but that wouldn't justify taking two of them out without a good reason.

But I had one. Didn't I?

I could only hope he saw the situation like I had.

Protection.

Pulling out a chair, Stone plopped himself into it and thrummed his fingers on the tabletop, the hammering noise rather annoying. Smirking, he gestured toward the chair to his right. Taking the invitation, I leaned back against the seat and folded my arms over my chest again.

"So, what happened to the two fucks afterwards?" he asked, taking a drink of water after asking me a question I didn't have the answer to. Well, not exactly. I only knew what Ryder had told me; I never followed up with him afterward to find out if he had any issues.

"Ryder said he was gonna drop them off at their club. And I'm gonna be honest. While I loved the idea, I wasn't sure it was the smartest move. Shoving the kill in their faces like that." Unfolding my arms, I rested my hands on top of the rounded table. "Especially after what his buddy told us right before Ryder put a bullet in his head."

"About coming for Sully?" When I looked confused, he added, "Ryder told me."

I looked down at my hands briefly before making eye contact with him again. "Yeah. That."

"Doesn't matter, brother. We already know Psych is planning something. We just don't know what or when. But rest assured, we'll be ready. No doubt."

I opened my mouth to ask him if he had ever thought about breaking away from Adelaide, before she got pregnant with Riley. Before his feelings for her had intensified and grown stronger. I wanted to know if he'd ever thought about sacrificing his happiness in order to keep her safe from our way of life, but the woman in question strolled into the kitchen with Riley on her hip and her purse slung over her shoulder.

After she passed their daughter to Stone, she kissed them both, whispered something in my buddy's ear and walked toward the front door. "Shall we?" she called over her shoulder, not waiting for me to catch up before disappearing outside.

CHAPTER TWENTY-NINE

Kena

FIVE DAYS HAD PASSED SINCE I'd laid eyes on Jagger. Boy, the guy ran hot and cold, his lack of presence certainly speaking volumes. I tried my hardest not to read too far into things, but what choice did I have? The only thing I had to go on was what he told me, which was zilch thus far. Lame excuses about having to work for the club, or handle business for the club. However he'd put it didn't make any sense to me whatsoever. In my head, if he truly liked me, he would make the time to see me, not confuse the hell out of me, day in and day out.

It seemed every day—no, every *hour*—I fluttered back and forth between deciding to give him his space and demanding answers to why he avoided being with me again. Sometimes my patience won out, and sometimes my aggravation shook the sense right out of me.

I was the furthest from a pushy person. In fact, I preferred to stay in the background, observing those around me instead of being up front and center. It was why I kept to myself, shielding myself from fully living. Until I'd met Jagger. Something about his soul spoke to mine, begging me to open up and give him a chance. So I'd stepped outside my comfort zone to meet him halfway. But his current behavior had me rethinking my decision to delve headfirst into what I'd hoped had been a budding relationship between us.

The way he looked at me whenever we were together was unlike anything I'd ever experienced before. His silent promises made my heart soar, but would whatever he held secret end up destroying us before we even got started? Did I think him worth it enough to take that chance? To risk my heart?

I didn't have to think about it too long.

Of course he was.

Any guy who would study sign language just to communicate with me, especially when he hadn't known me very long, ranked high on my list of keepers.

After he'd showed up at my house at two in the morning, kissed me silly, then cuddled with me for the rest of the night, I'd mistakenly thought we'd moved forward with whatever was happening between us. But I'd been wrong. When I woke, I saw he'd left a note. And sure, he stayed true to his word and texted me later that day, but that was all we'd been doing.

Texting.

I wanted nothing more than to see his face. Hear his voice. Feel his arms around me. Savor his kiss. But something bothered him and I had no idea what it could be. Maybe his fights weighed heavier on him than he cared to let on, but I wanted to let him know I would be there for him if he needed to unload and talk about . . . whatever.

Deciding enough was enough, my fingers glided over the letters as I typed out a text which cut straight to the point.

Kena: Why are you avoiding me?

Sitting on the couch, a glass of wine on the end table waiting to be consumed, I impatiently counted the minutes until he answered. *I could be here all night, or he could decide to put me out of my misery and respond right away.*

Five minutes.

Ten.

Twenty minutes later, my phone finally dinged.

Jagger: I'm not avoiding you at all. Is that what you think?

I should've made him sweat a little, but I didn't want to drag this out any longer than necessary, so I responded immediately.

> *Kena: You confuse me. You show up at my house late at night, looking like you've just been in a terrible fight, kiss me until I can't think straight, and then end up holding me until we fell asleep. Never once did you tell me what happened to you, and to make things worse you left before I woke up.*

> *Jagger: I left you a note.*

Grinding my teeth in frustration, I threw the phone on the cushion next to me and grabbed my glass of wine. Not having the patience to savor the red liquid, I swallowed a few large gulps, allowing the alcohol to permeate my aggravated mood.

Finally, I reached for my cell and typed out my retort to his pitiful excuse. *Men.*

> *Kena: Just because you left me a note doesn't excuse your rude behavior. If you don't want to see me anymore, just tell me. Be a man about it.*

Before I could stop them, tears flowed down my cheeks, frustrating me even more than before I'd contacted him. Sorrow washed through me that whatever I thought was happening between Jagger and me would die before it even took flight. The chance I could have found "the one" quickly disappeared, evaporating into thin air before I could even hold the possibility close. I knew my emotions ruled me, as they always had. I just never had anyone on the receiving end before. Harmless crushes, sure, but nothing like this.

> *Jagger: I'm calling you.*

> *Kena: I'm not answering.*

> *Jagger: Yes, you are.*

> *Kena: No, just tell me.*

My breath caught in my throat, threatening to suffocate me if he made me wait much longer. The chime from my phone pushed the air through my nose in relief. Or was that delayed frustration?

> *Jagger: Please answer your phone when I call.*

Realizing I desperately wanted to hear his voice, I gave in and agreed to hear whatever it was he wanted to tell me.

Kena: Fine.

Instead of another message, my phone vibrated in my hand, my generic ringtone slicing the air around me and managing to startle me, even though I'd been expecting his call.

Swiping the Answer option, I placed the device next to my ear. I'd learned to accept my challenge a long time ago, but during times such as this, all I wanted to do was speak my confusion. Unload all my uncertainties in a way which would make sense to him. But instead, all I could do was to either text with him or allow him to speak his mind.

"Kena, listen," he started, breathing heavily as if he'd just run a mile. "I'm so sorry for making you think I don't want to see you anymore, because that's simply not true. In fact, I want to be with you more than ever. The other night. . . ." He stalled, and if I had to guess he was probably pacing back and forth, his words temporarily failing him. Thankfully, the silence didn't last long. "There are things I'm trying to work out. Take care of. And until they're finished, I can't really talk about it. I hope you'll give me the time I need and not give up on me. I care about you. A lot," he confessed, the deep timbre of his voice unraveling any doubt I'd held about his feelings toward me. "Can I see you? Tonight?"

I hadn't expected for him to ask me such a thing, and right then I regretted my sort-of ultimatum. It hadn't been blatant, but he'd surely read between the lines. Not wanting him to feel as if he *had* to see me, I let the silence exist between us, perpetuating uncertainty on both our ends.

"I *want* to see you," he stressed. "It's not because you gave me some sort of half-ass ultimatum, either." I heard the lightheartedness in his tone, his amazing ability to read me without being anywhere near me.

I wouldn't know the true depth of his feelings until I could look into those penetrating amber-colored eyes of his, so I gave him what he wanted.

What *I* wanted.

I pressed a number on the keypad one time, the sound booming in my ears, releasing the tension I'd carried since I'd first texted him that evening.

"Great. You won't regret it, Kena. I promise. Can I pick you up in an hour?"

I pressed the key again. One time.

Yes.

"See you soon," he promised, hanging up the phone and in turn erasing some of the reservation I'd allowed to rattle my emotions.

CHAPTER THIRTY

Kena

TRUE TO HIS WORD, JAGGER showed up on my doorstep an hour later, looking as fantastic as ever. The cuts and bruises I'd seen days earlier had turned different shades, but he appeared to be healing nicely. My eyes lingered on his mouth; I couldn't help it. Every time I saw the guy, I wanted to throw myself at him, wrap myself in his embrace and latch on to those delicious lips of his.

I knew what he held within his kiss, and I'd wanted to feel the promise of something more right then. But I held back. How would I look to him if I attacked him, when only a short while ago I'd come off as upset? Never mind what kind of precedent that would set for us going forward. If there even was an "us" after that evening. He'd know that all he'd have to do was be near me and he'd get his way. And let's face it; he'd mess up a lot.

He *was* a guy, after all.

Stepping to the side, I allowed him to enter my house, his arm brushing mine as he walked past. A tiny shiver coursed through me at the slight contact, and I berated myself for being so weak.

The thick rustle of his leather vest tore me from my inner ramblings. The way he moved throughout the small space had me gasping for my next breath. He reminded me of a predator, assessing his surroundings before pouncing. Even though he tried to give me space by keeping his distance, the pull between us encapsulated my entire being.

I couldn't think.

I couldn't breathe.

I couldn't wait to be consumed by him once again.

My eyes wouldn't stop devouring the very sight of him. Dark, loose jeans hung low on his hips. His grey T-shirt clung to his torso as if it had been made specifically for him. All I wanted to do was run my hands over him, head to toe, but I remained unmoving. I wanted him to make the first move. Explain why he'd been avoiding me, even though he'd said he hadn't been.

I fidgeted with the hem of my tank top, hoping and praying he would end the silence soon. Although I could spend all day just staring at him, the uneasiness of the quietness drove me insane.

Jagger's eyes lit up the closer he stepped, his gaze lingering on my mouth, as I had done to him moments earlier, and I couldn't help but to wonder if the thoughts running through his head mirrored my own.

Without notice, he brought his hands up in front of him, and at first I couldn't focus on anything other than the scrapes and bruises desecrating his knuckles still. Wanting so desperately to reach out and touch him, I held back. Whatever he wanted to say to me had to happen in order for us to move forward.

Placing his fist against his chest, he rubbed it in a circular motion. *I'm sorry*, he signed, the apologetic look on his face replicating his message.

Although I appreciated the sentiment and effort, I couldn't help but wonder how many times I would see that specific gesture.

Why? My one-word question was all I could think of to ask in response.

Reaching out, he captured my hand and led me to the couch, jerking his head for me to take a seat. Once I settled in, he joined me, continuing to hold my hand as he turned his body toward me. "I know we don't know each other that well yet, but I hope you'll give me the chance to stick around. I really like you, and I think we could be really good together." I tried to tug my hand from his but he only tightened his grasp. "I need to get this off my chest before you start asking me more questions."

More questions? I'd only asked him one, although it *had* been an all-encompassing one.

He licked his lips and exhaled a heavy breath. "There are some things I can't divulge right now. Things that have to be secured, taken care of so there's no more threat to me or my club." I knit my brows at his unexpected statement. "I'm just trying to be honest. Well . . . as honest as I can be right now." Shifting closer, his knee bumped mine, the slight touch distracting me. "I'm just asking that you be patient and not get angry when I can't explain certain things. Can you do that? Can you give me the time I need to straighten some things out?"

His thumb danced back and forth over the top of my hand, his gentle touch a complete contradiction to the guy sitting next to me. His intimidating appearance warned the world not to get too close, his club's emblem etched on the back of his leather cut enough to scare most people. But from what I could tell, Jagger—and his friends I'd had the pleasure of meeting—seemed to be good men, even though a secrecy shrouded them, clinging to them so closely it was hard to see them for the people they truly were.

I realized my impression of them could've been misguided, but my gut told me they were good people.

I gave him a simple nod before brushing my lips against his. I hadn't meant to fold so easily, but Jagger's words, combined with his pleading look, assured me he was telling me the truth. As much as he could, anyway.

Surprised, he leaned back and searched my face for an explanation to my complete one-eighty. But he didn't find one, because I couldn't explain it myself, except to say I trusted him.

Explicitly.

For the next twenty minutes, we made out like a couple of teenagers, although we weren't too far removed from that age group. He'd repositioned me so I straddled him, his apparent arousal pressing against the most sensitive part of me.

Hands explored.

Kisses promised the world.

My heart beat so fast I feared it would burst from my chest the longer Jagger continued to tease me. A warmth flooded my insides as an ache I'd come to recognize well blossomed deep within, pulsing and demanding release. My body reacted to his, no doubt threatening to detonate if I continued to refuse what should have come naturally.

Although inexperience held me captive, I knew Jagger would be the one I'd give myself to.

Utterly and completely.

He'd already captured my mind and soul.

The only thing left to offer was my body.

With trembling hands, I gripped the hem of my top, inching the material higher until air flowed across my belly. Jagger's fingers had been entangled in my hair, but when I attempted to remove my shirt, he pulled back, resting his hands on my thighs and gently kneading my skin.

"What are you doing?" he asked, a reserved smile tentatively lifting the corners of his lips.

Letting go of the material, I answered. *Removing my shirt.*

"Why?"

A sudden flush doused my skin, but irritation quickly replaced the abrupt embarrassment I'd felt. *Why do you think?*

"I'm not ready for that," he said, chuckling once he realized what he'd said. "Let me clarify. I'm not ready for *you* to be ready for that. Does that make sense?"

No.

"Kena," he huffed, "I don't wanna rush you into something I don't think you're ready for."

But I am ready, I pouted, the incessant ache intensifying between my legs.

Removing me from his lap, he rose from the couch before reaching out and waiting for me to place my hand in his. Once I did, he led me toward the front door, completely disregarding that we were just talking about possibly having sex. Tugging my hand from his, I took a step back.

"What are you doing?" he asked, turning around to face me.

Where are you taking me?

"To eat. I'm hungry. Aren't you?"

Yes . . . but not for food.

Clenching his jaw, Jagger decimated the space separating us and tugged my arms behind my back, pinning my wrists with one of his hands. Spinning me around, he trapped my back against the wall and leaned close to my ear.

"Trust me, I want nothing more than to sink inside you, but not here. Not now." Nipping my earlobe, his warm breath prickled my skin, a shiver my sole reaction to his teasing. The smooth skin of his cheek rubbed against mine, the closeness undoing the last strand of my restraint. But I kept myself in check because the last thing I wanted was for Jagger to keep refusing me, landing blow after blow to my suddenly fragile ego. "Understand?"

A nod from me and he released my wrists, pulling me behind him out the front door.

We spent the next few hours enjoying a meal at a small Italian restaurant we both loved, talking about everything under the sun, from my job at the restaurant, to our favorite movies, to places we dreamed of visiting someday. Surprisingly, we both wanted to travel to Europe, taking in as many countries as could be afforded.

That evening, the connection we'd shared snared deeper than before. We'd learned a lot about each other, and when he dropped me off at home, walking me inside and giving me another heart-melting kiss, I knew he was it for me.

The one.

The person I wanted to spend all my time with.

But for now, I'd keep those feelings tucked safely away, patiently waiting for a time when I could express them. When I knew he felt the same.

CHAPTER THIRTY-ONE

Jagger

THE NEXT COUPLE WEEKS FLEW by in a blur. Our club hadn't heard a peep from the Reapers, much to our amazement. I'd talked in length to Marek about what had happened that night, and he assured me he would've done the same thing.

His icy demeanor toward me had certainly started to melt, accepting me more and conversing with me at length many times. Sully had visited the club often, and whenever I saw her we talked without the fear of her husband retaliating. Oftentimes, Sully and I communicated strictly using sign language. Her assistance helped me to hone my silent skills until I'd become completely comfortable, only messing up a few times when talking with Kena.

Kena: Can't wait to see you later.

Her message made me smile. Amongst everything else going on in my life, the club, the fights, she'd become my constant. My rock. Someone to turn to when things weighed heavy on my mind. Granted, I could only reveal so much, choosing to keep a lot of my life hidden until the time I deemed necessary to fill her in, but her support gifted me with a calm I hadn't even realized I'd needed until she came into my life.

I loved Kena's sense of humor, poking fun when I'd sign the wrong thing, innocently teasing me until I'd break out in laughter, being sure not to take myself so seriously.

I never thought I would feel joy, the concept of such an emotion foreign to me my entire life . . . until I met the woman I was put on this earth for. The first time I'd laid eyes on Kena, I knew my life would change; I just hadn't realized to what extent.

Jagger: I'll be there soon. You're staying over tonight, right?

The first time she'd spent the night was a little over a week ago, and I'd been thrilled to share my bed with her, although we didn't have sex. She'd wanted to, at least I thought she did with the way she kept rubbing herself against me while we made out on the couch. Then again, I returned the favor, seeking comfort for my constant hard-on. I was sure if I'd made the suggestion she would've been onboard, but something told me to hold back. To allow her more time to be sure.

Tonight, however, I was gonna broach the topic, and if I didn't see any hesitation in her response, I'd give in to what we both wanted. On every other occasion, there had been a tremble in her hands, or she would avert her eyes when she'd let me know she was open to having sex. All signs pointed to her being slightly unsure.

I didn't want her uncertainty.

I wanted her to *want* it to happen. Without a doubt.

A half hour later, I pulled up in front of her house. I'd brought my truck, the chill of the night air a bit too much for a ride on my bike. Hopping out of the driver's side, the front door swung open and Kena rushed outside, slamming the door behind her in haste.

Rushing forward, I asked, "Is everything okay?" Her face flushed, her lips turning up into an awkward grimace.

I think Braylen's having phone sex with Ryder.

Not able to contain it, I burst out laughing, having no doubt the man was talking all sorts of dirty to Kena's sister. What surprised me was that Braylen had given him the time of day. I thought she couldn't stand him. However, I had witnessed a few tiny cracks in her façade whenever he was around, or was mentioned.

"That's awesome," I chuckled.

Ewww. It is not. She acted as if the thought of it repulsed her, but secretly I thought she enjoyed the idea of the two of them together.

Drawing her close, I nuzzled my lips against the underneath of her ear, kissing her slowly and teasing both of us. She squirmed, often telling me I gave her the chills when I did that, but no way would I release her without gettin' my fill.

She lovingly slapped my chest and I finally pulled back, giving her a quick kiss on the lips before walking her toward the passenger side of my truck. As I opened the door for her, she turned and gave me a sexy smile, earning her a smack on the ass before she climbed into the vehicle.

I can't wait to get my hands all over her later. Adjusting my raging arousal, I circled the truck, taking an extra second to compose myself before I ended up attacking her, lifting her dress and taking her right on the front seat.

Grabbing some takeout, we headed back to my place for the evening. I'd actually been proud to show off my apartment, all the new furnishings having been delivered a few days before Kena had come over for the first time. I'd forever be in Adelaide's debt for helping me pick out some things which helped spruce up the drab space. The furniture was a mix of modern and contemporary, sleek lines and beautiful craftsmanship going into every detail of each piece. I ended up being drawn to the darker wood, although the coffee table was a mix of glass and metal, only adding to the overall layout and design of the living room. I'd painted the walls a cool beige color, adding colorful pictures and pillows as accents, extending the same concept into the bedroom.

The small fortune it had cost to decorate had been the best money I'd ever spent. Now when I opened the front door, it felt like a home.

The hours ticked by way too fast for my taste, but it did mean one thing: time to see if Kena was ready to fully give herself to me. As the final credits rolled on the comedy we'd just watched, I reached over and seized her wrist, tugging her toward me. Patting my lap at the same time, she took the hint and straddled me, her thighs pinning me on either side.

Gazing deep into her beautiful browns, I knew she was it for me, and tonight would only solidify that she belonged to me. The final step in her becoming mine. As my mouth captured hers, my kiss asking permission to forge ahead, my hands drifted under the hem of her blue sundress. Running my fingers up and down her back at first, she seemed relaxed, complacent even. Until I gripped her backside and pushed her against my thickness; then she broke the kiss and stared at me with her mouth wide open. Surprise and expectation laced together in one simple response.

"You ready for this, sweetheart? Because if you're not, we can wait a little while longer." While I prayed for her to say yes, I knew I cared about her enough to wait as long as it took.

Placing her hands on my chest, she pushed herself back until she found her footing and stood in front of me. Reaching out, she wiggled her fingers, letting me know she wanted me to take her hand.

An offering of herself to me.

And I readily accepted.

I led her down the hall to my bedroom, kicking the door closed behind me once we were inside. I'd left the bedside lamp on, so there was plenty of light without being overpowering for such an intimate moment. I wanted to see her, every part of her, but since this was all new to her, the bright overhead would make her that much more self-conscious.

I let go of her hand and allowed her the time she needed to direct the scene. For her to run the show. While I couldn't wait to be inside her, I wanted her to take all the time she needed.

Giving me her back, she swept her long dark hair over her shoulder, turning her face slightly toward me. It took me a couple seconds, but when I realized she wanted me to help her out of her dress, I stepped forward and took hold of the zipper. Each inch of exposed skin aroused me further, her silky skin begging for my kiss. Taking my time, I drew the metal fastener through its teeth, my racing heartbeat drumming in my ears.

When I placed my lips on the side of her neck, I felt her pulse strumming underneath, and I couldn't help but smile. No hesitation; I knew she was finally ready to give her body over to me.

Would her heart follow?

Once her dress hit the floor, she kicked it aside, turned around and stood before me in nothing but a white see-through lace bra and matching panties.

Gorgeous.

The only word fitting to describe her right then.

Taking my fill, I raised her chin to meet my eyes. "We'll go slowly. You stop me anytime you feel it's too much, okay?"

A simple nod from her was all I needed.

I'd never taken my time with anyone before. I'd never relished the feeling of just being with a woman, always in a rush to fuck and get it over with so I could move on.

But with Kena, I didn't want any of our moments to end. I wanted to savor every second with her. Sitting on the edge of my bed, I drew her close, spreading my legs so she could move in further. Her perfect breasts were directly in my line of sight, but her bra still shielded her from me. Without allowing another second to pass, I reached around her back and unhooked the clasp, pushing the straps off her shoulders and tossing the material to the floor to join her discarded dress.

My eyes were alight with pleasure at the mere sight of her exposed skin. So appreciative she'd picked me to give her virginity to, I treated her with gentleness until the rapture of the moment became too much. Threading my fingers through her long strands, I brought her mouth to mine and nibbled at her lips, begging to enter her warmth.

I needed to taste her.

To breathe her in.

After I'd bruised her mouth with my kiss, I trailed my lips down her throat, the moisture from my tongue eliciting goose bumps across her skin. I reached her collarbone, my teeth coming out to play for a brief moment, something I found she liked. Next I moved toward her pert breasts, begging to be tasted.

Sucked.

Pinched.

So I gave her what her body demanded.

Taking a pebbled nipple into my mouth, I swirled my tongue

around the heated flesh, gently biting and teasing her until all she could do was throw her head back in pleasure. She pushed herself further into me, and I ravenously accepted. Once I was done, I switched to the other, giving it as much attention as she deserved. I went back and forth, mouth over sensitive skin, fingers pinching the erect buds until I felt a rumble in her chest, telling me she enjoyed the torture I offered her.

I claimed her lips once more, spinning her around and pinning her to the bed beneath me while our tongues danced together. Spreading her legs, I broke from her delectable mouth and moved down her body, taking my time to experience every bit of her she'd laid bare to me. Hooking my thumbs in the waistband of her flimsy panties, I drew them down her toned thighs, stopping by her calves, too entranced with seeing her bare pussy to go any further.

Daring to glance up at her, realizing the look on her face would spur me to hurry, I held my breath and controlled my movements. With a sexy smile, she bit her lip as she writhed on the bed, widening her thighs to display more of herself. Her modesty fled, pleasure and want taking over and driving the course of the evening.

"Should we get rid of these?" I teased, tugging the lacey material the rest of the way down until they finally fell from around her feet.

Kena was the most beautiful woman I'd ever laid eyes on. She was shy yet eager. Reserved yet willing. She bit her nail while she looked down at me, my head nestled between her opened legs. I'd thought for sure she would've been more reluctant when we'd finally ventured to this point, but instead I saw desire driving her to expose her vulnerability.

"I've wanted to taste your pussy for so long," I groaned, running my fingers up the inside of her leg, quickly following the touch with my mouth.

When my warm breath caressed her core, her muscles tightened, and I knew what she'd offered was a true gift.

CHAPTER
THIRTY-TWO

Kena

AS SOON AS HIS TONGUE swiped through my innocence, I knew I'd never be the same. Every touch he laid on me I treasured. It'd seemed as if I'd waited forever to be with Jagger, and I couldn't believe it was finally happening.

I thought I would've been more reserved, but the way he loved my body, the adoration in his eyes when he looked at me, all of me, was nothing short of glorious. How could I want to hide any part of myself when his gorgeous stare undid me? Before I realized, my hands snaked down my body and found his hair, tugging his strands tighter each time his tongue flicked over me. When the tip of his finger entered me, I tensed, but his words worked to soothe me.

"I'll take it slow. I promise. The last thing I want to do is hurt you." I trusted him, so I relaxed and reveled in the pleasure he brought me. Just when I thought his skill couldn't get any better than his mouth and finger working me simultaneously, he buried his tongue inside my heat. My back arched off the bed, and in turn I shoved his head further into my pussy. He laughed, pulling back to ask, "You like that, huh?" My only answer was thrusting my hips back toward his face. "So greedy," he mumbled, before continuing to devour me as if he'd never have another taste.

I'd brought myself to orgasm many times before, but the build-up Jagger offered became so much more. My breaths came quick and short, my heart ramming against my chest in expectation for what my body prepared to do. Throwing my head back, I clutched the bedsheets with my free hand and ground my pussy closer to Jagger's mouth, silently begging for him to push me over the edge. To make me come so hard I wouldn't know which way was up.

His ministrations increased, his mouth promising the sweetest release. Fingers teased my opening, dipping inside every few seconds to add to the sweet torment.

"I know you wanna come," he spurred, driving his finger further into me while his lips wrapped around my clit. I would have shot off the bed had it not been for his hand splayed across my belly and holding me as still as possible. Pulling back, he blew his breath across my wetness, the chill he created making me jerk back in surprise. Nothing sexier existed than witnessing Jagger positioned between my thighs, licking me and bringing me to the brink of explosion. The sight alone almost undid me.

"Come on my tongue, Kena. Please," he begged, sucking on my clit once more, his hand working to make his plea come to fruition.

A harsh buzz deafened me. The light from the corner lamp became dimmer the closer I flew to heaven. At one point I thought I forgot to breathe altogether.

"I can feel you holding on. Let go," he urged. "Let go and come for me, baby." The deep rumble of his voice added to the pleasure, the vibrations from his throat tickling my clit, splintering my last shred of restraint.

My body locked up.

My muscles contracted and released, spasms throwing me into paradise.

Lights danced behind my eyelids the more intensely my orgasm racked through me. I gave in fully to the bliss, my thoughts so scattered I couldn't even think straight. All I could do was feel, ride the wave of ecstasy for as long as it lasted.

Finally my release subsided, allowing me to slow my erratic

breathing. My limbs felt like jelly. I couldn't move. I couldn't even bring my hands up in front of me to answer Jagger when he asked, "How was that?"

All I could do was smile, locking my gaze with his in hopes he understood.

And he did, the wicked grin on his face proof enough for me.

When I'd finally regained some mobility, I raised up on my knees.

"What are you doing?" he asked as I moved toward him, my intent obvious. Or at least, I thought it was.

I want to taste you.

"No."

No? Oh, you don't like that?

"I'm a guy. Of course I like that. I love it. But tonight, I just want it to be about you."

Can you at least take off your clothes, then? I don't think I like being the only naked one here.

"That I can do," he replied, kicking off his shoes and socks while he removed his shirt. His intricate tattoos only added to his sexiness, dark lines mixed with colorful swirls painting his skin so beautifully. I'd been staring so long at his chest and arms that I hadn't even noticed he'd removed his jeans . . . and his boxer briefs.

Standing in front of me in all his glory, his sweet smile did nothing to detract me from the huge erection he sported, his cock jutting out as if it had a mind of its own. Maybe I should have reconsidered. I thought I was ready. I mean, I wanted to be with Jagger more than anything, but I hadn't truly considered what would happen.

Don't get me wrong. I knew exactly what he and I would be engaged in, and I hoped I would love it, but looking at his thickness, realizing that part of him was going to be deep inside me, made me hesitate for a few seconds.

I berated myself for acting so childish, but for someone who'd never had sex before this moment was a huge deal. For me, at least.

"Are you okay?" He moved toward the bed, his fingers circling his excitement. As if second nature, he lazily ran his hand up and down his shaft, keeping his eyes on me the entire time. Averting my gaze from that part of him, I watched the way his muscular thighs carried him closer. The way his stomach muscles clenched with every pump of his hand.

Jagger crawled up the bed and moved his body over mine until my back hit the mattress, all before I could answer. "I know you're nervous. I can see it in your eyes. In the way your breaths skip. But please realize we'll only do what you want. What you can handle."

My heart melted. Placing my hands on the sides of his face, I pulled him to me and crashed my lips against his. I didn't want to wait one moment longer to connect with him.

"Fuck," he groaned. "You have no idea what you're doing to me." He continued to nip at my mouth, lavishing me with kisses, stopping briefly when he jumped up to snag a condom from his back pocket. Sheathing himself, he lowered on top of me again, bracing his weight with his forearms. "Are you ready?"

I nodded. I wanted more than anything to appear sexy and confident, but the truth was my nerves fired off every which way.

"Open your legs. Wider." His lips brushed over mine again, distracting me when the tip of his cock pressed slowly inside me. "Don't tense up," he cautioned. "You'll only make it worse."

Worse? I thought. Right then I couldn't help but give in to my unease, knitting my brow and digging my nails into his biceps. I swore if I bit my lower lip any harder I'd taste blood.

Pulling back a little, I saw his concern. "Okay, we're gonna stop. Maybe it's not the right time yet." When he tried to move away, I clutched on to him for dear life. The last thing I wanted to do was come across . . . well, as I had been. It was time for me to woman up and do what I'd wanted to do for quite some time now. There wasn't another man alive who I wanted to be my first, so before Jagger leapt off the bed, I wrapped my legs over the backs of his and tightened my hold. Reaching down, I grabbed his delectable ass and ground myself against him, his cock sliding through my folds with ease.

He didn't ask me if I was ready, or if I still wanted to do this. Instead, with as much gentleness as he possessed, he pushed himself inside my tightness, stopping every few seconds to allow me to adjust.

The way he swirled his tongue with mine when he ravished my mouth helped take my mind off the sting of pain once he'd fully sunk inside me. Eventually, we melded together, the friction of our bodies coming together, eliciting a pleasure I'd never even thought possible.

"Goddamnit!" he growled. "I'm not gonna last much longer." Slowing his thrusts, he breathed deeply before pulling back to rest on his haunches, taking me with him so our bodies remained connected. Seizing my waist, he pulled me roughly toward him, slamming into me with a controlled frenzy, withdrawing slowly before repeating. "Is that okay? Am I hurting you?"

No.

The last thing I wanted to explain was that while my body ached with delicious pleasure, I didn't want him to stop. I needed him to take me the way he wanted, trusting him to not go overboard and fuck me with wild abandon. I craved his lust, his unabashed desire for me. So yeah, *no* would be my only response.

Jagger's mouth parted and his head fell back, his grip on my waist tightening all while he tried not to speed up. "I can't . . . I can't hold back."

Just when the familiar tingles began, sprinkling their tease throughout my insides, he withdrew completely. Moving quickly up the bed, he turned me on my side until his body cradled mine from behind.

"I wanna be close to you," he whispered, kissing the shell of my ear. "Plus, I'll have better access to this," he said, trailing his hand down my belly until he rested the pad of his finger over my clit.

I reached behind me and threaded my fingers through his hair, opening my legs when he nudged them apart with his thigh. Pushing into me from behind, his fingers continued to play with my sensitive bundle of nerves, heightening the thrill until I thought I'd shatter into a million pieces. I rocked back into him, finding my rhythm rather easily. Restrained panting hit the side of my face, Jagger's tongue lavishing the skin of my neck, nipping and sucking while his body claimed mine.

The pressure built.

My muscles locked up tight. Again.

Like the sweetest of roller coasters, dragging out the ascent to the top, the anticipation of the strongest climax teased me.

"I can feel you start to clench around me," he grunted. "And it's the best fucking feeling in the world, baby."

Lowering my hand from his hair, I gripped his thigh, my nails digging into his skin and anchoring me in place. I tried to hold out as long as I could, never wanting his sweet assault to stop, but my body had other plans.

"Are you gonna come?" he asked, adding more pressure to my clit. All I could do in response was nod, one hand clutching the covers while the other held his leg. "Then fall with me, Kena. Let go and crash," he grunted, his speed increasing until he'd shouted out his blissful release.

The sounds he made thrilled me, ramping my own orgasm even higher. Our bodies continued to rock together until both of us had come back down from our sexual high, tangled in each other for the next five minutes. Eventually, he rolled onto his back, taking me with him so my head rested on his chest.

The wild thud of his heart slowed with the tick of the clock, and it wasn't long before I'd drifted off to sleep. Thoughts of Jagger infiltrated every facet of my mind as I gave in to some much needed rest.

CHAPTER
THIRTY-THREE

Jagger

IN THE PAST, EVEN THOUGH I hated to even think about it now that Kena was in my life, the girls I'd fucked had no problem letting me know when they were about to get off. Their moans and pleas for me to fuck them harder because they were right on the edge were a constant.

But with Kena it was completely different. I had to rely on her body to tell me how she was feeling. Watching her eyes glaze over in the sexiest of ways, or the way her nipples became erect, or the way her pussy drenched my cock in her excitement. She'd pushed me to the brink faster than ever before, her tightness fisting me until I had no other choice but to give in to the speeding train of pleasure barreling down on me.

I'd managed to make her come twice, and that was only the beginning. While I had to take it easy until she became accustomed to me, I looked forward to having quite a bit of fun with her, teasing her endlessly for hours . . . or minutes, depending on how hyped we both were. Images of all sorts of positions enticed me, and I couldn't wait.

Slowly rolling Kena to her side, I managed to sneak off into the bathroom without waking her, tossing the condom in the trash before returning. The mattress dipped from my weight and still she didn't stir, too wrecked from earlier. I sported a huge grin as I nestled in behind her, pulling her close so I could fall asleep as well.

I'd only known Kena a short time, had only slept in the same bed with her as many times as I could count on my fingers, yet it was as if she'd always been in my world. I knew I was falling for her, in a big way, and although the thought terrified me, for various reasons, I knew in the end she was the woman I wanted by my side.

I'd go to the ends of the earth to protect her, to shield her from harm any way I could. The fear of the unknown rattled me, but I couldn't focus on the "what ifs." I had to take each day as it came, hold on tight and enjoy the motherfuckin' ride.

Lost in a dream, it took me a minute to realize the shrill sound cutting through the darkness of the room was my cell. Fumbling through my jeans to find it, I quickly pulled it free from the pocket and squinted at the bright light on the screen.

"What?" I whisper-barked, pissed that whoever called had no concept of time.

Hurried breaths flew down the line, instantly putting me on alert. Swinging my legs over the side of the bed, I grabbed my clothes and walked into the hallway. I knew I'd have to leave. I just didn't know why yet.

"Get to the clubhouse now, Jagger!" Stone yelled, hanging up before he'd even allowed me to ask questions. Once I finished dressing, I scribbled out a quick note to Kena, reached for my keys and quietly closed and locked the door behind me.

I shouldn't have, but I sped all the way to the club, ignoring all the traffic lights. Lucky for me, there weren't many people out on the roads, seeing as how it was still very early.

There was an urgency to my step as I pulled open the door, entering the common room and absorbing the electric somberness drifting through the air.

Stone stood in the corner talking to Marek. Zip, Cutter and Breck lounged on the couches, drinks in hand and looking a little worse for wear, while Trigger busied himself serving alcohol to whomever requested it.

"What the fuck is goin' on?" Ryder shouted, entering the clubhouse looking like he'd been hit by a truck, hair all disheveled with red-rimmed eyes.

No one answered, serving to annoy him as he took a seat at the bar. Finding my own words, they caught in my throat when I heard shouting, followed by a barrage of curses coming from the hallway. Whoever was back there was angered beyond all rational thought.

Then I heard a door slam.

The eruption of noise floated toward us all, the expectancy for something explosive to follow. First I saw Tripp, his downcast eyes a telltale sign something bad happened. Then I saw Adelaide, and it was then I realized shit had hit the fan. In a big way, grand enough to warrant her presence. No doubt she'd been called in to help patch someone up; otherwise, there was no way Stone would have his woman here so late.

Still I kept my questions buried, watching and waiting for everything to unravel.

"How is she?" I heard Marek ask, moving closer until he'd reached Adelaide, a stolen look of concern and anger in his expression.

"She's pretty awful," she answered. "They did quite the number on her, so bad it's going to take her quite a while to recover. She really should go to the hospital, but I get why you don't want that, so I did the best I could." Sidestepping our prez, she saddled up next to Stone, turning her head into the crook of his arm and curling into his protective embrace for support.

For what, I still had no idea.

Until I saw Hawke slowly walking down the same hall Tripp had just emerged from, someone frail huddled next to him. At first, I wasn't sure who he shielded but the closer he stepped, the more I realized he was holding Edana. His woman. Only she didn't look like herself. She wore a baggy T-shirt and grey sweatpants, no doubt Hawke's clothes. But why? I'd never seen her in anything but skintight jeans and shirts which left little to the imagination. Her auburn hair was pushed back off her face, wet and tangled from a fresh shower.

When they both stood only a few feet from me, I saw the damage that had put everyone on edge. Nasty welts and bruises covered her face, her right eye swollen shut and her upper lip split open. The haggard way in which she walked indicated there was more damage to her body; she winced every few steps when Hawke unknowingly picked up his pace.

"Sorry, baby," I heard him mumble as they passed by. Up close, Edana looked worse, the red and purple bruises distinct and grotesque. Hawke dwarfed her small frame even more than normal, the fragility of her presence screaming out to all of us.

What the hell happened?

"I'll fuckin' kill every last one of 'em, Prez," he roared, walking toward Marek, coming to a brief stop while still sheltering his woman. "They raped her. I don't . . . I can't. . . ." Hawke stopped speaking. Anyone close enough to hear the pain in his voice knew that if he'd continued talking, he would've broken down right then.

"We'll get them for this," Marek promised. "For fucking everything." A quick glance between them, a silent plan of action already formulating in their heads, I was sure, and Hawke led Edana toward the exit.

Once they were gone, I walked toward Stone, pulling him to the side once the conversation ended between him and Marek, our president turning his attention to Tripp who'd been firing off questions as soon as an opportunity presented itself.

Adelaide stuck to Stone's side, but I didn't care. I wanted to talk to both of them actually.

"What the hell happened to Edana? And who does Hawke want to punish for it?" A niggling sense of who'd attacked her whispered in the back corners of my brain, but I needed to hear it out loud.

"Those goddamn Savages jumped her outside Indulge. They beat her with their fists, forced themselves on her and taunted her, telling her the only reason they were gonna let her live was so she could pass along a message."

Indulge was the club's newest titty bar, and normally security was pretty tight, so I was surprised to find out some of the Reapers were able to not only sneak near our establishment, but attack Edana.

One of our brothers' old ladies.

Without me pushing, Stone continued. "She went there looking for Hawke, no doubt to chew his ass out, boundless guilt he's no doubt dealing with. Anyway, they told her they were comin' for everyone we loved, and they wouldn't stop until Sully was back in their club." Marek had heard Stone's words, no doubt not for the first time, and threw a punch at the wall behind him, pushing his fist through the crumbling drywall.

We all knew our enemy wouldn't stop until they had Marek's wife back with them, her father orchestrating the ambush. We'd been waiting for quite some time now for him to make his move, and it looked like the wait was over.

But who would be next?

I hesitated leaving the club, needing to stick around in case I was needed, but I wanted to head back to my place. Kena was no doubt still locked in sleep, but she was there alone.

All of a sudden, my heart skidded to a stop, loathsome fear fueling my choppy gasps.

Her image filtered in, her innocent smile slicing me apart because I knew what I had to do.

CHAPTER THIRTY-FOUR

Kena

ROLLING OVER, I THRUST MY arm outward and expected to feel Jagger sleeping next to me. But his side was empty. And cold, indicating he'd left the bed quite some time ago. I'd glanced to the alarm clock next to the bed and saw the bright red numbers, reading 6:08 a.m.

Stretching to chase away any residual sleep, I threw off the covers and planted my feet firmly on the ground, shuffling from the room and toward the living area, expecting to find him there.

But again . . . nothing.

He was nowhere to be found. His place was small, and unless he was holed up in the bathroom, he'd left me alone in his apartment. Trudging toward the kitchen to find some coffee, it was then I saw a small note lying on the counter. Barely legible handwriting told me he had gone to the clubhouse. He didn't say why, but I knew enough about him to realize it had to have been important for him to leave me.

Thoughts of the previous night rushed over me and I smiled. I'd never felt like this about anyone before, and the notion that he cared for me as I did him made me the happiest woman in the world.

The way Jagger looked at me, touched me, whispered concerns in my ear as he worked inside my body thrilled me. His gentleness soothed my worries about my first time, and it couldn't have been more perfect.

I wouldn't have traded that moment for anything in the world.

Bringing the brewed tastiness to my lips, my hand shook in surprise when I heard the jostle of keys in the lock. The front door flew open and in walked Jagger, looking like he'd been put through the wringer. What had happened during the time he'd been gone? Walking across the threshold, he closed the door behind him and headed toward me, his eyes on me the entire time.

Once he was close, he circled his arm around my waist and pulled me in to him, burying his face in the crook of my neck, inhaling me before placing a lingering kiss on my skin. His tensed shoulders and re-served demeanor instantly put me on alert.

Stepping back, he held my hands in his and looked at me, saying nothing. He just stared, as if his goal was to memorize my every feature.

Finally, after a few intense moments, he dropped my hands and walked toward his bedroom. "I better take you home now, Kena," he called out over his shoulder as he disappeared down the hallway.

I was left standing in the kitchen in nothing but his T-shirt and a dumbfounded look on my face.

Following him back into his room, I searched for my clothes, lo-cating them half kicked under the bed. Gathering them in my hands, I walked toward the bathroom, closing the door behind me. I felt vulner-able right then, and the last thing I wanted to do was expose myself to Jagger—physically or emotionally.

Re-entering his space, I saw him sitting on his bed, his hands cra-dling his head. It wasn't until I knocked on the wood of the nearby dresser that he looked up. Slowly rising to his feet, he crossed the room and brushed past me without a word.

When he opened the front door I stopped him, grabbing his hand and tugging him back toward me. Once I had his attention, I asked, *What's wrong? Why are you taking me home so early? Did I do something wrong?*

The look on his face told me something serious was about to come flying out of his mouth, and as his lips parted, I held my breath, not wanting to hear any of what he was going to tell me.

Bracing my hands against my sides, I counted the seconds, but no sound ever left him. Instead, he looked like he was going to break down, so before that happened, he turned back around and walked out into the hallway, expecting me to follow.

Which I did.

Confused.

Angry.

Scared.

The entire ride back to my house was in silence. Had I misread his feelings for me?

Had he tricked me into bed, telling me whatever I wanted to hear in order to steal my innocence?

Did he view me as a challenge, nothing more?

If he would only talk to me I'd be able to find out what was wrong, but he remained tight-lipped, only asking if I was cold when he saw me shudder. The temperature had nothing to do with my shivers, just the obstinate guy sitting next to me.

He pulled down my street, the time ticking by too fast, bringing me closer to a situation I knew would upset me. Shutting off the engine, he gripped the wheel tightly, dipping his head for a brief moment before reaching for the door handle. Stepping out, he came around to my side, but I'd already exited the vehicle, standing next to his truck with my arms clutching my purse.

Part of me wanted to walk ahead and disappear inside, never giving him the opportunity to tell me whatever it was that weighed so heavy on him. But the other part of me wanted to demand he tell me why he wanted to get rid of me so fast.

I struggled between the two, but in the end I remained standing exactly where I was, leaning against the passenger side door, fiddling with my keys.

"I'll walk you inside," he finally said, speaking quickly before ushering me forward. The heat from his palm on my lower back warmed and chilled me at the same time.

He remained silent while I jabbed the key into the lock, pushing the door open and walking inside. I took a few steps to the side and watched as he hovered in the doorway, uncertain if he should come inside or turn around and leave.

Not being able to stand whatever this was between us any longer, I raised my hands in front of me and let loose, a bit of anger jerking my motions to let him know he'd upset me.

Why the silent treatment? Tell me what I did. I deserve to know.

I advanced toward him but he retreated, his back hitting the door, a conflicted look crossing over his face.

Listen, Kena, what happened last night was a mistake. It should have never happened. I found it odd he chose to sign to me instead of speak, but I had no time to wonder before I saw his expression change, appearing resolute and void of any feeling. As if I'd just been another notch on his bedpost, which I knew in my heart wasn't the case. Although he was making a strong case to prove otherwise.

Why would you say that?

He didn't answer, instead shoving his hands in his pockets, averting his eyes from mine every few seconds.

When I signed again, he stared at my hands, avoiding my face at all costs. Until he couldn't.

Stop being a coward, Jagger, and tell me what's going on. Tensed moments pinged between us, my heart beating so fast I feared it'd burst from my chest.

Did you use me? Did you just want to get me into bed? Was that your main goal? I lowered my arms to my sides and fisted my hands. My nails bit into my palms and I welcomed the sting of pain.

Would you hate me if I said yes?

Inhaling a ragged breath, I took a step back, my backside bumping into the chair behind me. My lips parted, as if I'd wanted to speak, but I knew that was just stupid. I didn't want to show him how hurt I was but I couldn't help my body's reaction, my heart breaking in two at the thought that the guy standing in front of me was nothing like I'd thought. I didn't know *this* Jagger. I hated this version of him, making me ache inside so badly I wanted to crumble to the floor and weep uncontrollably.

Instead, I held back the tears and answered. *Yes. I would.* For as much as I tried to convince myself that my answer had been truthful, I knew it was a lie. I wanted to hate him, to despise him for hurting me, but I knew I loved him. Even though we'd only known each other a short time, my feelings would seem silly to anyone else, but they were real to me.

And I told him my secret before I could stop myself.

But I love you, I signed, finally allowing the first of many tears to escape. I detested my vulnerability, but I couldn't shield it any longer.

His sharp intake of air told me I'd managed to shock him. Then again, if he'd only chased me because he wanted to get me into bed, I was sure telling him I loved him was the last thing he expected from me.

But didn't he know?

Couldn't he feel it in my kisses?

Couldn't he see it written all over my face when I looked at him?

Didn't he feel it last night when I gave myself to him?

Apparently not.

I'd been the biggest fool.

You don't love me, he replied, running his hands through his hair, his eyes appearing glassy . . . until they didn't. *I'm not the guy for you, and I'm sorry if I led you to believe that I was. We had fun, but I don't wanna see you anymore. I'm sorry,* he said, dropping his hands.

I don't believe you. Tell me, I demanded. *I want to hear you speak those words out loud.*

Shaking his head, he turned his back to me before reaching for the door handle.

I couldn't shout at him to turn around and look at me.

I couldn't yell at him, demand he take back his soul-wrenching words.

The only thing I could do was watch him disappear as the front door closed behind him.

CHAPTER THIRTY-FIVE

Jagger

CONSUMING A LOT OF ALCOHOL was the only way I could stop the pain, my heart feeling as if it had literally splintered in half. Two weeks had passed since I'd lied to Kena, and each day it only got worse.

She'd called me out, saw the weakness splayed all over my body when I told her I didn't want to see her anymore. She knew damn well I wouldn't be able to speak those wretched words out loud, so I had chosen to sign them instead.

The ache in my chest blossomed rapidly, making it difficult to breathe, the slow burn of whiskey dulling it only moderately. Hunching over the bar at The Underground, I embraced the liquor, not paying much attention to anyone around me. Until I had no choice.

A strong hand gripped my neck, and because I'd invited the drink to soothe me, my reaction was nothing less than . . . well, immobile. Trying to raise my head, the weight of my world too heavy to accommodate such a simple action, it fell forward before I could stop it, the hard wood of the ledge catching it instead of my hands.

"Fuuuuuck," I moaned, rubbing the affected area with fingers that felt like lead. Even the slow rise of my arm should have screamed I'd had enough to drink, but since I could still somewhat form a thought, I knew I wasn't done yet.

"You're a fuckin' mess, brother," Ryder growled from behind me, releasing my neck before settling in the seat next to me. He didn't say anything for a moment, or maybe he had and I hadn't heard him, too lost to the numbness finally encasing the tortured parts that remained.

"I got . . . got this," I mumbled, bringing the shot glass to my lips and tipping my head back, the motion throwing my entire body backward. Thank God Ryder had been there to catch me; otherwise, I'd have been lying on my back, hopefully knocked the fuck out.

Barlow approached, giving me a once-over before shaking his head. "How did you get that, Jagger?" Before allowing me to answer, he turned his attention to Ryder. "I cut him off two drinks ago, but apparently the slick little fucker still managed to snag some more." A harsh crack of his cleanup towel hit my neck, the sting just what I needed to push myself back into reality, albeit slowly.

"Ow! What the fuck, Barlow?"

"That's for not listening to me," he yelled over his shoulder, already walking toward the other end of the bar.

"I think you've had enough," Ryder confirmed, "but before I drop your ass off at home, I wanna know why you cut her loose." From my peripheral I saw him lean forward and rest his forearms on the bar. Although he hadn't been looking at me, it didn't mean he didn't expect me to answer.

I played dumb, however.

"Who?"

"You know damn well who. Braylen's been calling me, screaming at me as if that shit was my fuckin' fault."

Wincing, I could only imagine what Kena's sister had said to him. She was one ballsy, speak-her-mind kind of chick. But her desire to protect Kena made me smile. Well, not smile, but glad she had someone willing to call the likes of Ryder and bitch him out for something he had no hand in. No doubt she'd left me some nasty voice mails as well. Only I'd been too consistently wasted to even bother to check.

Barlow walked back in our direction, placing a tall glass of water in front of me. "Drink it," he demanded, stepping away before I could argue.

"Hey, gimme a shot," Ryder yelled. "You know what I want."

"Fuck no," Barlow shouted back, flipping that damn towel over his shoulder before busying himself with pouring a beer. Ryder opened his mouth to protest, but the bartender cut him off. "There's no way I'm serving you hard liquor, Ryder. I actually like you."

Thankful I had something else to pull my focus, I glanced back and forth between them, curious who'd win out. The two men were pretty much even in height, weight and muscle. The only difference being that Barlow had a shaved head covered in tattoos, his appearance giving him slightly more of a menacing edge.

"What the hell does that mean?" Ryder adjusted himself, one foot planted firmly on the ground while the other rested on the rung of the barstool.

"I don't want to have to call in reinforcements to beat the shit outta ya once you get out of hand." Advancing toward us again, he slid the beer toward Ryder, smirking before turning his back.

"Fuck you."

"You're welcome," Barlow responded, completely ignoring us for the next fifteen minutes.

I expected Ryder to press me for answers, but instead he let me wallow in my self-pity. Because Barlow wouldn't serve me anymore and I had my own personal watchdog hovering over me, I couldn't even lean over the bar when the bartender wasn't looking and snag a bottle, the one I'd taken earlier resting at my feet. Empty.

But the silence was short-lived, Ryder bumping my arm with his before he began his interrogation. "So, why did ya do it? I thought you really liked this one," he goaded, forcing me to talk, although he wouldn't like my response.

"Mind your business. I'm not sittin' here spillin' like some sort of bitch," I slurred, my head lolling from side to side, the room spinning so fast I had to close my eyes to make it stop. Only my lack of sight made it worse.

"It became my business when you dragged me into it, fucker." The bass in his voice dropped threateningly low.

"I don't wanna be with her," I lied, tapping the bar to get Barlow's attention, even though I knew he was simply gonna ignore me.

"Why?"

"Let it go," I shouted, pounding my fist against the wood that time.

"No, I won't. Not until you give me a good reason, one I can tell Braylen when she no doubt shows up at my fuckin' place. Again."

Snagging the opportunity to switch the subject, I dove right in. "She been to your place? So, what . . . You datin' her?" I grinned, my smile no doubt lopsided as all hell. Taking a few gulps of water, some of it dripping down my chin, I patiently waited to see if he'd take the bait.

Sadly, he didn't.

"We're not talkin' about me. Now, if you don't give me a reason why you're not seeing Kena anymore, I'm gonna drag your ass back to her house, drunk or not, and leave you there."

My heart sped up, fear he'd actually do that making me sit up as straight as I could manage. "I'm not good enough," I finally revealed. "She's in too much danger bein' with me." Gripping my hair, I said, "You saw what happened to Edana, man. I'd die if they ever got their hands on Kena." It was the absolute truth. If something bad ever happened to her because of me, I had no idea how I'd go on afterward.

"You can't stop livin' because you think somethin' bad might happen. If that was the case, no one would ever get with anyone." Pushing out a breath, he continued. "You think Marek doesn't worry about Sully every minute of the day, especially knowing Psych's plannin' on coming for her? Or that Stone isn't sick with worry every time Adelaide and Riley are out of his sight?"

"What about Braylen?"

"What about her?"

"Don't you worry she'll get hurt?"

"Nope." Swallowing half his beer in a few gulps, the glass clanked against the bar when he put it down. "Besides, we're just fuckin'. And ain't no bastards gonna stop me from gettin' my dick wet." He spewed his nonchalant words my way, but I saw the hesitation on his face. Braylen meant more to him than just someone to stick his dick in. But I decided not to call him out on it, although I should have because then it would've diverted the conversation. I was too drunk to mentally play games with him, though, his sobriety no doubt giving him the advantage.

So I settled on a dismissive approach. "Whatever."

Finishing off the rest of his beer, he stood and reached for my upper arm, pulling me to my feet. "Let's go."

I tried to shrug him off but it was futile. "Where we goin'?"

"You're gonna fix this. If not for yourself, then for me, 'cause I'm tired of hearing Braylen's shit." Effortlessly pulling me toward the exit, he added, "I can think of better things to occupy her mouth." He laughed at his own joke, continuing to force me outside and into his vehicle.

Realizing fighting him was useless, I tried to convince him I was too far gone, using my inebriation as the perfect excuse. "I'm too goddamn drunk to see her."

"That you are," he agreed, kicking over the engine and throwing it into gear. "I'm gonna get you some coffee. And Jagger?" I turned toward him. "If you puke in my truck, I'm gonna kill ya."

"Then stop drivin' like an asshole."

"I'm only goin' five miles an hour," he retorted, shaking his head. A few miles down the road he stopped at a drive-thru, ordering two large coffees. Black. Handing me the first one, he jerked his head at me. "Drink it."

Knowing I'd see Kena sooner rather than later, I didn't argue, bringing the hot liquid to my mouth, burning my tongue at first contact. But I soldiered on, needing to be somewhat sober when I finally laid eyes on her.

Ten minutes passed without either of us speaking, the tension between us faltering some. "How do you know she's even home?"

"I already checked with Braylen." That's all he said, keeping his focus on the road ahead.

Settling further into my seat, my alcohol-induced haze lessening with each fleeting mile, my brain formed many questions.

Did she know I was on my way?

Did she even want to see me?
Would I give in and beg her for another chance?
Would she forgive me?
I guess I'll have answers soon enough.

CHAPTER THIRTY-SIX

Kena

BRAYLEN HAD BEEN ACTING EXTREMELY weird for the past couple hours, looking out the window every once in a while. When I asked her why, she'd waved her hand at me and shrugged, not giving me a definitive answer.

Every day over the past two weeks crawled by, each passing second consumed with thoughts of Jagger. I knew I should have never been involved with him, fearing my sister's warning would eventually come true. That he'd break my heart.

And it was exactly what he'd done.

Although, I felt much worse than I ever thought I would. With Jagger, I pictured us making it for the long haul, envisioning us moving in together someday and forging a future.

I was old enough to know that not everything would be perfect, but I wanted to explore the next chapter of my life with him. Unfortunately, the first time I laid my heart on the line it'd been sliced from my chest and crushed under the weight of his rejection.

I'd chosen Jagger to give myself to, and he'd taken advantage of my vulnerability.

The thought that he'd only chosen me because I presented as a challenge enraged me. Did he laugh at me with his buddies? Brag about getting into the mute girl's pants? Anger washed over the hurt when I'd allow myself to fully contemplate what had happened between us, coming to grips with the fact Jagger was a bastard, feeding on my innocence any way he saw fit.

Braylen backed away from the window, mumbled something to herself and walked toward the front door. Glancing at the clock on the wall above the television, I saw it was closing in on eleven, the later hour nudging me to let out a full yawn.

When she looked in my direction, I signed, *I'm going to bed. I'm tired.*

A knock rapped on the door, drawing my attention right away. "Don't be mad at me, but for as much as I want to punch Jagger in the face right now for hurting you, I know he truly cares about you." I rose from the couch and took a step toward the hallway. She held her hands up in front of her as a sign of surrender. "I know. I know. I can't believe I'm even asking you to give him a chance to explain why he did what he did, but trust me. There's something more he's not telling you. Ryder texted me before and told me he's been miserable for the past two weeks, drinking himself silly just to get through it."

I didn't want to hear any more of what she had to say. Taking another tentative step away from her, the pounding on the door broke the building tension between my older sister and me. *How dare she do this? How dare she make me face the one person who crushed my entire world?* At first I thought I was being a bit overdramatic, but try telling that to my heart, to the sadness embedded in my brain every time I thought about him.

But although I hated that he'd destroyed me, I couldn't just stop loving him.

Is that him? I knew the answer before she responded.

"Yes. Ryder's out there with him. He had to sober Jagger up before he got here."

So it wasn't even Jagger's idea to come over, then? It was yours and Ryder's? That's even more humiliating.

Never mind that I felt like shit, I looked like it too. My hair was pulled back into a messy up-do, not having washed it in five days. I wore a yellow cami and wrinkled pajama bottoms, not caring that they hadn't been cleaned in as much time either.

Braylen moved toward the front door, her fingers circling around the handle, ready to welcome the two of them into our house.

Don't you dare, I warned.

"I hate seeing you like this, and if there is anything I can do to help . . . I'm gonna do it." On her last word, she flung open the door, stepping to the side as Ryder entered first. Jagger followed behind, making sure to stay near the entryway. *Smart move*, I thought.

I could have strangled Braylen right then. She'd been all over the place when it came to Jagger and me. First she liked him. Then she couldn't stand him. Then she liked him again. *Come on, woman, make up your mind already.*

"We're gonna give you some privacy," Ryder announced, seizing my sister's hand and pulling her from the house, her astonishment heard all the way to his truck, complaining she wasn't even dressed. But somehow I thought he wouldn't have a problem with the lack of clothing she wore, an oversized T-shirt the only thing covering her decency.

A rumble of the engine and a slight squeal of tires told me they'd really left me alone with Jagger. And while I was infuriated, my eyes couldn't stop drinking him in. I thought I looked bad, but it was nothing compared to him. His hair was a mess, and a faint shadow of a beard prickled his jawline. He looked tired, haggard even. Faint lines were etched into his face, accentuating his hollowed appearance. While he looked a little worse for wear, he was still the most handsome guy I'd ever seen.

But I couldn't think like that. No way would I allow him to affect me like he had before he broke my heart. I couldn't take it if he said something endearing or begged for my forgiveness. Because I just might crumble and give in, opening myself up for a bigger disaster down the road.

He continued to stand near the door, his eyes following my every movement. Knowing he wouldn't leave until I broached the topic of him being there, I took a step closer. I held steady, glaring at him to try and mask my true feelings.

Devastation.

What are you doing here?

"I had to see you," he answered, licking his lips in nervousness.

You had to see me, or you were forced here to see me?

"Both," he replied, surprisingly admitting that Ryder had dragged him to my house. "Kena," he started, advancing on me until I held my hand up for him to stop. "I'm so sorry for the way things ended between us. I didn't mean to hurt you. I hope we can still be friends."

So . . . you're not here to get me back?

"No."

I'm not gonna lie and say there wasn't a part of me that was distraught from his admission. While I'd vowed not to give him another chance, I at least thought he'd come to his senses and realized he had feelings for me. Feelings that hadn't disappeared just because he had.

Now I was beyond irate with Braylen, and whatever part Ryder had played in this whole charade. Why compound the hurt I'd felt? Just to see if there was a chance he'd come back around and want to be with me again? Had they even asked him if he *wanted* to see me? Talk to me? Try and get me back?

It was obvious they hadn't.

So then, what are you doing here? I asked again, fisting my hands at my sides so I didn't rush forward and slap the shit out of him for turning me into a pathetic person, drowning in hurt all because he'd bested me. Lied to me. Made me believe he'd cared.

"I wanted to apologize for my behavior and tell you that I didn't just go after you to get you into bed. That wasn't my intention at all. I genuinely cared about you. Fuck," he grumbled, running his palms down his face in frustration. "I still do. I just . . . I can't be with you."

I refused to beg him to explain further. He stood before me, telling me again that he didn't want me. And no matter how much I wanted to throw myself into his arms and plead for him to change his mind, I stood strong. I valued myself too much to act like such a fool.

Then there's nothing left for you to say. You can leave now. Besides. . . . I dropped my hands before I finished, realizing I'd only be inviting drama into my life, when all I wanted to do was forget everything and crawl into bed. Sleep until my sister forced me out of bed days later.

But it was too late.

I'd piqued his interest, his brow furrowing while he continued to stare at me. "Besides what?"

I just shook my head, refusing to fulfill his curiosity.

"Besides what, Kena?" he asked, a hint of anger lacing his voice when he'd said my name. "Are you trying to tell me you're seeing someone else? Is that it?" His entire body tensed, the flare of disbelief lighting up his eyes. "Tell me," he demanded, taking a step toward me, his carefully orchestrated reserve slowly crumbling.

He deserved to feel hurt, or betrayed, or jealous, or whatever emotion sliced through him right then.

"Is it Kevin?" His question shocked me, but it shouldn't have. He'd obviously had an issue with our friendship, although he'd never given me shit about it before.

I never answered, biting my lower lip in nervousness, a tick I'd seen him do before. But it was enough to appear as if I'd answered yes. A barrage of expletives flew from his mouth before his eyes turned dark and he snarled at me in fury.

My initial intention was to make him jealous. Of course it would've been with a lie, but I hadn't followed through. Although, it seemed I didn't have to; his imagination ran wild, and I did nothing to stop it.

The wildfire of his emotions cut through the air, engulfing us both in its tight grip.

"Let me tell you something right now. If I ever see his hands on you, I'm gonna rip them from his body and beat him with them. Don't test me, Kena. I mean it," he threatened, stepping closer until he stood only a couple feet away from me. The growl in his voice kicked me back into the reality of the situation. He had no right at all to threaten Kevin, even if he was my fictional boyfriend. Something he'd come up with all by himself. All right, I knew I hadn't dissuaded him otherwise, but still . . . He was the one who tossed me to the side, and in a cruel way I might add.

You have no right to say that to me. You broke up with me, so why do you care who I date? Again, I fed into the lie but I couldn't stop myself, part of me smug that he was jealous.

"So I broke up with you, and already you're spreading your legs for someone else? Is that it? Now that you're no longer a virgin, you'll jump on any cock ready and willing?"

I gasped at his audacity, but of course he could only see my reaction, not hear it. His words mixed with his hateful tone triggered me to do something I never thought I would.

Especially to him.

I slapped him so hard I'd jolted his head to the side. From the shocked look on his face, he clearly hadn't expected it either. Clenching his jaw, trying to keep his temper in check, he turned around and strode toward the front door, whipping it open before slamming it hard behind him when he left.

Tears coursed down my cheeks that I'd been reduced to someone who would strike another person.

And Jagger, of all people.

But he'd deserved it. Hadn't he?

CHAPTER THIRTY-SEVEN

Jagger

"WHAT THE FUCK DID YOU do?" Ryder roared, knocking me off the barstool before I'd even realized he was near me. Lucky for him, I was drunk. Again. Otherwise I would've knocked him the fuck out for coming at me like that.

Lolling my head to the side, rubbing my jaw from the impact of his fist, I slowly climbed to my feet, clutching the ledge of the bar and using it as an anchor until I found my footing.

"What the hell?" I muttered, continuing to rub my face. The man packed one hell of a punch, and like I said, he was lucky I was incapacitated.

"What did you say to her?"

"Who?"

"Kena."

"None of your damn business," I said, righting myself on the stool and tapping the bar to get Trigger's attention. The clubhouse was practically empty, except for a few men milling around. Marek and Stone had been holed up in Chambers a lot recently, only breaking away to ensure their families' safety. Hawke appeared every now and then, wanting to hear details of retaliation, but so far there hadn't been any.

Marek knew what had to be done, even though some of them

disagreed. Patience, although not our strong suit, had to be practiced. But I had a feeling he had something else up his sleeve, even if he denied it. I could've been wrong, however. I didn't even know how to run my own life, let alone how to run an entire club, or at the very least, offer any suggestions.

"Like I told ya before, it's my business when Braylen won't give it up because she fears I'm just like your dumb ass."

Finding some liquid courage, I asked, "Thought you guys were just fuckin', so what do you care? Can't you find another slut to stick your dick in?" Yeah, liquid courage wasn't always the smart way to go.

No one would have ever believed I was a trained, undefeated fighter right then. Not with the way Ryder managed to grip me up and pin me against the side of the bar. "If you don't fix whatever you said to Kena, I'm gonna make you regret it." His fists clenched tighter, the rustle of my cut echoing in my ears.

"Fine," I agreed. I made him believe his threat scared me, but in reality I knew I had to apologize for what I'd said to her. I was out of line, even if the thought of her with Kevin enraged me all over again.

Releasing me, he strode across the empty space and disappeared outside, leaving me alone with my thoughts. Trigger had taken off somewhere as soon as Ryder started in on me, and the other guys lounging around were now outside, probably tinkering with their bikes.

Straddling my seat once more, I pulled my phone from my back pocket and brought up the keypad. I doubted she would respond, but I had to send her a message regardless.

Jagger: I'm sorry.

Right away, my phone chimed.

Kena: GO TO HELL!!

Jagger: I'm already there. Trust me.

A half hour passed before she finally responded again, although my last text probably confused the hell out of her. It did me. I couldn't differentiate my emotions. At first, my heart broke that I had to set her free, realizing the danger she would be in if anyone knew she was attached to me. Then I was enraged at the thought she was seeing Kevin so soon after we'd broke up, but it wasn't her fault. I was the one who ended things, so why was I upset?

Because you love her.

And I did, although I could never tell her that because I knew we couldn't be together. Telling her those three words would kill us both, offering a hope that neither one of us could grab on to.

> *Kena: I'm not seeing Kevin. Never was. I just let you think that because you deserved it.*

I had to re-read her text five times before it fully sank in. My lips kicked up in a smug grin, happy what I'd thought wasn't even true. The palm of my hand smacked my forehead, remembering what I'd accused her of, the reality of the situation hitting me like a freight train.

So I broke up with you, and already you're spreading your legs for someone else? I can't believe those words actually came out of my mouth. And just because I'd still been partially drunk didn't excuse my behavior. Not at all. That wasn't me, but my anger had gotten the best of me.

> *Jagger: I'm so sorry. Can you forgive me? Can we still be friends?*

> *Kena: I don't want to be your friend.*

Ouch! But I totally deserved it.

> *Jagger: I understand. Just know that I'm really sorry.*

> *Kena: I can accept that you don't want to be with me anymore, although it hurts because you know how I feel about you. I'll forgive you someday, just not right now.*

I had no idea what to respond, so I didn't, dropping my phone on top of the bar. Once Trigger had returned, coming out of the kitchen with a big fat sandwich in hand, I asked for another shot.

"Don't you think you've had enough?" he asked, chewing while talking.

"Not nearly," I admitted, drumming my fingers on the wood and irritating the both of us.

Sliding my order toward me, he moved closer, a genuine look of concern on his face. I'd always liked Trigger, although the guy was quite intense on occasion. Mainly when it had to do with Adelaide. Protecting his niece was crucial to him, and when Stone had overstepped those boundaries, I thought he was gonna kill our VP. For Christ's sake, he'd shot him! But in his eyes, Stone deserved it. Thankfully, they'd moved on—but only barely, Trigger still giving him shit every now and again.

My phone dinged but I ignored it, choosing numbness instead.

CHAPTER
THIRTY-EIGHT

Kena

OVER THE COURSE OF THE next few weeks, Jagger had texted me numerous times, asking how my day was, apologizing over and over for the things he'd said and telling me he still wanted to be friends. But again, I'd told him I wasn't interested in only being his friend. Although my face lit up every time my phone did, it didn't mean I'd forgiven him for hurting me.

I had a decision to make, and every time I thought I had it figured out, I'd change my mind. Wasn't it my right as a woman? Braylen went back and forth just like I did, some days being Team Jagger, telling me I should give him another shot. Although what she wasn't understanding was that he didn't want another chance, he only wanted to be my freaking buddy.

Then other days, she cursed the day he'd come to our rescue, insisting he'd put some kind of voodoo hex on me. Her moods depended on whether or not Ryder had been giving her a hard time about something, pissing her off so badly she'd needed a glass of wine as soon as she stepped foot inside the house.

I figured only time would tell what would transpire between Jagger and me, but I did know one thing. I'd force him to tell me the real reason he broke it off.

So help me God . . . I had a right to know.

———— • ————

SNATCHING MY PHONE OFF OF my dresser, I decided tonight was the night I'd agree to meet up with Jagger. He'd asked me a few times to come over and have dinner, or for him to come to my place. I didn't think he was suddenly embarrassed to be seen with me in public, but not once did he suggest actually going out to a restaurant. Yeah, the only options were his place or mine.

Either way, he had no idea I planned on ambushing him with my need-to-know question. If he'd told me the truth, maybe I would've been more understanding. Less hurt. Although I didn't see how the last part would ever have been true.

I still hurt.

A lot.

And I continued to suffer because there wasn't a clean break between us. Yet, I continued torturing myself for some reason. Case in point, the message I'd sent to him.

Kena: Are you free tonight?

I wondered if he'd been waiting for me to message him, his response coming through right away.

Jagger: Of course.

Kena: Wanna cook me that dinner?

Jagger: Absolutely.

Kena: 7?

Jagger: Works for me. I'll pick you up then.

Kena: I'll just drive over.

I wanted to be the one able to leave at the drop of a hat, in case anything happened and I needed to make a hasty exit.

Jagger: No, I'll pick you up.

Kena: Then I'm not coming.

Jagger: Kena . . .

Kena: Jagger . . .

His response took a few minutes to come through, no doubt hating that he had to concede and give in. He couldn't control the situation and I knew it irked him.

Jagger: Fine. This time.

This time? Did he think there was going to be another time? The only reason I'd set up these dinner plans was because I wanted—no, I *needed*—answers.

Kena: See you at 7.

Jagger: Can't wait.

I took extra time preparing for the upcoming evening, choosing the perfect outfit, a pair of dark skinny jeans paired with a billowy cream-colored top. A pair of heels complemented the ensemble, making me appear sexy yet not over the top. I wanted him to take one look at me and instantly regret tossing me aside. I desperately needed it for my ego.

I chose to wear my hair down in loose waves, while going light on the makeup. I wanted to look good, but I didn't want to appear as if I'd been trying too hard.

Heading toward my car, I stopped abruptly when I saw that I had a flat tire. Stomping my foot, I made no qualms about cursing—inside my head, of course. Pulling my cell from my purse, I texted Braylen and asked when she'd be home. Her response was immediate, telling me not until late.

I had two choices to make. Either I could cancel on Jagger or I could convince him to just come to my house instead. No point in him coming to pick me up just to drive all the way back over to his place. Tapping my foot against the pavement for a solid minute while I thought things through, I finally decided to ask Jagger to come over.

Once back inside, I threw my purse on the couch, my phone still in hand.

Kena: I have a flat. Can you just come over here for dinner?

Braylen would be gone for hours, so there was no chance she'd run into him, probably giving me shit about letting him come over. Depending on her mood, of course.

Jagger: I made lasagna, so let me pack it up and I'll be there soon.

As soon as I read his message my stomach rumbled.

I had a decision to make. Either I wanted to forge ahead and accept him as my friend, or cut him from my life altogether. Looking at my pathetic self in the mirror, running my fingers through my hair and checking my lip gloss, I knew I wasn't strong enough to cut him out completely. Not yet.

Thirty minutes later, three knocks sounded. Checking my reflection one last time, I blew out a nervous breath and opened the front door. And the sight before me was worth every internal debate, every mixed emotion and every self-doubt I'd possessed over the past few weeks.

Jagger stood on my stoop, holding a tray of lasagna. He was the dish I wanted to devour instead of the carby goodness he held in his hands. As soon as he looked at me, I knew the night would become complicated. For me, at least. The intensity in his eyes gave away his secret, one he'd probably deny if I'd asked. He still desired me, but would he act on it? Go back on his ridiculous notion of us not being . . . well, *us?*

Widening the door, I stepped aside until he'd entered. Without instruction, he walked toward the kitchen and placed the pan on the counter.

"We're probably gonna have to nuke it for a few seconds before we eat. It's still warm, but it'll taste better piping hot. Don't you think?" he asked.

Sure.

Reaching into the upper cabinets, I took down two plates, grabbed a couple of forks from the drawer and removed the lid from the tray.

"I'll get that," he offered, suddenly appearing behind me, his warm breath hitting the back of my neck. His closeness rattled me. I didn't want to feel vulnerable around him, but I couldn't stop my heart from speeding up, or tamp down the need to turn around and press my lips to his.

Placing his hands on my waist, he gently moved me aside, busying himself with dishing out a piece of lasagna for us both, popping them in the microwave for ninety seconds to ensure the temperature was just right.

The clattering of dishes called my attention back to the table. I'd been staring at the back of him, watching the way his muscles flexed every time he moved. His jeans fit him perfectly, teasing me with the image of what I knew lay just underneath. He'd worn a white button-up shirt, the sleeves rolled up to his elbows, exposing muscular, inked forearms. And so help me, I swore it was arm porn.

Clearing his throat brought my attention back to his face. Blushing lightly because I knew he'd just caught me staring, I moved to the seat next to where he stood, sitting down and focusing on the plate of food he'd set in front of me.

Don't look at him. Don't look at him. I kept repeating this over and over, not wanting to give him any indication that he'd been affecting me since he'd walked through that damn door.

"Kena." I kept my eyes on the table. "Kena," he called a bit louder. "Look at me."

Slowly raising my head, I raked my eyes over every button on his shirt, the skin of his throat, his chin, his lips, his nose . . . and finally his eyes.

He didn't say anything at first, instead taking his time studying me in turn. His scrutiny put me on alert, and I swore if he didn't say something in the next few seconds, I was going to jump over the table and attack that perfect mouth of his.

"Ready to eat?"

Yeah, not what I'd expected him to say, even though the food he'd cooked sat directly in front of us.

Nodding, I picked up my fork and cut into the steaming dish.

Funny thing was I'd suddenly lost my appetite, my nerves making me semi-nauseous. But I didn't want him to realize how uncomfortable I'd suddenly become so I started eating, appreciating how tasty the meal was.

I smiled between mouthfuls.

"I hope you like it. It's the best thing I can make." He laughed, the tiny dimple in his left cheek appearing.

I gave a simple nod.

Jagger looked like someone people should be afraid of, his tough exterior the first thing everyone saw. But when he smiled, I saw the guy underneath. When he'd made love to me, I'd felt his gentleness. When he looked at me like I was the only person in the world, I saw his vulnerability.

Too bad I couldn't claim him as mine anymore.

Just a friend.

But I'd take what I could for the time being, until it became too much and I became tired of torturing myself.

After dinner we retired to the sofa. I kicked off my shoes and tucked my legs underneath me, sitting far enough away from him that we wouldn't accidentally touch. I needed the distance, craved it for my sanity to remain intact.

Awkward moments passed until I couldn't take it anymore. *So what now?* I signed. *How does this friend thing work?* I smiled but I was anything but happy. Nervous was more like it, sitting but a couple feet away from Jagger, trying to appear unaffected, but I was anything but.

Shrugging, he replied, "Not sure. I've never been friends before."

Never?

"Nope."

Leaning back, I untucked my legs and brought them up toward my chest, resting my hands on my knees. *We'll figure it out together, then.*

"Okay." He smiled and reached out to touch me, his fingers briefly running up and down my arm. Pulling back, he settled into his seat again, his eyes drifting over my face before focusing on the television. I'd flicked it on before we'd sat down.

"Hey, my club's having a cookout this Saturday. Do you wanna go?

And before you say no, I think Ryder invited Braylen, so at least you'll know a few people." He grinned, lifting his glass of water to his mouth. I watched him swallow the cold liquid, and I wanted more than anything to lick the droplets of water off his lips. "Kena? Did you hear me?"

Startled, I looked away, but not before I heard him chuckle.

I don't know, I answered, still avoiding his face while literally twiddling my thumbs.

The cushion next to me dipped, and when I looked up, Jagger had moved closer, our thighs brushing against one another's.

What are you doing?

He moved closer, cupping the side of my face, and even though I fought it, I leaned in to his touch.

"I don't know," he confessed, his lips only inches from mine, his warm breath tickling my mouth. So badly I wanted him to kiss me, and I think he wanted that as well, but we were toying with very dangerous territory.

With my hands pressed against his chest, my fingers playing with the fabric of his shirt for a brief moment, I pushed him back. I needed the distance. I could barely breathe, his closeness suffocating me in some strange way.

Don't.

"I'm sorry. I shouldn't have done that."

I hadn't meant to ask him, but I couldn't help myself. *Why did you break up with me? Why throw away what we had only to settle for this?* I asked, waving my hand back and forth between us.

Irritation lit up his face as he rose to his feet. "Do you think I wanted to let you go? Do you think I like feeling like my heart is missing from my chest? I had no choice," he mumbled, gripping the back of his neck and squeezing. "It's not safe for you to be with me right now, Kena. There are things happening in my life that I can't get into. Just know I would be with you if I could. Maybe in the future, after everything gets sorted out . . . but not until then."

Rising to stand in front of him, I let my anger take hold and dictate which words my hands would form. *So, what? You're gonna string me along, keep me in the shadows until you deem it time for us to be together again?*

"It's not like that."

I think it is.

"Kena, please," he begged, stepping closer, but I backed up, knowing if he touched me I'd break. "I swear I wish it were different. I really do. We're trying to deal with the threat, and then we'll be good."

He spoke in code, not making any sense at all. *I don't know if I can hang on until then*, I confessed.

Completely disregarding my last statement, a pretty important one, he proceeded to ask me the question he'd asked minutes earlier.

"Will you go to the cookout with me on Saturday?"

You just said I wasn't safe with you, I countered.

"There's no safer place than the clubhouse. All of us will be there." He didn't elaborate or even fully explain what the hell he'd been rambling about seconds prior. His back and forth made me dizzy, and before I said something I would forever regret, I gave him an inch.

No doubt he'd find a way to take a mile, though.

I'll think about it.

For once, he was the one nodding, words escaping him for a response. Soon after, we called it a night, him kissing my cheek before finally leaving.

As I lay in bed, tucked comfortably under the covers, I couldn't help but wonder where I stood in Jagger's world. Would fate allow us to be together again soon, or would her sometimes cruel hands tear us apart for good?

CHAPTER THIRTY-NINE

Jagger

IT TOOK EVERYTHING IN ME not to pin her on her back and attack that luscious mouth of hers, but I knew if I had, I would have hurt her more than she already was. But there were times, like when I was sitting right next to her, inhaling her sweet scent, entranced with the way she stared at me, that I wanted to throw caution to the wind and go for it. Fuck the consequences.

Fortunately, the next day, after some much-needed prodding, Kena agreed to go to the cookout. I tried to pretend I was the sole reason she'd agreed, but I knew Braylen had a hand in it.

After our mini argument, I knew I had to back off a bit and give her the space she needed. It was just as hard for me as it was for her, dealing with our relationship, whatever status we were in.

Jagger: What are you wearing?

Kena: Are you trying to get cute with me?

Her slight flirtation shocked me, but I loved it. It meant she was on the slow road back to forgiving me.

Jagger: Damnit! You caught me.

Kena: Nice try, but I'm not telling you. You'll just have to see for yourself.

Jagger: Seriously, asking because I need to know whether I should bring my bike or truck.

Kena: Oh . . . Truck.

Jagger: See you soon.

———— • ————

THE PARTY WAS IN FULL swing by the time we arrived, men and their women socializing as if we weren't on the cusp of a war. But I understood. Sometimes, we needed to take a step away from it all and enjoy what's important in life—friends and family. The carefree day only shielded the stress we'd been experiencing, however. And by stress, I mean the daunting horror that any one of us, or someone we cared immensely about, could be snatched away in a heartbeat.

Willing myself to focus on the happiness playing out right in front of me, I reached for Kena's hand, surprised she'd given it, and strolled across the lot. A small clearing came into view the further we walked, a couple large tents pitched with picnic tables underneath.

The smell of steak and burgers made my stomach rumble, reminding me I hadn't eaten very much. "Do you want me to fix you a plate?" I asked, still gripping tightly to her hand. My eyes drifted over her face, down her body to her feet, and then back up until our eyes connected. I hadn't meant to do it, but I couldn't help the way she made me just want to stare at her. Her hair was pulled back in a ponytail, her face makeup-less but for a sheer sheen on her lips. It was under the bright sun that I noticed a splattering of freckles across her nose, making her appear younger than her twenty-one years.

The way her body looked in the outfit she'd chosen made me want to hide her from every brother's sight. The red tank top she wore fit her like a glove, a hint of cleavage popping out and making me want to strip her naked just so I could caress her skin with my tongue. And don't get me started on her shorts. Yes, they were modest, not hot pants or coochie cutters or shit like that, but the cut of them hugged her ass and made her toned legs look longer than they actually were. A pair of flip-flops adorned her feet. Her required casualness for the cookout was a win, although she looked sexy as hell to boot.

Tugging on my hand, I turned to look at her, wondering why she wanted to escape. She did it again. "You don't want to hold my hand?" I asked innocently, though a slight tremor of hurt mixed in with the words.

Again she tried to pull away, the annoyance on her face quite telling. As soon as I let go, I found out why she'd been trying to dislodge her hand from mine.

How easily you forget I need my hands to answer.

Quirking up the side of my mouth, I apologized. "Sorry."

She smiled and my heart leapt inside my chest. *You just wanna show all the other guys that I'm off-limits.* As soon as she lowered her hands she looked away, instantly regretting her response.

Hooking my fingers under her chin, I lifted her head so she would look at me. "Yes, that's partly the reason, but more than that, I love touching you."

Gone were any traces of playfulness. *You can't say things like that to me. I'm really trying to give this friendship thing a chance, but when you look at me like that, and tell me you love touching me, and admit that you're warning other guys to essentially stay away from me, it confuses me. And quite frankly, it hurts.*

I reached for her arm but she quickly walked ahead, spotting her sister and Ryder sitting under one of the tents. Tentatively walking up behind her, I placed my hand on her shoulder and leaned in to whisper in her ear, Braylen glaring at me the entire time.

"I'm sorry. I didn't mean to hurt you. Again." Inhaling her vanilla scented skin, I kissed her temple and rose back up to my full height. "I'm gonna grab some food. I'll surprise you." Trying to make light of a tense situation, I headed over to where Cutter was manning the grill.

Call me the master of mixed signals, but I simply couldn't help it. *I was conflicted, so I had no doubt Kena's warring emotions matched my own.*

"Who the hotties sittin' with Ryder? And what the fuck do they see in that grumpy bastard?" Cutter asked, flipping a couple of the steaks before tending to the dogs and burgers.

Cutter was a strange sort of guy. And by strange, I meant I could never get a good read on him. He mostly kept to himself, often called upon for his skills with disposing of people. I'd heard about it with Vex, and I'd seen it firsthand with Yanez. I wouldn't go as far as calling him creepy, per se, because he only did what was necessary, but I sure as shit wouldn't want to be on the receiving end of his "attention."

His son, Breck, on the other hand, was the complete opposite. They barely shared the same features, let alone a similar personality. I liked Breck just fine, most times. Other times, he was lucky I hadn't knocked him out, his cockiness getting the better of him. Especially when he was three sheets to the wind. Besides, I was a prospect; I couldn't touch a full patched member unless I was defending myself, which thankfully had never been the issue with him. Or any of the other brothers.

Slapping some cheese on two of the burgers, I stood back when Cutter gave me an annoyed look. "The blonde, Braylen, is sort of dating Ryder, and the gorgeous creature next to her is mine." I hadn't meant to claim her so possessively, but I had no doubt a few of these guys would make a play for her if they thought she was single.

Technically she is single, dumbass.

Shaking the absurd yet poignant thought from my head, I reached for one of the hotdogs and got my hand slapped with the spatula. "Fuck, that hurt," I groaned, giving him a death glare, one he returned ten-fold.

"Don't touch the food while I'm cooking, prospect." Raising his bottle of beer, he took a few gulps before placing it down on the side of the grill, its own perfect little holder grooved into the cut of the steel appliance. "I didn't know ya had a woman," he grunted, never once turning to look at me.

"Yeah, although . . . Yeah, it's complicated."

"Complicated? You postin' some fucked-up status on Facebook or somethin'?"

"What the hell do you know about social media, old man?" I laughed, still keeping watch over Kena out of the corner of my eye.

"I know enough. And if I were you, I'd un-complicate that shit. Otherwise, my son is gonna have her on her back before you know it." His words cut right to the heart of me. Sure enough, when I turned fully around to face the three of them—or should I say four of them—I saw Breck sitting across from Kena, laughing at something Ryder said but keeping his eye on my woman. Where the hell had he come from?

"How the hell did you see him? Your nose is in the goddamn grill."

"I don't miss shit," he said, tossing some food on a plate and shoving it toward me. "Here. Now go away."

Swiftly walking toward the table, my adrenaline fueling the anger coursing through me, I stopped right next to Kena and set the plate in front of her. I'd meant to grab some sides and drinks, but no way would I allow Breck any more time in her presence without realizing she wasn't available.

Single or fucking not, Kena was taken.

She was mine.

Placing my hand on her shoulder, I glared at the guy brazen enough to try and grab her attention, staking my claim like some sort of animal. "Here you go, babe," I said, talking to her but keeping my eye on Cutter's son.

"What's up, prospect? Can we help you?" Breck laughed, the lilt of his tone indicating he was well on his way to feelin' good. No doubt he'd started drinking hours before.

"Yeah, you can stop hittin' on my woman," I said with a controlled tone. All I wanted to do was reach across the table and knock him on his ass, but I refrained. Sliding into the seat next to Kena, I threw my arm over her shoulder and pulled her close, scowling at Breck the entire time. I knew my behavior was less than stellar, but I was powerless against the surge of testosterone rapidly flowing through my veins.

"No way this fine piece is yours," he countered, pissing me off even more. Before I could respond, Kena elbowed me in the side, dislodging my arm from around her. Turning toward me, her face scrunched in annoyance. Bringing up her hands, she signed so fast I almost missed a few of the words.

Your woman? Why are you all of a sudden being so possessive? Are you trying to show off or something, because I don't like it.

Trying to figure out an apology, I was caught off guard when Breck opened his mouth.

"Holy fuck! You got you a woman who can't talk?" Slapping the table, he continued his drunken rambling. "You lucky sonofabitch. How awesome is that? You don't have to hear her yapping all the time, naggin' you and shit."

I hopped to my feet and reached over the table, but Ryder had already beat me to him, grabbing Breck in a choke hold and lifting him from his seat so quickly he stumbled backward. He slurred his words while trying to figure out why Ryder had attacked him. And while a few of the other guys turned their attention toward us, none of them approached, realizing that Breck had probably deserved whatever was coming his way.

And he did. Without a doubt. The rule about a prospect not putting his hands on a full patched member unless it was in self-defense? That went right out the fuckin' window as soon as he said what he did about Kena. Surely Marek would have pardoned my actions, had I been the one to teach Breck a lesson.

I'd been so amped up with attacking him I'd failed to see how Kena had been faring from his heartless comments. When I sat back down, I turned my body toward hers but she moved away. It was only by an inch or so, but I hated any distance between us.

I'm so sorry about what he said. I'd decided to sign, hoping it would somehow alleviate whatever embarrassment or anger she'd been feeling right then. She shrugged as if she hadn't been affected, but when a tear danced down her flushed cheek, I knew she was upset. And I didn't blame her. Not one fucking bit. Hastily wiping away a few more tears, she rose from her seat and started walking away from the table.

"Where are you going?" I jogged up next to her and tried to take her hand but she pulled it back, continuing to walk ahead of me. "Kena!" I shouted. "Where are you going?"

She turned around, signed, *To the bathroom*, and continued on her way. I kept my distance but there was no way in hell I was gonna leave her alone, especially when she had no idea where she was going.

CHAPTER FORTY

Kena

EMBARRASSMENT COURSED DOWN MY FACE the further I walked away from the whole scene. I heard Jagger's steps behind me, but I knew if I turned around I'd start sobbing uncontrollably, seeking comfort in the arms of someone who may or may not want me.

Coming across the first building I saw, I turned the handle and entered, the wide open space shocking me with its sheer size. A few couches littered the area, with single leather seating spread throughout. A large bar occupied the entire back wall, an area I was sure got a lot of use. There were a few closed doors, so I walked to the nearest one. My fingers curled around the knob, but before I could turn it, Jagger's hand covered mine.

"Oh no, sweetheart, you can't go in there," he warned, a softness to his voice abating his command not to enter.

Withdrawing from his touch, I asked, *Why? What's in there?*

He opened his mouth to respond, but someone beat him to it. "Chambers. No women or nonmembers allowed inside their sacred meeting room," a beautiful woman mocked, smiling big while her eyes raked over me. She seemed rather friendly, so why did a twinge of jealousy grapple with my good senses?

Placing her hand on Jagger's shoulder, she shoved him out of her way, bringing her hands up in front of her and signing, *Hi. I'm Sully.*

My smile widened because there was someone besides my family—and Jagger, of course—who I could communicate with. She obviously wasn't deaf, or mute, so I wondered how or why she knew sign language. Was she a teacher for the hearing impaired? Or was it because of someone in her family?

I'm Kena. Nice to meet you.

You as well. Jagger has told me a lot about you.

"Yeah, and you're not supposed to use any of it against me," Jagger cautioned, smiling as soon as his eyes connected back with mine.

Continuing to smile at Sully, I hoped she hadn't seen my unease bridled underneath my façade. The day had been trying enough, and it was still early. Whatever was going on between Jagger and me—or *wasn't* going on between us—bothered me. Add that asshole with his comments, and I was ready to go home.

"Sully! Where are you, woman?" a man hollered, striding across the room until he came to stand behind the black-haired female. His tone indicated he'd been frustrated, but as soon as he touched her, he seemed to calm. The man was very attractive, his blue eyes quite entrancing. Unnervingly so. Circling his arms around Sully's waist, he pulled her close and kissed her neck, taking a few extra seconds before he raised his head in our direction. "Who's this?" Apparently he was a right-to-the-point kind of person.

"Kena. Jagger's girlfriend," Sully answered, instantly making me even more uncomfortable. Not so much because I didn't like the title, but I knew for sure Jagger would rebuff the statement, hammering home our odd situation for everyone.

But he never made the correction. Instead, he put his arm over my shoulder, the heat from his hand resting on my skin burning me up. I squirmed, my body suddenly engulfed with a blush I couldn't control, no matter how hard I tried. Ever since I'd met Jagger I'd started to slowly come out of my shell. His attentions for me brought out some of my hidden confidence, but being surrounded by people I didn't know, I started to revert back to my old shy self.

And it only got worse when more people filtered in.

"What do we have here?" Stone shouted as he approached, carrying a baby girl, the sight so precious . . . yet odd. It was strange to see someone like Stone, a tough-looking guy whose skin was covered in more ink than Jagger's, cradling a baby to his chest, making funny faces and noises every few seconds. I assumed the baby was his, but maybe not. Maybe he loved kids so much he snatched one up right from under an unsuspecting woman's nose. "Hi, Kena," he said, before handing the baby to Sully. I watched the interaction, Sully's expression tugging at my heartstrings, even though I didn't know her at all. But it was hard to miss the look of longing clinging to the gaze she fixated on the child.

Another female's voice cut through my thoughts, bringing my attention to someone strolling up to our newly formed group.

"Hey, babe," Stone greeted. "I think Riley needs her diaper changed." He smirked, kissing the blonde woman on the mouth quickly, but passionately.

"So you handed her to Sully?" she admonished, slapping his arm in mock annoyance. "Why didn't you just do it?"

"Because I did the last two. It's your turn."

"I'd be happy to do it," Sully interrupted, shifting the attention back to her. Watching everyone's interaction helped reduce my pang of anxiety—until they turned their attention back on me, of course.

"So . . . this must be Kena," the blonde said, stepping forward and pulling me in for a hug. She'd surprised me, but I appreciated her kindness. "I'm Adelaide. Sorry, I'm a hugger," she chuckled.

"As long as your hugs are directed only toward females, we're all good," Stone griped, the look on his handsome face showing he was riling her up.

"Don't even start," Adelaide grumbled, flipping her hair over her shoulder. Turning her focus solely on me, she asked, "So, Kena, tell me. Why is it that Jagger has kept you hidden until now?" She flicked her eyes toward the guy in question before looking back at me.

I had no idea what Jagger had told his friends and what he'd decided to keep secret, so I shrugged, not knowing how else to respond. Honestly, I'd thought Adelaide had asked a damn good question, one I was curious about myself, even if he'd given me some lame-ass reason.

"Well, she's here now," Sully shouted over her shoulder, walking down a hallway with the baby. My eyes followed her because I wasn't quite sure where else to look.

"Yes, and we're going to take full advantage," Adelaide said, smacking Jagger's arm off my shoulder only to replace it with her own. "Any woman who can get Jagger to settle down is a keeper in my book." Again I blushed, hating how much everyone kept referring to me as his girlfriend. But I wasn't about to correct all of them right then, causing more of an uncomfortable scene than necessary. I'd talk to Jagger later, begging him to tell these people we're just friends, even though the thought killed me. I wanted to be so much more, but apparently he didn't. Or did. What he'd told me conflicted with the way he'd been acting ever since we arrived earlier.

"Don't scare her, Addy," Stone said, coming to my defense and stealing his woman from my side.

"Oh shush," she muttered. "Kena, are you free tomorrow? I have to pick up something I ordered for Jagger's place, and it finally came in. I'd love to hear what you think, seeing as how you probably spend a lot of time there." Her smile was infectious, and for a few moments I allowed myself to live in a world where Jagger and I were together, and this was just one of many conversations I'd had with people who obviously cared for him.

So that's why your apartment looks so nice? She helped you decorate?

"Yes, she's the reason my place looks so good," Jagger confessed, grinning at Adelaide before turning his heart-stopping smile in my direction. All I wanted to do was throw my arms around his neck, pull him close and kiss him silly. But of course I couldn't—or wouldn't, to be more accurate.

"So are you? Free, that is?" Adelaide repeated.

What could it hurt? I nodded.

"Great, I'll get your number from Jagger and I'll text you tomorrow."

Sully re-entered the room right then, heading straight for our little circle.

"All done," she stated, passing the baby to her mother. "Well, I'm starving, so I'm going back out to grab some food." Turning toward me, Sully affectionately touched my upper arm. *It was great to meet you, Kena, and hopefully I'll see more of you. Maybe we can hang out sometime.*

Adelaide and Sully had been so nice; it was a shame I'd probably never get the chance to forge any kind of friendship with them. I feared my visits to the club were not going to be too often, today being a special occasion because of the cookout. But I told her what she wanted to hear.

I'd love that.

Once everyone had disappeared outside, I found the perfect opportunity to tell Jagger I wanted to leave. I'd loved meeting more of his friends—well, most of them—but I was tired, still reeling from all the emotions pinging back and forth inside me.

Can you take me home now?

He looked shocked. "Why? Is it because of what Breck said before? Don't pay any attention to him."

It wasn't just what he'd said. It was everything. My uncertainty about what was going on between Jagger and me, being overwhelmed with the sudden intrusion of his friends, although they were lovely, the heat, my hunger, my sudden headache. The list could go on and on, and all I wanted to do was go home and lie down. Maybe dissect Jagger's behavior toward me today.

I raised my hands to respond when a group of men entered, their laughter and shouting ensuring Jagger and I wouldn't be having any sort of conversation in front of them.

My gaze was still locked on the strangers who'd entered our space when Jagger intertwined his fingers with mine and led me down the same hallway I'd seen Sully walk down before.

He ushered me into a bedroom, closing the door and locking it behind him, the click forcing my heart into my throat. When I dared to look at him, knowing full well something was about to happen, I did my best to stay strong. The pull he had over me was palpable, desire wrapping its arms around me and urging me to fall into his embrace. To allow his mouth to claim me.

"Kena." He said my name on a groan, as if I'd been torturing him simply by being in the vicinity. Moments passed in silence, me stand-ing in the center of the room while he remained by the door. All but a few feet separated us, yet it felt like miles. The way he looked at me confused me. His eyes devoured the very sight of me, promising me endless hours of pleasure, but his body language remained on reserve, fighting the urge to walk to me and do God only knew what. His con-flictions were contagious, and I knew right then I needed to leave.

I didn't think my heart would be able to handle another letdown.

CHAPTER FORTY-ONE

Kena

I WANT TO GO HOME, I repeated. He took a step forward, forcing me to retreat.

"Why are you putting distance between us?"

Because you're being cruel. You're confusing me, saying one thing yet doing another. You've told me we can't be together because it's not safe, yet you take me to meet your entire club.

"I told you it's—"

I cut him off before he continued spewing his pathetic excuse.

Then you get all possessive when your buddy says something to me, although I thank you for putting that ass in his place. But still, you act like I'm yours, when in fact the opposite is true. Either be with me or don't. I can't take the back and forth, the stolen moments between us before you act like we're nothing more than friends again. We both know we're more than that, but I fear it'll be too late when you realize you let me slip through your fingers.

I witnessed his inner struggle. The frown now apparent on his face, the quick breaths to gain some sort of semblance of control, the way his hands fisted and relaxed over and over again. Finally, when I figured he'd made some sort of decision, he stalked toward me and drew me into his arms, slamming his mouth over mine before I could even think to react. To prepare myself for some sort of sexual onslaught.

Our kiss became frantic, holding on to each other as if we'd simply slip away otherwise. There were so many things I wished to say, but there was no way I wanted to pull my hands from his body. Winding my fingers into the strands of his hair, I tugged harshly, my excitement getting the better of me. He moaned, apparently more than a little turned on. The evidence of his excitement pressed against my belly, no mistaking what else he wanted to do with me.

Jagger took a step forward, forcing me back. Much like before . . . minus the space between us. He kept advancing, making me retreat until the edge of the bed stopped me. The gentle yet firm caress of his tongue made all my thoughts jumbled, halting all rationale.

I was lying on my back before I could protest, Jagger's body covering mine completely, his mouth stirring up all sorts of sordid desires. We'd only had sex once, but it was enough to know how amazing he'd felt deep inside me, throwing me into wave after wave of immense pleasure.

I certainly had my reservations, but the way he nipped my lips and swept his tongue through my mouth to taste me excited me. The way his breath mixed with mine as if we were one thrilled me.

Nothing less than exhilarating.

"I need you so much," he growled, trailing his hands down my body, slowly lifting the bottom of my shirt and ghosting his fingers over my heated skin. I squirmed beneath him, trying to dispel the effect he had on me, but it was useless.

I thought he would've moved his hands toward my breasts, giving me more time to consider the idea of stopping him, but instead he popped the button of my shorts, pulled down my zipper and tugged at the waistband of my panties. His fingers disappeared inside, running through my swollen folds all while he continued to ravage my mouth with his dominance. Slipping a finger inside me, I inhaled a sweet breath before biting his lower lip at the shock of the sudden, yet welcome, intrusion.

"Fuck!" he groaned. "You're drenched." Taking his time, he pleasured me, crooking his finger inside me and hitting that perfect spot. Widening my legs, I'd accidentally trapped him, making it so he couldn't move his hand. He chuckled before withdrawing his finger. Switching positions, he knelt at the foot of the bed, gripping my shorts and trying to drag them down my legs. But I stopped him, my hands on his persistent.

"What's the matter?"

I had to let go of him in order to respond, so I only hoped he'd allow me to answer before continuing to try and undress me.

I don't think we should do this.

"Why?"

Because I don't think it's a good idea. Given the circumstances.

"That we're at the clubhouse?" He truly looked confused.

No, not that. Well . . . yes, that. But more because of the fact that we aren't together.

"Yes we are," he stated matter-of-factly, looking at me as if I'd gone crazy.

Maybe I *was* crazy. His back and forth certainly confused the hell out of me so badly I couldn't even think straight. Had I missed something? Had we gotten back together and he hadn't told me? When he hadn't corrected the girlfriend comment from his friends, was that when it happened?

Instead of giving in, I disputed the entire concept, even though it was the last thing I wanted to do. I wanted the words he'd spoken to be the truth, but the little voice inside my head told me to stop hoping for such things.

Jagger, we're not together. You broke it off with me, remember? Then you wanted to be friends. Only friends. Until you deem it safe to bring me back into your world and out in the open. But technically, I'm not yours and you're not mine. Not in the way that counts.

Placing one hand on his chest and the other on mine, directly over our hearts, he said, "This is where it counts."

While the sentiment made me well up with a whole new batch of emotions, I knew he'd never see our situation from my point of view.

I'd planned on some elaborate speech, but all I could come up with was, *It's not enough.*

His face fell and all I wanted to do was comfort him, when in reality I was the one who had been the most affected by his decisions. It seemed that way to me, at least. While I'd witnessed his affection for me every time he looked at me, touched me, kissed me, it was *my* heart breaking every time he averted his eyes. Or withdrew his hands from me. Or broke the intoxicating connection between us by removing his lips from mine.

I'd meant to remain strong, but when Jagger rose from the bed and held his hand out to help me up, a lone tear escaped the corner of my eye. I tried to quickly wipe my sadness away before he saw. But it was too late.

"I'm so sorry, baby," he soothed, pulling me close and wrapping his strong arms around my trembling body. And it was then I allowed Jagger to witness my frailty, sobbing until I was sure I'd released every last tortured heartache. He never said another word the entire time he comforted me, simply stroking my hair and kissing the top of my head every now and again.

After what felt like forever, I managed to calm down. Pulling away from his embrace, I fastened my shorts and flattened my slightly twisted shirt.

Reaching for my hand, he said, "Come on, I'll take you home."

We re-entered the large common area when I saw Braylen and Ryder come in from outside. As soon as she saw me she rushed forward, frowning at what I was sure was my disheveled state.

"Are you okay?" She didn't even give me a chance to respond before she seized my free hand and ripped me away from Jagger, dragging me clear across the room. "What happened? Why were you crying?"

I'm fine. Really. It's just a little too much all at once. Being here with all these people. Dealing with Jagger and our feelings for each other. Not being together but being together. I don't know. I lowered my hands because I knew I wasn't making any damn sense, her drawn features proving as much.

"Men!" she exclaimed, sneaking a peek at Ryder when he wasn't looking. I'd thought for sure she would've pummeled me for information, but luckily she didn't press. "Do you wanna leave? We can veg out at home if you want." While I appreciated the offer, I knew damn well my sister didn't want to leave Ryder yet, so I let her off the hook.

Jagger is taking me home. We were actually on our way out to find you to say good-bye when you came in.

"Are you sure? Because if you don't want to go with him, I'll take you. Just say the word."

Thanks, but I'll be fine.

A swirl of activity erupted, giving Jagger and me the perfect opportunity to escape without too many questions. More so for him than me.

As I lay in bed later that evening, I dreamed of a life where Jagger and I could be together without issue. Praying someday that we'd get back together, forging ahead into what I knew would be a great life together.

Little did I know we'd have to travel through hell first.

CHAPTER FORTY-TWO

Kena

MY PHONE DINGED, SHOVING ME away from the remaining shadows of sleep. Turning my head, I noticed my alarm clock read 10:08 a.m. Stretching my limbs before sitting up in bed, I couldn't believe I'd slept so late. Normally, I was quite the early riser. Although, ever since becoming involved with Jagger, I'd noticed all my old habits flew right out the window. The very thought of our predicament drained me, no doubt pushing my mind, as well as my body, into total exhaustion.

Hence the late hour. Or rather, it was late for me. Braylen, on the other hand, could sleep until noon if I'd let her. Swiping the screen, I saw I had a text message from an unknown number. Curiosity took hold, so I opened it and started reading.

Unknown: Did you still want to get together today?

Poised to type a response and ask who it was, my phone pinged with another message.

Unknown: BTW, this is Adelaide.

Duh! It was then I remembered she'd invited me to go shopping. But was I up for traipsing around town with a woman I'd only just met? Besides, she didn't know how to communicate with me like Sully did, so would our day be spent in silence, nodding and quick smiles filling up the uncomfortable pauses?

As if reading my mind, she'd sent another text.

> *Adelaide: I've sat in on the occasional lesson with Jagger, so I know a small amount of SL. Although I'm sure I'll mess something up, so please be patient with me.*

Some of my nerves melted away. The people Jagger surrounded himself with seemed wonderful. Their support of him shone through, and anyone could see they genuinely cared for him.

I seriously contemplated backing out of the day's trip, but something inside nudged me to forge ahead. To get out of my comfortable little bubble and make new friends. I had a good feeling about Adelaide and knew she and I would get along well, despite the communication barrier.

> *Kena: I'd love to. Just tell me where to meet you.*

> *Adelaide: Nonsense. Zip will be joining us. Only to keep an eye out, per Stone's crazy request. I hope you don't mind.*

Assuming Zip was one of the members of Jagger's club, I should have listened to my instincts when she'd said he'd be joining us, wondering why he'd been asked to tag along. But I didn't.

> *Adelaide: I promise you won't even know he's there. Besides, if he becomes a pain, I'll just threaten him with my uncle. Fill you in on that little trick of mine when I see you. ☺*

Adelaide's ease for the situation soothed me, so I typed my response right away.

> *Kena: Looking forward to it.*

I added her name and number to my contacts and texted her my address, informing her I'd be ready in an hour.

———— ♦ ————

SLIPPING INTO THE BACK OF a red muscle car, Adelaide turned in her seat and smiled at me, the excitement on her face brightening my mood. Any hesitation I'd held slowly evaporated into thin air. The driver, however, stared at me through the rearview mirror, never cracking a grin or saying anything to either of us before pulling out onto the street.

"Don't mind him, Kena. Zip's just grumpy because he was tasked with escorting us." The guy in the driver's seat grumbled incoherently before tightening his grip on the wheel. "Besides, he knows if he doesn't lighten up, I'll tell my uncle he misbehaved." She laughed, but Zip didn't find what she'd said funny.

"You better not sic that ol' man on me," he warned, being sure to keep his tone toward her respectful.

"Ol' man? Wait until I tell him that."

"Shit!" he grunted. "Adelaide, have mercy on me. Please." He looked unsure as to whether he should take her seriously or not.

Ten minutes later, Zip pulled the car into a parking lot, shutting off the engine before turning toward his passenger. "You know the drill. Please don't get me in trouble by ditching me. You know damn well Stone will hand me my ass if you do. Never mind what Trigger will do to me." His expression was serious.

"Fine. But don't hover over us. Deal?" Adelaide reached for her door handle, staring back at Zip and waiting for him to tell her what she wanted to hear.

"Deal," he conceded.

I watched him exit the car, my reaction kept in check when I noticed the gun tucked in the waistband of his pants. The dark black weapon screamed that maybe this wasn't such a good idea. Adelaide caught me staring and assured me, "Don't even give it a second thought, Kena. All the men carry."

All the men? Did Jagger?

As if sensing my inner turmoil, she continued with, "It's just a precaution. Nothing more." Somehow I feared she wasn't being completely honest, but not knowing much about the two of them or their club, I only had her word to go on.

I was still a nervous wreck, but I tried to overshadow my thoughts by listening to Adelaide talk about how excited she was that Jagger asked for her help in decorating his place.

"You should have seen his apartment before I got my hands on it," she cringed. "There was a ratty couch and crappy TV in the living room. That's it. Can you believe it? And his bedroom was even worse, just a mattress on the floor and a single, broken-down dresser. I think the door fronts were falling off too."

I frowned thinking of Jagger living in such a place, but at least that was no longer the case. Thank God.

I'm sure he was stubborn at first, I signed.

"Did you say he was stubborn?"

I nodded, a little surprised she'd understood me.

"I know the sign for that word," she laughed. "Sully used it a lot when she was teaching him." Leading me toward a small, trendy-looking furniture store, Zip jumped ahead of us and held the door open. At least he was a gentleman, although I was sure most of the public didn't view him as such.

When he relaxed, he looked to be a little younger than me. He wasn't overly tall, probably just shy of six feet. His leather cut and baggy jeans did well to hide his thin build, but I was sure he was lethal with that gun of his. Otherwise, I doubted Stone would have asked him to watch over his woman.

Zip's dark hair was slicked back, his green eyes watching every move Adelaide and I made, while remaining at a distance which allowed us to float around the store with ease.

"Don't worry about him," she said when I glanced back at him a few more times.

Are you scared?

I had no idea why I'd asked her such a question, but my hands were gesturing before I could stop them.

"I'm not sure what you just asked me." She looked embarrassed, and I hated we couldn't talk freely. But I was aware this would happen, so I spelled out the last word, hoping she knew the alphabet.

Thankfully, she did.

"Scared? Am I scared? Is that what you're asking me?"

I nodded.

"No," she answered without hesitation. "Zip's temper is enough to scare off anyone if they rile him up. Besides, he's a good shot." She chuckled, but quickly stopped when she saw the uneasy look on my face.

Linking her arm through mine, she led me toward one of the sales associates. "You're safe, Kena. And I know there's something amiss with you and Jagger. No doubt his stubbornness," she said, bumping my shoulder with hers, "is getting in the way. But he'll come around. I've never seen him this over the moon about someone before. It'll work out. Have faith."

Have faith. Easy-enough concept. Or was it?

After Adelaide spoke with the associate, we headed back toward Zip, his nose buried in his phone as we approached.

"You almost done?" he asked.

"Yeah. They'll bring out the lamp, and then we can go." Turning her attention toward me, she asked, "Are you hungry?"

Yes.

My stomach rumbled from the mere mention of food. I hadn't eaten anything before I'd left my house, too nervous.

"I can run through a drive-thru but that's it." Zip's nose was still buried in his phone.

"No," she countered. "I want to go to the diner next door and sit down."

"Can't do it," he pushed back. "Prez wants me back as soon as possible."

"Why?"

"You know I can't tell you that." Zip and Adelaide squared off, staring at each other while I stood off to the side, not knowing what to do with myself.

After a few more tense seconds, she huffed and gave in. "Fine."

"Here you go, miss," a man said, handing Adelaide the most beautiful lamp I'd ever seen. I knew it was only a lighting fixture, but it was gorgeous. The top part was a sphere, etched lines of colors swirling around its entirety. A curved spine connected with the base, dark, thick wood making up the rest of the piece. Jagger made the right move in asking his friend to help decorate his place. She certainly had an eye for design.

We decided to skip the drive-thru, Adelaide offering to whip us up something back at the clubhouse before taking me home. I wasn't sure who would give me a ride, however, seeing as how Zip had been the one driving. But I knew they wouldn't leave me stranded, so I didn't give it another thought.

Adelaide had chosen to sit in the back with me, chatting away about various topics, her daughter most of all. I smiled, nodded and listened intently, thoroughly enjoying our day together.

"I'm going to have Sully teach me sign language just like she did Jagger. I have a feeling you're going to be sticking around for quite a while." Her enthusiasm for my place in Jagger's life tugged at my heart. I had no clue if what she spoke was the truth or not, but I loved the idea.

I continued smiling at her when all of a sudden we were both thrust back into our seats, Zip having picked up considerable speed.

"What the hell?" Adelaide grumbled, clutching the door for support. "Slow the hell down!" she shouted.

"Fuck!" he yelled in response. He grabbed his phone before shouting, "Put your seat belts on. Now!"

Reaching for my restraint, I buckled it into place while having no idea what was going on. Adelaide had done the same, Zip speaking again right after the click of her belt sounded.

"Someone's followin' us. Hold on while I try to lose 'em."

I never had time to look and see who was behind us.

To ask Adelaide a question.

To contemplate whether or not my life was in danger.

To wonder if I'd see Jagger again.

To think anything at all.

Another vehicle slammed into us from behind, sending us careening into the opposite lane. Closing my eyes and holding my breath, all I heard were screeching tires at first. Then it was as if we'd been thrown into the air, the car tumbling down the highway, rolling over and over until we'd finally halted, skidding to a stop with the roof of the car beneath us.

Everything had happened so fast, I barely had the opportunity to dissect our predicament when I heard heavy, booted footsteps running toward us. Mumbled voices shouted to each other.

Had someone come to help?

My head throbbed as soon as I pried my eyes open, my vision blurry when I looked around the inside of the car. Broken glass was everywhere, so I was careful where I placed my hands when trying to support my weight upside down. Turning my head to my left, I saw that Adelaide was awake, taking in the scene just as I was, but the look on her face was more alert than mine. I couldn't see Zip, but I heard him groaning, no doubt hurt from the accident.

It was an accident, wasn't it?

Or did someone purposely run us off the road?

Before I could allow my brain to contemplate whether or not that was true, I heard people just outside the car. Then I heard the driver's side door open, the metal screaming with every pull. At first I thought the men who'd approached were there to help, but the thought was quickly doused when I heard someone say, "Kill him then grab those two."

My heart skidded to a stop when I saw two arms reach inside the car and drag Zip from his seat, flinging him into the road with no regard as to whether or not he'd been hurt. Then I remembered what had just been said.

From my position in the back of the car, I saw Zip roll onto his side and reach behind him. He was going for his gun, but before he pulled it free, a deafening, soul-piercing shot rang out.

His arm fell awkwardly behind him, his lifeless body kicked onto its back, pinning his limb beneath him. A river of blood seeped from his head and coated the concrete. I would've screamed right then if I'd had a voice. Instead I started to cry, my fear of being shot like an animal in the street so overwhelming I could do nothing but release my terror in the form of tears.

"Oh my God! Oh my God!" was all I heard Adelaide cry. She was just as terrified, but neither of us had time to comfort the other with false promises before both of our doors were ripped open, the same ear-piercing sounds of metal being jarred away from the frame of the car.

Two men clad in leather and smelling like alcohol and smoke leaned inside and freed us from our seat belts. Grabbing us underneath our arms, they roughly yanked us from the car. With whatever strength I had, I started to flail about, figuring there had to be other people sur-rounding our accident.

Someone besides these cold-blooded killers.

But I never had the chance to see before I was struck on the head, darkness stealing my hazy sight.

CHAPTER
FORTY-THREE

Jagger

SO MUCH COMMOTION STOLE MY focus. Various screams and shouts blocked my chance to concentrate on any one man or the enraged words they spewed amongst each other.

Having no idea what had happened, I braced myself for the worst, but nothing could have prepared me for what happened next. I had no idea my world was about to be flipped on its goddamn ass. That my heart would be ripped from my chest and sliced into such tiny pieces there was no possible way it'd ever be whole again.

Gathered around the table in Chambers, every man stopped their rantings when a phone rang. I looked around the room, trying to decipher where the noise had originated from. When I glanced toward Marek, I saw the small device in his hand.

A look of rage mixed with fear shadowed his hardened features.

After pressing the Answer button, silence ensued.

Until a harsh voice destroyed the quiet, tearing our world apart.

Our leader had put the cell on speaker, allowing all of us to hear the caller. Which should have been the first thing to alarm me, but I was too focused on trying to figure out why every brother beside me looked like they wanted to kill.

"After all this time, did you really think I'd just let it go? Let you take my daughter without retribution?"

Oh shit! Psych!

I leaned as close as I could, making sure I didn't miss a single word. At least now I had one piece to the puzzle, but I was still confused as to what was going on.

"What do you want?" Marek asked in a slow and dangerous voice. The muscles in his neck strained, and I knew as soon as this call ended he'd let loose and explode for all of us to see. Focusing on Stone next, I saw that he'd mirrored his friend's body language. He was also enraged, but there was something about his expression that unnerved me to my very core. The fear that bound him frightened me, a shiver racing through me at what was going to be revealed in the next few seconds.

"I want Sully. You give her to me and I'll give you back the two bitches we rescued on the highway." He said the word "rescued'" slowly, telling us with the inflection of his tone that he'd done the opposite. Whoever he'd "rescued," he'd kidnapped. No doubt about that.

"And what about Zip?" Marek growled.

What the fuck happened to Zip, and who are the two "bitches" he's referring to? With everything going on, I hadn't even noticed Zip was missing from the room.

"He's dead. My men left him in the middle of the road." Psych spoke so matter-of-fact it was as if he'd been talking about a car that'd broken down on the side of the highway.

Marek slammed his hand down on the table, the thunderous sound vibrating throughout the room. Dread pulsed through my veins, and it was all I could do not to rush from the room to retrieve our fallen brother.

"Mark my words, you soulless fuck. My face will be the last you'll see before I rip your fucking heart from your chest," our leader threatened, pounding the table a few more times for emphasis. Stone leaned back in his chair and ran his hands over his face, terror seizing his expression while waiting for Psych to speak again.

"Mark *my* words, *Marek*," Psych taunted, "I'll fuck your VP's woman until she bleeds. Until she begs for death. Then I'll move on to her little friend. Although I don't think that one can speak, so that'll be a whole lotta fun."

Stone kicked his seat behind him when he suddenly jumped to his feet. "Don't you fucking touch her!" he yelled, whirling around and punching his fist through the wall. The sound jerked me out of my daze. It'd taken my brain a few seconds to catch up to what was going on, my denial surely trying to protect me.

But when Stone's eyes latched onto mine, when he watched as Psych's words slowly registered, I knew this shit was for real. I froze in place, unable to move. The breath in my lungs stilled as I fought back the vomit creeping up my throat.

"GIMME BACK MY DAUGHTER!" Psych roared through the phone, gutting everyone in the room. The hair on the back of my neck stood up, and I knew right then there was a very real possibility I'd never see Kena alive again.

Would Marek give up his wife in exchange for Adelaide and Kena?

Did he even have a choice?

If he didn't comply, he'd ensure their deaths for sure. And while he might not lose too much sleep over Kena's, I was sure he would torture himself over Adelaide's demise.

His best friend's woman.

Trigger's niece.

Before Marek could deny the demand, Stone stole the phone from the table and answered. "When and where?" Three simple words, but when put together, they meant a shift in everything we'd ever known.

Marek jumped from his chair the same time I had. In fact, all of the men were on their feet, realizing something was about to go down right here inside Chambers. Volatile looks and controlled fury threatened to annihilate anyone daring to move the wrong way, or say the wrong thing. And it wasn't just from Marek or Stone. It was from Tripp. And Ryder. And Hawke. And Trigger. And Cutter. And Breck.

And me.

Before one of us went nuclear, a noise erupted from the other end of the line, silencing the rage we'd all felt by replacing the emotion with stifling dread.

Screams.

Haunted screams.

A woman's screams.

Adelaide's screams.

"Don't you fuckin' touch her!" Stone thundered again, punching the wall behind him once more in his haste to expel some of his fury.

"She sure is a looker, Crosswell. I bet her pussy's real nice." Psych's eerie laughter made us all cringe, the idea that he'd violate his captives a very real possibility. If he hadn't done so already.

Thoughts of Kena rushed over me. I tried to keep it together, do my part in whatever needed to happen before allowing myself to feel the mixed bag of emotions threatening my sanity. But the flood of rage, despair and heartache took hold and I feared I'd never be the same again.

"I'll call back with the information. Oh, and boys, don't even think about pulling a fast one. If I get a whiff you're up to something, I'll gut them both like the whores they are."

Psych ended the call, and as soon as the silence creeped in, the entire room exploded into chaos.

CHAPTER FORTY-FOUR

Kena

HUDDLED IN THE CORNER OF a dank, musty room, I clutched my knees to my chest for solace. I had no idea where I was or who had taken us, too terrified of the possibilities of what could happen to properly think straight.

Clutching my hands to my head, I tried to soothe the thunderous pounding between my temples, but nothing I did helped. I'd cried enough over the past few hours to last me a lifetime, so I'd eventually stopped. Whether that was because I'd willed myself to do so or because my body had finally depleted the emotion, I couldn't say.

The door creaked open and someone stepped inside. But I couldn't look. If I saw who it was, then this was all too real. I buried my head deeper into my hands, my elbows coming together while my fingers touched at the base of my spine. But no matter how much I shielded my sight, my ears continued to prick at every noise.

"Get up," the rough voice demanded, stepping closer when I didn't budge. A strong grip wrapped around my wrist, hauling me to my feet. He started to walk toward the door, and something told me to fight. I had no idea where he intended to take me but I knew it wasn't somewhere safe. All I had was my struggle, so I allowed it to pour from me in waves.

I jerked my arm back the best I could, but it was ineffectual. The large man standing in front of me looked pissed off. And scary. His face was shadowed with a heavy beard, his dark hair cropped close to his head. If I hadn't known any better, I would've thought he had been in the military at some point in his life, the haircut very similar to those of Marines. But I knew from one look into his dark eyes that he had done no such thing. There was nothing honorable about him.

He yanked me forward. "No use resisting. Prez wants a test drive." No remorse. No concern or amusement in his tone. Dead. He was empty inside, alarming me even more than I had been before. "Says the other one is too much trouble."

My thoughts flew to Adelaide. I hadn't seen her since the accident—or rather, the intentional car crash. When I came to, she was gone. I'd thought I'd heard her screams, but tried to convince myself I'd been hallucinating. My denial served as self-preservation, but right now this man was shattering it to pieces.

Again I tried to resist, but that time it only served to anger him, delivering a backhand so harsh my head whipped to the side and I stumbled backward. I hadn't fallen, though, his hold on my arm too fierce to allow a slap to break the connection.

I whimpered.

I cried.

But of course he heard none of it.

"Tough little cunt, aren't ya?" he laughed, pulling me out of the room and down a narrow hallway. "Maybe when Psych's done wit' ya, he'll let me go a round. I like a bitch who resists."

I may have been inexperienced before Jagger, but I was smart enough to know exactly what he'd been referring to. I steeled my reserve the best I could, covering my cheek with my free hand to help stop the blossoming ache. I'd never been struck before, the radiating pain becoming worse and worse with each step I was forced to take. Licking my lip, I tasted blood. But at least the pain served as a distraction, blocking me from thinking about what was going to happen next.

We stopped outside a steel door. I tried to free myself from his grasp again, but to no avail. He knocked three times before the door swung open, an intimidating man appearing on the other side. As soon as he looked past my captor, he grinned, raking his eyes over me from head to toe. I cursed my earlier decision to wear a dress that day, wishing I'd thrown on some jeans instead. But how was I to know the car I'd be in would be run off the road, the driver would be killed and I'd be one of two people kidnapped?

Oh my God! Guilt tore at me that I hadn't thought of him before now.

Zip.

I can't believe they killed him.

Right in front of us.

I didn't know the guy, that was true enough, but he seemed to be friendly with Adelaide. Plus, he was a member of the Knights Corruption, and therefore someone of importance to Jagger, as well as the other men of the club.

Jagger. Oh my God! Did he even know we'd been taken?

Had our kidnappers made contact?

Was it even about the club?

Or were we going to be sold into slavery? I'd seen my share of documentaries before. Sexual slavery happened all over the world, even in America. The thought I'd be sold to strangers for nothing more than pleasure heightened my terror.

"Bring her in," a gruff voice called out. Passing by the man who'd answered the door, I was thrust toward another standing in the middle of the room. The guy in charge, I assumed. He was older, probably somewhere in his late forties. Maybe even early fifties. Haggard lines had stolen the remnants of whatever youth he'd had, the signs of a hard life certainly lived. His dark, shoulder-length hair greyed at the temples, the strands shaggy and unkempt. He licked his thin lips while assessing my body, inhaling the air around me as he advanced closer.

"You smell nice," he said, his compliment certainly a lecherous one. I averted my eyes, quickly taking in the room. I noticed a worn, stained mattress in the corner, an unconscious Adelaide lying across it. Her hair was matted with blood, either from the accident or from whatever she'd endured at the hands of these men. Only one side of her face was visible. And from what I could see, they'd beaten her. But had they done something worse? The man who'd brought me here indicated they hadn't, but I didn't know if that was the truth or not. I prayed it was.

"Can you hear me?" he asked, reaching out to touch my breast like he had every right to violate me. I shouldn't have done it, but I couldn't stop my body's reaction, slapping him across the face the second his hand fell away.

The man behind me grabbed my hair and yanked me back, slamming me into his hard chest. "You're gonna pay for that," he seethed, shoving me toward the man I'd just assaulted.

The older man tilted his head, running his fingers over his cheek, a redness starting to appear from where I'd struck him. He grinned, as if he'd found what I'd done amusing. "Now, let's try this again," he sneered. "My men tell me you haven't uttered a sound since they found you." My eyes must have bulged out of my head. Found me? What a warped sense of reality he possessed. "Can you hear me?" he repeated through clenched teeth.

I nodded.

"Good. Then you'll understand when I tell you that you and that bitch over there are being traded for my daughter. But that doesn't mean I can't have some fun with you until then."

Vigorously shaking my head, I raised my hands in front of me even though I knew he'd never understand me.

Jagger will kill you if you touch me.

"Put your hands down," he growled. "I don't understand retard, so save it." His insult shouldn't have hurt, not in the least considering what type of man he was, but it did. Turning his attention to the man behind me, and the other standing near the door, he waved them off with a flick of his wrist. "You can leave us now. Make sure to keep an eye out. Just in case the Knights try some slick shit. For all I know, these two have trackers on them."

"You got it, Prez." The clank of the closing door made me jump, my fright amusing this horrid man I was now alone with. Well, technically Adelaide was also there, but the poor woman was still unconscious. I pushed the thought away that she could be dead. He'd just said we were being traded for his daughter, so would he be stupid enough to kill one of us? And who was his daughter?

"Do you have a tracker on you?" I shook my head, but he stalked toward me anyway. "I don't think I believe you," he taunted. "Looks like I'm gonna have to check for myself." A few more steps and he'd backed me against the wall. Trapped. Nowhere to go. I was at his mercy and we both knew it.

I tried to make a run for the door, but he caught me mid-stride, wrapping his hand around my throat and squeezing. I clawed at his hold but it was useless. "Nice try, but you're not goin' anywhere until I say so. But I can let you in on a little secret." He licked the side of my face, his rancid breath making me instantly sick. "No one is gettin' out of here alive except me and my men. When your precious little boyfriend comes for you, along with his buddies, we're gonna slaughter them all."

Surprised he was able to read my mind so well, or rather the look on my face, he spoke again, his rough voice no doubt the product of too many years of smoking. "Yeah, I know who you are, sweetheart. You're the fighter's woman. Since I couldn't snatch back my daughter, I grabbed the next best thing. Stone's woman. You just happened to be with her. Two cunts for the price of one," he laughed, the evil sound strangling the hope out of me.

Snaking his free hand down my body, he hoisted the hem of my dress, trailing his fingers up my inner leg until he reached the apex of my thighs. I tried to squirm away from his touch, but he only tightened his grip on my throat. Moving my panties to the side, he shoved a finger inside me. I winced, the burn of his intrusion rocketing through me. I closed my eyes to block him from sight, needing the shield of darkness to help my brain flit off to somewhere else. But it was useless.

"Nope, no tracker up there. How about your sweet little ass?" My eyes flew open when his hand trailed toward my backside. Before he could enter me there, his attention was drawn to the other side of the room.

"Leave her a . . . lone, you bas . . . tard," Adelaide croaked out, her voice raw and throaty.

"Well, well. Look who decided to join the party." He released his hand from around my throat and propelled me toward Adelaide. "Go join your friend while we wait."

I thought for sure he was going to do something to one or the both of us while we waited for the men to show up, but he didn't. He walked from the room and left us to ponder our future.

Or lack thereof.

CHAPTER
FORTY-FIVE

Jagger

"THERE'S NO WAY IN HELL I'm letting Sully go!" Marek shouted, pacing back and forth like a caged animal. His head whipped up every few seconds to look at his VP. His best friend.

"So you're gonna let Addy and Kena die? Is that it?" Stone yelled back, doing a bit of his own pacing.

I was torn. I wanted to shout at Marek to listen to Stone and allow Sully to be traded for the lives of our women, but then I didn't want Sully to come to any harm either. I could only imagine the torture he grappled with; I had no idea what I'd do if I were in his shoes. My initial answer would be the same, but would I eventually come around and devise a plan that would enable me to save my woman, along with the other two?

My thoughts turned to Kena, my heart breaking at the thought they were touching her. Hurting her. I knew I should have never brought her into my life, but I'd been a selfish prick, wanting her up close and personal. Then shit went down with Edana, and it was enough to wake me up. But it'd been too late. I wondered if I hadn't allowed her to go with Adelaide, if she would be at home safe and sound right now.

But she never would've allowed me to get away with forbidding her from accompanying Adelaide, nor would Stone's woman tolerate such pigheadedness from me.

I should've left Kena alone after coming to her rescue the first night I met her. My decisions would forever haunt me, but now was not the time to focus on such things. I had to do my part in the planning of what we were going to do next.

"I don't know what to do, Stone, but I sure as fuck am not handing my wife over to her father. He'll kill her and you know it."

"Well, he'll kill Addy and Kena if you don't," Stone countered, his face red with bridled rage.

"Fuck!" Marek roared, throwing his chair against the wall, his predicament weighing on all of us. The rest of the men sat in silence, waiting for orders. We were all ready and willing to act at a moment's notice.

A soft knock rapped against the large wooden door, our heads whirling toward the sound. Since I was closest, I rose from my seat and turned the handle. Sully stood in the doorway, her eyes red and puffy, indicating she'd been crying. I hadn't even realized she was there. When I'd been called in, I knew it was an emergency but I had no idea what had happened. I'd later come to find out Zip had managed to call Hawke, allowing him to hear everything that had transpired after he'd been dragged from his car. Marek must have brought his wife to the only place he knew was safe. The gates were locked and armed, so there was no fear of someone sneaking in while we were held up in Chambers.

Marek attempted to block Sully from entering but she shoved past him. No women were allowed in here, but no one said a damn word, realizing the circumstances warranted a bit of leeway.

"Baby," Marek soothed, "what do you need?"

"You need to take me to him, Cole," she said, preparing herself for one hell of an argument.

He looked shocked that she not only knew what we'd been discussing, but that she'd offer to go back to her father. The man who'd raped and beaten her throughout her life. The man who'd passed her off to Vex and who'd so freely given her to Yanez.

"Never," he growled. "I'll never let him get his hands on you ever again." When he saw the look on his wife's face, he pleaded with her instead. "Don't ask me to do that, Sully. I can't. Please," he practically begged, a trait none of us were used to.

"He won't kill me." For her to even speak those words about her own kin made my blood run cold. It spoke to the true evil of her father. Shit, he was worse than my old man, which was saying a lot.

"He will and you know it. Maybe not right away, but he'll end your life as surely as you stand before me." He shook his head. "No, forget it. It's not happening."

"Then I'll leave you," she warned, standing tall with her head held high. She never took her eyes from her husband, challenging him to comply before things got out of hand.

"What?" he asked, astonished she'd threatened such a thing. Grabbing her before she could retreat, he pulled her close, his face mere inches from hers. "What the fuck did you just say?"

Sully never flinched. "I'll leave you if you don't let me go. I'm the key to saving both of them, and I can't sit by and do nothing. If my father wants me, then make the trade. He won't do anything. I promise. He'd rather keep me alive and torment me than end my life. Besides, I can endure him again until you come for me, because I now know what love is." She placed her hands on either side of his face and kissed him gently. "You've saved me, in every way possible, and it's you I'll think of when things get tough. But I'll survive. I promise. Just come for me soon, okay?" She smiled, but it quickly faded.

"I can't do it," he repeated, resting his forehead against hers. At some point, Stone had approached his friend from behind. He placed his hand on Marek's shoulder, but his touch was quickly dislodged. "Don't fuckin' touch me," he barked, never breaking away from his wife.

"Don't be mad at him, Cole. Wouldn't you ask the same of him if the roles were reversed?" Marek never responded, but we all knew his answer would've been yes.

"So either way I lose you."

"But if you trade me, you'll get me back. The time frame just depends on you."

"Fine," he conceded before releasing her. "But you're coming back with us right along with Adelaide and Kena." Grasping his wife's hands, he pulled her toward his seat at the head of the table. "Now we wait for him to call back with instructions."

———— ◦ ————

AN HOUR LATER WE TRAVELED north toward Modesto. The place we were to make the exchange was an old abandoned warehouse, a building so dilapidated I was shocked it hadn't been torn down yet. What Psych hadn't realized was that I knew the place well. I'd fought there quite a few times, finding hidden back entryways into the building for the sole purpose of avoiding all the hoopla that went along with the fights. All I wanted to do when I battled was get in, win, collect my money and get the hell out.

No doubt Psych would have half his fucking club waiting to ambush us, but we had a plan of our own. Stone and I sat in the front of his truck, Marek and Sully huddled in the back, capturing their last fleeting moments before she was handed over.

Marek had placed a call to Salzar, the head of our Laredo chapter, as soon as he'd heard about the kidnapping. And again when Psych had given him the directions to the warehouse. So we had men hiding out everywhere, waiting for orders to attack. Some were hidden around the warehouse we were headed, some were back manning our compound, and others had been dispatched to hide out near the Reapers' compound and wait for instructions.

Stone turned down an unpaved path, the warehouse about half a mile down the road. My heart sped up, fear and adrenaline fueling the erratic thumping. What if something went wrong and Psych killed Adelaide and Kena anyway? Were they even still alive? Stone had asked to speak to his woman when the Reapers' president called back a second time, to which he heard Adelaide screaming, but that was a while ago. A lot could have transpired since then.

As we approached the building, the garage started to open, two men standing guard just inside and guiding us through. Both Reapers were armed, their weaponry strapped across their chest, probably not the only ones they had on their bodies. Coming to a stop a few feet after entering, our doors were yanked open and three additional men appeared, extracting us from the vehicle and shoving us forward, but only after patting us down and stealing our weapons. The entire way, Marek had his arms wrapped tightly around Sully, protecting her as best he could with Psych's men crowding them.

We were ushered through a narrow hallway, down two flights of steps and around a few corners. It would've been easy to get lost, which was probably why Psych chose that place in particular. It was enormous, and anyone inside was like a rat in a maze. Unless you knew your way around, of course. Which I did.

Eventually, we came to a stop, one of the men knocking three times on a large steel door. It opened right away and none other than the president of the Savage Reapers stood before us, grinning like he was privy to the biggest fucking secret.

Little did he know *we* were the ones who held the secret.

"Come in," he said, stepping back and allowing us to enter. The room was huge, but my eyes instantly found Kena. She was crouching in the far corner, hovering over Adelaide's body, when she saw us. The look on her face gutted me, and I'd never forgive myself for putting her in danger. Stone had seen them at the same time I had. Both of us moved to rush forward but we were shoved back, guns pointed directly at our heads. "Don't fucking move until I tell you to," Psych warned.

"Adelaide!" Stone shouted. "Is she okay?" His voice became frenzied when he couldn't get to her. Sully buried herself in Marek's embrace the entire time, clutching on to him knowing she would have to stand next to her father soon enough.

She's unconscious, Kena signed.

"What did she say?"

"She said she's unconscious," I translated.

Turning his fury toward Psych, Stone shouted, "What the fuck did you do to her?"

"Your woman has a mouth on her." That's all he said, but we were smart enough to fill in the blanks. The gun pointed at Stone's head wouldn't have stopped him from attacking Psych, but the fear Adelaide would be killed in the struggle somehow was the only thing that stopped him from crushing the Reapers' leader. I knew because it was the only reason I hadn't rushed him either.

Leering at his daughter, Psych motioned her closer. "Come here, Sully." She withdrew from Marek and stood straight. After a single step, her husband stopped her.

"Not until you release them."

"Well," Psych huffed, then turned to Stone. "Seeing as how your bitch is out cold, how do you think that's gonna happen?"

"Then let Kena come over," I interjected, desperately needing to touch her. Protect her.

I'm not leaving her, Jagger.

"This isn't up for debate," I responded, pissed she was putting herself in more danger by not listening to me.

She shook her head, refusing to budge.

"Kena!" I shouted, taking a single step forward only to be shoved back once more, the same gun now pressing into my forehead. Kena's hands flew to her mouth, but she finally listened and rose to her feet. When she tucked her hair behind her ear in nervousness, I saw the side of her face was swollen, her lip cut and bleeding.

"Come now," Psych demanded, his patience nonexistent the longer his daughter kept him waiting. Marek leaned in close and whispered in Sully's ear before reluctantly releasing her. Both women walked at the same speed, Kena coming to stand next to me as Sully reached her father.

While I welcomed Kena into my arms, careful not to explode and kill every motherfucker present because someone had hurt her, Psych's reaction to his daughter was the exact opposite.

"You know you'll be punished for consorting with them, don't you? You married the president, for fuck's sake," he said, his anger on a slow simmer. "You disgust me."

Sully never said a word, waiting to see what he would do next.

We all were.

Then it happened so fast, none of us saw it coming. Psych clenched his fist, raised his hand and punched his daughter, the slam to the side of her face sending her crashing to the floor. Her hand flew to her cheek to hide the damage as she crawled toward the wall. Unfortunately, I knew some of the abuses Sully had suffered at the hands of her father, and this wasn't the first time he'd struck her. She knew what she was agreeing to when she'd insisted Marek trade her for the lives of the two other women. Observing her abuse firsthand, however, was entirely different than hearing about it, and if I ever got the opportunity to repay him for what he'd just made me witness, I would. And I'd take every bit of pleasure I could squeeze from it.

"You're gonna pay for that!" Marek roared, quite possibly shedding the last of his sanity right before our eyes.

"Don't," Sully squeaked, raising her hand to warn Marek not to retaliate.

"Yeah, don't," Psych mocked, the evil smirk on his face making me wish I could kill him where he stood. But all in due time. "You know I never intended to let you leave, right? Any of you. Our clubs' war will end tonight, retribution for everything you've done to us, mainly cutting off our supply with Los Zappas. That one really hurt," he said, scratching the top of his head as a deranged look took hold.

His men flanked us, promises of our ultimate demise drifting in the air. Before anyone made good on any threats, though, gunfire was heard faintly in the distance, pulling us all back into the severity of the situation. Not that we hadn't resided there to begin with. Swinging his eyes toward Marek, our prez shocked the fucker when he announced, "And you know you're not walking out of here either, right?"

Psych laughed.

He actually laughed, making me believe he'd truly earned his road name. He was definitely psychotic, teetering on the line between reality and madness.

"I knew you'd bring all your men with you," Psych said. "That's why I sent my men to your compound. So even if you made it outta here alive, you'll have nothing to go back to." The leader of the Reapers grinned, thinking he'd bested us. Yet again. When would he ever learn?

"Seems as if we anticipated each other's moves."

Psych's brows knit tightly together.

"What does that mean?" he asked, glaring at Marek with intent to do him harm very soon.

"It means your compound is already in ruins. So, if by the grace of God, *you* somehow get outta here alive, you'll have to run and hide because you'll have nothing to return to. No shelter."

Both men locked eyes, their fierce intentions battling the other for dominance. Little did Psych know we would be the victorious ones. We'd always win when it came to them. They may have bested us here and there, attacking our brothers and now our women, but in the end it would be their club that would perish into dust. Not ours.

From the look on Psych's face, the time for talking was over. The gunfire we'd heard in the distance had breached the warehouse's walls. There were men yelling, their words still muffled enough we couldn't make out what they were saying, but we all heard the urgency in their tones.

Someone pounded repeatedly on the other side of the door. I wasn't sure if they wanted to get inside, or wanted someone on our side to come out. It could've been one of our men, or one of Psych's. Either way, we weren't to open that door until the situation had been handled.

By handled, I meant the men holding us hostage no longer had breath in their lungs, and Psych was shackled, ready to be transported back with us.

The plan was to keep him alive long enough for Marek to make him pay for everything he'd ever done to us, but more importantly everything he'd ever done to Sully. The latter taking precedence.

My eyes stayed glued to Psych. All it would take would be a nod, or a wink, or a flick of his wrist to tell his men to pull their triggers.

All of us remained stock still.

We had a plan.

All we had to do was wait to make our move.

CHAPTER
FORTY-SIX

Kena

MY EYES FLITTED FROM ADELAIDE'S unconscious form, to Jagger, who continued to stand close to me, to the man who'd orchestrated our kidnapping. I briefly glanced at Stone, Marek and Sully as well, struggling with the belief that she was related to that madman.

It wasn't until I was taken that I fully realized Jagger's hesitation to be with me. I had no idea. How could I? My world before him had been all butterflies and roses compared to the way he lived. While I believed the men of his club to be good people, they'd obviously been involved in things which put their lives and their families' lives in jeopardy. I felt horrible for giving him such a hard time about us, never in a million years seeing things from his perspective. But again, I didn't know any of this danger existed, another facet he'd tried to protect me from.

Jagger's hand brushed against mine, pulling me back from my drifting thoughts. My eyes connected with his and I saw his warning. It was quick and subtle, but because I'd grown up honing my ability to read people's body language, I instantly knew he was telling me to get down with a simple flick of his eyes toward the ground.

One moment there was an unsettling silence inside the room, all of us waiting to see what would transpire in the seconds ahead.

And the next there was complete anarchy.

"Now, Sully!" Marek shouted. At the same time his voice rang out, Jagger shoved me toward the corner before swiftly ducking away from the gun pointed at his head. He swept his leg out and the man standing closest to him lost his footing, his arms flailing, dropping his gun in the process. The weapon skidded across the floor and stopped in front of me, but instead of picking it up, I kicked it back toward Jagger. Thankfully he'd been able to retrieve it before one of the other men saw the exchange. Marek and Stone had been able to disarm their men as well, their opponents no match against their fighting skills.

When I looked toward the opposite side of the room, I saw Psych on the ground, clutching his upper thigh. From my position, I couldn't see anything other than he was still alive and looked to be in tremendous pain.

My eyes darted back toward Jagger, watching him stand over the man he'd disarmed. Without looking at me, he said, "Kena, look away. Now!" The urgency in his tone was enough to make me shut my eyes and bury my head in my hands.

A gunshot rang out, the thunderous sound making me jump. Two more shots sounded, and I knew all three previously armed men were dead.

"Are you okay?" Jagger asked, crouching next to me and pulling my hands from my face. "Look at me, baby. It's okay." When I finally pried my eyes open, I saw blood spattered on his face, hands and clothes, the result of shooting someone at close range. But fear didn't shake me; gratitude that he'd survived did. Tears poured from my eyes as I swung my arms around his neck and pulled him impossibly close.

Jagger helped me find my footing, kissing me as he removed my hands from around him. "I'll be right back." I nodded my understanding before he walked toward Marek and Sully.

Stone had run to Adelaide as soon as the threat had been eradicated, bending down to gather her in his arms. Stopping next to his brothers, he'd demanded they leave immediately because he was worried about her still-unconscious state.

Marek turned toward Jagger. "Can you get them outta here?"

"Yes," he simply answered.

"I'm not going anywhere without you," Sully cried, throwing herself into her husband's arms. "I can't . . . I won't survive if something happens to you."

"Nothin' will happen to me," he reassured, lifting her chin so he could look into her eyes. The love between them was palpable, and I felt like an intruder watching their interaction, but I couldn't look away. With everything that had just happened, I clung to the love they shared, allowing it to fuel my strength to survive. To get out of here alive and forge ahead with Jagger once more. If he'd have me. What happened may have solidified his need to stay away from me, but I simply wouldn't know until after we got ourselves away from this place.

Clasping my hand, a gun in his other, Jagger pulled me toward everyone else. "Follow close behind me. I'll take you the back way." Looking toward Marek, he said, "Once I get them out of here, I'll call Salzar. He should be close by." No one said another word as Jagger cautiously opened the door, peering into the hallway to see if it was safe for us to leave.

We followed him down multiple winding passages, stopping every hundred feet or so and waiting for the threat of armed men to pass. Luckily the lighting inside the building was dim, some areas left in complete darkness. After hiding out in one of the numerous rooms, Jagger deemed it safe to continue on. Finally, after walking up two flights of stairs and down a few more narrow hallways, Jagger led us into an area which looked like a dead end.

"Are you sure you know where you're going?" Stone whisper-shouted from behind me.

"Yeah. The back exit is just up ahead."

Sure enough, after a few more feet we came upon an old run-down-looking exit. Jagger withdrew his hand from mine and passed me the gun while he pried the weather-beaten door open, the squeak of the metal hinges sounding much louder in the quiet space.

"Hurry up, man," Stone grunted, shifting Adelaide's weight in his arms.

Flinging the door the rest of the way open, Jagger walked ahead of us. "Hold on a sec. I wanna make sure no one is waiting to ambush us outside." He disappeared and my heart leapt inside my chest. Fear of the unknown fueled the tremor of my hands. I could barely catch my breath when Jagger popped his head back in, giving me a half smile before reaching for my hand once again. "Come on. All clear."

Sully walked close behind me, followed by Stone carrying Adelaide. We trudged through an open field for what felt like miles, but it probably only seemed so long because I was utterly exhausted. Mentally as well as physically.

Jagger shoved his gun into his waistband, reached around me and held out his free hand to Sully. She clasped on to him without hesitation. I suspected she and Jagger were close, and I couldn't have been happier he was looking out for her. Witnessing the brief encounter between her and her father told me she'd endured horrible abuse at his hands. I saw the fear in her eyes when she'd stood next to him, the complacent acceptance when he'd hit her, as if she were not only expecting his backlash, but was used to it.

We eventually came across a clearing, jogging the rest of the way, conscious of Stone having to carry Adelaide. Otherwise we would've run as fast as we could just to put that much more distance between us and the place where we could've spent our last moments.

My ears pricked when I heard a whistle off in the distance. I squeezed Jagger's hand. "Don't worry. That's for us." And sure enough, just a few more yards ahead, there was a large SUV waiting, men jumping out and surrounding us. I didn't recognize anyone besides the guy who'd insulted me at the cookout, and Ryder.

Filing into the vehicle, Sully and I huddled close together while Stone continued to cradle Adelaide in his arms, the worried look on his face increasing the longer it took her to wake. She'd flitted in and out of awareness the entire time she and I were held captive in that room. My only guess was that they must have hit her in the head at some point.

"Gimme a phone," Jagger demanded, holding his hand out to Ryder. Walking in front of the truck, he blocked out some of the illumination from the headlights. Returning moments later, he came around my side and leaned in, clasping my hand. "Kena," he started, the tense flick of his jaw preparing me for what he had to say. "Wait for me back at the clubhouse. You'll be safe there."

Instantly I tried to snatch back my hand. I vigorously shook my head, trying yet again to tug my hand from his. But he wouldn't let go.

"Go. I promise I'll meet you there. I have to help Marek." He released me. Bringing his fist to his chest, he rubbed it in a circle. *I'm sorry.* Then he did something completely unexpected. Unclenching his fisted hand, he held up his thumb, index finger and pinky, the two remaining fingers bent forward.

I love you.

I sobbed, clutching the area over my heart to help ease my despair. It didn't work. Sully comforted me the entire way back, offering as much support as she could. Her husband had also chosen to remain behind, and I couldn't help but wonder if either of us would see the men we loved alive again.

EPILOGUE

Jagger

LEANING BACK IN MY CHAIR, my hands folded on top of the table, I wanted to be engaged in the conversation but I was too distracted. Looking around Chambers, my eyes stilled on the vacant seat diagonal from me.

Zip's chair.

He was a good guy. Occasionally a little hot under the collar, but his anger was often fueled by his need to make the Reapers pay whenever they'd crossed us. Zip was loyal to the club one hundred percent. And he would be missed.

Hawke and Tripp had gone to the site of the accident, but they never found Zip's body. After calling every hospital in a fifty-mile radius, we learned he'd been picked up by paramedics who'd arrived at the scene shortly after Psych's men had snatched the women.

Marek had been the one to claim his body, seeing as we were his only family. And since he spent most of his time at the clubhouse, it was only fitting he be buried behind it. The Knights owned close to ten acres surrounding our compound, so we designated the perfect spot for his grave, a shady area under an old, strong oak tree. We gathered to pay homage and said our good-byes four days after his death, drinking to the lost soldier of our group well into the early morning hours.

Before we'd walked into that warehouse, we had devised the plan that Sully would smuggle in a knife. We knew she'd be checked for weapons, just like the rest of us, but we'd prayed they'd overlook the one hidden in her boot. They had. Luckily. She knew to wait for the signal before striking, to plunge the blade deep in his leg and twist so the wound refused to close. We didn't want her to kill him, just temporarily put him out of commission. Thankfully, she'd succeeded.

For as evil and corrupt as Psych was, he wasn't very smart; he'd only had a few men in the room to protect him. The absence of his own weapon continued to baffle me. The only thing I could chalk it up to was arrogance. Which had been his downfall. Sure, he probably figured since his men had disarmed us, he had the upper hand, but he should've known better.

After calling Salzar and giving him detailed directions as to where he could find us inside, I headed back toward the room we'd escaped from. I wasn't shocked to find Marek standing over Psych's bloodied body, his knuckles raw from beatin' the hell out of Sully's father. Seeing the look of gratitude on Marek's face when he saw me return was all the thanks I needed.

"Stone will let you know whose shift is up next," Marek said, smirking at his VP. The tension between the two men had finally dissolved. They threw themselves back into the daily running of the club, focusing more on their immediate plans for Psych, who just so happened to be shackled in the basement of the safe house. For the past two weeks.

Our prisoner of war, I supposed.

The men took turns checking in on him to make sure he was as destitute as possible. We fed him the bare minimum, only giving him the amount of water needed for survival until Marek decided to finally end his wretched life. I knew he was cooking up something good, and Psych's death was definitely something I wanted a hand in. Not only had he hurt Sully her entire life and injured Adelaide, who thankfully was recovering nicely, but he'd had the audacity to touch Kena as well.

She'd told me what he'd done to her. He'd violated her, and for that alone he needed to pay dearly.

Every day Kena's face looked better and better, the bruises fading to a light yellowish color. She wore her hair down a lot, trying to shield the damage from me because she knew how angry I became seeing evidence of what I'd essentially allowed to happen. Even though she argued, telling me it wasn't my fault.

I didn't believe her, though. Most times I would concede because I wanted to move on and not focus on the guilt that ate at me on a daily basis. I'd talked in length with Stone about what I'd been going through, and he asked me one simple question: Did I love her? I told him the truth. I did. I had no idea how I'd lived on this earth without her by my side all these years, but I thanked fate for bringing us together.

I vowed to never leave her side again. Something she seemed more than pleased about, except of course when I'd become overprotective about her going places alone. But because of what had happened, she hadn't argued too much, realizing her safety was my number one priority.

We spent a lot of time joined at the hip, the guys in the club referring to me as pussy-whipped, but I didn't care. I welcomed their jabs because it meant Kena was really mine. Hell, we'd already started talking about moving in together someday in the near future.

Lost to thoughts of my woman, I missed most of what the men had been discussing. Until Marek shouted my name. "Prospect! Are you fuckin' listenin'?" he yelled, glaring at me.

I knew he'd been under a tremendous amount of stress dealing with Psych. Then add to that he worried about Rabid, the Reapers' VP. Our prez wanted to make sure the man stayed hidden. He'd never been an issue before, seeing as how the man had no backbone, but things sometimes changed when a leader was dethroned, so to speak. People sometimes rose up and wanted to assume power, even though the Savage Reapers had no sustainable source of income to speak of. Once the cartel cut them off, they'd been slowly drowning, selling subpar product they'd either stolen or bought off one of the local gangs, the drugs utter shit. And their customers knew it.

"Prospect!" Marek yelled again. Shit, I was two for two. I really needed to pay attention.

"Sorry," I said, waiting for him to speak again.

"Come here," he demanded. When I finally stopped in front of him, I glanced around the room, but none of the other men gave me a clue as to what was going on, their faces expressionless. "Gimme your cut," Marek said, grabbing my vest as soon as it slid past my shoulders. "Ever since you came to this club, you've done as asked, no matter how degrading or dangerous the request." Stone handed Marek a knife. I glanced down at my cut lying on top of the table, the prospect patch being pried away from the leather. Every stitch being ripped apart.

"Over these past few months, you've really proven your loyalty. First with helping to dispose of Yanez, then with being the reason we all made it out of that warehouse alive. So I think it's time," he said, pulling something from the inside pocket of his vest, "that you become a permanent member." On his last word, he handed me back my cut along with a full member patch.

Two words sewn onto a thick piece of material.

Knights Corruption.

No more prospecting.

"If your woman can't stitch it on, I'll have Sully do it," he offered. I stared at the patch for what felt like forever, my eyes becoming glassy, but I knew they'd never let me live it down if I allowed my emotions to escape. So I tipped my head back, allowing the water building in my eyes to recede.

When I finally looked at Marek, he was smiling.

Full-blown.

At me.

The gesture alone almost made me gasp in shock. But I returned the sentiment, beyond thrilled that I'd finally been accepted as an equal to all the brothers in the club.

———•———

Kena

WAITING OUTSIDE THEIR MEETING ROOM killed me, but I was so excited for Jagger. Braylen had grabbed me as soon as I came out of the bathroom, shouting for me to get dressed, that we had to get to the clubhouse as soon as possible. At first, I thought something was wrong, but she quickly explained it was a good thing.

Today was the day Jagger was being fully patched into the club.

Ryder had told my sister it would be real nice if I was there when he came out of Chambers. His exact words.

In past conversations with Jagger I knew most of the hierarchy of his club, some of it confusing me so he'd go over it again. To which I'd give him a blank stare. But the one thing I did know for sure was that it was a huge deal to become a fully patched member. He loved that club, almost as much as he loved me. At least that's what he'd told me. I wasn't fully convinced it was true—not yet, at least—but he was making promising strides to prove it to me.

I heard shouts and laughter behind the large wooden doors, hyping my excitement to the next level. A few moments later, the handle turned, the large room coming into full view.

And there he was, standing tall and proud, a smile so big I would've thought he'd won the lottery. Then again, in his eyes, I was sure that's how he felt.

Jagger was a good man. He deserved life's every happiness, and I was thrilled he'd chosen me to join him in this next chapter of his life.

"Hey, babe!" he shouted, breaking away from the others and heading straight for me. The prospect patch on his cut missing, nothing in its place.

Why is there nothing in place of the patch?

"It's right here," he answered, holding up his hand. "Do you know how to stitch?" His smile was infectious, my breath catching in my throat looking at the pure joy on his face.

I do.

Drawing me into his arms, he pressed his eager lips to mine, his tongue teasing me in the most delicious way. Just like that, I wanted to be alone with him. To celebrate privately.

Breaking the kiss, his mouth found my ear, whispering, "I think I like those two words. I might just make you say them again real soon." His warm breath tickled the side of my neck. Leaning back, I stared at him, waiting for him to tell me he was joking, but he never did. Instead, he winked before kissing me once more.

"How about we go back to my place and celebrate?"

I loved it when he read my mind.

COMING SOON

Tripp
Knights Corruption MC Series, book 4
January 2017

ACKNOWLEDGEMENTS

TO MY HUBBY- THANK YOU for your continued support while I lose myself for hours on end in my office. Thanks for holding down the fort and entertaining our furry children while I'm lost inside my head. Love you, baby!

A huge thank you to my family and friends for your continued love, encouragement and support. What a wild ride this journey has been, and hopefully will continue to be for many years to come.

To the ladies at Hot Tree Editing, both editors and beta readers, I can't say enough great things about you. You continue to amaze me and I can't wait until our next project together. You have been beyond fantastic!

To Clarise from CT Cover Creations, what can I say other than you're freaking amazing, woman! Your work speaks for itself. I'm absolutely thrilled with each and every cover you've magically created for me. They just keep getting better and better, Jagger being number 9! Can you believe it? If you lived in the same country, I would track you down just so I could give you a huge hug. ☺

To Kiki, Ruth and all of the other amazing ladies at The Next Step PR- You work tirelessly to promote my work, and "thank you" just doesn't seem adequate enough. For all of your love and support, and for helping to guide me through this wonderful book world we all love so much, I'm eternally grateful. I'm beyond excited to see what the future holds for us all.

To Beth -Your love and support is truly priceless. I'm beyond thrilled we've become such dear friends. I don't know what I would do without you! You cheer me on when I'm nervous, and celebrate when I succeed. Love you! Here's to many more wonderful years to come.

To all of the bloggers who have shared my work, I'm forever indebted to you. You ladies are simply wonderful!

To all of you who have reached out to me to let me know how much you loved my stories, I am beyond humbled. Thank you so much, and I'll continue to do my best to bring you stories you can lose yourself in, even if it's only for a few hours.

And last but not least, I would like to thank you, the reader. If this is the first book you've read from me, I hope you enjoy it. If this is yet another story from me you've taken a chance on . . . THANK YOU from the bottom of my heart!

ABOUT THE AUTHOR

S. NELSON GREW UP WITH a love of reading and a very active imagination, never putting pen to paper, or fingers to keyboard until 2013.

Her passion to create was overwhelming, and within a few months she'd written her first novel, Stolen Fate. When she isn't engrossed in creating one of the many stories rattling around inside her head, she loves to read and travel as much as she can.

She lives in the Northeast with her husband and two dogs, enjoying the ever changing seasons.

If you would like to follow or contact her please do so at the following:

Website:
www.snelsonauthor.com

Email Address:
snelsonauthor8@gmail.com

Also on Facebook, Goodreads, Amazon, Instagram and Twitter

OTHER BOOKS BY
S. NELSON

Stolen Fate

Redemption

Addicted (Addicted Trilogy, Book 1)

Shattered (Addicted Trilogy, Book 2)

Wanted (Addicted Trilogy, Book 3)

Torn

Marek (Knights Corruption MC Series, book 1)

Stone (Knights Corruption MC Series, book 2)